Torc of Moonlight : Book One

...Fast-paced and thrilling, the novel captures the reader from start to finish. The language that Acaster uses is full of vivid imagery and rich descriptions that are sure to engage the reader; painting either a beautiful image of the various landscapes or of the chilling moments filled with tension.

'HullFire', Feb 2010 issue University of Hull Student Magazine

...The historical detail is immaculate, as is the authentic detail of modern student-life, the whole suffused with a rich pagan sexuality... Superbly gripping

Linda Acaster, in starkly elegant prose, builds a powerful novel of possession and psychological breakdown in 'Torc of Moonlight'. She writes the male point of view very well indeed...

An excerpt from Book Two: ***The Bull At The Gate***
follows at the end of this novel

Further information can be found at
http://lindaacaster.blogspot.com
http://www.lindaacaster.com

For Evleen
Dropping coins in moonlit Yorkshire pools can get you into BIG trouble!
Enjoy!

Book One

TORC

of

MOONLIGHT

Linda Acaster

Linda Acaster

Torc of Moonlight

This book is a work of fiction. Names, characters, places and incidents are either the product of the author's imagination or are used fictitiously.

Second Edition
This edition copyright © 2013 Linda Acaster
ISBN: 978-1482073232

An excerpt from Book Two
The Bull At The Gate
follows at the end of this novel

Also available as an ebook in Kindle and ePub formats
© 2013 Linda Acaster

First published in print form © 2009 Linda Acaster
by NGP/Legend Press, UK

All rights reserved.
No part of this publication may be reproduced or transmitted in any form without the express written permission of the author. This book is protected under the copyright laws of the United States of America. Linda Acaster also asserts the moral right to be identified as the author of this work under the UK Copyright, Designs and Patents Act 1988.

Acknowledgements

Fiction is nothing if not based on fact. Special thanks are due to:

Edna Whelan & Ian Taylor, for their inspirational book *Yorkshire Holy Wells and Sacred Springs*;
The staff and students of the University of Hull;
Kingston-upon-Hull Museums, especially the Hull & East Riding Museum;
The people of Hull, for keeping the faith, and the city green;
The people of Malton, for not hiding their history beneath a car park;
The North Yorkshire Moors Steam Preservation Society, for retaining the railway halt at Newtondale;
The Forestry Commission, for opening a path to Newtondale Spring, and for the conservation and maintenance of all the other sacred waters within its domain.

Prologue

He could hear dogs, far off — big dogs, hunting dogs — and he knew he had to run because the hunting dogs were hunting him.

There was a Sanctuary. He kept the knowledge a beacon in his mind. He knew the path, had trod it years before, but it was overgrown now, so overgrown, and he had no flame to light the way. The Keeper was gone, but the Presence would be there, locked among the thorns. The Presence was all powerful. She would embrace him, surround him, protect him. He still had the gladius, the jewelled and flashing blade. She would take it in payment. She could not refuse. She would protect him, disarm his enemies, turn them to stone, to pillars of fire, to hares to be hunted by their own dogs.

He faltered. His chest was aflame, his legs close to collapse. There should be a path, another path. The sword was brought up, its hilt glinting in the night's weak light, its blade a blur of shadow against the silhouetted trees as it swept through tangled briars. And he was running again, down an incline. The trees were thinning, the earth becoming softer underfoot, water and mud squelching as he ran, forcing between his toes, splashing up his legs, burning into his torn skin.

Ankle-deep now, he stood at the rim of the Pool, not a ripple stirring its surface. Trees crowded the edges as if they had backed away in deference, leaving a ring of sky so brightly starlit that he drew breath in wonder at the spectacle.

He spied a fallen tree, its roots lost in the darkness of the woodland, its leafless boughs reaching into the centre of the Pool. Splashing across, he heaved himself up. The trunk was covered with moss, and the water cascading from his legs turned the surface to slime, but his balance was good and he did not fall.

A single slapping of the water focused his attention and he brought up the sword two-handed against the leaping dog. Its dark shape grew to fill his vision, the starlight catching the bared fangs, coating the glistening tongue with frost. It did not yelp as the blade parted its ribcage. Blood spurted hot over his arms as he turned along the axis of the animal's leap to heave the body from the blade. It flew by his shoulder as if still under its own momentum, landing on the jutting branches to be impaled there, dripping gore into the dark liquid below. The initial sacrifice.

He could hear his hunters crashing through the woodland, men as well as dogs, see yellow fire-torches flashing between the trees, but the Pool filled his senses: scents of rotting wood and peaty earth, of deer musk and boar dung. Most of all there was the Presence, waiting in her domain, waiting for him.

Anticipation made the hairs rise on his skin. It powered his blood and fired his sexual desire. He called with a voice deep and challenging. Again he called, and again, followed by an invocation fast and rhythmic. The gladius was taken in both hands, its blade pressed flat across his thigh. All his strength was applied, but it did not even bend. The dogs were close; he could hear them splashing at the edge of the Pool.

Lifting the weapon to shoulder height he sang out a second invocation, a third invocation — three by three by three — and the sword was tossed skywards to meet the twinkling stars. It turned as it rose, twisting along its length, the jewels set into its pommel blinking and winking against the darkness of the woods. Its thrust exhausted, it began to descend, out of the sky and the stars, down through the column of silhouetted trees, and into the yielding water with less sound than a pebble's drop.

On tip-toe he stood on the narrow trunk, head back, arms outstretched, every muscle tensed for the moment, for the coming of the Presence.

There was splashing, much splashing. A spear flew by his

arm. He gave a great whoop of indrawn breath, a gasp, his eyes widening to the brightness of the stars, to the silence of the Pool below his feet. He called afresh, a great shout filled with horror. The name again, fear gripping the tone. He howled the name, bellowed it, fists clenched in anger. He railed at the Presence, jabbing at the air in front of him as if it were a person, seething abuse at an unseen form which gave no answer.

He did not see the dog. He felt its weight, its claws at his back. When the great fangs burst through his shoulder the night turned red to his eyes and he screamed until his lungs had no more air to make the noise. He was falling, the weight of the dog bearing him down, twisting in the air as the sword had twisted, man and dog together. The cold waters of the Pool enveloped him, breathing fire into the wounds on his back. And still he railed at the Presence, cursing and swearing vengeance until the bubbles frothing from his lips sparkled no more in the starlight, and the chilling liquid poured into his lungs, water hissing over red hot stone.

There were no trees.

The sky was a clear tempering blue. Burnished by the noon sunlight, it was the exact shade of the enamelled decoration borne by the gladius. A glorious colour, it seemed suspended so close that he might have raked its surface with his fingers and watched it ripple like an Otherworld pool.

But there were no trees.

Without trees there were no birds, and no bird's song to break the desperate keening of the wind across a land shaded from his sight. A desolate land, he reasoned, devoid of all living things except the sky above him and the water that bore him and refused his release.

He set aside anxiety. Had there ever been a time when none had sought to conspire against him: Senecio, his sword brother; Yslan, the Shrine Keeper; the Presence herself?

He spat his contempt in a string of phlegm. The Presence did not speak against him now, had never spoken but in the mind of the Keeper and through her twisted tongue. All those years wasted in trepidation of that which did not exist. The songs, the rituals, the very memory of her false existence—

How he *hated* her.

A sound caught him unawares, a cry as mournful as the wind. Focusing, he strained to hear it afresh, quartered the sky with his sight to catch a glimpse of beak or feather. A curlew! Its dagger-sharp wings set rigid against the air currents, it skimmed at the speed of an arrow to bank and return across his vision.

Oh, for such movement, such freedom...

It would be his. The summer was dying. The chill winds hugged the dusk and the dawn, dragging the mantle of winter behind them. There would be no mistake this time. The rite of passage would be fulfilled.

Drawing together an image of his sword-arm, he reached out to grasp the weapon's jewelled hilt with its enamelled decoration of sky-riven blue. The lure never failed to draw them. Let the warmth of the sun kiss his form spread among the water droplets. Let it lift him to the bosom of the darkest cloud. Let the wind carry him to the chosen. This time nothing would conspire against him. He, Ognirius Licinius Vranaun, he would pass through.

Chapter One

His lungs were on fire and his legs felt like lead. If he had not been able to see the wall looming towards him, Nick would have thrown in the towel and collapsed on the grass. But Murray was behind him, stomping on his heels with the power of a raging bull elephant, the same height as himself but twenty kilos heavier, and Nick knew that he should have burned him off the park, should have been standing at the finish with his usual quip about the beer growing warm and the girls all being taken. But he wasn't. Was nowhere near it. Murray was gaining on him. Was going to catch him and pass him. And there wasn't a thing he could do about it.

Summoning his last reserves, Nick willed himself another half metre. Too late he realised he had misjudged the distance to the wall. It had jumped forward to meet him, its stark geometric pattern filling his vision, offering no route of escape. He tried to lift his arms, to turn aside his head, but he had not left himself enough time, enough space. His shoulder connected with the rough red brick with such force that his feet left the ground and he was propelled through the air to land in a heap on the grass. Murray's booming voice filtered through his daze.

'Fuck me, Blaketon! I nearly had you!'

Nick tried to drag his sprawling limbs into some semblance of order, but the initial numbness was fast transforming into throbbing pain. At the very least he had dislocated his shoulder and broken his collarbone; at the very worst he was not long for this world.

'Christ, look at you. This is what happens after a summer of licentious debauchery.' Murray breathed hard, catching his wind. 'I, on the other hand, am reaping the benefits of a temperate and soul-enriching sabbatical.'

'Wanker.'

The profanity was meant to convey all the emotions of a first fifteen battle song, but it left Nick's lips a damp gasp. Murray guffawed. Nick couldn't understand where his friend was drawing his energy from. He'd felt better after being dragged semi-conscious from beneath a collapsed rugby scrum.

Murray was on his feet again, pumping his arms and jogging on the spot. The ground beneath Nick reverberated with each footfall, sending an oddly undulating spasm down his spine and along his ribs. At first it felt curiously soothing, how he imagined riding a water bed, and then came the realisation that the sloshing was inside him, and a prickle of perspiration erupted over his body. He rolled himself over to watch the remains of his breakfast spread across the grass beneath his nose.

Strong hands raised him to his knees.

'Any more where that came from?'

Nick thought about it and shook his head. His senses swam. He hoped Murray wasn't going to let go of him. Without support he would end nose first in the lumpy slime seeping into the earth.

'I'm going to sit you back. Ready?'

An arm slid round his ribs, and Nick felt as though he were floating in some dreamscape where actions were uncoordinated and strangely out of time. Was he passing out?

'You look like shit.'

'Feel it.'

Murray's fingers gripped the back of his neck. 'Drop your head between your knees.'

'No!' He had not meant to sound so panicked, but at least it stilled the insistent pressure of Murray's hand.

'Is he okay?'

The voice was unrecognised. Nick saw a pair of neatly creased denims move into his line of vision. That was all he needed: a spectator.

'Will be soon,' Murray was saying. 'Do me a favour: watch him, will you, two minutes, while I grab our gear from the changing room?'

Murray stood and Nick started after him, to be forced back on to his haunches by a hand on his shoulder.

'Don't move or I'll bounce you.' Murray left, trotting along the side of the Sports Centre to its entrance.

The spectator didn't say anything. Nick didn't look up at him. The seconds ticked by. Two minutes came and went. The spectator moved his weight from one foot to the other. Not a sportsman, Nick concluded. He wished he would just leave.

'A bit hard on the ale last night, were you?'

The voice was full of forced camaraderie bordering, Nick felt, on scorn. He let his gaze rise up the ironed denims until it reached a clutch of volumes carried uncomfortably by a thin-fingered hand. Although it was partly obscured, the silver print of the facing title screamed its worth at him. The spectator was a Sciences student. Nick had fallen foul of those supercilious bastards the previous semester when they had played an interfaculty friendly.

His vision cleared. The world was moving in real time again, but when Nick looked up he squinted at the face of the spectator as if he were having trouble focusing.

'Malaria,' he said quietly. 'Sometimes there just isn't the warning.' He watched the youth's expression cloud. 'Damned debilitating,' he added.

'Oh. Yes. Er, I can imagine.'

Nick dropped his head to chortle low in his throat, and chalked one up for the Arts.

The ensuing silence was broken by the return of Murray who threw down his sports bag and proceeded to wrap Nick's tracksuit top round his shoulders. The spectator sidled away and Nick rose to his feet, waving aside Murray's help.

'Feeling better, are we?'

'Much.'

'Good. For one awful moment I thought I was going to have

to resort to mouth-to-mouth resuscitation.'

'Spare me.'

'Just what I thought. That's why I left you with him. If you were going to infect anybody it wasn't going to be me.'

They grinned at each other, sharing the relief of the moment.

'Feel strong enough to walk to the Med Centre?'

'I'm not going to the Med Centre.'

Picking up his sports bag, Murray took a step towards him. He didn't have the height to tower over most people, but his bulk could blot out the sun.

'Read my lips, lover: you are going to the Med Centre.'

Nick shook his head and started walking towards the complex of buildings at the further side of the sports field. 'Don't do a number on me, Murray. I've had it all fucking summer.'

They fell into step.

'I guessed things hadn't run quite according to plan when I saw the suntan Louise is sporting. What did she tell you?'

The muscles in Nick's neck began to tighten. 'I haven't seen her.'

He nipped across the access road in front of a group of cyclists. One swore at him, but he paid no attention. The paved walkway between Staff House and the Sciences block had seen none of the early October sun, and the breeze which had seemed almost summer-like on the playing field tunnelled between the buildings with an edge that spoke of frost. Murray was at his shoulder before he reached the square.

'Well, you can certainly step it out now, but what about tonight? The posters are up, y'know. There'll be a lot of young blood wanting to show off their talent. After last season Hodgson has a scent for glory, and he'll want only the best. You put in a replay of that little stunt and he won't just shunt you off to the Med Centre, he'll call an ambulance.'

'I feel fine now.'

'All I'm saying is it might be an idea to put a word in his ear. Y'know, immune system fighting a virus, not able to put in a peak performance, going to dose yourself up and get an early night, etc, etc. Then if you do shit out your place is covered. And if you end up with 'flu you can go sneeze all over him to prove it.'

'I told you, I'm fine.'

They made their way through the people funnelling beneath the arch of the main Science building. Most seemed to be coming in the opposite direction, and half of them were pushing bicycles. Murray exchanged greetings with students he knew, and back out in the sunshine he drew level with Nick.

'I would have thought you would have hoped to go down with something like 'flu, just to put your mind at rest that it's nothing more serious.'

'I really worried you, didn't I?'

'Let's just say that I had this thought of dropping Law and taking up Medicine.'

'I'm fine. Honest.'

'Yeah, sure. Do us both a favour, eh? Get a shower and climb into bed for the rest of the day.'

Nick shook his head. 'I've a seminar at 11.15.'

'Give it a miss.'

'I missed too many last year.'

Murray kicked out at an empty crisp packet on the flagstones and didn't answer. As they cornered the Chemistry building Nick glanced at his wristwatch.

'Look, I've not got long. I'll see you tonight.'

'And if you start feeling weird again you'll go to the Med Centre, right?'

'What is this? Are you trying to imitate my mother?'

They laughed and parted company. Nick had only gone a few paces when a theatrically falsetto voice pierced the general hubbub.

'And change your underclothes. They're dis-*gusting*.'

Waving two fingers in the air, Nick kept walking.

Leaving the ivy-covered walls of the older buildings, he passed alongside the grey concrete rear of the Law block and on to the narrow path that wound through the thin scrub birch separating the campus proper from the first of the public roads.

When he'd come to Hull he'd been pleased that the original blood-red brick buildings, with their small-paned windows and incongruously peaked attic rooms, had made up such a small proportion of the university's campus. A year on he was grateful for the trees, and for the forethought of those who had planted them in every conceivable nook and cranny. In spring the squares were ankle deep in pink and white blossoms. Now, on breezy days, leaves sang out their death rattle as they clung to swaying branches, or ran before him, crisp and golden, to be caught in a root and crushed underfoot. Concrete, no matter the style, was concrete, stark and uncompromising. Ivy would never grow up the walls of the Law block, but the birds sang in the trees below it, and the hedgehogs grubbed in their roots to scurry across to the gardens opposite as soon as the traffic quietened.

He was becoming sentimental, there was no denying it. Emotional even. Perhaps Murray was right, perhaps he was sickening for something. Or perhaps he was just wallowing in his own self-pity. No matter how he tried to keep his thoughts in check, Murray's voice was in his head telling him of the tan Louise was sporting, and the memory of that never-changing, ever-cheerful voicemail message kept kicking into play, laughing at him.

The gate was stuck again. He released the latch and pushed at it with his thigh, managing only to reinforce the bruise he had been cultivating since taking up residence at the house. He freed the latch, this time lifting the gate clear of the sneck. It swung easily on freshly greased hinges.

'Sodding thing,' Nick muttered, and he pressed it back further, catching it securely in the rose bushes which separated the small front garden from its neighbour.

Gaining a house on Salmon Grove had been the finest coup of his entire first year. The hall of residence he had been allocated had been no dump, of course. With its park-like gardens and in-house entertainment committee it had been all he had imagined university life to be. The problem was that it was situated two miles from the main campus, and, as the year progressed, those two miles had lengthened into twenty and then into two hundred. At Salmon Grove he could fall out of bed straight into a lecture and be back before the sheets had cooled.

Closing the door behind him, he waited for his vision to become accustomed to the gloom. The only window in the hallway was above the solid front door, and the mature trees growing out of the pavement restricted the light as well as screening the concrete edifices across the road. Walking into the handlebars of Maureen's bicycle had been an incident he did not wish to repeat, though why she insisted on having a bicycle when she was less than a stone's throw from the campus was beyond him.

Her bike wasn't there, only a bulging black dustbin liner which he purposely ignored. Both downstairs doors were closed, and there seemed to be no movement coming from above. Hopefully the other occupants were out and he had the house to himself. Separating his room key on the ring, he laid a hand on the banister and dragged himself up the stairs.

The door swung back revealing his front bedroom exactly as he had left it earlier that morning, hardly changed from the Saturday before when he'd double-parked the rental and heaved the contents of his life up the stairs. He would have to empty the boxes soon; he could hardly remember what was in them.

The unmade bed beneath the window looked inviting, and if he was going down with something it made sense to get it out of his system with as little hassle as possible. It also made sense not to rock the boat, especially after the one-to-one he'd endured at the end of the previous semester, and the lies he'd told back home.

'So how did Murray do? Is he struggling, too?'

His parents had sat together on the sofa. He couldn't remember them ever sitting together on the sofa before. The sofa had always been for him and his sisters.

'Everybody has found it hard. It's just so different. You think it's simply going to be an extension of 'A' levels, but it's not.'

His father had remained tight-lipped, his mother quietly understanding. He would have felt better if it had dissolved into a row. And then, of course, had come the bombshell.

'You said that you hadn't much studying to do over the summer. Your father's managed to get you a job, holiday relief at the plant.'

All he'd said was, 'Oh.'

What the hell could he have said? His mother had taken on extra hours to help with his student loan, and his sisters had made it perfectly plain that they held him responsible for their not having a holiday. To cap it all Louise had dropped him like a steaming turd and was now sporting a suntan that had made Murray's eyes water.

Stripping off his running gear, he grabbed a still-damp towel and walked on to the landing and into the shower room.

It was good to have a shower with an uninterrupted flow of water. No one filling kettles or flushing toilets. No sudden spikes in the temperature, freezing one moment, scalding the next. He rested his forehead against the cool tiles, letting the water play directly on to his neck and shoulder. He had jarred them badly when he had collided with the wall, but had not realised how stiff the muscles had grown. The particles of red brick embedded in his skin were a surprise, too. He must have hit the wall with the power of an express.

Water poured on to his head, fanning his hair, running along his cheekbones and down his nose. He opened his mouth to breathe, and his breathing became slower as the warmth of the water lulled him. The building steam felt damp in his lungs, but soothing, the noise of the jet hypnotic in its unending hiss.

He snapped round the dial and the water shut off. How long had he been standing there? His fingertips looked like gnarled tree bark. He pushed his hair from his face and blinked. He was supposed to be at a seminar.

Towelling himself as he went, he dripped his way back across the landing to probe the discarded paper cups on his study table for his wristwatch. Five minutes. Shit.

The clothes he'd discarded the night before still lay at the foot of the bed and he dragged them on, regardless of how they looked. His socks were stiff, but he had no idea of where a clean pair was and no time to search one out. The orange wallet file shrieked at him from across the room like a well wound alarm clock. There wasn't much in it: some paper and a pen, a few notices he'd picked up, a copy of his timetable, but it looked good, looked as if he'd got his act together. He laid a hand on it, grabbed his keys and slammed the door behind him.

'So nice of you to join us, number 28. I hope we haven't dragged you away from anything interesting.'

Nick stood in the doorway looking across the heads of the students to the lecturer, one hand on her hip, the other knuckles down on the table beside her. It didn't seem like a good idea to answer, especially as he couldn't remember her name. The door behind him opened with a groan of its spring and the lecturer's gaze realigned on a point beyond his shoulder.

'Number 29! Well, *hello* there.'

Jesus, was she really counting them in? Nick took the opportunity to reach one of the vacant seats in the centre of the group. Almost immediately he realised his mistake. Sunshine was pouring through the skylight with the efficiency of greenhouse glass. He looked around for a seat in the shadows, but they had all been taken.

'For those of you who have forgotten, or for those who simply never bothered to find out, my name is Janet Duval. I am on an exchange from Lancaster, and it is my dubious pleasure to be acquainted with you for the entire academic year. I am reliably informed that my bark is worse than my bite, but I feel it only fair to warn you, especially the late-comers, that a full series of rabies shots may be considered beneficial.

'I expect full sittings at my seminars and my tutorials. Those who feel their eyesight too precious to waste upon the set texts will also find themselves at a distinct disadvantage as questions will be asked during meetings, including this one.

'You are now free, for fifteen seconds, to gasp, groan or wince, whichever is your desire, and then we shall make a start.'

There was a distinct lack of gasps or groans, Nick noticed, but a marked amount of shifting about in seats. And then the door opened and Janet Duval raised an overly benign smile and diverted her attention from the group.

Nick recognised most of the people within his line of vision, though there seemed to be a higher than usual proportion of mature students in this class. He had expected *Myth & Reality of the American West* to be one of the less daunting options, but Janet Duval was making it perfectly clear that she had written scripts for Billy the Kid.

Perhaps her attitude would prove to be a mixed blessing. On secondment for a year, it seemed she was determined to make her mark. If she made it on him hopefully he would forgo a repeat of the interview he had endured the previous semester, and he would have something cheery to email home.

The seminar room dimmed and Nick let out a slow stream of breath, angling his head to glance at the skylight. A cloud was drifting across the sun, an orange corona sparkling round the edge of the grey mass. He hoped that it would be a big cloud, twenty minutes' worth at least. His brains felt as if they were being fried.

Luxuriating in the drop in temperature, he took time out from listening to Duval to review the jottings he had made. He hadn't read the books, of course — Damn! He had a lot of reading to do — but it was probable that few on the course had, either. He felt reasonably safe in that area.

The questions began without any preamble, and bore no relevance to what had gone before. Duval was testing the general climate, and no one was offering a reply. Each silence was met with a hardening of her expression, a stiffening of her angular frame. Nick sagged into his chair. She was going to point to someone and demand an answer, he could tell. It wasn't going to be him.

'Does this mean that not one of you, *not one of you*, has the guts to chance an answer? Not even to get the rest off the hook?'

The silence seemed interminable.

'The consensus of opinion, then, is for extra assignments?'

There was a general shuffling and clearing of throats, and then Duval's attention focused near the front and the disquiet subsided. Some stupid sod had offered themselves as a sacrificial lamb. Nick breathed a sigh of relief.

The voice was female. Nick had no idea what she said. All he caught was an aural impression, a richness in the timbre. He eased himself to one side, trying to locate her through the line of shoulders and heads. What he noticed was Duval's reaction, her surprise and the softening of her features. Dear God, had their sacrificial lamb turned into a saviour?

'Very good,' Duval was murmuring. 'I trust everyone heard that?'

There was a hum of agreement around Nick. It threw him for a moment. He hadn't heard the answer; how could those behind him? And then he realised that standing so close to the abyss the group would have agreed with anything the lecturer offered.

Duval was partway through another question. Nick had missed the beginning — something about fur trading companies. No one was going to answer again.

But Duval hardly waited. Her gaze drifted across the group to return to the oracle before her. Nick made a concerted effort to see who it was, and caught a glimpse of shoulder-length auburn hair and part of a green sweater. The sound of her voice swirled around him, its peaks and troughs enticing in their clarity. It brought to mind the rim of a crystal glass being smoothed by a damp fingertip; more than a note, but not quite a tune.

Duval was nodding and smiling, smiling not only at the girl but at the entire group. Who was this wonder? She had Duval eating out of her hand.

Nick pulled his chair to the left, its rubber feet squealing across the glossy tiles. The student beside him frowned, but Duval didn't seem to notice. She was into a new phase of her lecture and heads bowed as notes were scribbled. Nick gained an uninterrupted view of the auburn hair and green sweater.

He tried to match a face to the outline, but no memory would stir itself. His gaze followed the gentle ripples of her hair from crown to shoulder blade and he wondered if it was naturally wavy or if she spent each breakfast clutching a hot brush the way his younger sister did. Her hand reached out to tuck a lock behind her ear, but her action gave him no more sight of her face. She touched her pens, the books and papers beside her. The hand withdrew.

Last year's English options? He didn't think so. One of the rugby groupies? Definitely not. With hair that colour he would have remembered. It was very likely that he didn't know her at all — yet he felt there was something familiar. He caught himself with a snort. Perhaps he just wished there was. Sporting a redhead on his arm would certainly put Louise's nose out of joint.

The cloud broke and sunshine poured unrestrained through the skylight. There was general unrest as the sudden brightness bounced off white paper and polished tiles. Nick blinked, squinting to bring his vision back into focus. The girl's hair was alight, sparkling through shades of autumn with each slight movement of her head. Duval was speaking to her.

'Can you give me three out of three?'

The girl was wriggling in her chair, small agitated movements. Duval had caught her unawares. Nick hadn't heard the question, either. He looked to Duval, hoping that she would repeat it. She didn't. She let the girl squirm.

'Er, Catlin. Er, *Notes and Manners on...* er... It's a two volume set.'

Hearing her properly took Nick by surprise. Her voice held none of the authority or rhythm he had anticipated. It didn't seem to fit with what had registered before.

Duval seemed only marginally disappointed in the answer. 'At least you know to which books I'm referring.' She turned her attention to the group. 'Which is more than can be said for the rest of you.'

There was a crash. Eyes turned, including Duval's. The girl with the auburn hair slid off her seat to retrieve her dropped file. Duval's voice demanded attention, but it became a drone to Nick as he watched the girl reach under her chair to reclaim an errant pen. Her outstretched fingers curled around the ballpoint and hesitated. Nick lifted his gaze up the sleeve of her sweater. Half hidden behind the chair she was looking at him, her expression full of doubt, her pale features framed by the corona of flaming hair which undulated through shades of amber and gold, russet and hazel, individual locks lifting from her shoulders.

They were lifting.

Nick stared in disbelief. Tendrils were lifting and swaying away from her head, fanning out as if caught in a shifting field of static, weaving and twisting, mesmerizing in its intricate pattern.

She moved, turned away, sitting in her seat with her back to him. Her hair fell in ripples from her crown in a palette of autumn colours, but not a tendril stirred against the pull of gravity. Another cloud passed across the sun plunging the room into a dull opacity. Nick fought to refocus his vision. When colours became clear again her hair had been leached of its fire.

Chapter 2

Everyone was standing. Nick rested back in his seat feeling witless. Had the class come to an end? It must have done. The students were leaving. Duval was sorting papers in her open briefcase.

Her hair had lifted.

It couldn't have done. What was he thinking? His eyes had been playing tricks on him. He wasn't well. He'd thrown up, hadn't he? Nearly passed out. Of course he had. He'd frightened Murray to death.

The girl with the auburn hair had left her seat. Nick looked to the crush at the doorway, but could not pick her out, not the auburn hair, not the green sweater. Most probably she had already gone. He felt oddly relieved.

Sunshine poured through the skylight, its intensity pressing on his head. Squinting into the light source, he could clearly see a flaring round the edge of the passing cloud. Stupid sod! That was what he'd seen around her head — an after-image of the sun's corona.

In the quad the breeze gusted about him, kicking up dried leaves and pieces of litter. Cornered by the buildings they chased round and round upon themselves, chattering on the paving slabs as if animated. It was cooler outside, much cooler. The clouds weren't wispy as they had been earlier in the day, but ominously thicker. He'd give odds that they would be training in a downpour. Slick grass and standing water. His kit would have to be scrubbed of its mud.

The memory of Louise's touch came unbidden. He tried to banish it, but it was insistent. She liked the rainy games the best, standing on the touchline with that huge red and blue panelled umbrella. She would rush on to the field to meet him when the final whistle blew, to lay a hand on his heaving chest, to draw her nails down the shirt that had become his second skin. She could pout when she didn't get her own way, and her way was for him to be unshowered, unshaven and still sweating after a game. And he'd gone for it like a dog with its tongue hanging out. Not any more.

He toyed with the idea of going back to the house, but he knew that he would drop on his bed and sleep if he went there. He needed food and he needed something substantial. If he ate later he would be liable to throw up again, and if he did so all over Hodgson's boots there would definitely be no place for him in the team. He checked his pockets for cash and made his way to the main refectory.

The noise in the high-ceilinged hall reverberated with a need and an excitement as if everyone was speaking in tongues. Nick couldn't see a free table anywhere and the queue to the counter was twenty deep. He groaned and considered his options. He could go to the shops on Cottingham Road, but he didn't want a takeaway. There were the campus' cafes, but he wanted more than a snack, and the queues were liable to be the same. A couple ahead pulled out and he stepped forward, and it was then that he saw her, leaning over to pick up a tray. Five up the queue was the auburn hair and green sweater.

He didn't think about it. He slipped his position in the line and pushed in behind her, raised his hand to touch her arm, hesitated, then let it fall on her shoulder.

She spun round more startled than he had expected, the tray held vertically, a shield between them, but he met her gaze with bright eyes and a face wreathed in smiles.

'I missed you at the end of the seminar,' he said. 'I'm so pleased I managed to catch you. Sara didn't say where I could get hold of you and I was afraid that I might not see you again until Duval's next session.'

It came out in a rush as he'd meant it to, giving her no time to voice automatic defences, and Sara was such a fantastic name to use. There had to be over 200 Saras on campus. If she didn't know one, she knew someone who did. He could see the confusion standing in her face. She was puzzling the name, trying to locate the connection. Sara was his foot in the slamming door.

'I'll be up front,' he told her. 'I'm here because I need help, and Sara said that you were red hot on the subject and— Hey, I'm sorry, I haven't even introduced myself. I'm Nick, Nicholas Blaketon.'

He offered his hand, half expecting her not to take it, but she did, even in the confined space of the queue. She had a light grip, a cool and damp hand, very small in his. He released it at once, wanting her to read nothing untoward in his manner. She was shaking her head, not a good sign.

'I'm sorry, I—'

'We met at a party last year—'

'A party?'

'Well, a gathering, anyway. I suppose it didn't quite get out of hand enough to be called a party.'

Didn't she go to parties? He reached across to collect a tray from the stack, hoping he could sever that thread of conversation.

'I'm sorry, I think you've got the wrong person.'

He was losing it. He watched her lift a prawn salad from the chilled shelves and turn her back on him to move a little further up the queue. Fibres of her sweater wavered iridescent under the intense lighting, her hair a shower of red-gold leaves.

'Alison,' he said. 'Your name is Alison.'

She half turned, one eyebrow raised. 'Alice,' she murmured.

Alice..? He had never been that close in his life.

Snapping his fingers, Nick tried to look contrite. 'Alice. I'm sorry. Alice, of course it is. This just underlines my problem. I don't have a retentive memory. You could answer Duval's questions just like that. I was floundering, believe me.'

The assistant behind the counter inclined her head towards him and he looked down the regimented line of stainless steel tins set into the heated work surface. 'Meat pie and everything. As big as you like. Thanks.'

The queue was moving. Alice was following it, leaving him. She paused to take a glass of orange.

'Can you get me one of those?' Nick called. She looked back at him, perturbed he thought, but she reached for a second orange and stood it on her tray. He caught up with her at the cash desk. She had her purse open, ready.

'Let me pay for these,' he said.

'No, I'm fine, thank you.'

'Hey, it's the least I can do. Excuse me, these two trays together, please.'

'No, honestly.'

But the cashier's fingers were moving faster than the eye could follow and the bill was for two meals. Nick slapped a note in the woman's hand. Alice put away her purse and picked up her tray.

'Thank you, but it wasn't necessary.'

'It's the least I can do as I'm imposing on you like this. Now where are we going to sit?'

Stunned surprise crossed her face, but he made out that he hadn't seen it. Thankfully the occupants of a table stood to leave and he shepherded her towards it.

He had expected them to sit opposite each other across the table, but as he was making himself comfortable she began moving along the bench to leave them sitting diagonally. He thought of moving up, too, but decided against it. Was it leg or eye contact she was avoiding? Either way, she was looking distinctly uncomfortable. He used the most obvious opening gambit.

'Thanks for picking up the orange,' he said, retrieving the glass from her tray.

A weak smile was sent in his general direction, but her flitting gaze didn't come closer than his elbow before returning to her lunch. He was going to have to work here, he could tell.

Lifting his meal to remove the tray from the table, the gravy slopped across his fingers, dripping from the edge of the plate to create a thickening pool on the Formica. Alice had collected a serviette for herself, but he had not thought of doing the same. Casting covetous eyes on it as he licked his fingers, he caught her studying the meal before him. He looked at the decorous salad in front of her and at his own meat pie, two veg and chips. He gave a Gallic shrug.

'She likes me. I remind her of her son.' He looked pointedly at Alice, hoping to elicit a response. 'I suppose I remind you of your brother. It's always the same.'

Her gaze flicked over him, never landing for more than a moment, direct eye contact not on the menu. 'I don't have a brother.'

Filing the information, Nick cut into his pie. 'I've got sisters, two, both younger. They can be a right pain. I suppose it's different if you're female yourself.'

There was no answer, and Nick read it that she was an only child. That might account for her reticence. University could be overwhelming when you were used to dealing with people singly. He decided to eat for a while and not say anything to see how she'd react. The silence was tangibly unnatural, but he persisted, wanting her to be the one to break it.

'You're not a History student, are you?' she said at last.

Thank you, God.

'No, I'm a joint American Studies and English.' Nick took a gamble on an almost certainty. 'I believe you're majoring in History.'

'Yes, I am. That's why I can't understand why you think I can help you.'

It stumped him, too. He was going to have to think fast and speak hesitantly.

'Basically... because you aren't from my main groups.' He pushed at the vegetables on his plate. Yes, this would do. He lowered his voice.

'I'm on a warning. I don't want the others to know.'

'How bad a warning?'

Nick shifted in his chair. 'How bad does it get? I'm here. I might not be next year if I can't pull it together by Christmas.'

This wasn't coming out the way he wanted. It was sounding too close to the real thing.

'I still don't understand. What do you want me to do? Write your essays for you?'

She was looking at him, directly at him, and for the first time he could see her properly, could sink into her clear grey eyes and pale skin. She wasn't wearing any make-up. None at all. Her eyebrows and lips were the only flashes of colour in her face, apart from her hair. Her auburn hair made her live. It was an effort to draw his gaze away.

'Is that what you think of me? That I could baldly ask you to write my essays? Of course I don't want you to do that. I just—' he opened his hands, trying to think on his feet '—I read the books, I do the studying, but I can't retain it. I miss things out, obvious things. All I ask is that you give me fifteen minutes, just to look over an essay before I hand it in. That's all. A few pointers, no more. I'd ask one of the group, but it's embarrassing. And I feel I can trust you.'

It was the biggest load of bullshit he'd uttered for weeks, but she was swallowing it. He could see her unbending.

'We're not due to hand any in for a while.'

'I realise that, but I had to ask, y'know. I mean, fifteen minutes doesn't sound much, but you are busy, everyone's busy...'

'No, it's all right.' Her fingers were touching unseen points in the air as she tried to placate him, to keep him at arm's length. 'We've a lot of reading now. It's the notes you take that make the difference. Do you use headings?'

He tried to look suitably fazed.

'You should put them under headings, each heading on a separate sheet, or digital file. And make sure that each note you make is marked with the title of the book and the name of the author. It's easier if you have a source sheet and...' She trailed off to pick at her salad. 'I'm sorry. You'll do this already.'

She was shy, that was what it was. Nick smiled. After Louise he could do with a bit of shyness.

'You seem to have it taped. It's the basics I seem to have missing.'

Her gaze rose to meet his. 'It feels like I've been doing research all my life. I guess it comes naturally.'

'Do you do anything else? Clubs, sports or anything?'

The locks of her hair danced around her face as she shook her head. Nick drew breath as he watched them lift, suddenly uncertain of what he'd seen during Duval's seminar.

'No, nothing. When I'm not studying I'm studying. I'm very boring.'

'I don't think you could ever be boring.'

He slammed his teeth down on the words, but they had already escaped. There was no change in her expression, but her grey eyes were open to the world and he could see that the barriers were going up again.

'I think you would bring a vitality to anything you put your mind to. I think you could lecture Duval off the park. Is that what you want to do, teach?'

She smiled at him, but it was all polite courtesy. The fragile rapport was broken. He felt a physical pain when she placed her knife and fork together on the remains of her meal and rose to leave.

'I have to go,' she said. 'I'll see you at the next seminar. We'll know what we are supposed to be doing then.'

'Thanks for agreeing to help me.'

'That's okay, just as long as you don't land your assignment on me five minutes before it has to be handed in. I can't work miracles.'

'However you want to play it.'

She wanted to play it away from him, he told himself; let her go.

'Bye,' he said. She nodded and left. It took him all his time to keep his eyes on his plate and not turn to watch her weave between the tables. And he hadn't even got her phone number.

Bastard.

The babble of voices crowded in on him, the clatter of plates and cutlery sounding as sharp as cymbals to his ears. He tried to continue with his meal, but it had no taste. When three freshers came to ask if they could share his table, he let them have it to themselves.

'You're sure about this?'

'Yes. Yes, I am.'

'The crucifixion is not exactly original, you know.'

He raised his gaze from the paper, ostensibly to stare into the middle distance while he considered alternatives. Instead, he let it flicker down her profile. Her nose was too prominent, but the line and height of her cheekbones compensated. She turned to face him, her brow creasing in a frown, and he shifted his gaze to the shelving beyond her head crowded with boxes and paint canisters and artists' utensils.

'Will that influence the marking?'

Drawing his gaze back to her face, he offered a protective smile. 'Not necessarily. The nuances of interpretation count for much.'

He watched her expression relax, her dark eyes return to the sketch on the bench. She was perspiring slightly, the coffee'd silk of her skin sheening on her throat. Choutelan, she'd said her name was, though he was not certain that he'd heard correctly. But Choutelan weighed well on the tongue, a whisper of the erotic that suited her natural grace.

'And you feel that the subject matter would not arouse censure?'

'This is Britain,' he said.

He wondered how she would feel about becoming the subject of a painting. It was far too long since he'd held a brush. The rangy limbs, the beguiling elegance of movement, he could capture in oils, tie down on canvas. Not in that absurd Shetland sweater, though. Maybe she was feeling the chill of the English damp; not acclimatised yet. He mused on her likely background. Her colouring, and the texture of her skin, didn't sit too well with the impeccable Surrey accent.

'You said you had reservations about the materials.'

She was uncomfortable, didn't like the silences. He relished that.

'I think the concept is unbalanced.'

He took the pencil from her hand, brushing the length of her fingers with his own. She was very, very warm.

'You have everything made from natural materials: the wood of the cross, the crown of thorned twigs, the Christ figure himself... And the scale is all wrong for the statement you wish to make. You should consider life-size—'

'*Life-size?*'

'It wouldn't be much more work.'

'I was not thinking of the work involved, but the storage.'

He lifted his eyes from the sketch to let his gaze, and his smile, wash over her. So young. The physical maturity of womanhood. The naïvety of the child.

'You could store it here, build it here, in the studio. Where better?'

'But... if all the students—'

'Not all,' he countered. 'Only those with vision.'

He watched her smile down at the sketch. He could envisage that smile transferred to a brush stroke, to the touch of his fingertips. To him.

'And the materials?'

'To return to the unadorned basics, Christ was God's only son. God made the land, the flora and fauna.'

'So, the materials for the Christ figure should be pure and natural.'

'Exactly.' The urge to touch her was building.

'And the instruments of his torture, his death, were all man-made.'

'Absolutely.'

He wondered how she would react if he placed his hand on

hers, how she would react if he reached across and drew his tongue along her throat.

'Nature subjugated by technology!'

'The vision,' he murmured. 'I could see it straight away. It doesn't come often, but it makes tutoring so worthwhile.'

He angled his body closer to hers. For a moment they touched, clothing to clothing, then she moved away. He smiled. Games of cat and mouse made these entanglements so much more fulfilling, and it was far too long since he'd indulged himself.

Chapter 3

The rain started as a soft drizzle around three. By four-thirty it was hammering against the windows, and by six any self-respecting boat-builder was looking to make a start on an Ark.

Nick lay on top of his rumpled bedclothes wondering if it was worth making a move. Surely Hodgson wasn't so obsessed as to have them tearing about the field in this? Then again, he probably was. He would rationalise it, wouldn't he? Professionalism, he would call it.

'If a little rain puts you off a mere training session, how can you expect to be picked for the big matches?'

Nick could hear the man's voice as clearly as if he were standing in the doorway, see him in his mind's eye, hands on hips, the muscle of his youth fighting hard not to turn to flab.

'When I had my trial for the England Under 21s...'

No doubt they would have to endure all that crap again, too.

He dragged himself up, crossing to the basin to rub the damp flannel over his face. It felt as if it had been dipped in iced water, not simply laid across the basin's side, and it brought him round faster than he had anticipated. Had he a temperature? He tested his forehead and neck with the palm of one hand. Could be. The glands below his ears were a bit spongy.

His kit still sat in its bag by the door, and he glanced across to it, wondering which way to jump. He didn't feel sick, did he? No, he didn't feel sick. Oh, what the hell. He'd risk it; do as Murray suggested and drop a whining line in Hodgson's ear to cover himself.

*

His supposedly rainproof jacket was seeping across the shoulders before he had turned the corner of the Law building. Why didn't this university have covered walkways? Yorkshire was hardly abutting the South of France.

Head down, he plodded along the deserted pavement, the rain thudding into his back and against his hood, blunt needles determined to reach his skin. And then something solid hit him just above the kidneys and he spun round, an arm automatically rising in defence. Murray was gesticulating from a doorway.

'Nick, you wanker! Didn't you hear me calling you? Where the hell are you going?'

Leaving the wide pathway, he crossed the sodden grass to stand just outside the shelter of the open porch. Murray was wearing a sweater over a white-collared rugby shirt, but it wasn't the sort worn to play a game. By his feet was a training bag, but it was full of books, Nick could tell by the regular shape of the bulges carved in the blue nylon.

'Rugby? First training tonight? Ring any bells?'

'You've got to be kidding. It'll be off.'

'Is it?'

He watched Murray look into the rain. It didn't feel as cold as it had. Quite refreshing, in fact. Lifting his head slightly, Nick let a squall pass the edge of his hood to dance on his face. If he were honest, it felt quite invigorating.

'Bastard!' Murray spat. 'It won't be, will it? Hodgson will use the weather for one of his separating-the-men-from-the-boys routines.'

He pointed to the bag at his feet. 'I've got to dump these and grab my gear. Do us both a favour, eh? You're passing the Union. Look in to see if a cancellation has been posted. If it has, pull a couple of beers in the Sanctuary. I'll look in on my way by. If you aren't there... Nick, are you okay?'

Nick blinked the rain from his eyelashes. 'Yeah. Sure.'

'Thrown up again?'

'Oh, for fuck's sake. Just get your arse in gear. The session will be on, I'm telling you.'

Turning to cut across the grass, he pushed back the hood of his jacket to let the full force of the rain pour over his head.

He hardly passed anyone on his way to University House, but it was the normal crush inside. He found it amusing how the other students gave him room as he mounted the stairs. There was a lot to be said for leaving a puddle as he walked.

There was no room to give on the floor above. The walls of the narrow corridor ran with society and club notice boards. The sports boards were on the wall in the wi-fi lounge beyond, and he was pushed and sworn at for drenching those he passed.

He drew alongside the section designated for the Union teams, and although he turned to face the ochre board he made no attempt to focus on the notices displayed. The short hairs on the back of his neck were horripilating, a frisson skittering down his spine. Something had caught in his peripheral vision back along the corridor. Six steps and he was standing before her, the individual locks of her hair rising around her head, defying gravity.

Alice.

Sounds rushed at him down a long echoing tube, and he broke into the real world, his eyes close to the poster, his fingers resting on the stylised pen-and-ink drawing. He glanced left and right, feeling awkward, checking where he was, checking who was with him. No one seemed surprised that he was standing so close to the wall. One of the employed admin staff passed, reading papers from a folder. A group of young women spoke breathlessly, their voices cutting one across another in their exuberance. Shrill laughter erupted from an open office door.

He returned his attention to the notice board, to the drawing beneath his fingers. It wasn't of Alice, not truly of Alice. It was a head and shoulders depiction of a young woman with tendrils of shoulder-length hair rising like leafy branches around her head, her neck extended, the picture giving the impression of a slender tree. His fingertips traced each undulating lock. Not

Alice, no. Not anyone. Just a female. Any female.

The background colour of the notice seeped into his perception. A pale leaf-green. Black lines focused into crisp lettering.

'Blakey?'

Mother Earth Society
Next Meeting: 18 October M/Room 3
Samhain Celebrations - Preliminary Discussion

A name inked out. Hankins? Hawkins? His gaze rose to the subject heading the board: Environmental & Conservation. There was a smaller notice, something about bats, another giving details of clearing a canal.

'Hey, Blaketon!'

Nick looked down the narrow corridor, now empty and strangely tunnel-like. Someone stood in the open doorway of the wi-fi lounge, the bright lighting of the area casting his mass into silhouette. Nick could see others crossing behind him, but they were oddly muted, curiously out of time.

Behind Nick a door opened, and a woman came hurrying along the corridor fighting her way into a bulky coat. She passed Nick almost at a run, the draught she created sweeping over him, bringing the clack of her heels and the smell of her perfume sharply to his senses. Noise rose around him — the rhythmic wheeze of a photocopier, the drone of distant conversation, the ringing of a telephone — filling the corridor with a normality he had not realised was missing.

'Blakey! It is you, y'bastard.'

Bernie Colwyn was striding towards him. Bernie Colwyn, prop-forward. He smacked both hands against Nick's shoulders and Nick shuddered beneath the onslaught.

'Good t'see ya, mate!' he enthused. 'Ready for the off? If you've come looking for a cancellation you've forgotten Hodgson's little quirks.'

Nick watched Bernie's smile dissolve into a frown, and then

erupt again into an eye-twinkling grin.

'Whatever you're on, mucker, save some for me. I'll have it later.' An arm waltzed him around. 'C'mon now. Let's go kick the shit outta these freshers.'

With the pick of the crop before him, Hodgson was strutting back and forth revelling in the choices it afforded. Already he'd had the company divide by experience. As expected, the freshers made up the largest group, those who had played rugby at their schools standing slightly apart from those who hadn't but fancied their chances — or a laugh.

Nick looked them over. He'd stood in that group the previous October, wondering what he was letting himself in for. Those hoping for a laugh were in for a rude awakening. Laughs were saved for the bar, after a game. On the field it was to the death.

'There's a lot of meat across there,' Murray whispered over his shoulder.

'Don't start fretting until you've seen them run.'

'Running is for fly-halfs, and there's not a fly-half across there. Your place is assured.'

'Nothing in this life is assured,' Nick told him. He thought that his own place on the first team might be, though, considering the look of the opposition.

An hour had passed before Hodgson had completed his form filling and team talks. Nick had worried that the warmth of the Sports Centre might have started another wave of dizziness, or whatever it had been, but he felt okay. The meal, or half the meal he'd eaten, had worked its charm. When Hodgson finally led them out under the floodlights he was looking forward to the exercise, even to the rain, though not everyone felt the same. There was a general chorus of groaning as heads were bowed into hunched shoulders.

The group broke into a jog. Nick stood apart to raise his face to the ink-black sky. The rain was cold. Iced. It stung as it hit him and he had to squint to protect his eyes, but he stayed there, breathing slow and deep to enlarge his lung capacity, feeling the rain gather at his throat to run under his shirt and down his chest.

He shuddered and blinked, pushing back his slick hair. The group were along the edge of the field now, a ghostly bobbing mass at the furthest reaches of the pooled floodlights. Nick felt energized, better than he had the entire day. He would catch them before they were two-thirds round the circuit, he decided, jog at Hodgson's shoulder and ask how his holiday had been.

Hodgson blew his whistle after the second lap. He had cones set out and the trialists running in relays around them. Some of the beefier participants came croppers on the corners, churning the mud as they slid full length, adding vital seconds to Hodgson's stopwatch. Nick saw it as he took the last corner on his run: the red and blue panelled golfing umbrella.

Murray welcomed his return to the fold, slapping him on the back. 'Good time! No problem!'

Cocking his head towards the Sports Centre doorway, he said, 'Have you seen who's here? You can't say that she's not keen.'

Nick turned his shoulder to the rain and looked through the blaze of floodlights. Her head was lost in the over-shadowing umbrella, her body a silhouette against the lighted doorway, showing the long, tightly-clad legs and waist-hugging jacket to best effect. He wondered if the suntan was as bright as Murray maintained, and if it stopped at her bikini line or covered every inch of her. The thought brought a bitter taste to his mouth and he spat a string of phlegm across the squelching grass as he shifted his stance to watch the last of the runners come in.

Hodgson blew his whistle. 'Okay! Okay! Three groups of two, now. Keep jogging so your muscles don't chill. Three groups of two. Leader takes a ball. Run and pass along the line, now. Run and pass!'

They ran and passed, the ball zig-zagging down the line as the players drew out across the field.

'What is this?' Hodgson demanded as the leaders returned to him. 'If you want to play fucking girlie-ball get the fuck off my pitch! Spread yourselves out and *throw* the bastard thing!'

And so the two lines spread further apart and the ball was arced across the space between them, its slippery surface glinting white under the floodlights.

Nick noticed the dropouts on the return run. Heads bowed, some had their hands resting on their hips, others resting on their thighs. One limped. Another was on his knees throwing up an ill-advised late meal. Nick chuckled. He was feeling good; a little winded, but good. His gaze followed a couple of stragglers walking towards the sanctuary of the Sports Centre. She was still standing in the doorway, waiting for him, the red and blue umbrella hiding her face.

Hodgson split the field again, this time into mixed ability groups facing each other across the width of the pitch. Nick placed his feet purposefully on the line. Murray sidled up to him.

'About time, too. A little hand-to-hand never did anyone any harm.' He clenched his fists and muscle tensed all along the soaked arms of his shirt to bunch around his shoulders. He growled at the opposing line.

'And who have you got in your sights?' Nick asked.

'Anybody who dares touch the ball.'

Nick chuckled.

'You watch yourself,' Murray warned. 'There's always some bastard wants to score points by tearing the ears off a little 'un. Remember last year.'

Nick glanced across at him. That was how he and Murray had forged their alliance. Some house-side had deliberately put the boot in and then crushed him beneath a belly-flop. Murray had dragged off the offending carcass and had been intent on making a corpse of him until he, too, was dragged clear.

'I can take care of myself,' Nick murmured. 'It's brains that count, not brawn.'

He watched Murray study him out of the corner of his eye,

expecting something to be said, but nothing was.

Hodgson threw the ball to the player at the end and blew his whistle. They ran forwards as an untidy line, each watching play to his left. The fool with the ball was going to try a solo up to the skirmish line. Nick gritted his teeth in annoyance, his protective plastic shield biting into his gums. That wasn't the objective. The objective was to practise passing at a run. Then the fool slipped in the mud, taking more care in his landing than in the safety of the ball. The opposition was on him, but too fast, carving furrows in the grass and fumbling the interception. Nick heard Murray bellowing to his right, and one of their team scooped up the ball and threw himself horizontally in the air, the ball flying through the sheeting rain to be caught and dropped. It bounced, once, twice, before falling dead in open ground. Murray roared in but Bernie Colwyn was the closer, smothering the ball and whipping it from Murray's reach in a shower of water and mud, to be buried himself the moment he skidded to a halt.

Arms and legs were disentangled and the ball was fed out along the opposing line. Nick held back, watching the play develop. A throw, a throw, a missed tackle, a call, a feint, and a mudman was through their line and running for touch. Nick felt his boot-studs slide then grip in the liquefying surface as he drove to narrow the angle between them. He powered on, aware of others around him, uncertain of their allegiance, dragging air into his lungs, forcing weakening muscle taut, until the familiar pain barrier was met and passed.

His pulse thudded loudly in his ears now, his arms pumping in a rhythm that seemed peculiarly slow. His field of vision narrowed to take in no one but the target. A fire burned in his chest, moving in a solid mass to his belly as the heels of his opponent grew larger. He clenched his teeth, telegraphing a signal to each ligament and sinew. Then he leaped, and reached, and sodden clothing and sticky flesh were sliding along his palms. The world revolved in alternating spokes of light and dark. The ground rushed up at him. He grunted as he bounced, his limbs as floppy as a rag-doll's, and real time burst upon him with the triumph of his victory.

It came out of the darkness, the sole of the boot, its gleaming studs multi-eyed talons winking in the searing white of the floodlights, the surrounding tangle of mud and grass tiny festering beards. He wrenched muscles trying to move aside, to turn away his head, but he was pinned somehow, an arm beneath his back, and the boot was filling his vision so he couldn't even shut his eyes against it. Then the night burst in upon itself, purple and yellow. Pain followed, searing through his head. Something was in his eyes, hot and stinging, and he was rolling on to his stomach, spitting mud from his mouth. Blood was mixed with it, blood running from his nose, blood on his hands, and on the cuffs of his shirt... *the bastard, the dirty bastard, the dirty fucking bastard...*

The ball stood white and unmarked a metre from the bastard's head. Nick felt his fingers dig into the soft ground as he propelled himself forward, the matted vegetation pressuring beneath his nails, the roar in his throat echoing in his mind. The bastard was on all fours. Nick tried to bring his leg round, to time the kick before the bastard raised himself, but his thrust was too wild and his heel skidded on the water-logged surface. The face lifted, the mouth opening, eyes wide and white as Nick's forearm smashed into him, catching him askew across the chin and chest, sending him back in a flail of arms and raised legs. Nick fisted with a left, feeling the knuckles strain against the skin; it slid along the ribs not under them. But the bastard was down now, and Nick drew back his foot for a kick that would finish it.

His field of vision whipped sideways. Caught on one leg he didn't stand a chance, in his temper hadn't seen his attacker coming on his blind side. Swinging his fist at the massive shoulders was as much out of frustration at his own shortcomings as in anger at the intervention. And then he was caught between the ground and this new opponent, and the ground was solid beneath him and his opponent as heavy as a side of beef. Nick's breath left him in an audible whoosh, but his right fist was in there, jabbing, jabbing, trying to get round the bulk of the body to the kidneys.

There was a discomfort at his throat that was building to pain. He tried to ignore it, to keep jabbing and reaching and clawing, and then he realised that he couldn't breathe, couldn't cry out. His windpipe was being crushed. He stared at the moon-face above him, brought his sight into focus, centring his gaze onto the slit eyes and taut-lipped grimace. Murray.

'...God's sake, Blaketon, quit it, I tell you. Quit it, you stupid sod, you screaming bastard. It was an accident. What the fuck are you trying to do? It was an accident for Christ's sake.'

Murray's words streamed away into the dark hole of the night as the skin around his eyes relaxed. The pinning arm moved to the top of Nick's chest, and Nick drank in air like a drowning man returning from the dead.

'Are you with us now?' Murray hissed. 'Speak to me, you prat.'

Nick couldn't get the words to form and instead shut his eyes. Exhaustion was cascading through him. Every limb ached. A pain was returning to his head, throbbing behind his eyes.

'Stupid sod!' Murray spat at him. 'It was an accident, you bastard. What the fuck were you trying to do to him?'

Nick lay panting, his brains scrambled. He wasn't sure he could form a thought that was coherent. He could hear a whistle, could feel the ground reverberating beneath pounding boots. Someone was shouting. Hodgson. Hodgson was shouting.

When Murray rolled off him, Nick thought he was going to float up from the ground. He dragged air into the furthest reaches of his lungs as if it would act as an anchor, and it hurt, it hurt like hell, each depressed rib springing up to resume its natural position. He struggled to his knees feeling oddly uncoordinated, and was hauled to his feet by Murray's powerful arm.

'What's going on?' Hodgson was demanding. 'What happened

here?'

'I... I had the ball and a clear run for the line, and... and I was tackled and... and I went down, we went down... and...'

Nick raised his head to look at the youth a couple of strides to his left. He was of similar build, his short-cropped hair making him seem almost bald. A hard man, except that he wasn't. He was scared, the hang of his shoulders shouting submission, his gaze darting between Hodgson and the ground, between the ground and Nick.

'I was right on their heels,' Murray was saying. 'I saw it all. The tackle was a bit iffy because of the mud. They both went down, and Blaketon caught a boot in the face. He thought it was deliberate...' Murray swung his attention to Nick, his expression full of grim warning '...but it was an accident, and as soon as I got here I separated them.'

Hodgson stepped forward. 'Let's have a look at that wound.'

Nick tried not to wince as he allowed his face to be prodded.

'I don't think it'll need stitching, it's mostly grazes, but you'd better get yourself to the Med Centre for a once-over and an anti-Tetanus jab.'

'Will it be open?' Murray asked.

'In the morning, then.'

'Sorry, mate,' the youth said over Hodgson's shoulder. 'I didn't even know I'd caught you. I didn't mean to.'

A hand was being offered, a tentative reconciliation. Nick looked at it, an alien thing, as colourless as pork rind in the weak floodlight. There was an urge to smack it aside and go for the youth's throat, but the urge was deep inside him, unconnected to the reality of his heaving chest and aching muscles. The way he felt he would be hard put to fight his way out of a paper bag. The thought amused him and he laughed. He nodded to the youth, and raised his hand in acknowledgement, but even that was a feat beyond him and the gesture was lost in a swaying of his arm. Enough, he decided. Enough. And he turned toward the bright lights of the Sports Centre, which spun in front of him as he staggered.

Murray was one side, peering into his face, Hodgson the other, holding him with one hand and waving at the muddied players who were all heading for the light.

'There's something wrong with him,' Nick heard Murray say.

'Probably just a touch of concussion,' was Hodgson's return. 'We'll know better once we get him inside.'

'What happened?' Nick asked.

'You're okay,' Murray told him. 'Just keep walking.'

Within a few strides he had walked himself conscious. The floodlight stood brilliant against the night sky, the lashing rain streaking diagonally across its stanchion. A blur of colour resolved into the Sports Centre. There was a crush at the entrance ahead of them, mudmen shoulder to shoulder seeking respite from the rain, and then they had funnelled up the steps, and he saw her.

The red and blue panelled umbrella had been furled. She stood back from the muddied path left by the players, but well within the cast of the porch lights. He could see her, but she hadn't seen him.

Nick drew himself free of Hodgson's support. His heart began to beat strongly, pumping his blood, releasing the fire.

He watched her, without blinking, as he and Murray and Hodgson matched strides across the spongy turf. Murray was easing the grip on his arm. Hodgson was turning to look behind.

There was recognition in her change of stance before it reached her face. The tip of the umbrella pecked at the glossy surface of the perron and was lifted as she moved towards the top of the flight, her eyes brightening, her dark lips curving into a smile. Hodgson hung back as they reached the steps. Murray and Nick mounted the first together, slowly, like dancers.

Nick saw her shift the umbrella from both hands to her left. They mounted the next step, and she drew it to her side. The studs of their boots clattered against the terrazzo. Her fingers were flexing. The next step was gained. The manicured nails were reaching out. He raised his head as he lifted his foot for the final flier and the fire in his blood ignited his lungs.

Her figure-hugging jacket was unzipped almost to her waist, the white shirt beneath unbuttoned to the swell of her suntanned breasts. His gaze rose up the contours of her neck, firm and swan-like, to the dipped chin and painted mouth, lips already pouting; the small nose, the blushered cheekbones, mascaraed lashes veiling hazel eyes which looked much lighter now they shone from the deep tan of her face. Her arm was raised, painted nails ready to claw his shirt, a wet and muddied second skin.

His straight-armed barge knocked her off her feet, but he never saw her fall. Murray's blow caught him in the chest and he plunged backwards from the steps. He heard the clatter of the umbrella on the terrazzo, saw Hodgson's shocked expression, saw Murray's bulky silhouette blocking half the lights from the porch and the windows behind.

The muddy grass broke his fall, partly on his side, partly on his left shoulder, and with the momentum Nick executed a backward roll that brought him to his feet. The cold rain washed his face and he laughed into the night sky, punching into the air as he jumped to give himself more height.

'Any port in a storm, Murray! She'll be grateful. See if she isn't!'

He turned, and at a jog, he crossed the pitch beneath the floodlights, increasing to a run as he entered the gloom beyond. The darkness was so welcoming, so enveloping, he shut his eyes to savour it, the wind-driven rain the only sensation to touch him.

He jarred his ankle as his foot dropped on to the hard surface of the road, and his eyes sprang open, surprised that he had covered the distance so soon. Easing back to a jog, he cut down the alley between the buildings, the noise of his studded boots setting up such a clattering on the concrete that he glanced behind for sight of pursuers.

Jogging through the Sciences quad he didn't pass a soul. The ungiving flagstones were taking its toll on his legs, and he changed course to stride along the grassy edge of the shrubbery separating the walkway from the glass and concrete buildings.

Behind the Law block the birches waved their sparse-leafed branches in welcome, and he slowed as he entered their shadowy domain. Gravel crunched beneath his boots as he walked towards the feeble street lamps of Salmon Grove. Rain didn't fall here, it splattered, and he stood a moment, breathing hard, to open his arms and fling back his head in willing acceptance of each drop that marked him.

At first he thought it was wind-driven leaves he could hear, but as he listened he realised that it was water, a stream of water tumbling over rocks, splashing and gurgling and bubbling, calling him towards it.

His boots sank up to their laces in mud and he looked down at the track the water had cut between the trees. It was wide enough to be called a stream, but not deep enough, not yet; but it was water, and it was running, running from a dark cleft in the windowless crag of the building's side. He moved between the tree trunks, keeping to the flow, his feet pressing through the sodden leaf litter into the fertile earth. The sucking of each lifted foot threatened to drag off his boot, but he did not change his course.

A broken down-pipe taking water from the roof. The disappointment left him stunned. What had he been expecting? A brook surging from rock? It almost looked like that, the rippled surface of the grey concrete blocks. It could be rock, natural rock, if his mind allowed it to be.

Lifting a hand he slipped it into the cascade, only to have it knocked aside by the sheer force of the plunging water. Cold. So very cold. He stepped beneath it so that it hit him on the top of his head, numbing his scalp and sending shivers of pain down his neck and his spine. The water moulded round him, forcing itself into his ears, in his eyes, over his nose, until all the flesh of his head was numb. His knees buckled. The water pressed down on him. He was sitting in the streambed, his fingers rooted in the earth. And he was breathing easily. He felt relaxed. In control. He would pass through. This time, he, Ognirius Licinius Vranaun, he would pass through.

Chapter 4

His body jolted and his eyes sprang open, but it took Nick a moment to appreciate that he was in his room. Everything seemed to be standing at an odd angle, almost reverse, and then the door shook beneath a heavy onslaught and he realised that it had been the noise which had awoken him.

He tried to sit up across the foot of the bed, but the pain was unexpected and sharp enough to make him gasp. It seemed to be coming from everywhere: his shoulders and legs, his back, his face, and then the hammering on the door began again, and he drew himself up with as much care as he could manage.

The duvet was covered in mud. He was covered in mud. It caked his arms and his legs, and the rugby kit he wore. He stared down at his boots, still tied securely around his feet. It looked as if he had waded through a marsh. With a growing sense of dread he gazed down at the carpet. A trail of mud, grit and shrivelled leaves led across the room.

When he opened the door John Wilson flinched back to the spindled rail of the landing, immediately straightening his shoulders and becoming more aggressive in his stance as if realising what he'd done.

'It lives,' he stated. 'Not that we were concerned one way or the other, you understand. A replacement of your calibre would be easy to find. Any wino dossing in a doorway would be more than capable of filling your shoes.'

Nick was looking past him, at the soil marks on the banister and the doors, on the pale green anaglypta covering the walls.

'Ah, you've noticed the attempt at redecoration. Good. May I also draw your attention to these.' John was pointing a bony finger to a line of cleaning utensils set out on the fouled carpet.

'Broom, dustpan, bucket, cloths. Get on with it. We'll be back around one and will expect to find the place looking the way it did when we moved in.' He laughed lightly, an affected girlish noise. 'Was that just over a week ago? How time flies when one is having such fun with one's fellow house-mates.' He turned for the stairs.

Nick began to lift an arm to stop him, but the pain in his shoulder made him wish he hadn't. 'I don't—'

'What was that? The beginning of an apology, was it?'

Closing his eyes against the sarcasm, Nick tentatively pushed his fingers over his temple and into his matted hair. A sprinkling of dried mud drifted down to the carpet. John raised a derisive eyebrow but didn't make a comment.

'I'm sorry, I don't remember—'

'You're sorry for the mess, or you're sorry that you don't remember being out of your mind?'

'I...' He shook his head. 'I hadn't been... How did I get in the house?'

'Oh, that's an easy one. You kicked in one of the panels of the front door until Maureen got there and opened it for you.

'And what did you say to her? Do you remember that at all? She won't tell me, or Bruce. Refuses to discuss it. But the front wheel of her bike is buckled, and she did that when she threw the thing in your path and locked herself in her room. And that's no exaggeration, because Bruce saw her do it from the top of these stairs.'

Nick tried to take it all in. John stared back tight-lipped.

'Doesn't look good, does it? Doesn't look as if an apology will be enough. Finding somewhere else to live might be on the cards, don't you think?'

With that he headed down the stairs. Nick didn't move until the front door slammed.

Standing before the mirror above his basin, he understood why John had flinched at the initial sight of him. He looked like some heavily made up actor from of a low budget scream 'n' slash movie. Mud, and what looked suspiciously like dried blood, caked his face, but it wasn't that which was causing the tightness around his left cheek and eye. His face was inflamed, and it took a lot of gentle dousing with luke-warm water to discover the extent of the damage.

Two lines raked his skin almost from eyeball to chin. His nose was badly grazed, and although there was no bleeding there obviously had been plenty at some time by the state of his shirt and shorts. But had it all come from him? That he'd been kicked in the face seemed obvious, and if he tried hard his memory could even glean snatches of the incident, but had he been fighting, too? His grazed knuckles and the pains in his muscles suggested that he had. Why couldn't he remember?

Cleaning himself was a long, slow process. First he showered to get rid of the excess dirt and then he filled the modern hip-bath and tried to soak away the aches and whatever might be lodged in the cuts and scratches. Blue and yellow bruises were blossoming all over him.

The warm water was soothing, and despite the lack of leg space he could feel himself drifting into that no-man's land of relaxation which verged on sleep. At least he'd had the forethought to sit his mobile phone on the shelf beside his head. John had told him that the others would be back at one o'clock. He wasn't sure that he wanted to wait around for them.

The mud came off the walls and paintwork easier than he had dared to hope. The stair carpet was the problem. He brushed, and vacuumed, but there were places where the dirt was deeply ingrained. His attempt at rubbing at it with a wet cloth was a disaster. He would have to hire a shampooer the way his mother did each summer. He remembered her constant grumbling about the expense and wondered if his finances would stretch that far. They would have to. Finding a new room was out of the question, but spending a year with individuals who refused to speak to him wouldn't be any fun either.

The front wheel of Maureen's bicycle was missing a few spokes and looked as if it had been under a truck. Or someone had deliberately smashed a very large boot through it. He didn't believe he'd done that, couldn't accept that he'd even had the strength until he saw the cracks in the bottom panel of the front door. He turned the Yale and pulled the door towards him. The damage was worse on the outside. Much worse.

One o'clock came and went in the Med Centre's reception area waiting for an anti-Tetanus jab. Priorities, he told himself. He would face the others later, around dinner maybe, but he was also toying with the idea of visiting the refectory again. He wondered if she would be there. Alison. Alice. And then he remembered the red and blue panelled golfing umbrella.

He had punched Louise.

He had *punched* Louise!

No, pushed her.

He nursed his head in his hands. Who was he trying to kid? He had hit her. Where? On the shoulder, he hoped. He tried to remember, but instead came up with a picture of a man silhouetted against the lights of the Sports Centre. He sat straight, a hand pressed against his painful solar plexus. Murray had hit him, knocked him clean off the steps. Shit. Why was all this just coming back to him now?

'Mr Blaketon?'

He looked up at the nurse who had read his name from a card. She gave him a cursory once over when he stood to follow her, but she didn't smile. Older than his mother, she had the sort of cynical air that was very short on sympathy.

'Which arm?' she asked as she closed the door of the cubicle.

'I'd prefer it in the left. Is there any mention on there of concussion?'

'No. What are the symptoms?'

He rolled up his sleeve to reveal a large bruise on his forearm. He decided not to meet the nurse's gaze. 'Loss of memory,' he said.

'Are you sure you can't put that down to the amount of alcohol you consumed?'

'I didn't consume any.'

'Drugs?'

'None.'

She cleaned his upper arm with a medi-swab. The smell of surgical spirit was strong enough to turn his stomach, and his arm stung. He had a sudden change of heart about the injection, but the needle was primed and moving towards his flesh. He held his breath and fought the urge to close his eyes. It hurt worse than at the dentist's. She wiped his arm again and turned away to dispose of the needle.

'Can you remember what you did today?'

'Yes,' he said. He rubbed his upper arm vigorously while she wasn't looking. It was turning numb. Was it supposed to turn numb?

'Then it's last night that's missing?'

She looked back to him and this time he held her gaze. 'I didn't take anything.'

'I understood that the first time. It could be no more than a glitch due to the kick you received. If pieces of today start disappearing then get back here at once. Do you want some antiseptic on that face?'

'Will it help?'

'Not much, but it'll hurt a damned sight more than the arm.'

Not trusting his judgement, he didn't weave through the traffic on Cottingham Road but waited at the crossing to re-enter the campus proper. There was a lot he had to do. His duvet cover needed washing; he'd sponged the feather insert as best he could and left it up against the radiator in his room. There were his clothes to collect from the Sports Centre. Most of all there were bridges to build: between himself and the others in the house, between himself and Louise, between himself and Murray. Louise was probably a lost cause, and he couldn't say that he'd shed too many tears over that. Murray was another matter.

There were plenty of puddles about, but the sky was surprisingly blue after the previous evening's rain, and the sun flared off each window in the upper storeys of the library drawing Nick's attention as he walked beside the building. He was almost to the arch beneath Sciences when he decided to retrace his steps. Murray might be in the library searching for the books he needed. He should be doing the same if he was going to keep ahead of his essays.

The warmth of the foyer enveloped him before he had passed through the security turnstile. All the catalogue terminals were in use, but Murray's shoulders weren't hunched over any of the keyboards. There were spaces at the inter-library terminals, and he considered logging on to see if there was anything different on offer from the previous semester. He sat down and tapped a few keys, but even before the main displays came on the screen he was up and moving away.

Murray wasn't on the ground floor. Nor was he among the Law references on West 2. Climbing the gloomy stairs again, Nick began to wonder what the hell he was doing. Perhaps Murray was among the Social History section — he'd been talking about the number of projects he had to get through this year — but he was just as likely to be at the launderette, or even still in bed.

Halfway up the flight Nick stopped to lean on the central handrail. His legs were complaining vehemently, his back hurting. Every time he breathed his ribs were giving him gip. He had to be out of his mind.

He turned to go down and the world turned with him, the smooth green walls breaking into sections and staggering towards him. He clung to the handrail, his centre of gravity swaying across the open stairwell, his sight caught on the black line of the handrail as it coiled down and down and down. Nick shut his eyes, shut them tight, and hung on, waiting for the dizziness to pass. A clanging echoed slowly around the shaft. It was deep, very deep. And empty.

He couldn't go down, couldn't even look down, and so he

went up, one step at a time, following the stairwell, the turbulence in the air brushing his cheek, clawing at his neck.

A landing appeared offering him a door, an exit. He took it gratefully, concentrating on the single chair standing vacant by shelves. He clutched at its sides, determined not to fall off.

His breathing eased. There was still some prickling at the back of his neck, a chill across his shoulders, but he felt stable now, if slick with sweat.

Nick stood to test his sense of balance. He even bent to retie the lace from his trainer without any ill effects. Only the prickling at the nape of his neck remained, and he rubbed at that with his left hand before remembering the injection. Go back, the nurse had told him, and he decided that he would. He hadn't a clue what he was going to tell her, but something was wrong. He should have gone to the Med Centre when Murray had first suggested it.

The plaque facing the door displayed a large number four. Nick hadn't realised he'd climbed two flights. It was very quiet, too. Eerie. He moved to the end of the nearest aisle looking for signs of activity. Rows of shelves tiered above his head, their tops close enough to the low ceiling to cowl the lights, creating banks of dusky shadow. Running above were cables and conduits and grotesquely curving pipes that the charcoal coloured ceiling did little to disguise, only seemed to bring closer to his head. The prickling at his neck began again.

The screen of the catalogue terminal flickered green on black as if demanding an urgent answer. Where was the assistant? Where were the browsers? To his left, a long way to his left, opaque squares of glass let in the only natural light. Behind a pillar of bookshelves a corner of a table was visible. A book lay open on it.

He walked towards the daylight, towards the table, sensing a need to tread with stealth. No one was there. There was no one sitting at any of the tables beneath the windows. Some of the chairs were set square and regimented; others looked as if they had been abandoned not a moment before. A modern *Marie*

Celeste. Even the windows were angled outwards, similar to the stern of a sailing ship. He splayed his feet a little, half expecting to feel the movement of the swell, as he tried to discern the view beyond, but the outer glass was hung with grime and corded cobwebs, and it was hard to make out even the colour of the sky.

There was a jolt of machinery which seemed to vibrate along the carpeted floor. Nick tensed as a high-pitched whine sang a steady note, but it was only the lift. He rubbed a hand across his ribs as he watched the lights play above its doors on the other side of the checking counter. A final thud and the noise stopped. He waited, but the metal doors did not open and the noise did not resume.

His attention returned to the line of tables beneath the windows, finally alighting on the open book in front of him. On one leaf was a badly exposed photograph, beneath it a line drawing, some sort of diagram. The opposite page was all text. He lifted the cover to glimpse its title. *Roman and Romano-British Mosaics in Northern England.*

History. Alice was a History Special.

A tingling started in his fingertips. He replaced the book on the table and shook his hand to restore the circulation. The tingling moved through his wrist and along his forearm, gaining in momentum until it was racing towards his shoulder. It caught at his neck and he clamped his other hand over it, willing himself not to panic. Someone was watching him. Someone's eyes were boring into him. He whirled round in defence. There was no one to be seen.

He was breathing hard now, and his ribcage ached. Someone was there. It wasn't his imagination. Someone had to be there.

In two strides he was in the adjacent aisle. A metal kick-stool stood directly under a light, but the passage was clear all the way through to the far wall. He stepped to the next aisle, and then to the next. It was like staring down corridors in a vast maze, the geometric lines of the shelving shooting away from him, taking the perspective to a dim vanishing point in the shadows. There was no one standing in the next aisle. He took another stride, and rocked back against the shelves.

She was crouching on her haunches, working along the books close to the floor. She wasn't wearing the green sweater, had on a pair of jeans and a dark blue body-warmer, but the trail of her auburn hair he would have recognised anywhere.

The prickling died at his neck, to be replaced by a surge of perspiration at his armpits and a stirring at his crotch. He wanted to speak to her, to say something overwhelmingly banal to catch her attention, but most of all he wanted to touch her, to stroke her auburn hair, to feel its silky strands slide through his open fingers.

He was almost upon her when she rose, a bag slung diagonally over her shoulder, a pile of books under one arm. She was turning towards him, turning but backing away. He caught sight of his own hand reaching out for her. Saliva was filling his mouth and he swallowed it down, the sour taste making him grimace. He snapped his fingers and pointed.

'Alice!' he exclaimed with unnatural enthusiasm. 'I forgot your name.' He half turned, retracting his hand to gesture in the opposite direction in an effort to get his hand away from her. 'I saw you from the end of the aisle and couldn't remember your name.' He gave an awkward chuckle, trying to look simply sheepish and not the complete imbecile he felt, but her grey eyes were wide in a pale face, and she held the stack of books like a shield against his attack the way she had held the tray in the refectory.

'What are you doing here?' Her question was sharp, halfway between a request and a demand.

'Er... Looking for a friend.'

Her eyes narrowed. 'Go away.'

Nick shrugged and smiled and looked down at the carpet tiles while he wondered what to say.

'Well, I'm... I'm touched that you consider me a friend,' he said, 'especially after such a short introduction yesterday, but I was looking for Murray. He said he'd be spending the afternoon up here.'

'Who?'

'Murray Symonds. Big individual. You couldn't miss him.'

'He's not a History student. I know all the History students.'

'Er, no, he's...' Nick caught sight of his grazed knuckles, the scratches across the back of his hand. 'We play rugby together.'

Of course. That was why she was backing away.

'You, er...' He chuckled again, trying to make light of it, and swept his fingers beside his face. 'You may have noticed.'

'Your friend Murray did that to you?'

'No, no. It, er, was an accident. I tackled someone and his boots... Are you interested in rugby?'

She shook her head and her auburn hair danced. Nick held his breath, wondering if it would rise around her head. It didn't.

'Ah. It's a bit difficult to explain, then.' He shrugged again. 'I left it too late to get out of the way. It... er... isn't as bad as it looks.'

This was getting him nowhere. He indicated the books tucked under her arm. 'Are you taking those out, or putting them back on the shelves?'

'I'm working on them.'

'They look heavy. Here, I'll—'

She pulled away. 'Leave me alone. Just go away and leave me alone.'

Taking two steps backwards she whirled on her heel to make her escape. The air seemed to follow her in a rush, the way it did when his motorbike was left in the wake of a juggernaut, and he swayed on the balls of his feet before pursuing her down the aisle. He was almost at the central intersection when he realised that she was walking in the opposite direction on the other side of the shelving. He doubled back, to find his way blocked by a student carrying a briefcase and a bulging sports bag. Both had to stop and press against opposing shelves to pass, so narrow was the aisle, and by the time Nick made it to the grimy windows he felt that he had lost her.

Two students were hunched over a pile of books at a table on his right. He stared at them, not quite believing they were real.

With their bags beside them and a half-eaten apple at one elbow, they looked as if they had been there for hours.

Alice was to his left, sitting at the furthest table, her back to the wall, facing him down the aisle. She had a book open in front of her, but Nick didn't think that she was reading it. When he began to walk towards her she raised her head and he knew she'd been watching for him.

As he closed the ground between them a familiar prickling attacked his shoulders and the back of his neck. His pulse rate mounted, increasing to a low drumming in his ears, and the injured muscles around his ribs began to tighten. She was on her feet ready to confront him by the time he reached the other side of the table.

'Stay away from me!' she hissed. 'This is harassment!'

He shook his head, but the movement seemed impossibly slow.

'No Sara pointed me out to you. There's no axe hanging over your head. There's no Murray, either, is there?'

'You've got the wrong idea,' Nick said.

He rested his hand on the table for his own support. He was trembling, feeling oddly frail. The wood was warm beneath his palm, the patterning grain undulating in sweeping strokes. Beech, perhaps. Or oak. Not pine, certainly.

'What do you want me to do here?' she demanded. 'Scream for help?'

The books were fanned across the table like cue cards. *The Brigantes and Their Septs*, *Roman Inscriptions of York*, *The Autumn Killing*, *Soldier and Civilian in Roman Yorkshire*.

'I... I only want to get to know you.'

'I don't want to get to know you. Do you understand? Leave me alone. I don't want to get to know *anybody*.

'Hey! Hold that!'

At first Nick thought she was shouting at him, but she was looking away. As he turned to follow her gaze she sped by him. There was a woman behind the checking counter, a student at the catalogue terminal. Behind them both a youth with ginger hair was holding open the doors to the lift. Nick gasped, throwing out a hand towards her.

'No! Alice! *Alice!*'

The student looked up from the terminal. The ginger youth frowned. The assistant raised a hand and said something he didn't catch. The doors of the lift were sliding together, sliding shut. Nick reached them, saw Alice through the narrowing gap, her grey eyes staring from her pale face, staring right through him, the surround of her auburn hair glinting like fire in the light above her head, all lost in the soft phush of pneumatics. He slapped his hands on the metal of the doors and closed his eyes as the whir of the mechanism took her down, down and away from him.

'Hey, you!'

The sharp tone made him turn. They were facing him in a semi-circle, staring, scowling.

'What's going on?' the assistant demanded. 'What's your name?'

Nick backed along the wall until he reached the door.

The chill of the stairwell embraced him, the noise of the lift echoing loudly in the hollow space. He kept close to the wall as he descended the stairs, didn't want to look towards the central well and its sheer drop. Anger and need and fear and sorrow crowded in on him, and he quickened his step trying to escape their growing howl. Faster he went, down flight after flight, his trainers slapping on the risers and scuffing on the turns, her name a hissing sibilant in his head. *Alice 'n' Alice 'n' Alice 'n' Alice...*

Chapter 5

It was after nine that evening before Nick found Murray. He and Bernie Colwyn were sitting in the Sanctuary bar in the Union, holding court before a gaggle of eager-eyed freshers. The talk was rugby, Nick could tell by the rise and fall of Murray's shoulders, the swinging movements of his arms. They'd been there for a while, going by the forest of empties on the table, and it didn't look as if anyone was going to plead poverty and head out. Not to be expected the first week, of course, even if half of them were still waiting for their loans to come through.

Nick hung back. He wanted to speak to Murray, needed to talk to him, to talk to somebody and Murray was all he'd got, but he also needed privacy, otherwise he'd be landed with more privacy than he bargained for. Like a padded room. Acting as if he were some sort of schizo wasn't funny when it was for real. And if it wasn't the onset of that, he didn't want to contemplate what was happening to him. Not on his own, anyway.

Bernie Colwyn was the first to notice him. Nick watched the big man's gaze jump to Murray, saw the nonchalant clink of glasses, the quiet phrase pass over his lips. Murray didn't look round, but others did. There was no turning back. He walked through the dim lighting to their crowded table.

'Room for another?'

'That depends whether you're planning to swing any punches,' Murray countered. Still not looking at him, he grasped his pint and downed the final third in one, smacking the glass back on the beer mat in a gesture alien to the Murray Nick knew.

One of the freshers was opening a tube of mints, another swilling the dregs of his beer round his glass. Around the table they were freezing him out, all of them, except for the one by the wall. He was staring.

For the life of him, Nick couldn't grasp at a name. They'd all been at the training session, but he didn't want to look too closely, to remember too well. Except for the youth in the corner, the one with the very short hair, almost a skinhead cut. Nick remembered his face from above Hodgson's shoulder. He recalled the offered hand and his own urge to smack it aside and... and go for the throat?

He wasn't sure what he was feeling now. If he didn't get a seat with them he'd never get one again, and if he did get a seat the atmosphere was going to be so strained they'd make a profit selling it in parcels at the bar. Why hadn't he read the situation and left?

'I just wanted a word. But it can wait until the morning.'

'A word?' Murray started to turn round. 'After your performance all you want is a— Ah, shit. Nick... Have you stood in front of a mirror lately? You look as if you've been dug up.'

'Yes. I know.' Without thinking Nick glanced across at the skinhead in the corner. He was shaking his head.

'I'm sorry,' the skinhead murmured. 'I'd no idea I'd even caught—'

'Don't be sorry,' Murray snapped. 'He wasn't going to be sorry about what he intended doing to you.'

Every eye but Murray's turned Nick's way, and the ensuing silence fanned out to nearby tables as onlookers grew curious.

Nick stood straight and held out his hands. 'Okay. It was my fault, my fault entirely. I over-reacted.' He looked at the skinhead pressed into the corner. 'I apologise for knuckling you. I'm sorry.'

Murray swung round. 'That was me, you prat! Can't you remember who you hit?'

Nick blinked at him. 'Not entirely. That's why I wanted to talk to you.'

'If you want to talk to someone, I suggest you talk to Louise. You remember Louise? She wanted to talk to someone last night. Black boots. Blue uniform. Silver car with a chequered stripe. Ring any bells in that fucking brain of yours? Remember *hitting* her?'

'I thought I'd... pushed her.'

All conversation in that part of the bar dropped away.

'*Pushed* her?'

'Excuse me, gentlemen. Just collect a few glasses here. We're running out at the bar.'

Long arms forced a path between Nick and Murray. Nick didn't look at the barman but stepped aside to give him room. Murray didn't take his eyes from Nick, acting as if the man wasn't there. The collective ching of the glasses sounded like the bell in a boxing ring, and as the barman started to pull away Nick matched the man's stride.

'I'll see you tomorrow.'

'I'm busy,' Murray slung after him. 'And I'm going to be very busy for a very long time.'

Nick didn't answer and he didn't look back. He half expected to have a glass thrown at him, at least some caustic language, but he walked to the door of the Sanctuary in a silence that didn't fall into itself, even when he began his descent of the stairs.

A soft wind sighed through trees. A distant, undulating note. A gentle breeze rustled grass. It rippled water, and water lapped a shore. But only in sound. There was no light. No form. No touch. No taste. Only sound. Wind through trees; breeze through grass; water caressing a shore. And the scent of flowers. Wild flowers. Thick and heady. Filling his nostrils. Overloading his senses. And he was falling. Falling into them. They were reaching up to him. Flowers. Stems brushing his ribs. Snapping beneath his chest. Being crushed beneath his weight. Giving up their scent. Overpowering him with their scent.

Nick felt the cry rush up his throat and jolted his face from the bedding to stare at shadows dancing across the wardrobe door. Tree shadows. Shadows from nightmares. Nightmares from childhood when doors opened and monsters stepped out.

He stared at the wardrobe door. It didn't open.

Lowering his face onto the sheet, he tried to relax. His heart was hammering and his breathing rapid, his skin slick with fast-chilling sweat. He lifted himself on to one elbow and groaned as he caught his erection among the crumpled bedding. Easing himself on to his side, he dragged free the pillow wedged beneath him, held it in one hand and stared at it, its white bulk coated with an orange cast from the streetlamp outside the uncurtained window.

Had he been cradling his pillow? He reached for the dream, but it was fading fast and he wasn't inclined to chase after it. Cushioning his head, he lay back to look about the room, to gaze at the wardrobe door. Tree shadows etched solid lines of black across the paintwork, but they weren't moving now. Part of his dream, perhaps. Perhaps his imagination.

He shuddered. The bed was cold, the sheet damp from his perspiration. He threw back the duvet and reached for a pair of jogging pants and a sweatshirt from the floor.

His mother had packed a hot water bottle somewhere. She'd been insistent about him taking it, about him not catching his death in the northern winter. But which box was it in? He gazed at the shadowed bulk of the three cartons stacked between the wall and his desk. Who cared? A coffee would be better.

The house was silent except for Maureen's subdued snoring. In the hall Nick did his best to keep his eyes averted from the bent wheel of her bicycle. He supposed he would have to do something about it pretty soon. He'd been lucky and had managed to sneak in without being seen, but that buckled wheel was a reminder to everyone, and everyone had to pass it to get upstairs to the bathroom.

On the return, the stairs creaked the way they never had on his descent, and Nick was pleased to be able to switch off the landing light and gain his own room again. He leaned against the door and contemplated the four metre square chamber that was his for the year.

It had seemed huge when he had first looked it over. Now, cluttered as it was, it felt peculiarly claustrophobic. Spiky shadows crossed every wall, corner to corner, even reaching out to leave their mark on him as he stood at the furthest point from the window. He regarded the wall of glass by his bed.

'How come the room's available?' he'd asked.

'You'd stay here, would you, if an exchange at Heidelberg came up?'

'So why haven't one of the others moved into it? It must be the biggest room in the house.'

'That's your answer. Single glazed; faces north; as draughty as hell. Wet and cold running condensation autumn and spring. Impenetrable Jack Frost all winter.'

Nick had pushed the single bed beneath the window, leaving just enough space to open the glazed door and squeeze on to the ledge that was the balcony. From there he could almost touch the leaves on the trees. That had been during early summer when the air was warm and the light dappled. In the chill grey of a damp autumn it seemed more that the trees were reaching inside for him. He took a sip of his coffee and nestled the hot cup to his chest.

The tingling started in his fingertips. At first he gave it no concern, thinking it was the heat of the mug or the tension in his grip, but as the sensation crept along his fingers and the backs of his hands, panic began to set in. Then the tingling roared along his arms to grip the nape of his neck. The coffee slopped over the edge of the mug to be soaked up by his shirt and burn his skin beneath.

He set the mug on the corner of the desk, but his hands were shaking so much that he slopped the contents again. There was a sucking sound, like air being drawn into constricted lungs, and the shadow-trees lunged towards him, wrapping their branches about his head and body.

The curtains at the window... If he could close the curtains...

He fell across the bed. The street light was bright in his eyes, blinding him against the shape of the trees outside. His hand reached for the curtain. He felt the soft material in his fingers; grasped it. The prickling at his neck was hurting, his gritted teeth forced so hard together they were being pushed back into the gums. He hauled at the fabric. The runners wouldn't give on the rail. The curtain wouldn't move, was snagged somewhere. Sweat was pouring from him. The glass was cold, so soothing against his skin, a balm against the pain. And the neon light was receding, receding to a flaring dot. He thought that he was fainting, but the streetlamp was to his left, behind the part-clothed skeleton of the tree, the flaring neon to his right. Across the road and between the blocks of the on-campus residence, small now, a dot, flaring neon and russet and gold.

The prickling faded but Nick did not blink his eyes, dared not in case he lost sight of it. His pulse leapt afresh, and he pressed his forehead closer to the pane. There was no mistake. Between the buildings of Taylor Court he could see her, sitting on a seat by the pond, the locks of her fiery hair lifting, beckoning him down.

His breath condensed on the cold glass by his lips but it did not obscure his view. He lifted his hands and grasped tight the wooden horizontal above his head. Desire was rising within him, strong and violent. He dug his fingernails into the paintwork, anchoring himself to the frame.

I won't go down. I won't.

Alice closed her eyes, crossed her arms over her abdomen and waited for the spasm to fade. Her back ached, her stomach ached, her legs ached, her head ached. She was three days late.

What on earth was the matter with her? She'd never been late in her life. Textbook regular, had been since the very first. And there was absolutely no reason. She wasn't ill. She wasn't run down. She wasn't under any stress.

A face filled her mind and she snapped open her eyes so as not to see it, but the scarred cheek and staring eyes followed her into the lamplight. For several seconds the dismembered head hung in the night air before dissolving away, to be replaced by a trail of willow fronds and the brick paving of the courtyard.

Alice fixed her gaze on the porch light above the yellow door in front of her, willing her heartbeat to slow. The stillness of the night crowded in as if the darkness were solid planes, and the distances, and the unnatural neon lighting, were no more than illusions in an ebony mirror. She refused to look left or right in case she caught a fleeting glimpse of something she preferred to believe did not exist.

It couldn't be. Not again.

Yet, it could explain so much.

A pain zig-zagged through her abdomen and wrapped itself around her kidneys. She gasped aloud, hugging herself once more, holding her breath until the cramp eased.

His face swam before her pale and cold. Alice tried to block it out. It was almost as if she were calling him to her.

The activity holiday had been part reward, part gift for her thirteenth birthday. She hadn't wanted to go, not wanted to leave the house and the Clarksons, but her parents had insisted, as they always did.

She'd seen Andrew that first afternoon, across the tumult in the reception area. His smile had been so warm and full of joy. They'd been teamed together for many of the activities that week. He'd explained the rules of badminton and she'd shown him how to read a map for the orienteering. She'd kept close when his gelding had tried to throw him. He'd insisted on partnering her in the canoe.

The dreams... It had been him in the dreams. The wind, the water lapping against the shore, the overpowering scent of that woman who had hugged her and hugged her until she feared she would never breathe again.

I mustn't think of him.

His arm was reaching out for her, his fingers, open and grasping, trying to tangle in her hair. But the hand was too broad, the knuckles skinned. Her gaze ran along the extended arm, across the shoulder. Even before she reached the scarred face she knew it was not Andrew but Nicholas Blaketon.

The splash sounded loud in the still air and Alice lowered her hands to look about her. Despite the lighting, the courtyard was edged with shadows, some surprisingly faint, others impenetrable. She could see no one, but that didn't mean no one was there, that he wasn't there. She'd felt his stare in the seminar room. Again in the library. There was no denying it now, no brushing the intuition aside as mere coincidence. If there was one thing her life had taught her, there was no such thing as coincidence.

She turned her attention to the trees at the edge of the wooden seat, to the weed-like reeds and ragged shrubs which had been allowed to choke the pond. A splash meant water, and water meant... Frogs? Rats? She drew her feet up on to the seat and hugged her shins. Had those droplets on the brickwork been there when she had first sat down? Were they a trail? Tiny paw-prints?

A wave of nausea surged through her and she closed her eyes as muscles spasmed. It was definitely getting worse. She was close now. She shouldn't sit there. The night air was not helping as she'd hoped.

As slim as an arrow, his aim had been true, but the exertion far beyond any agony he had experienced or devised. It had felt as though the air was shredding him with barbed talons. If he had not hit the water... But the water was his sustenance as well as his torturer, and he was below her now, savouring the essence of the female: the fiery warmth radiating from her body, the pungent scent of peaking womanhood. He absorbed every facet, allowed it to uncoil within him, took strength from it as he had once taken strength from a battle-potion. As ephemeral as mist, as silent as smoke, he rose between the slats of the seat to stand over her.

How young she looked, despite her years, like the boy who

thought himself a man, the boy whose battle-training was as hollow as his heart.

Drawing on memories, he lifted an arm and his arm rose before him. He didn't need the water! He could conjure in the air!

He stared at his arm in wonder, astonished at the power he had harnessed. Even the jewelled rings had returned to his fingers, flesh to bone, bulk that was rounded, sustainable. His hand rose to his chest, feeling muscle, rose to his throat, his knuckles catching on the roundels of the torc. Even the torc from so long ago. He could feel it, lift it, see it. Colouring was weak, though. Watery milk. Milky water. Faint silver, instead of bright gold.

He banished the thread of doubt. Did he crave everything at the first attempt? Had he not gained more than anticipated? One step at a time. One step at a time.

He lowered his head to breathe in her scents. Something new. Something unexpected. The tang of bitter fruit. Lemons. She had squeezed lemons in her hair. The triggered memory made him salivate, and the knowledge that he could kindled his heart. Everything would return.

'How good you are for me.'

His fingers delved gently within the locks of her hair. With a sudden twist, he clenched his fist and dragged up his forearm, but not a strand of tawny hair was disturbed. She did not know that he was there. She could not feel his presence.

The firm lines of his body began to blur as disappointment ran from him. He crushed the emotion. Was that not why he had command of the boy? One step at a time.

He'd been too eager. He'd let his exhilaration run before him. He should have stayed with the boy. The boy was not fully broken, and now his grip was weakened.

But the freedom... How wondrous it was to see and touch and feel, and not to have that liquid glaze dimming his perceptions.

He let his gaze fall on the auburn head. She might not sense him, but he could smell her and touch her and taste her, and she could feed him as the boy fed him.

His fingers gripped her throat, then slid forward over her collarbone and beneath her clothing. Her breasts were engorged, straining against their bindings, forcing the hard nipples back into the flesh. As he cupped their weight she groaned, and he smiled as though his touch had been the cause. He raked his nails across her tender belly, imagining the blossoming weals. She gasped, and tensed, as muscles spasmed, and he knew that she was ready. She offered no resistance as he forced his hand into her crotch and felt the soft tissues envelop him. When her body lifted to walk through him and away, he remained by the trees and the pond, his fingers glistening with her blood.

Chapter 6

Beneath the shadow of the covered entrance way, Nick stood on the edge of the brick pavement looking into the enclosure of Taylor Court. The barrack-like blocks seemed forbidding, even in the morning sunlight, the square net-curtained windows yielding nothing of their interior, or their inhabitants.

Alice had left the seat and walked out of his line of vision towards one of the buildings. He wondered how many houses there were in total. He could see semi-circular steps to five doors, individual names printed clearly above — Lincoln, Brough, Kirkella — house names and place names of the area.

He rubbed at his eyes as his vision began to blur. God, he was tired. As far as he could recall he'd collapsed on the bed and slept like a log after Alice had left the courtyard, even sleeping through his alarm. If Maureen hadn't decided to play opera at full volume beneath his floor he reckoned he'd have been out for the count still. She'd put it on deliberately, no doubt about it, but he was grateful, nonetheless. He had to get out of this habit of turning up late for lectures.

Taking a lungful of air to help oxygenate his system, he returned his attention to the forlorn trees and dishevelled undergrowth beside the wooden seat. There was a pond there, somewhere. He remembered looking in it during his previous year when he'd been exploring, finding his bearings around the campus. It had been new then. Sticklebacks had been swimming in the clear water. There'd been dragonflies, too, he remembered. It hardly seemed possible now.

A girl on a cycle startled him as she flashed by. He'd have to do something about Maureen's bike. He was sure he'd seen a shop on Cottingham Road. He'd check after the lecture, after lunch; hell, after breakfast, whenever that was liable to be. He shouldn't have chickened out on the others in the house. He should have faced them all in the kitchen and dealt with the confrontation. He'd have to do it sometime. He couldn't keep dodging them until next June.

Hugging his wallet file across his chest he contemplated the route ahead. There was nothing to stop him cutting through Taylor Court, coming out at the opposite entrance. It was a shorter path, now, after all, and had been his original intention.

The seat and the trailing willows loomed large in his vision. Alice had been there last night, sitting alone in the darkness. She lived on the courtyard. One of the faceless windows was hers. She could be sitting there, watching, waiting for him as she'd been waiting last night, calling him.

He retreated on to Salmon Grove to take the longer route.

He was much too early for his English lecture. Not only was the theatre still locked, but no one was waiting. Nick was relieved about that. Louise was bound to be there, it was their first of the semester, but he didn't feel up to facing her, or her friends. He bought a jam doughnut from the snack bar along the corridor, a can of Cola from the machine, and proceeded to eat breakfast on his way to the Union building.

The narrow corridor on the first floor was thronged with people and with noise, not at all as it had been the last time he had walked along it, yet as he stood looking down its length goose-pimples rose along his arms and tightened the skin at the back of his neck. Panic clawed at him and he balled his fists waiting for the eerie tingling to follow. Muscles ached from the tension, but nothing else manifested.

He felt stupid and embarrassed. Didn't he have enough to contend with without self-induced paranoia?

Careful to keep his gaze away from the notice boards, he made his way down the corridor. Relief swept through him when he passed the societies' boards. He emerged into the wi-fi lounge and turned to the ochre pin boards. Only drawing pins adorned the rugby's space; there wasn't a single notice.

He and Murray had used the space as a private bulletin board when Murray's mobile had disintegrated and he'd been waiting for a replacement. They'd played the one-upmanship game of making each note more lurid than the last, gleefully anticipating the reaction of casual readers; all so childish now he thought about it.

He pulled his own mobile from his pocket. There were no messages, not even an abusive one from Louise. He clicked through the Phonebook, his thumb hovering over the connection button as he stared at Murray's name on the screen. Not a call, no. That would get him an earful. A text. Give Murray time to think about it, to come round. His fingers slid across the buttons. He read the message: *Sorry. Urgently need to talk. Zucchini 1pm today.* He considered it. It didn't seem enough but what else could he say? He pressed Send and the mobile sang its little routine and cut its backlight. Murray wouldn't respond immediately. Or if he did Nick didn't want to read it. He switched off the mobile and slipped it in a pocket.

It was a weight lifted. As he walked back down the corridor, he felt better, in fact so positive that he decided to face his anxiety head on and seek out the poster on the Environmental / Conservation board.

Her oval face, her leafy hair. He'd tried to tell himself that it was no more than a stylised drawing. Any woman, any age. It wasn't. It was definitely Alice. What he couldn't understand was how he had noticed it. Including her leafy locks the drawing was hardly bigger than a fifty pence piece, a mere logo.

Mother Earth Society
Next Meeting: 18 October – M/Room 3
Samhain Celebrations - Preliminary Discussion

And that name inked out at the bottom. It had to be Hawkins. He stared at it. Hawkin, perhaps. He'd not come across the name, he was sure, but he disliked the man, instinctively knew that the name belonged to a man. No woman would draw another looking like that, looking so... voluptuous.

Nick pulled himself away. He wasn't sure he trusted the path his thoughts were taking.

As he passed through the glass doors to Larkin East, he slowed his pace. There was a crowd waiting outside the lecture theatre. They lounged against the wall, chatting in groups that blocked the corridor, females outnumbering males. Louise was bound to be among them. He looked for her slim outline and short dark hair.

Someone brushed his shoulder, hurrying down the aisle. Bulging briefcase, worn jeans and an amazingly old fashioned jumper; it had to be Dr Cavley. Nick watched him unlock the theatre door and enter, the waiting students funnelling in behind him. He joined the cortege. One or two glanced his way, to look again in a mixture of horror and surprise, but Nick made out that he hadn't noticed. The left side of his face had begun to tighten considerably. He'd hardly looked at it in the steamy mirror that morning as he'd pressed a damp flannel to his torn skin. It was probably beginning to scab.

As others descended the stairs in the tiered seating, Nick made a line for the furthest bench on the back row. The strip-light above had blown. From there he would be able to see everyone below him, but hopefully anyone looking up might have trouble making out more than a silhouette.

The restlessness eased as files were opened, notebooks produced. Dr Cavley was passing a pile of handouts to the front row. Unless Louise had drastically changed the colour of her hair, she was not on the front row. She wasn't on either of the next two either. Nick made out Cheryl and Suzanne sitting together three tiers below him, and had expected that Louise would have chosen to sit with them. He'd hardly been able to separate the trio when he'd been doing all the running the previous year. With hindsight, that had probably been the plan. Had she sunk her claws into someone new already? That would be hoping for too much.

Cavley slapped down a book to catch everyone's attention and pushed his glasses further along his nose. Nick had come across Dr Cavley before, had been in a couple of his seminars during the previous semester. His voice was clear but he was intimidated by numbers. This would be the last time he looked up at his audience.

'Welcome, one and all, to Victorian Literature 1837 to 1880. If that's not what you were hoping for, you are in the wrong lecture hall.'

He gave a broad smile and a few of the students tittered in response. If Cavley went true to form it would also be his last joke.

The dwindling sheets were passed to Nick. It was the forthcoming lecture and tutorial schedule, together with the inevitable booklist.

Victorian Literature had seemed a relatively painless option when he had plumped for it. Half the books he'd either covered in his 'A' levels, or his mother had as dramas on DVD. The rest would be available at any bookshop in Hull at £2.49 a throw. There seemed to be an awful lot of them, nevertheless. His gaze slid down the list. *Alice's Adventures in Wonderland (1865)*. An involuntary shiver climbed Nick's spine. He wondered what Mr Carroll would have made of Nick's own journey into the unknown.

'As you can read,' Cavley continued, 'this lecture is to be an introduction, an overview.'

Nick rubbed the tiredness from his eyes and pulled out a pen.

'Hi. Nice to have you with us.'

The dated jumper swam into Nick's focusing vision and he knew it belonged to Cavley. It seemed ridiculous to have to look up into the lecturer's face, but look he did. The man was grinning.

'It seems they sneaked out round you.' His glasses were in their usual position, teetering on the edge of his nose. He pushed them back into place to peer over Nick's arm at his notebook.

'Ah, Darwin. Does that to me, too. Glad I won't be taking the lecture. It would be terribly bad form for your snoring to drown out what I was saying.'

'I wasn't snoring, was I?' Nick shook his head to make his brain function. Of course he hadn't been snoring. It was Cavley's idea of sarcasm. 'I'm sorry, Dr Cavley.'

'That's okay. It's your degree. I get paid regardless. I only came across to check that you hadn't died. Good party, was it?'

Nick began to collect his notebook and pens, and stuff them into the wallet file. 'Party? Er, no.' He indicated his cheek. Two could play with straight-faced wit. 'I ran out of pain-killers and spent most of the night pacing the floor.'

Cavley's manner changed immediately. 'Oh. I'm sorry. I didn't realise. Have you been to the Medical Centre?'

'First thing.' He gave the man a half smile, making out that it hurt more than it did. 'I think I took too many.'

'You must be careful. Are you sure you're all right?'

Dr Cavley was as solicitous as a mother hen all the way from the theatre to the outer glass doors, where Nick was grateful to part company with him.

It was 12.50 when he entered the café. Most of the tables were taken, but Nick queued at the counter all the same. There was no sign of Murray. He bought a coffee and a strip of pizza and went to lean against the wall until a table became free.

Murray still hadn't turned up by 1.10. At 1.20 Nick switched on his mobile, watching its screen as the phone sang through its wake-up routine. Murray's reply, texted seconds after he'd sent his own, consisted of two words. Nick knew that he was on his own.

*

His afternoon was free. He ambled round the Waterstone's bookshop for a while, buying a couple of editions specified in Cavley's list, then began to make his way back through the campus to the house. Despite trying to convince himself that he would spend the afternoon reading, or perhaps catching up on some much needed sleep, when he stood at the entrance to Taylor Court it had to be admitted that hadn't been his plan at all. He had to stop this... this haunting.

The courtyard was busy with students moving through, or coming in and out of the houses. Feeling like a condemned man, Nick walked slowly across the brick paving, making for the scrubby vegetation and the wooden seat. He watched a door snap shut with the certain thud of an automatic lock, and his gaze rose to the push buttons and speaker grille on the adjoining wall. Room numbers only; no names.

He was going to have to face Alice before he left the courtyard, he knew that, willed himself to accept it as a fact, but with no last name to hand he wondered how he was going to find her, who he was going to ask for directions. He thought about it logically, covering everything that had happened to him since he'd first set eyes on her, and hoped to God that he would need to ask, that the prickling wouldn't start at his neck, and that he wouldn't just know.

The sky had clouded since the morning and the breeze had picked up. The willow tree by the pond was shaking its tentacled limbs, a dervish in slow motion. Dried leaves chased one another under the legs of the wooden seat. No one was sitting there.

Reaching out an unsteady hand, Nick curled his fingers about the top horizontal of the backrest, and waited. His heart was thudding and he realised that he was breathing heavily, but there was no tingling in his hand, no prickling at his neck. The weather had been fine that morning. Others would have sat there, talked there, laughed there, probably obliterating all trace of her.

The concept was idiotic. Wasn't it? Something from a bad

ghost story? Could a person be haunted by the living?

He walked to the front of the bench, but decided against sitting there. Instead he took the extra step and peered into the degenerating undergrowth. The pond was choked with grass and weeds, almost silted up, as if an attempt had been made to fill it in. The occasional flash of water he glimpsed was swirling with sediment. He wondered what lurked beneath the mud, what he'd unwittingly disturbed. Frogs, perhaps. Sticklebacks couldn't swim freely any more, but he was sure frogs would like the mud.

He was looking for diversions; he had to stop this and achieve what he had come to do.

Positioning himself so that his calves were almost touching the seat, he gazed across the courtyard. Alice had walked out of his view — he turned to check his line of vision with the Salmon Grove houses — she'd walked out of his view and towards... either Kirkella or Brantingham. A red door. A yellow door.

The houses were at the ends of two blocks standing at ninety degrees to each other in the corner of the courtyard. Which one? Who to ask? Two students were cycling through the open space. Others were talking outside one of the houses at the further end. It wouldn't look suspicious if he walked up to the two doors, he reasoned. Who was going to question him, think him a burglar? At worst he could make out that he'd forgotten his key.

He strode across to Kirkella and mounted the semi-circular steps to the red door. He'd sensed Alice when he'd been close to her, known that she'd been in the vicinity. He waited for the tingling to show itself; passed his palm within an inch of the push buttons on the metal plate. There wasn't a spark, even of static.

Through the glass pane of the upper door, he peered into the hall beyond. A pin board and a ribboned letter rack adorned the wall, a black and white poster advertising some band he'd never heard of. The walls were a light yellowy wash, the staircase an even paler wood. He could see through another half-glazed door into what looked like a kitchen. There was nobody there. He considered pushing a few buttons to see what happened; decided against it.

The walk across to Brantingham was short, but he was sweating so much now that greasy fingerprints were being left on the wallet file in his grasp. In turn he wiped each palm down his jeans' legs. It didn't seem to help.

There was no eerie calling from beyond the glass as he stepped in front of the square net-curtained windows, no tingling as he stood at the yellow door and ran his fingers lightly over the push buttons. He checked over his shoulder, checked the line between the seat and the door. She hadn't got up and walked away between the buildings, had she? He stepped off the top stair to gaze over the rough ground. No, not in the dark, surely.

There was a click and he looked round to see the door being opened by a girl with blonde hair piled up into some sort of nest.

'Nobody answering?' She blinked, and the initial smile faded. Her eyebrows rose and her lips parted. Nick was beginning to get used to the effect the sight of his face was having on people, and he waited for her to finish her reassessment of him.

'Good grief,' she murmured. 'Who did you annoy?'

'Rugby injury.'

'Macho man, eh? Perhaps I should come and watch.'

Nick's heart gave a lurch. It was Louise in another guise. Why were all these women so bastard predatory?

The blonde averted her gaze as if suddenly embarrassed. 'It's quiet upstairs. I think the fellas are out. I can stick a Post-It to a door if you want to leave a message.'

'I've come to see Alice.'

Her eyes flitted back to him, swept over him from hip to hair. 'Alice?'

'Yes. I need to speak to her, but she's not answering her bell. We had a bit of a row. About my playing rugby.' He hardly dared take a breath.

'You're, er, some sort of—' she angled her head '—boyfriend?'
Voila!

He gave her a quick taste of his sheepish look. 'That's a bit of an old fashioned term.'

The blonde shrugged. 'Well, our Alice is a bit of an old fashioned girl. Y'know, university life should be study, study, study. It's not blood that flows through her veins, it's ink. Or iced water. I guess you'd better come in.'

As the door snapped shut behind them, Nick followed her past the light tones of the wooden staircase to the glass door of the kitchen. She half opened it, then turned to indicate to his right.

'Help yourself. I'm going to put the kettle on for a coffee.'

Slipping inside, she left him standing in a short, windowless corridor which ran as a T-junction through the middle of the house. Everywhere he looked stood natural wood, not just the doors and skirtings, but the walls were faced with panels of the stuff to a height well over two metres. Daylight filtered from the kitchen and the stairwell, giving the impression of a secret passage in an old mansion.

There were four doors on the right of the entrance hall. Alice lived in one of them. Taking a firm grip of his English file, Nick walked slowly along the carpeted floor.

He passed the first door without incident. By the second he stopped to drag a breath into his aching lungs. It was there. The tingling was in his fingertips. He tried to lick his lips, but his tongue was dry. Two more steps and he was by the third door. The tingling had intensified to pins and needles, though there was none of the intense pain he had experienced the night before. Should he knock?

His gaze sought the final door. His breathing was rapid now, his adrenalin high. It was that one. Something told him. Intuition. Instinct. It was the one furthest down the hall.

He didn't rush. Wanted to be sure. Was sure. The pins and needles were cramping his hands, the hairs on his neck rising like the hackles of a dog. Room 8 belonged to Alice, and Alice was inside.

He knocked.

There was a sound from within, but whether it was a call to enter he wasn't certain. Closing his eyes, he laid his hand on the knob and twisted.

Nick's heart pounded high in his throat as he pushed the door ajar and slipped through. It closed automatically behind him.

He was in a tunnel, a dim tunnel, sandwiched between a set of doors so close either side of him as to almost touch both shoulders. At the far end was a window, its curtains partly drawn. To the right, in some sort of long recess, was what looked like an overloaded work station. A wheeled chair was pushed beneath. In an opposing recess he could see the bottom part of a bed. The shadow cast by the drawn curtains obscured it, but Nick's vision was growing used to the gloom. There was the definite outline of legs beneath the duvet. Was she asleep?

He cleared his throat, but decided that wasn't enough. 'Alice?'

There was a drowsy murmur, a pained murmur. Gooseflesh ran along his arms. He stepped forwards, leaning to gain a view of the top of the bed.

Cushioned by up-ended pillows, Alice was wedged into the corner where the walls met. He saw her eyelids flicker, her head turn a little. There was something wrong with her hair, something wrong with her whole posture.

Throwing his file on to the bottom of the bed, Nick strode to the window and ripped back the curtain. Light poured into the room, over the bed, over Alice. She grimaced, bringing up a hand to shield her eyes. Her hair was lank to her head, the undulating waves flattened, the colour no more than a dull brown. Her pale complexion had a blue tinge; her thin lips an opaque cast. Her eyes seemed shrunken in their sockets, the surrounding skin bruised dark.

'Alice! What the hell's happened to you?'

Chapter 7

Her eyes opened wide as she stared at him. 'What are you doing here? How did you get in? Aren't I safe even here?'

'Alice, what's happened to you? You look as though you've been mugged.'

'Get out!'

She was becoming animated now, and Nick realised that she'd been dozing when he'd entered. He stepped back as she pushed herself from the wall. The duvet, high up under her chin, peeled away from her, revealing a thick-knitted jacket and a high-necked jumper. Her hand came up clutching a hot-water bottle, which she flung to the far end of the bed. Nick watched it flop against his file. She couldn't be cold; it wasn't possible. The heating was on.

'Get out!'

She made to climb from the bed, but doubled up, her arms pressed into her abdomen. The groan she gave made Nick's eyes widen. He glanced at the hot-water bottle, then back to Alice, leaning once more against the pillows.

'Are you ill? Or is it..? Are you..?' He wasn't sure which words to use, how she would react.

Her head raised a little, her eyes glaring at him from deep within their hollowed sockets.

'I'm menstruating. Are you happy now? Go away.'

'Jesus, Alice. And I thought my sister had it bad. Are you taking anything for it? I can call the Med Centre.'

She turned back into her pillow, all fight gone. 'Leave me alone. Just go away.'

Nick stared at the duvet, following its blue ribboned edging. He hadn't expected this. What a pillock he was. He'd lied to

Cavley about being up all night in pain, lied and passed it off as if it had been no more than a small discomfort, when Alice must have been going through hell.

His attention fell on a mug by a pile of books at her bedside. Hours cold, the brown liquid inside was topped with the scum of separated milk.

'I'll make you some coffee and refill your hot-water bottle.'

'For goodness sake, just leave.'

Nick took no notice.

The blonde had gone from the kitchen. The kettle was still warm, but empty, and he refilled it at the sink. He didn't bother washing Alice's cup, just took a clean one from the crockery stacked on the drainer. Took two. If he was drinking with her, he reasoned, she might think twice about throwing him out.

Spoons were easily to hand, but he couldn't find the coffee. No doubt they'd run out; the jar seemed forever empty in the Salmon Grove kitchen. Tea bags were on a shelf in the wall unit, and it was as he was reaching for them that he realised there were no pins and needles in his hands, no tingling in his fingers.

He flexed them, tapped the tips together. There was no sign of it; no discomfort at his neck, either. He tried to remember when it had disappeared. Had it still been irritating him when he'd first spoken to Alice?

The kettle threw a cloud of steam from its spout, but didn't seem in any hurry to turn itself off, so Nick tripped the switch manually. There was milk in the fridge — better and better — and sugar in a canister on the counter. He added half a spoonful to one of the mugs.

With the hot-water bottle he'd tucked under his arm beginning to burn his ribs, he made his way down the corridor to Alice's room. He expected the tingling to return to his fingers as he approached her door, but the sensation remained elusive.

A mug in each hand, he had trouble with the door knob, and for an awful moment he thought that she'd locked him out, but the door gave eventually, and he was pleased to be able to let the bottle fall on to the bed. Alice slipped it beneath the duvet without a word.

'I've made tea. Do you take sugar?'

'No.'

He proffered one of the mugs, and she took it without comment. There was still no tingling in his fingers, no prickling at his neck. He couldn't understand that, couldn't understand it at all. Wheeling over the operator's chair, he sat in the aisle between her bed and her work station.

Alice sipped her tea. Nick sipped his. He didn't know what to say to her, or if he should say anything. Her eyes were closed most of the time, making it difficult to start a conversation. And then there was what to talk about. Everything that filed through his mind seemed trivial compared to her condition, and he could hardly broach what he had originally intended.

He took to looking about the room. Books were everywhere. For the full length of the recess that housed her bed, a double tier of shelving had been fixed close to the ceiling. Another shelving unit was standing guard over the work station, itself a mass of books and papers almost suffocating a closed laptop. Beneath the bench was another bookcase, the bottom shelf given to over-stuffed wallet files. Beside it large format glossy books were piled one upon another half as high again.

Nick let a low whistle escape between his teeth. If ever he'd been glad that he was a joint English and not a straight History, this was it.

He noticed her steady gaze on him and smiled. She didn't smile back.

'You have a sister?' she asked.

'Oh, yes. Two. Natalie is taking her GCSE's this year. She sails through her monthlies without a hiccup, creates more about getting a pimple on her face. Joanne will be fourteen at Christmas. She has a hell of a time. And so do the rest of us. You don't go near her for a week beforehand. She's like death when it hits, and afterwards it takes her nearly a week to get straight.'

'Not much of the month left for normality.'

'I guess not.'

Nick had never thought about that, had only seen it in terms of himself being on the receiving end of her mood swings.

He looked back at Alice. 'Are yours always this bad?'

She shook her head, closing her eyes, closing him out.

'Do you want something to eat? You haven't eaten today, have you? Joanne is just the same. Mum has to practically sit with her, forcing the stuff down her throat. I'll make you some soup.'

The cupboards in the kitchen yielded a bowl and a tin of vegetable soup, and he had it heating in the microwave in no time. Alice sat up when he brought it in. She even thanked him, though it was expressed so quietly he nearly missed it. He didn't press the point, but sipped at the dregs of his tea taking an interest in the maps pinned on what wall space there was, and the rows and rows of books.

Some were obviously secondhand, a few were paperbacks, but the majority were glossies, and looked new. He picked one at random from the shelves. £24.50. Another, no price. A third, £32.95. His gaze ranged over the length of the shelving above her bed. There was a small fortune perched around the walls, a small fortune.

'Is, er, Roman history your main subject, or are you in business as a specialist book dealer?' He chuckled, trying to make the quip an ice-breaker. He didn't need to see Alice's face to know that he was failing miserably, but he continued undeterred. 'What I don't understand is, if you are so heavily into Roman stuff, why are you taking Duval's American lectures?'

'I'm not *into* Roman stuff, I'm *into* Celtic stuff. Late Celtic and Romano-British.'

Nick noted the biting sarcasm, and bent his head, duly chastened. She took her history seriously, without a doubt. The blonde had said it, hadn't she? Ink in her veins. Yet, the maps were modern Ordnance Survey, and ringed and marked as they were, spoke of hands-on practicalities.

'You interested in archaeology?'

'Why are you here?'

He licked his lips and turned to look at her. She was frowning at him, as suspicious as ever.

'Here? Honest answer? To get as far away from home as possible. How about you? You haven't purchased all these books while you've been in Hull, have you? You've brought them from home. And Special or no Special, I'm sure the syllabus isn't covering just Celtic and Romano-British history.'

He'd said too much, he could see it in her face. He'd not meant it to sound like an attack, but in trying to change the course of the conversation that was how it had turned out. He considered apologising. He considered averting his gaze, acting docile and submissive.

Her sudden chuckle, weak as it was, came as a surprise.

'It's my... hobby. I told you in the refectory. When I'm not studying, I'm studying. I'm very boring.'

Nick forced a smile to mirror her lightening mood. 'Each to his own. I play rugby and get my face kicked off.'

'Why, Nicholas Blaketon, are you so intent on following me?'

He looked down at her, and knew that he couldn't side-step the issue again. He turned, taking two paces towards the window.

'Look, you're going to think that I'm crazy.' He shook his head, and faced her. 'This is ridiculous. You're going to think that I'm crazy even when you're fully compos mentis and can take it all in. We don't have a hope in hell while you're like this. When you're back to normal we'll sit down quietly with a big pot of coffee and discuss it like rational human beings.'

He nearly laughed. *Rational?* Who was he trying to kid? Hair that rose like leafy tendrils and shone in the dark? Pins and needles in his hands and his neck? Tree shadows trying to reach for him through his window?

'I've told you,' she said, 'I'm not interested in a relationship. Not with you, not—'

'Yeah, yeah, I know. Not if I was the last man on earth. I get it all the time, believe me. But that's not part of the equation.'

'Don't lie to me. I'm not a bimbo.'

'I'm not lying to you. Ask any bimbo you meet. They all know me. I move in their circles. They sure aren't as much work as you.'

Their eyes remained locked. Nick wasn't going to back down now, he wasn't even going to consider it. He was lying, though, lying through his teeth. There might be no sexual aggression driving him on this time, no flaring hair beckoning him down, but given the barest encouragement he would sit beside her on the pillows and cradle her in his arms.

The stirring at his crotch startled him, the sudden flush of perspiration, the prickling at his neck. He turned back to the window, grasping the sill with a pressure that tensed the muscles all along his arms.

'Let's just change the subject, shall we?' He swallowed, breathed deep. He was okay, he told himself. He was in control. The prickling was ebbing; his body was still. He was going to be okay. He was. He was.

He tried to look engrossed when finally he faced her. 'Explain this hobby of yours, this love of Roman Britain. What's the great attraction?'

She didn't speak for a time, just gazed at him with her pale grey eyes set deep in their darkened sockets. There was a fluttering across Nick's chest, as if she were trailing her hair over his skin. He caught his breath and held it, perspiration breaking free from him again. Was she doing this to him? Was he doing it to himself?

And then she shuffled on her pillows and looked away. He heard the ripple of liquid in the hot-water bottle.

'I've always been interested. My— A relative used to tell me stories when I was very young. Myths and legends. Near my parents' house there is a series of burial tumuli. I used to dream about the people who were interred there.'

'Dream?' His muscles tensed again, this time deep in his gut. 'What sort of dreams?'

She shrugged. 'Well, fantasise. Like children do. I made up

stories about them. When I was a bit older there was a dig on the site, and that kindled the interest. By that time I was reading well and... and I bought books.' She glanced above her head. 'I've been collecting them ever since.'

Nick eased his stance against the wall. 'I went to some Roman Palace near Chichester once,' he said. 'School trip. I can remember walkways above mosaics. Can't say I was that enthralled, though. I thought more of the earthworks on the Common, to be honest. Great scrambling area. You'd call it desecration, of course, and I suppose it was, but it had been used by generations of kids.'

She was staring at him. He looked down at the bed, not wanting to be captured by her incessant gaze.

'We didn't know any better. Besides, it was healthier there than on the road. I can't think of one of us who got a licence before his bike.'

'Scrambling?' There was a long pause. 'With a... motorcycle?'

'Of course a motorcycle.' He extended his arms, curling his fingers as if gripping handlebars. He twisted a wrist. 'Brum-brum!'

It was her shudder that caught his attention, a shudder that turned into a shallow rocking motion as she closed her eyes and wrapped her arms about her body.

'Alice?'

'Get out.'

'What?'

'Get out.'

'Alice, you're being unreasonable. I was fifteen years old.'

'Get out, get out, get out, get out!'

Despite burying her face in one of her pillows, she let out a scream that echoed from the ceiling.

'Alice!' Nick spread his hands wide and looked about him. What the hell was the matter with her? Half the building would be able to hear.

Nick made a move towards her. Again a scream, longer this time, more sickening. An animal caught in a trap.

'Okay! Okay! I'm going. For God's sake, Alice, you're unbelievable!'

He wrenched open the door and slammed it on another ear-splitting shriek. The blonde was striding down the corridor towards him, her expression thunderous. A door opened behind her. Another questioning face. He felt very, very angry.

'Don't even think it! That woman has a screw loose. She's totally out of order. Totally!'

There was a clattering on the stairs as he turned into the entrance hall. In the periphery of his vision he caught the impression of a lanky youth with a mop of tousled hair.

'What hap-pen-ing?'

With one hand Nick released the lock on the outer door, with the other pulled the door towards him. The youth was near the foot of the stairs, and Nick turned to face him through the glass, a foreign student, probably: dark eyes, dark hair, sallow skin. Angling his head, Nick curled back his lips either side of gritted teeth. 'Fuck off!'

He was down the stone steps and into the cold air of the growing twilight by the time the door snapped shut behind him, halfway across the courtyard before he realised his English file lay on Alice's bed.

'Alice, calm down and tell me what happened. Let go of the pillow, Alice. You're all right now. He's gone. Do you hear me, Alice? He's gone and we won't let him come back.'

Alice knew he hadn't gone; she could still hear the engine of his motorcycle roaring behind the house. He would wait until she made a run across the lawn and then he would zoom between the flowerbeds and circle her, circle her, all the time revving the engine and staring at her, just staring and not saying anything, not smiling, not showing that it was a game and that he was teasing her. Mrs Clarkson said that he shouldn't tease her, but sometimes it made her giggle, when it was a game, and sometimes she was frightened, when he didn't smile and he brought the big motorcycle so close she could feel its exhaust coughing on her legs. But if she stayed here, in the rhododendron hedge, she was safe, and if he kept revving the engine, kept on revving it really loudly, Mr Clarkson would find him and tell him to go home, and he would roar down the drive and the leaves on the rhododendron hedge would shake around her as he passed, but she'd be safe, even though she'd miss him and ask Mrs Clarkson when he would be coming again. Except that he wouldn't be coming again, wouldn't be coming ever again. So she shouldn't be hearing the engine, even though it was getting louder now. She shouldn't hear it because it wasn't there, wasn't there, wasn't there. She wasn't even hiding in the hedge, she was in her bed, wasn't she? She was safe in her bed. He couldn't bring his motorcycle into her bedroom, but her bedroom wasn't there, only her bed, in the darkness, and he was revving the engine, close now, coming out of the darkness, the headlight blazing, the engine roaring, and he was circling her, circling her, and her bed was turning with him so that she could see him all the time, see the big motorcycle in the darkness, the shiny surface of his leathers black against the night. And his gloved hand kept revving the engine, pulling the cycle closer, until she could feel the exhaust coughing on her face, until the front wheel turned towards her, the light from the headlamp streaming yellow over her. She couldn't ask him to stop, couldn't beg him to go away, because there was nothing above the black leather shoulders. He'd lost his head in the accident. It had been cut clean off, that's what she'd heard Mummy say, he'd lost his head in the accident. But he hadn't lost it; Mummy was wrong. His head sat above the front wheel of the motorcycle, his large yellow eyes shining the light all over her as his hand revved the engine. And he was never going to go away, never going to go away, never ever going to go away.

Chapter 8

Nick stormed out of Taylor Court and on to Salmon Grove. There were no vehicles on the street, but he could hear the low drone of the early rush hour traffic building beyond the houses, the roar of a high performance motorcycle accelerating along Cottingham Road.

Alice was a cow. He'd made her coffee, cooked her soup, felt sorry for her, even. And she'd *screamed*.

He couldn't believe it. He hadn't made a move towards her and she'd screamed loud enough to wake the dead. And who was going to believe him? What an idiot he was! How fucking naïve! It had been only two nights ago that half a dozen people had witnessed him hit Louise. He'd been set up. The pair of them were in league.

A car drew round the corner ahead of him, its dirty headlights pooling yellow on the tarmac road. Without a signal it pulled over to the opposite kerb, stopping outside number fourteen. Nick stepped behind the sturdy trunk of the next beech hesitating in its shadow to see Bruce and Maureen alight on to the pavement. They exchanged words with the driver, and Bruce let fly with that wounded chortle of his. They waved as the car pulled away, walking through the open gate and up the path. Nick willed them inside, but they just seemed to be standing there. It was difficult to see what they were doing, cloaked in the gloom of the recessed porch. Had neither of them a key?

At last the door was opened and the hall light switched on. It became obvious, then, what they were doing. Maureen was pointing to the bottom of the door, pointing to the panel he'd practically kicked through, reliving the night in detail.

Nick closed his eyes and snarled. He'd had quite enough for one day and could do without walking into an inquisition. He was going to have to wait until they settled themselves before he could sneak up to his room.

Leaning his shoulder against the tree, he slipped his hands beneath his armpits. It was damned cold outside after the central heating of the Taylor Court flats. The wind was light, but it had an edge he didn't trust. It was probably going to rain again.

Maureen's room lit blinding white beyond the gauze of the net curtains. She entered, removing her jacket as she walked towards the windows. Nick had never seen the inside of her room. Even before their exchange she'd had a downer on him. It was as if she resented him being there, above her.

She didn't reach the window, but turned to answer a call. The next moment she left the room, the door to the hall standing open. She wasn't going to be long. Coffee, probably, if someone had bothered to buy any.

The sky grew darker, the traffic noise increased. Vehicles passed down Salmon Grove; a convoy of students on bicycles, most without lights. The pavements either side became thronged with a steady stream leaving the campus, people clutching bags and files, talking and laughing.

Nick altered his stance, moved to the other side of the tree. If he stayed where he was much longer someone was going to accuse him of being a stalker. What was Maureen doing? Growing the bloody coffee beans?

There was a metallic snap to his right, and he whirled round, startling the girl lifting an umbrella above her head.

'Sorry,' he mumbled.

She didn't reply, just stared at him with eyes wide in an expressionless face. He made to walk away, trying to act the innocent, but she didn't make a move, and he found himself being forced to walk along Salmon Grove a good distance beyond the house.

It was drizzling. He ducked behind the knobbly trunk of

another beech and gazed up through the spread of its boughs. He couldn't see the rain. It was falling in a mist so fine as to be invisible, but it was definitely falling. In the neon from the streetlamps he could see moisture glistening on the branches, could see it in the heavy droop of the sparse leaves still clinging there, not wanting to give up their ghost of life. He felt it damp on his upturned face.

A squirrel sprinted across above him, stopped, and angled its grey head to fix him with a worried eye. It scampered off, darting from branch to branch as if there were no separate trees, the canopy just one gigantic hedge.

Light still shone from the open curtains in Maureen's room. The door to the hall still stood open; she hadn't returned.

Enough, he decided. He was cold and wet and fed up to the back teeth. He'd as much right to be in the house as the rest of them. If they even looked his way he would tell them what they could do with their damned front door.

His foot was already in the gutter when a car drew round the corner and slewed across the road, the same car as before. Nick watched John climb out of the passenger side not six metres from him. The driver alighted, too, a girl wearing a sloppy hat and a dress that nearly touched the heels of her Doc Marten's. John opened the door to the house and waited in the fall of light from the hall until the girl had checked round the vehicle. She was going to be staying some time, it seemed.

'Come on, Lisa. These will be getting cold.'

John was carrying something; Nick hadn't taken much notice. Now he could see quite clearly: pizza boxes, stacked one on top of another. And a bottle of wine, too, by the weight of the slim carrier hanging from his arm. Nick had walked in on a couple of their little pizza parties the previous semester. All conversation had stopped dead, food and drink halfway to their mouths.

We'd love to have you join us at the house. But they only wanted his money to make up the rent, not his body sitting at the table in the kitchen or blocking the bathroom doorway, certainly not his rugby-playing friends cracking cans of lager in his bedroom.

'Is this what he did?' the girl was asking as she paused by the door. 'Is he in now?'

Her voice was a shrill gasp. What had they been painting him? Some sort of Neanderthal?

The front door closed. The hall light remained on. Maureen returned to her room followed by the Lisa girl who threw down her coat and fiddled with her blonde hair in front of a mirror. Nick focused on her, his pulse quickening. No, it wasn't the blonde from the Taylor Court flats; thank God for small mercies.

Lisa and Maureen laughed together, then their posture changed. Small gestures, faces close, confiding. The Lisa girl threw back her head and stared at the ceiling, said something more, and slipped her arm round Maureen's shoulder. Nick felt his chest tighten. He watched as the girls left the room. The door still stood open, but he knew they wouldn't be returning, not until the pizzas were eaten and the wine was drunk.

Leaning heavily against the tree, he let the rough bark press into his forehead, texturing his skin. Moisture collecting on his hair ran down his neck in a single chilly rivulet.

Bastards.

Bastards, bastards...

'Bastards!'

Slapping the tree, he lurched down the road towards the campus buildings.

Zucchini was closing; the Refectory was swamped; the café behind the library was in darkness. He was damned if he was going out on to Cottingham Road in the drizzle to eat a takeaway out of polystyrene, and he couldn't go across to The Mare in case the team ended up in there.

In the McCarthy in the Union he downed a pint in two, slapping the glass on the counter to demand a refill. The barman squinted at him before returning his glass to the pumps. No conversation was exchanged.

Nick sank the top from the pint. The first was already racing through his bloodstream and he was beginning to feel light-headed. A doughnut for breakfast, and not much more for lunch, was asking for trouble. Perhaps trouble was what he wanted. He grinned at his reflection in the mirror behind the bar, watching as his lips drew back from his teeth. The vertical lines of scabbing on his cheek, together with his slick hair, made him look wolfish, he thought. He narrowed his eyes, adding to the threatening demeanour.

Fuck them. Fuck the lot of them.

He took another draught, relishing the feel of the icy liquor slipping down his throat. Replacing his glass on the beer mat, he raised his gaze to his reflection.

What was he doing chasing Alice in the first place? She didn't want a relationship, did she? Not with him, not with anyone. Except that had been a lie, hadn't it? She'd got a relationship — or had had a relationship — with that Hawkins individual who'd drawn her likeness on that poster.

Nick took two more gulps and swilled the remainder round the glass, staring at the bubbles which rose from the base.

Mother Earth Society? What was that supposed to be, anyway? Morris Men and flower garlands? Nymphos in white, dancing round—

He closed his mind on the thought, closed it faster than a steel trap, but the image had escaped and was multiplying, searing his emotions. He could wait it out, he told himself. It would dissipate if he remained calm. He picked up the glass to down the rest, liquid hissing over red-hot stones, and his turbulent thoughts organised themselves into a crystal clear sequence.

He'd seduced her.

That's what had happened. Hawkins had seduced Alice, seduced her and used her and thrown her aside.

The bastard. No wonder she didn't want anything to do with him. No wonder her only outlet was her work and her books. *The bastard.*

He picked up his glass again, but it was empty. No one was serving. Nick looked round the pine tables, wondering where the barman had gone. His brain seemed to be floating free of his skull. What was the matter with him? He'd only had two.

Outside the door to the McCarthy people swirled about him, clattering up and down the stone steps. He stood a moment in the maelstrom listening to the ebb and flow of their happy chatter. He'd been happy once. Alice would have been happy. Once.

The steps led up to the canteen, offices, and the Sanctuary bar. He ignored them all. Down the long corridor, far down the corridor, Alice's poster was tacked to the wall. One tug had it free, the single red drawing pin spinning away to the tiled floor. The next moment he was pushing through the door of the *HullFire* office.

The girl behind the computer screen looked up with a smile that faded to a suspicious frown. Nick slapped the poster across her keyboard.

'Hawkins,' he snapped. 'Who is he?'

The girl blinked, and pushed herself back on her wheeled chair. 'What?'

'Hawkins,' Nick repeated, stabbing a finger at the blacked-out name on the poster beneath Alice's head. 'Who is he and where can I find him?'

Her gaze followed his hand, and then took in the poster as a whole. 'Oh,' she said.

Nick leant over her desk. 'Who is he?'

The girl stood, pushing her face towards his, matching his aggression. 'What's your problem? Never heard of *please* and *thank you*?' Her eyes flashed. 'Our lecherous lecturer laid your girlfriend, has he?'

Nick straightened, catching his breath. The girl eased her stance in return.

'Figures,' she said. 'We thought this little interlude was too good to be true. Helen is the one you need to speak to. She did an exposé a couple of years back. Nearly had him turfed out.'

'Where is he?'

'Forget it, or you'll end up turfed out. And that prat isn't worth your future.'

'I've never heard of him. Lecturer in what?'

'Forget it. Acting the jilted lover isn't going to score you any points around here.'

'Helen, then. Where will I find this Helen?'

'Right here.'

Behind him the door swung gently on its hinges to reveal an angular woman in her late twenties wearing a mauve silk jacket and a short black skirt. In her heels she was taller than Nick. At sight of the poster she raised a darkly pencilled eyebrow.

'Mother Earth Society, eh? Not a devotee, are you, desperately trying to be one with nature?' Her gaze washed over his scarred face. 'I guess not. Hardly the bardic type.'

'He's looking for Harkin,' the girl told her.

'Hawkins,' Nick corrected.

The woman shook her head. 'Leonard Harkin, our celebrated hippie that never was, chief practitioner of free love and peace, man.' She swayed, giving an imitation of being stoned. 'Except he wraps it up with candles and secret invocations.'

The girl shot her a warning look. 'Helen...'

'But not everyone,' Helen continued, 'only the impressionable ones, the ones he wants to shag. Your girlfriend. Presumably.'

'Where will I find him?'

'Now? Pass. His studio's in Loten. You could try there. Of course, at this hour he could be scraping his reptiles on Cranbrook.' She looked beyond his shoulder to the girl behind the desk. 'Time to call it a day, Jenny.'

Nick frowned. 'This Harkin lectures in...?'

Helen unhooked a coat from the back of the door and passed it over the desk. Jenny flicked the switch on the computer and its incessant hum fell silent in the tiny office.

'You're not listening,' Helen told him. 'Loten. Studio. You'll find it if you want to. Can hardly miss it really.' She gestured towards the corridor. 'Would you like to go ahead of us so we can lock up?'

Nick stepped by her and kept on walking. Helen followed him out of the office, watching his determined stride with interest as Jenny turned the key.

'You shouldn't have done that,' Jenny said. 'If he flattens Harkin he'll get thrown out. If he mentions your name you'll get thrown out. They'll bring up that harassment claim he made against you.'

Helen smiled, unperturbed. 'I hope he does flatten Harkin. I hope he beats the shit out of him. Justice has been a long time coming.' She narrowed her eyes. 'Besides, you never can tell. A scapegoat might come in handy.'

Down the outer concrete steps, beneath the bare-limbed trees pushing through the pavement, a hard right immediately after the Gulbenkian Theatre.

Nick hesitated at the mouth of the walkway. No lamps lit the path. On his left the windows of Staff House were as dark as the louring sky. The theatre block offered no windows at all. Standing sentinel at the far end was Loten Tower, patches of inner light etching its bulk against the night sky.

The drizzle had hardened to a determined rain, filling the pavement with puddles. Nick wiped his face with an open hand as he let his gaze climb the illuminated floors. He'd never been inside, had never had the need. Somewhere in there was a studio and Leonard Harkin, the hippie that never was.

The women's contempt oozed through Nick's mind. Harkin preyed on women. He had preyed on Alice.

The building loomed before him, the lighted vestibule, its walls covered in notices. Nick pushed on the glass door and stood inside, dripping water on to the tiles. Photographs of professors and lecturers were mounted in an alcove. He scanned each one looking for Harkin; drew a blank. His name wasn't on any of the notices, either. No studio was listed on the board between the stairway and the lift.

Nick retraced his wet footprints across the vestibule. In an unlit alcove, through a glass firedoor, a small sign caught his eye. An arrow. Nick followed its line. At the top of a short flight of steps was a solid wooden door: Art & Design Studio.

The head was to be classical, Roman rather than Greek, but the curls in the hair wouldn't lie at the angle Leonard wanted. He wiped the spatula across the sleeve of his smock leaving a trail of yellow clay on the dark blue material. Was it balanced above the ears?

Releasing the catch on the turntable, he swung round the head and stood back a pace to weigh the effect. Of all the bronzes he had cast in his life, none had caused these problems. The nose, the eyes, the mouth, they were perfectly proportioned, but the hair... It was as if the hair was straightening as he looked at it.

The door to the studio snapped open and Leonard automatically raised his gaze, not that he could see it for the height of the intervening shelving units.

'I'm round here if someone wants me,' he called.

He hoped no one wanted him. He'd had a full day of syllabus work with students who couldn't draw a straight line without the aid of pixels and a mouse. This time was his and he needed it to commune with his own creativity. It had been nearly a year since he had undertaken such a professional assignment, and he wanted it to be perfect. And then there were the drafts for that painting he wanted to begin. His tongue caressed her name. *Choutelan.*

Breaking free of his thoughts, he touched the spatula to the head again, but his attention was drawn to the young man who appeared from behind the loaded shelves. A cursory glance told him that the youth was not one of his students, and his gaze realigned on the clay curls.

'My last group left over an hour ago,' he said.

'You're Leonard Harkin.'

The words were spoken quietly, but Leonard caught their accusing edge. He raised his eyes again, noting the bunched shoulders, the slightly lowered head, the scarred cheek set almost like a mask on the expressionless face, the dark, unblinking eyes. Leonard wiped the spatula on the arm of his smock and slipped it into a jar on a shelf to his right. From the same jar he took a slim, steel, palette knife.

'And you're dripping water on to my studio floor.' He smiled, trying to keep the exchange light. 'Can I help you?'

As the youth stepped towards him, Leonard judged the length of his reach. He'd not get across the double-width bench and its accumulated clutter, and Leonard could seal himself behind it if he pushed the dump bin in the aisle. Enraged boyfriends had confronted him before, and despite being more than twice the youth's age Leonard knew he could out-face this one simply by remaining calm. They were always full of temper, hurling more threats than fists, a sop to experience every time. But why a visit now? He'd given no cause since before...

Small hairs started to rise along his upper spine and curl around the base of his skull, quickening as his gaze fell upon the Mother Earth Society poster the youth was pressing on the bench.

They were using his graphics. They were still using his graphics.

Leonard shuddered as the youth's finger jabbed at the picture.

'You drew this.'

'No. I mean—'

'You drew this from life.'

'No. No one sat for it. It's stylised. It's from the sixties. Sixties psychedelia.'

'This is Alice Linwood.'

A solid piece of gut seemed to rise up Leonard's throat and wedge there. He fought for breath, for the power to swallow it down. The slicked-back hair, the tilt of his head, the hooded eyes above the long nose... It made him look... look almost...

Leonard struggled to regain his composure. 'I don't know anyone called— by that name.'

'Don't lie to me. Don't ever lie to me. You abused her. You abused her trust.'

Leonard shook his head. He couldn't speak now, couldn't draw his gaze from the fixed stare and the scarred cheek, from the overwhelming sense of controlled menace the youth was projecting.

'Stay away from her.'

He moved to pick up the poster, and Leonard watched a droplet of water detach from a lock of his dark hair and splash onto the bench. It stood there a moment, a tiny crystal dome, before sinking into the heart of the wood.

'Stay away from her,' the youth repeated. 'Stay away from her even in your thoughts, or I shall come for you, and I shall tear out your fucking heart.'

His legs didn't feel strong enough to support him, and his hands were shaking so much that he had trouble reaching inside his smock for his pack of cigarettes. Leonard needed to hold the lighter with two hands to keep the flame steady, but the draught... The draught was nectar. Unbelievably soothing. He filled his lungs on a single slow pull, held it tight within him before exhaling in a steady stream. His gaze lowered to the tall filing cabinets and the paper chest before being whipped away to refocus on the bench in front on him.

They were still using his graphics. After all this time they were *still using his graphics*. Dear God, why hadn't he checked?

The sight of her head, the rising tendrils of her hair...

Sucking hard on the cigarette, he turned to lean against the bench. The cobalt blue night crowded against the glass of the near floor to ceiling window, mirroring the room and himself. The smock made him look bulkier than he was. Perhaps that was what had saved him from physical assault.

He chuckled at his own conceit. The faded jeans, the long

hair, they were nothing but illusory trappings. He was middle-aged, Goddammit. He wasn't fit. He smoked too much. He liked his malts. The youth had not attacked him because he had not been *instructed* to attack him. And next time, maybe next time, she'd tell him to strike and there'd not be a warning.

The taste of the burning filter made him grimace, and he stubbed the remains of the cigarette on the surface of the bench. He knew why she was contacting him again, how she was able to contact him again.

Stupid! Stupid!

The dark image of the filing cabinets standing against the wall behind him filled his vision in the reflecting glass. His breathing was becoming ragged. He considered lighting another cigarette, and admonished himself for trying to postpone the deed.

Boxes and packaging were stacked on top of the cabinets and had to be moved. Grimacing against the strain, he slid his hand behind the wooden paper chest, laying himself across its top in an effort to extend his reach. The cold of the plastered wall and the metal filing cabinet sandwiched his extended hand.

Where was it? It had to be there.

Panic gripped him as he considered the possibility of her coming into the studio and taking it herself, but then his fingertips brushed the rough card and momentarily he felt relief.

By degrees he pulled it free of its hiding place, drawing it up into the fluorescent lighting to lay it on the top of the chest. Slightly smaller than a portfolio case, its purpose was the same, except that all four sides had been glued and stapled tight. He didn't struggle with the bindings, simply took the dust-laden package across to the guillotine and sliced off its head.

The bench was cleared with a sweep of his arm and the paintings tipped out in a pile. Leonard didn't attempt to spread them. He didn't think he could cope with seeing them all at once. He lifted the protective sheet of the first and gazed down at Alice Linwood.

The rendition was less stylised than the graphic. A head and shoulders depiction. Her flaring hair had depth and was a myriad of autumn shades. He'd caught a hint of summer sky in her grey eyes, perhaps a hint of water. The soft line of her cheek and chin were as accurate as any photograph, yet there was a sense of *being* that no flat machine-made image could portray. From the tips of her flowing hair to the lower edge of her shoulders, it seemed feasible that in the blinking of an eye she could leave the confines of the medium and be as animated as any human of flesh and blood and bone.

How innocently it had been painted. How innocent in heart and in soul, in spirit and in purpose. How easily he had given his mind to her.

With trembling fingers he replaced the protective sheet and turned the board face down on the bench.

The next painting showed itself through its translucent sheet: a full figure study, almost the same, but the naïvety gone, the obsession rising. He slipped it free of its cover, biting his lip as he gazed on it. There was a bloom in her cheek now. She was dressed in a long white gown that clung to her limbs, its fine draperies emphasising, rather than hiding, the engorged swell of her breasts and her belly.

Leonard slipped the cover over the painting to lay it face down on the first. He withdrew the third quickly, wanting this to be over.

Alice stood naked. The pose was the same, the bloom on her cheek was still there, the hint of summer water in her eye, but her confinement was long overdue. Bloated breasts leaked milk over a distended belly so enormous as to be obscene.

The fourth was a Sheela-na-gig. Leonard closed his eyes on it. He knew he'd painted it, knew it was Alice. He wanted to sob, but daren't let free the fear.

The bloom had gone from her cheek, the pregnancy from her belly. There was a hint of madness in her eye as she lay on her back peering manically through her widely held legs, her tongue lolling in a deformed mouth as she opened her genitalia. It was

Alice. Her hair, more green than auburn now, rose to surround her like a cloak, its locks feathering to leafy vines as they wound about her limbs.

In the next painting all humanity was gone. A toad. The markings on its head and back were the colour and texture of Alice's hair. There were human feet on the muscled green legs, a glimmer of her features in the raised eyes and extended snout. Its mouth was opening, the tip of the tongue poised to lash out. For him.

The picture was placed with the others, leaving the last, the unfinished. It didn't have a protective cover. Leonard was shocked to see that it didn't have the detail he remembered. Where was the woodland? The torchlight? The milling, chanting throng? Had that been in the dreams alone? In his imagination, but not beneath his brush?

He lifted his hand to trace his fingertips across the raised brushstrokes; faltered; drew back. The naked man was bound tight in blackthorn, his skin dark with gashes, the boughs' spines red with blood. A sacrifice. A sacrifice without a face.

A tremulous gasp escaped Leonard's throat as he gazed upon the base wash surrounded by its cowl of detailed blackthorn. He had given the man no features. He had managed to pull himself free of her grasp before the face had been completed, before he felt the blackthorn tear through his own flesh. But he'd kept the paintings. She had traced him through the paintings, restored the link when he'd believed it severed. All because he'd kept the paintings, because the Society was still using his graphics. Why had he been so stupid? *Why?*

He turned the last picture face-down on the rest and shovelled them all into the art-board case.

It wasn't too late. If he acted quickly, it might not be too late.

Chapter 9

Sunshine fell through leafy boughs to dapple across Nick's face. White flashes danced in the air around him. Birds, he thought, but he couldn't be sure. There was no sound, only a smell, of earth and cut grass, and something richer he couldn't place. And then the noise began, coming to him from a long way off. The scents started to recede and the white flashes grew more sustained. He opened his eyes expecting to see trees, but it was only the pattern of the closed curtain bright with the daylight behind it. Maureen was in the shower-room, singing opera.

Stretching his limbs beneath the duvet, Nick heard his joints crack. His neck was stiff, his shoulders ached. He felt centuries old. With a groan he swung his feet from the bed to sit on the edge of the mattress, his head in his hands. The room stank of vinegar and stale fish and chip grease.

On the other side of his wall the singing stopped as abruptly as the spraying of the water. Nick pulled himself to his feet to pad across the carpet and lean on the basin. Tentatively he touched his cheek. The puffiness seemed to have gone. He pulled a series of faces in the mirror. The broken lines of dark scabbing altered his expressions, but his cheek wasn't tender. It felt just odd. There seemed to be an awful lot of overnight stubble. He tried to remember if he'd shaved the day before, but the memory eluded him.

There was movement in the shower room. Picking up a towel and his toiletries, Nick stationed himself behind his door to wait for Maureen to step on to the landing. For a woman she was never long in either bathroom; his sisters could do to take notes.

He waited until he heard her tread on the stairs before opening his door. The last thing he wanted was to confront her on the narrow landing. He would have to face her soon, though. That bicycle wheel needed mending.

Nick had listened at the top of the stairs long enough. He knew that Bruce was in his own room. He wasn't sure about John. The most important person was Maureen, and she had just come out of the kitchen and closed her bedroom door behind her. It was now or never.

He glided down the staircase making hardly a sound on the creaking boards. Her bicycle stood in the dim hallway, its accusing front wheel for all to see. Nick didn't hesitate; gently he tapped on her door.

'It's open!'

Maureen stood beyond the bed jamming books into a large ethnic holdall. Nick didn't say anything, didn't make any move towards her, just waited until she looked up. The happy smile froze, fading as she stood straight, the bag in her hands.

'Good morning,' he said. 'I figured it was well past the time for me to apologise.'

She was holding the bag in front of her like a shield, her expression, her stance, exactly the same as Alice's had been in the refectory the first time he'd spoken to her.

He started again. 'I've come to apologise for my behaviour the other night, and to ask if I can take your bike to be repaired.'

Pulling his gaze from the holdall, he realigned it on her face, feeling a sudden sense of relief that it was Maureen's face, Maureen's tight and tidy brown hair.

'Do you have tools for it, that I can use to take off the wheel?'

There was a movement to his left, in the hallway. One of the others. John, he thought. Nick didn't look, kept his eyes on Maureen, but he could feel a sense of purpose coursing through his veins, pumping up his muscles. If the little weasel made a wrong move he would straight-arm him off his feet.

'Do you have any tools?' Nick repeated.

It was John to his left, and he was moving towards him,

slowly, deliberately, full of his own little importance. Nick relaxed his shoulders and his arm. He'd practised the move a thousand times in his rugby training, knew he could execute it without breaking sweat.

John walked into the room, close up to Nick, so very close, but instead of speaking to him, he peered round the edge of the door.

'You all right, Maureen?'

She blinked at him. 'Yes,' she said. 'No.' She moved her head, refocusing on Nick. 'No, I don't have any special tools for it. There might be some under the sink. I'm not sure.'

Flustered now, she started to check the contents of the holdall.

'I'll take the bike as it is,' Nick told her. 'I'll have it back as soon as it's ready.'

She stopped rummaging to look at him. The three of them stood a moment, statues locked in time and space, and then Nick turned and moved past John out into the dim hallway.

'Can't you just put me through?'

Leonard took a fast drag on his cigarette and leaned further into the acoustic hood in an attempt to hear what the girl was saying above the din of the Union reception area.

'As has already been explained to you, Mr Harkin, Ms Marshall has a full diary. No doubt she will return your calls when a window opens for her. She has both your numbers, and I will relay the fact that you have rung again. Good day to you, sir.'

There was a click and the line was disconnected. He glared at the receiver and pushed his cigarette back between his lips. 'Pompous bitch!'

The man in the greasy blue overalls looked as if he should have been tending hot rods, but he came from behind his counter and squatted next to the bicycle.

'Can it be mended?' Nick asked.

The man tried to spin the wheel in its fork, but the buckling was so bad that it jammed.

'Oh, aye,' he said. 'Anything can be mended. The point is, is it worth the work?'

Nick let the front wheel return to the floor with a bump, almost snagging the man's fingers as he inspected the broken spokes. 'How much?'

The man rose to face Nick, keeping his own eye contact solid and unblinking. 'Probably more than a new one. Labour's not cheap, not even in Hull. Son.'

Nick ignored the derisive tone. He wasn't certain where the next nearest cycle shop was and he didn't want to carry the damned machine all over the city.

'Fine. Put on a new one. Can you do it while I wait?'

'It's an odd size, not kept in stock. I can get you one, though, by tomorrow.' The stoic expression softened and he gave Nick the scornful smile of a man holding all the aces. 'Tomorrow afternoon. Late tomorrow afternoon.'

A double-decker shot by, too close to the pavement's edge for comfort, followed by a line of cars. There was something odd about Cranbrook Avenue, something Nick didn't like. The terraced houses were all built of the same creamy brick. Perhaps that was it: the same drab uniformity. The same bay window, the same round-shouldered porch, the same sized front garden leading on to the pavement. The lack of trees seemed to make the long ribbon of tarmac stretch away to some infinity point beyond the horizon.

The previous semester he'd tried for a room in one of the houses further along — most of the houses on the road were either leased by the university or belonged to landlords who let them direct to students — but he was pleased, now, that those lodgings had fallen through. He was having his share of problems at the moment, it couldn't be denied, but as he turned into Salmon Grove there was a welcome in the air for him, in the trees and in the birds, in the great swathes of muddy green grass, in the sheer openness of the place.

He slowed as he drew level with the entrance to Taylor Court. He wouldn't look, he told himself, he didn't care. But he did look, and when he didn't see Alice cross his line of vision his heart fell and his spirits with it.

She'd screamed, he reminded himself, screamed as if he was some damned rapist, but he still wanted to ring the bell to her room and ask if she was okay. He tapped his fingers together, shrugged his shoulders. There wasn't a sign of the tingling now. He hoped he hadn't lost that, too.

The rest of the morning was spent in his room, his bed a clutter of American Studies books, as he tried to formulate a plan of action to kill the required reading list. He'd fallen behind early in his fresher year and had never managed to make it up. That he'd limped through on the modules he'd gained had been a sheer fluke. Making the same mistake again would mean he'd be out on his ear. Murray might have a photographic memory, but Nick's needed to be spoon-fed.

He wondered about Murray, wondered how their friendship could have taken such a dive over such an— But hitting Louise hadn't been an infantile act. It had been something far darker. And he hadn't asked how she was, had he, or sought her out to apologise. He'd simply ignored her as Murray was ignoring him.

At one o'clock Nick threw in the towel and made for the refectory. He told himself that it was about time he had a substantial meal down him, but it was Thursday, training day before the Saturday match. No rugby player had a big meal on a Thursday evening, only at lunchtime.

The refectory was crowded, the cacophony of noise shrill and excited as voices fought the clatter of crockery and trays. He stood his turn in the queue searching the faces of those eating at the tables. He didn't see Murray. He didn't see Alice's auburn hair, either, and wasn't certain which gave him more regret.

There was a seat at a table for six. The occupants had finished their meal. Plates had been stacked in an untidy heap in the spare place and the rest of the Formica was covered in glossy pamphlets.

Nick rested his tray on the edge of the table and pushed their stained crockery towards the girl opposite. The group's animated conversation faded as each member turned to glare at him. He looked back, first at one, and then another. A scarred cheek, an expressionless face, a little unblinking eye contact... He'd never realised how easily people could be cowed.

After an initial hesitation, the conversation returned as if he had not joined them, and it wasn't long before he caught the gist. They were freshers, pooling their knowledge of what the city had to offer. There was talk of the ice arena, and the up and coming films at the cinema complexes. One was desperately trying to drum up support for a bowling tournament, but was being scorned. A gangly youth held up a fistful of garishly coloured leaflets.

'Is this it? Is this the sum total of nightclubs this place has to offer? We might as well stay on campus with the Asylum.'

'What do you want with nightclub prices? Have you seen what the Union has lined up this semester?'

'What I want to know,' drawled the girl next to Nick, 'is which wally picked up these.' With a flourish she fanned the offending pamphlets. 'The treasures of Ferens Art Gallery. The Town Docks Museum, showing the now defunct whaling industry. I really can't understand why it could possibly be defunct, can you?' A ripple of laughter ran round the table, but Nick was staring at the sepia-toned picture on the last leaflet now in her hand.

The girl raised her voice to regain her friends' attention. 'And the pièce de résistance: A Celtic World at The Hull & East Riding Museum!'

Hoots of derision rose in a cloud. Nick watched the pamphlet fall to lay face up on the rest.

'Whose idea of a good time is this? Come clean and we'll see about getting you medical attention.'

'It was Melanie! I saw her take them.'

'I did not! I get blamed for everything.'

Nick put down his fork to reach across for the discarded pamphlet. The conversation dwindled, but he took no notice. He'd seen that sepia-toned picture before, on the cover of one of Alice's glossy books.

Visit the Iron Age village and meet
the tribal queen with her followers.
Hear the sounds and voices of ancient times.

There was movement around him. The group were picking up their flyers and their crockery and were leaving.

'Here,' offered the girl beside him. 'Another two for your collection.' Pamphlets advertising the art gallery and the whaling museum were pushed in his direction. Nick ignored them.

The archaeological remains left by the Iron Age
people of East Yorkshire are some of the richest to be
found in Britain. Now you can walk into the past
and stand face to face with an
East Yorkshire Celt over 2,000 years old!
Admire their skills, fine swords and jewellery.
See the spectacular chariot burials and rich grave offerings.
A Celtic World – It's another life.

There was a clatter of a tray and two students took the empty chairs at the far end of the table. Nick glanced at them. One smiled back.

'Okay if we sit here?' he asked, indicating a foursome. 'Not saving the table for anyone, were you?'

Nick shook his head and returned to gazing at the sepia-toned picture. Bearded men with checked cloaks and stiffly combed hair were burying another in a shallow grave. A sword, a shield, and large, spoked wheels were being laid in the depression with him. Nick picked at his dinner and began re-reading the blurb.

Two more students arrived and the conversation turned to the Council, to personality clashes, to a possible coup. Nick showed no interest, and the others made no attempt to include him. Then a youth sat in the free chair opposite. Nick didn't recognise the bright blue eyes or expansive grin, but the skinhead haircut was so out of place as to be unmistakable.

'We were never actually introduced,' the student said, formally offering his hand across the table. 'I'm Toby Medavoy.'

Toby's hand was warm, his grip firm. Small hands for a rugby player, Nick thought. He folded the museum pamphlet and pushed it into his pocket.

'Nick Blaketon. But you know that already.'

Toby smiled as he separated his knife and fork. 'You were pointed out to me, yes.'

'I can imagine.'

'Well, we got off to a bad start, didn't we, so I thought I'd come across and even it up a little. Your face looks a lot better. Are you training tonight?'

'I hadn't given it much thought. Somehow I don't think I'd be made welcome.'

Toby waved his fork in a dismissive gesture. 'Ah, that's all politics. You're a damned good fly-half. Natural flair.'

'You haven't seen me play.'

'Hey, I can run, I know I can, and I was away clean. You came out of the dark like a bullet.'

'So what position do you prefer?'

'I've played some fly-half, but I like the wing.'

Nick took a sip of his Cola and gave Toby Medavoy a calculated perusal. 'So you want to know if I'm going to fight for first team fly?'

The forkful of shepherd's pie hesitated on its way to Toby's mouth. He looked pointedly over the top of it. 'No. I want to know if you'll support me if I make first team wing, or whether we'll be playing some pitched battle of our own every match. Accident or not, after the crack I gave you I could understand a harboured grudge.'

Nick shook his head. 'You're safe with me. Only on the understanding that we play in the same team, though. We end up on opposing sides and that's a whole different ball game.'

He watched Toby's gaze wash over him, trying to work out if he was joking or not. Deep inside, something twisted at the youth's uncertainty, making Nick smile. Toby grinned back and ploughed on with his meal.

'Do you think Hodgson will give you any grief about, er... that other matter?'

'Other matter?'

'The brush with your girlfriend.'

Nick didn't answer him, and Toby filled the gap too quickly. 'I wasn't there, of course. I didn't see it. But, er... well... It was the talk of the changing room. Only to be expected, I guess.'

'Did you see her afterwards?'

Toby licked at the side of his mouth, then wiped at the spot with his fingers, trying to get at something he couldn't see. Time, Nick suspected, a chance to think.

'Hodgson was sort of taking care of her. She'd hit her head on the floor. I was detailed to get a compress and a cup of water.'

Nick knew then. Nick knew exactly why Toby Medavoy had come to the table to introduce himself and to make friends. He looked at Toby and shrank back into himself, wondering how he felt about him, how he felt about Louise.

'How is she?'

Toby looked perplexed, but it was a performance so obviously being played. 'You haven't patched it up between you?'

'There's nothing to patch. It's a free and open field.'

He placed his cutlery on the remains of his meal and knocked back his glass of Cola. He could see that Toby was watching him, but Nick had had enough of the conversation, and rose to leave.

'Will you be there tonight?' Toby asked.

'Wouldn't miss it for the world.'

The telephone rang once, twice, and then there was that ominous click. Leonard's heart sank as the answering machine kicked in and Julia's modulated tones — her business voice — asked him to leave a message. He took another deep drag of his cigarette and balled his fist to rub it slowly up and down the tight ridges of his forehead as he waited for the tone.

'Julia, this is—' There was another click, louder this time, as if the connection had been cut, and he hesitated, waiting to see if the dialling tone would fill the line.

'I know who it is, Leonard.'

'Julia! Thank God. I've been trying to get you all day. Doesn't that girl in your office pass on any messages?'

'Every time, Leonard, every time. But I have clients, Leonard, and they pay me for my undivided attention.'

He wanted to snap at her, to scream down the phone that he was the one who needed her undivided attention. Instead he took another draught to calm himself. Julia was his salvation. His only hope.

'I expected you to call after they'd gone, before you left for home. I started leaving messages on this—'

'I know, Leonard. The last one was only fifteen minutes ago.'

'Then why didn't you answer it?'

'Good God, I was just walking through the damned door. Aren't I allowed to take off my coat? Now what's wrong, Leonard? And please make it quick. I've a speaking engagement at eight.'

'It's started again. She's coming for me again, Julia. Why is it you even need to ask? Can't you feel it?'

'Leonard, I am not attached to you via an umbilical cord. Stop being so hysterical. We've been through this before. She cannot come for you. We broke all the connections. There is no way she can reach for you. This is self-induced, and if you don't stop it will end up self-fulfilling.'

He closed his eyes and leaned his head against the wall by the telephone. 'You don't understand, Julia. I'm not just being twitchy. She's sent a go-between. He had a poster from the Society.'

'You're still going to meetings? You idiot!'

'No, no, I've not been near. I've not even read their bulletins. If only I had, Julia, if only I had! They're still using my graphics. My graphics are all over the damned campus!' His hands were shaking. He took a drag on his cigarette.

'I told you to destroy the originals.'

'I did, but they must have photocopied one of the blanks. Julia, I need your help. I need you here.'

'Don't be ridiculous. I can't drop everything and come up to Hull. What else has happened?'

'I– I've started dreaming.' He shuddered. The sounds, the flashes, the smell of bracken and pine... A wave of memory washed over him. He dragged in another lungful of nicotine.

'Specifics?'

'Not yet, but they'll come, I know they will. I need you, Julia. You've got to help me.'

'What are you taking, Leonard?'

'Nothing. Honestly. I swear. Nothing.'

'Don't lie to me, Leonard. Don't you ever lie to me again. I had enough of it in the spring and I'm not going through all that with you a second time. What are you taking?'

'Marlboro and malt. That's all, I swear to you. I'm smoking them like I've got shares in the bloody company.' He took another drag. The cigarette was almost down to the filter. He patted his shirt front, but the pocket was empty.

'Get rid of the malt, Leonard. Now. Down the sink with it.'

'Julia, it's fifteen year—'

'It's alcohol, and it's a depressant. Down the sink with it now. I'll keep on the line.'

'But—'

'Do it now, Leonard, or I'm hanging up and unplugging the phone.'

'Okay, okay.'

He let the handset dangle down the wall and crossed the untidy sitting room to the bay window. Through the thin curtaining the streetlamp shone in a direct line with his eyes. So much light was comforting. He only wished there was as much straining to get through the curtains of his bedroom at the back of the house.

The Dalwhinnie stood on a table by the television. Julia was right. It had only been opened the evening before and already it was half empty. He looked at the finger of malt in the glass that stood by the bottle, hesitating only a moment before reaching for that as well. Both went down the sink in the kitchenette. The smell was magnificent, and he stood, savouring it. Below him there were voices in the hall, and then the front door slammed shut. He returned to the phone.

'Hello? Julia? Are you there?'

'Yes, I'm still here. Leonard, you've got to be frank with me. You're not smoking anything, are you? And the toads have gone, haven't they?'

He glanced across the room at the empty vivarium next to the place where the malt had stood. 'Yes, months ago.'

'Do you know if she's still in that flat?'

Leonard closed his eyes. He could feel perspiration beading on his upper lip. Of course she was still in the flat. She'd be in that flat for three damned years, wouldn't she?

'I've no idea,' he said. 'You told me not to make enquiries.'

'You did destroy the paintings, didn't you?'

Leonard turned in a half circle so he could glimpse out on to the enclosed landing where the art-board case stood against the door to the stairs.

'Yes,' he said. 'Yes, I destroyed them.'

Julia's voice lifted. 'Then you're inducing this yourself because we're entering Samhain. I know you, Leonard. You've lapsed with your meditations. Get back to them. Stay off the alcohol and the drugs, and keep busy. Go swimming, Leonard. You'll find the exercise invigorating. I've got to go; I'm due out. I'll call in a couple of days to see how you are.'

'My mobile. You've got my mobile's number?'

'Leonard, I have every damned number you've ever used.' She cut the line.

Leonard hung the phone back on its cradle. His tenants downstairs had gone out. He could do it now and there'd be no one to stand at his shoulder and ask stupid questions.

Checking the pocket of his denims for his lighter, he walked into the hall and opened the door on the stairs. With one hand he lifted the art-board case, with the other the tin of solvent.

The changing room was crowded when Nick walked through the door. He'd deliberately arrived late, wanting his entrance to be seen by the group as a single body and not in dribs and drabs with them talking to one another through the sides of their mouths. He noticed a couple blink as he slipped his bag from his shoulder. Murray had his head down, tying his boots, and didn't see him, but as Nick walked past Bernie was jabbing him in his ribs.

'Nick! Over here, mate! I've saved you a peg!'

Toby Medavoy was waving his T-shirt above his head as if it were a flag. There were spare pegs all over — not as many had turned up for this training session as the first, despite the calmer weather — but Nick played along and slid his way through the half-naked bodies to Toby's side.

'Glad you could make it, mate. I was beginning to think that we'd be losing a good fly. Hodgson's picking his preliminary teams on tonight's show. The practice match is going to be on Saturday.'

Nick wished he wouldn't talk so much or so loudly. He knew it was only an act for the others, but this mate business was a bit over the top, considering that his intention was to play rugby like a brother and then shag the pants off his ex.

How did he truly feel about that? Nick had been pondering the question all afternoon. How would he feel when Louise stepped up to the touchline with her brolly and her tight jeans? How would he feel when the others realised she wasn't waiting for him?

Hodgson called for order. When the group was round him in a semi-circle he made a big deal of looking at his watch and tapping at its glass.

'Somebody put the hour back while I was getting changed? Is this it? Is this the entire crew?' He pulled in his chin and pushed out his chest. 'If I'd given up the ghost because of a little mud and some pittling rain I would never have made the England Under 21s.'

Heads bowed as all along the line the players shut out Hodgson's voice. Nick counted bodies, wondering if there were enough to make two full teams plus substitutes, and his eye caught Murray's. He was chewing gum, slack-jawed, his lucky green headband flattening his ears and cutting a groove into his hair. He had the look of some illiterate yob, not a solicitor in the making. He regarded Nick and then spat the gum into his hand, leaving Nick in no doubt as to his train of thought.

'Okay,' called Hodgson. 'Everyone outside, and I want two laps of the field before we start. Moyngarth, switch on the floodlights. Blaketon, are you fit to train? Wait here until I can look at that face. Symonds, pick up the cones as you go out.'

The milling throng became a snake which picked up speed and slithered out of the changing room. Hodgson did a thorough job of inspecting Nick's face, but both knew that wasn't the reason he'd been kept behind.

'Am I going to get a repeat performance of Monday?'

'No.'

'Your relationships in order now, are they?'

'I think so.'

'They'd better be, Blaketon. If I catch you doing something like that again, on or off the field, I'll ensure you never even pick up a paddle for ping-pong. Understand?'

It didn't take long for Nick to understand a sight more than that. Not only wasn't he acknowledged on the field, but those who were forcibly partnered with him managed to mis-kick or mis-throw a resounding one hundred per cent. He knew what it was leading to. When the running tackles began the ball was passed to him immaculately every time, and every time he was cut in two by a tackle that verged on the vicious.

Once he was allowed to run with the ball. At first he thought he was out-swerving the opposition, but none on his side wanted to take the ball from him either. As he pounded down the length of the field, further and further from Hodgson's careful eye, he realised what was awaiting him and his mouth turned dry. It wasn't going to matter if he touched down cleanly or not, there was going to be a pile and a ruck and he was going to be on the receiving end of every fist and boot they could muster.

When it happened, he closed his eyes, protected his head and curled up. The sheer bouncing weight knocked the wind out of him. Someone stamped on his lower thigh, and he tried not to cry out. A fist found its way through his forearms and then there was blood in his mouth, and all he could think of was what a stupid sod he'd been for not wearing his gumshield. A boot clipped his ribs, but there were too many covering him with their own bodies to do him a great deal of damage, and then, oddly, he seemed to be standing over himself, high above the ruck, watching the fists and hearing the grunts and obscenities as if it wasn't happening to him at all but to someone else. And he was laughing, high above himself, delighting in it, a hard raucous laugh that didn't seem to be coming from his throat, but was bubbling through his bloodstream like a narcotic. He could feel the lunges, the kicks, but he didn't care. They couldn't hurt him.

As the weight began to lift, and his other self closed in on him again, he realised that it was Toby Medavoy who had lost his cool.

'You bastards!' he was shouting. 'You bastards! What need

was there for that? You've just side-lined our best fly-half!'

Nick opened his eyes a fraction, saw stems of grass, brown mud, white floodlight shooting between his arms, the dark shadows of night beyond. Nobody tried for a last jab.

'Nick, mate,' Toby was saying. 'Nick?'

He could feel him at his shoulder, locking his fingers round his left wrist, prising free his arm. It hadn't hurt. Why was it hurting now?

'Can you hear me, Nick? No sudden moves, now. Take it gently. Where the hell's Hodgson? A bloke could die out here.'

Nick half sat, half kneeled, and spat free a mixture of grass and blood. 'I'm okay. Give me a hand.'

Once on his feet the pain kicked in with a vengeance, but he'd already decided that he wouldn't let any of them see him stooped or hobbling.

Toby was visibly relieved that he could walk unaided. 'I mean,' he said, 'what the hell was all that?'

Nick didn't look at him, just kept walking towards the Sports Centre. The rest of the trialists were filing in through the door. He wondered if Louise would be standing there on the terrazzo, sunglasses covering her black eye.

'They all know her, Toby. Remember that when it turns to shit in your hands.'

He felt another raucous laugh echo inside him, but it only surfaced as a lopsided smile.

Leonard lit the rag and threw it. A yellow comet, it arced through the night air before disappearing into the black hole of the metal dustbin. Nothing happened. Be patient, he told himself.

He kept his eyes on the mouth of the dustbin, but in the darkness it took on the characteristics of some slavering maw, the projecting angles of the art-boards pointed teeth. He shivered, and stepped back into the light from the downstairs kitchen window.

Creamy brick walls, head high, extended either side of him from the house enclosing the narrow paved garden down to the shed. It felt like some sort of extended cell. Geraniums fought their way through the weeds in the tubs. He was surprised they were still alive. Green plastic patio chairs stood in an empty foursome to his left, the dirty barbecue a little further on. The wheelie bin, already overflowing, was parked by the side gate waiting for collection. Blue-black shadows filled all the spaces. Shadows climbed the Russian Vine and slithered over the shed roof from the campus grounds beyond, from the trees, and from the pond he'd dug with love and filled with fear and loathing.

There was a whoosh and the dustbin lit, a comet itself, belching out a vertical tail of black smoke over the art-boards he'd sliced and slashed and ripped into manageable pieces. He closed his eyes and let the acrid smell play in his nostrils, a soothing balm on the cool night air.

But his eyes began to water, his throat to close. He coughed, and blinked, and his heart grew large in its hammering as he saw the swirling pall tracking across to engulf him. She was coming for him. She was going to step out of the smoke and transfix him where he stood. She was going to reach out and— and—

It was he who was reaching out, to the wall, to grasp the bolt, to drag it back, pulling open the side gate. The smoke eddied around him, pouring through the gap and out into Salmon Grove.

Leonard was across the paved garden in three strides, forcing himself against the brick wall which separated his property from the next. He wiped at his streaming eyes with the cuff of his shirt, and stared at the dustbin. Smoke no longer billowed from its lip. Orange and yellow flames reached spiky fingers up the art-boards. Occasionally a strong blue light fizzed and died as a block of paint fuelled its own demise. But she was there, staring at him as the flames licked at her shoulders: the bloom in her cheek, the hint of summer water in her eye.

He'd sliced her face, cut through her rising locks of hair. He *knew* he had. How could she look at him like this?

He swallowed hard and made a move, pouncing on the dustbin before its contents could leap out at him. He pulled at the jagged pieces of board behind her head, pushing her down into the flames. The heat scorched his fingers, but he didn't care, just as long as she burned.

'Cremating the evidence?'

Leonard gave a cry and sprang back against the wall. Standing beside the back door was a tall girl in a white sweater. She pushed her dark, shoulder-length hair away from her face and behind an ear.

'Good grief, Len. I'm not the ghost of Christmas Past.' She moved into the light thrown from the kitchen window. 'I'm going to be most affronted if you don't remember me.'

The curve of her smile, the incline of her head, the soft roll of her hips as she moved towards him... 'Clare,' he whispered.

She clapped her hands and spread them wide. 'Heeey!'

'What are you doing here?'

'Oh, great. Nearly six years and it's *What are you doing here?*'

Leonard stepped towards her. 'No. I mean... It's wonderful to see you, Clare. It's just... so unexpected.'

'And so it should be. That's what surprises are all about. And while we're talking about surprises, I might as well come clean and tell you that I'm camped on the downstairs sofa.' She pulled a face. 'I know what a stickler you are about your rent.'

'No, no. It's wonderful. *Wonderful.* Clare, I'm so pleased to see you.'

His mind was alight, his spirits soaring. Clare was back in his life! He made a move towards her, but she stepped away.

'Whoa! Not with those dirty hands, you don't. Have you eaten yet?' He shook his head. 'Good job I bought enough for two.'

She turned back for the house and Leonard followed her. The pale sweater was so long it covered her jeans almost to mid thigh, but it did nothing to hide the wiggle of her hips as she crossed the threshold.

The light from the dustbin was subsiding, overtaken by faint wisps of rising smoke. The front board collapsed upon itself, sliding down the face of the ones behind. A flame kindled briefly. The green and brown head of the Alice-toad was almost untouched. A charcoal streak reached from its opening mouth across to the board partly held beneath. The blackthorn spines had crazed over the marks of the knife, cowling closer the head of the victim whose features were stark now, smouldered in place by the sacrificial pyre.

Chapter 10

Nick took one look at the queues forming at the ATMs and almost changed his mind, but he wasn't sure how much the repair to Maureen's bike was going to cost and he'd had enough of a run-in with the mechanic when he'd dropped it off. He didn't want to look a complete imbecile by going to collect it without enough funds to pay for the new wheel, and some of those shops could be peculiar about taking a card. Besides, he reckoned it would be little different at the bank on Cottingham Road and so stepped behind a thin shouldered Sikh juggling folders as he plunged fingers into pockets, presumably trying to find his own debit card.

It wasn't until his chosen queue had moved up a metre that he glanced across and noticed Murray hunched over the adjacent machine. Nick measured his shoulders, wondering if one of the blows he'd received the evening before had come from his friend's fist. The idea would have been unthinkable a year ago when Murray had first waded in to rescue him from a maul.

When he turned from the cashpoint he was stuffing notes into an envelope, and didn't lift his head until they were almost shoulder to shoulder. Seeing Nick so close seemed to take him by surprise. He hesitated, averting his gaze, then walked on.

The girl in front of the Sikh didn't have one card, she had two, and pulled cash out on them both. The other queue moved on. Nick tapped his toes on the paving and glanced at the sky. There were a couple of pale blue patches among the clouds, but most were heavy with rain. He hoped the girl hurried up. Eventually his turn came and he received a pleasant surprise. There was £50 more in his account than he'd expected. His mother probably, worrying as she always did. He'd have to ring her, though neither would mention the reminder. He slipped the notes in his wallet and his receipt in his jeans' pocket and stepped aside.

Murray was leaning against the wall on the corner. They made eye contact, but Nick was careful to betray no emotion. He'd just about prostrated himself in the Sanctuary bar. He'd been told to go forth and multiply by text. Even in the changing room before the practice he'd been left in no doubt as to how Murray felt about him. It seemed that things had changed. Nick didn't know why but, from the hang of his shoulders and his contrite expression, Murray wanted to talk. The point was, did he want to talk back?

Nick decided that he didn't, and changed his route. Murray fell into step by the Chemistry building.

'We need a truce, Nick. Things have got out of hand.'

'I hadn't noticed.'

Murray's arm came down, a barrier in front of him, and they stopped to face each other.

'Sure you had. You got beaten to a pulp last night. I could have intervened.'

'I thought you'd helped.'

Murray looked down at his feet. 'It all just got out of hand.'

Nick moved off, turning in front of the Law building. Murray followed. They walked under the Wilberforce elevation and alongside the first of the large car parks.

'Hodgson's set the teams for the morning. We both made First. Do you think you'll be fit enough?'

'Of course I'm fit enough. A couple of bruises and you think I should keel over?'

'For Christ's sake, Nick. Don't you ever look in a mirror when you shave? Your own mother would be hard pressed to recognise you. I'm surprised you speak as clearly as you do with that lip. How's the rest of you?'

Bruised but unbowed, though Nick wasn't going to give him the satisfaction of saying so. He'd been surprised that he'd slept so well, that he didn't ache more. Perhaps his body was just getting used to the punishment. Perhaps he was getting battle-hardened.

'The stupid thing is,' Murray continued, 'you and Medavoy act like the best of buddies now.'

'But that wasn't what the kicking was for, was it?'

Murray lashed out at a loose stone on the edge of the roadway. It careened into the bushes.

'No, it wasn't. But we shouldn't have got involved. None of us. It was none of our business.'

Ahead the bushes merged into thicker undergrowth and screening trees; beyond could be seen the first blocks of Taylor Court. Nick wondered if he'd meant to come this way, and decided that he had.

'Medavoy's got First team wing.' Murray kicked at another stone, more vehemently this time. It cracked through the shrubs and a blackbird skittered out of the cover, shrieking its alarm.

'Have you a problem with that?'

'Only in the fact that I feel I've been taken for a ride. You might have a problem with it, though. Medavoy didn't join us in the Sanctuary after the practice. We thought he'd stuck with you. He hadn't, had he? He was seen in The Haworth. With his arm around Louise.'

He pushed his hands deep into his jeans' pockets and looked askance at Nick.

'So?'

'Christ, Nick! She's going to turn up on the touchline tomorrow, isn't she?'

'I've no idea. And what's more, Murray, I don't give a shit.' He drew up short, reaching out to grab Murray's arm and pull him to a halt. 'Look at that!'

At the edge of the shrubs leading to the covered gateway of Taylor Court sat a mottled green and brown amphibian nearly half the size of a rugby ball.

'Good God,' whispered Murray. 'What the hell is it?'

'Well, it's a frog, you fool. It was so still I thought it was a coloured rock. Then it blinked. There, it's blinked again. Did you see it that time?'

'That is not a frog, Nick. My grandfather has frogs on his allotment. I know what a frog looks like, and I'm telling you, that is definitely no frog.'

Nick slowly lowered himself on to his haunches.

'Don't start imitating the bloody thing!'

'It's looking at me. Do you see it angling its head?'

'Of course it's looking at you. It's probably sizing you up for lunch. Any second its tongue is going to shoot out, lash around your throat and drag you inside its mouth. The bloody thing's huge.'

'Keep your voice down. You'll frighten it away.'

'Good. It gives me the creeps.' Murray peered about him. 'Makes you wonder what the hell is lurking in all this damned undergrowth. The Council worries about muggers. There could be half a zoo hiding here, waiting to get their teeth into you.'

Nick edged closer. The creature inclined its head again, seeming to consider him with one black and gold eye. Its skin was rough, knobbly in places, but its camouflaging markings made it difficult to tell which was raised flesh and which was variegated colouring. It was beautiful, immensely beautiful, and Nick was fascinated. Would its skin feel damp and slimy, or dry and soft? If he was fast enough he might be able to pick it up.

He crept closer, and the animal did a little shuffle beneath an overhanging bush. Nick put out his hands and started to make his move, only to find himself being pulled on to his backside.

'Don't touch it! They're poisonous!'

The noise, the sudden movement, was too much. It raised itself high on all four legs and ran — Nick couldn't believe his eyes — it ran for the thicker cover closer to the housing.

'What did you do that for?'

'They're poisonous, I tell you. You know, ...*hubble, bubble... wing of bat and skin of toad...*'

Nick stepped into the bushes, moving foliage aside in an attempt to locate it, but there weren't even any tracks in the soft earth into which his trainers sank so easily.

'I don't think that's quite how *Macbeth* goes,' he said.

'Fuck *Macbeth*. Those things give off toxins through their skin. Explain to me how a girl kissing a frog can turn it into a prince if it's not giving her a mouthful of hallucinogens.'

Nick guffawed, and started scraping the soles of his shoes against the edge of the concrete path. 'So that's what they're doing when they've got their tongue down your throat — trying to turn you into a prince!'

'Well, it's nice to see you laugh for a change. These past few days you've looked positively murderous. Where are we going, anyway? Back to your place for a coffee?'

'Might as well. I've a bike to pick up in an hour or so.'

Trailing muddy footprints, he followed Murray under the covered gateway of Taylor Court. On the other side the sun was shining, the brick buildings glowing yellow in response. Nick kept a lookout for a glimpse of the frog, or toad, or whatever it had been, but despite the expanse of paving there was a lot of natural cover for it. Trees still clung to their faded gold leaves. Ground-hugging shrubs were still verdant. Flowers had green growth and buds waiting to blossom. Nature was still alive in the courtyard, whereas the trees on Salmon Grove had already embraced the coming winter.

'You getting a motorcycle?' Murray asked.

'What? No. A pedal bike. It belongs to Maureen downstairs. It's, er, sort of a favour.'

'I thought you didn't get on with the others in the house.'

'I don't.' Nick waved his hand in front of him, dismissing the conversation. 'It's a long story.'

The exit on to Salmon Grove was in sight now. To his left was Brantingham House. He wouldn't look, he told himself, but he stopped a moment, and made a point of gazing at the yellow painted door in the yellow brick facia. He couldn't see her window from the front, but he knew where her room was, and he could sense a part of him walking through the glass doors and along the dim corridor where the wooden panels rose higher than his head.

'Could you imagine living here?' asked Murray. 'There's not a soul, is there? Not the sound of a radio, or a TV, or a CD player, or anything. It's like a ghost town. Gives me the creeps.'

Nick walked on. 'Everything gives you the creeps. If you're not surrounded by people and chatter and...'

There was a tingling in his fingertips. It was slight, but growing, as was the prickling at his neck. He knew she was there, watching him. His breathing deepened as his heart-rate increased, but it wasn't until Murray squinted beyond his shoulder that he dared to turn around.

Breathless, Alice drew to a walk a few metres from him. Nick shortened the distance between them, his hands sticky, now, with perspiration.

Her face was very pale. Dark smudges still underlined her eyes, but the colour was back in her lips; it was fanning around her head in the dancing locks of her hair. He wanted so much to touch her, to reach out and draw her close to him, to run his fingers through her hair and press his face into her neck. He ached to touch her.

'I saw you from the kitchen,' she said. She looked down at the orange file in her hands and offered it. 'They're your English papers. You left it when...' Her gaze dropped. 'I'm sorry about that.'

Nick glanced at the offered file. If he took it she would have no reason to stay. Besides, he didn't want the file. He wanted to wrap his fingers around her wrist, to capture her and make her his.

'How are you?' The words seemed deeply guttural, partly slurred. He cleared his throat. 'I mean, you looked very ill.'

'I wasn't ill. It's just— It's just the way it is sometimes.'

She squirmed a little, glancing beyond him, and he remembered Murray almost at his shoulder.

'I'll let you go,' she said, proffering the file again. 'You're busy.'

'I'm not.' He angled his head and shot Murray a look. Murray stepped backwards, turned, and walked towards Salmon Grove.

'I'm not busy at all,' Nick repeated. 'Are you sure you're okay now?'

He watched her blink at him, watched the tip of her tongue moisten her lips. She looked away again.

'I don't mean to embarrass you, Alice...' he let the sound of her name whistle softly across his tongue '... but Alice, you screamed, Alice.'

She hung her head, pulling the file close to her body. 'I'm sorry. I explained it to the others, though. I wouldn't want—'

'Explain it to me.'

She lifted her face to look at him with pale eyes that this time did not blink or try to move away. They grew large in Nick's vision as he focused on them. He'd thought of them as grey, but they were as translucent as sun-kissed water.

'Death,' she said. 'You brought memories of death.'

He looked at her afresh, let his gaze wash over the curves of her cheekbones, the soft draping of her auburn hair. 'A relative?'

'No. Sort of, I suppose. The brother I never had. He was killed in a motorcycle accident. You were talking about your motorcycle.'

'My bike's in bits back home. I'm afraid it'll be walking or bus when we go into the city centre.'

She frowned at him. 'Pardon?'

'Tomorrow. There are no lectures, no seminars. I'm taking you to a museum.'

She was shaking her head, but he took no notice, pushing his hand into his jeans' pocket to bring out the leaflet he'd picked up the day before. Straightening it out, he showed her the sepia-toned picture.

'I remembered seeing it on the cover of one of your books. You'll love it. It's just your subject. *Face to face with an East Yorkshire Celt*. We can't go in the morning, I've got a match, but we've got all afternoon. It doesn't close until five.'

'No, I don't—'

'Better still,' he said, 'come and watch me play. Yes, come and watch me play rugby.'

'I thought you'd been playing.' Her hand began to move towards his face. 'You didn't have that bruising when I last saw you.'

He leaned in towards her approaching fingers, the anticipation of her caress rising fast within him, for it only to fall as her hand faltered and drew back.

Touch me, he willed her. *Touch me just once.*

'Was it another practice?'

He nodded, not trusting himself to speak.

'Are you sure you want to take part in the real thing?'

He forced himself to smile. His whole body seemed to be trembling. 'Come and watch. I'll play so much better if you come and watch.'

'I wouldn't dare.'

'In case I got hurt?'

'In case you were killed.'

She moved so fast that he hardly had time to react. The file swung between them. He covered it with his arm, his hand locking around hers, pushing her fingers against his ribs. Her touch was beyond his expectation. He felt he'd been impaled. Heat radiated from the point of impact, sizzling along his chest wall and into his gut, streaking along his arm and across his shoulders. He couldn't breathe, barely moved when she slipped her hand from under his. So cold a hand. So numbingly cold.

He watched her blink at him, once, twice. He wanted to speak to her, to tell her about first seeing her lifting hair, about protecting her from Harkin, about needing her, needing her more than life. But it was all an incomprehensible howl in his mind, and she was stepping back from him, moving away, ripping out his heart and dragging it across the brick paving.

'One-thirty,' someone said, and it took him a moment to realise it was him. 'I'll be here at one-thirty.'

*

Letting slip the tendrils which clamped him firmly to the boy, Ognirius Licinius Vranaun allowed himself to float to the surface. The boy murmured in his sleep state, in pain, Ognirius hoped. A little pain was always good, and the boy was unimaginably fragile. When he'd glided into his consciousness he'd thought the boy battle-training and his own heart had soared at the memories it stirred, but what he'd found had made him laugh aloud. Nineteen summers? What had the boy done in his nineteen summers to commend himself to the gods? It was beyond laughter. The old women would have torn their hair and wailed at such a child-man, calling him cursed, calling the village cursed for sustaining him.

At nineteen summers three heads he had held aloft and had been vaunted for his bravery. He had brought wolf and bear to the village and displayed the wounds he'd gained in killing them. Nineteen? He'd had his shoulder decorated with thorn and woad when he'd barely been able to take his first slave to his loins. He'd seen the Foreigners twenty-fold times and more by his nineteenth summer, but only once had he set eyes on their Derventio.

Derventio. The memory was sweet, still. Buildings of white stone that dazzled in the sunlight. Paved squares and rising columns gave witness to its wealth and the power of its people. At nineteen summers he had seen the splendour that was Derventio but once, but once had been enough. That day he had known where his destiny lay. It hadn't been with the weakened gods of his own people. Not with the Presence in the Pool.

Yellow doors in yellow buildings.

The opportunity had presented itself like a reflection in a bronze mirror, a detail he had not planned but welcomed as a sign that a veiled god was aiding his course. Perhaps, even, he was aiding his own course unknown. Perhaps, even, his power was becoming that of a veiled god.

He smiled as he thought on it. A veiled god for days only. He would soon pass through, then the name of Ognirius Licinius Vranaun would live as had been destined, for ever on the lips of men.

Chapter 11

For twenty minutes there was nothing in it. The First team took ground, lost ground, fumbled passes. The Seconds won every line out, but collapsed in the scrum. Hodgson stood on the touchline tearing out his hair as again and again the whistle was blown for a knock-on.

'None of us will see our names on the First team sheet next week if we can't do better than this!' roared Murray. 'Anyone would think we were a load of frigging girls.'

'It's the pitch,' a brawny fresher threw across. 'It's like a ploughed field.'

'You want Twickenham? Wait 'til we're playing the teams from the sticks. They pull a plough for a living. It'll make this look like a fucking bowling green.'

The whistle sounded shrilly and Toby Medavoy came to jog alongside Nick as he moved back into position.

'Is he usually like this?' Toby asked.

'He makes a good captain.'

'He wasn't made captain.'

'He will be next match.' Nick peeled away, not wanting to be near Toby Medavoy.

The ball was kicked, and the game began again, as scrappily as ever. Just before half-time Bernie Colwyn cradled his massive arms round a lobbed ball and took out his following opponent with a shoulder barge that laid the man flat. He was off at the run, head down, legs shuddering with the pressure of the drive. For his size he ducked and weaved with surprising agility, first fending off one defender, then selling the next a dummy. If Murray hadn't brought him down with a side-on tackle he would have been over the line and celebrating under the uprights.

The near miss spurred both teams and the game play snapped into focus. There was still no score when the half-time whistle blew, but a few supporters had gathered to straddle the touchline and shout encouragement. Alice wasn't one of them, Nick noted, but neither was Louise. He kept his distance from Toby Medavoy and tried to concentrate on the team talk.

The new half started as the last had finished, and soon the Seconds had a try. The angle, though, was so oblique that the conversion was well outside the uprights. The Seconds weren't too disappointed, but the First team was relieved, and again Murray went round rallying the troops.

'Come on! We can do this! Once more into the breach!'

Everyone looked at him and chuckled.

The passes began to mesh, the tackles were good, and suddenly Toby Medavoy was away, only two Seconds between him and the line. Nick swung in behind him, the roar of the supporters and his own backs surging through him as his boots sank into the turf and the muscles in his calves stretched sinew-tight.

The Seconds were closing. Medavoy kept on, his eyes forwards, looking neither side for support. Nick shouted to him, letting him know he was there, but received no indication that he'd been heard. There was an exchange of looks and the Seconds altered their course. Nick knew what they intended: to herd Medavoy one into the other. He called a warning and willed himself another half metre to be in the optimum position for the pass. There'd be only the one. The timing had to be perfect.

Medavoy saw him at last. The ball was transferred from one hand to two and... and the dummy was too early and too obvious. The Seconds didn't even falter. Medavoy was not going to pass the ball. He was determined that he was to be the one to cross the line, he and no one else. Nick couldn't believe his stupidity. As in the training session under the floodlights, Medavoy was going straight and true, his only thought being to outrun his opponents. He hadn't done it then; he wasn't going to do it now.

Nick glanced over his shoulder to check the position of the ref. The gods were with him. The ref wasn't up with play, his line of sight obscured. Veering like a hare, he launched himself at the nearer of the Seconds, catching the man at hip level. They hit the ground, but Nick did not let go, wanting to keep the man pinned long enough for support to arrive and regain possession when Medavoy lost it. Players thudded past them, and the Second struggled free of Nick's embrace, flinging him aside. He bounced on his left shoulder and rolled, coming to rest almost on the sideline. There was a tremendous roar, and spectators danced around him. Despite the idiocy, someone had scored. Nick squirmed in the mud to see who it was and caught sight of Toby Medavoy being hoisted aloft in the shadow of the uprights, his face a grin from ear to ear.

Tensed muscles relaxed, and Nick felt the waiting aches and pains swarm over his limbs and across his ribs. He groaned as he raised himself from the grass, hesitated as his eyes locked on to a pair of black trousers clinging to long, rangy legs. Louise was standing close enough to kick him in the face, but she simply looked across his shoulder as he stood, and clapped with all the rest in salute of Toby Medavoy.

Leonard Harkin slid his arm across the sheet and basked in the warmth still lingering there. She hadn't been up long. He pulled the edge of the cover over his face and breathed in her scents: her man-made perfume, her more earthy perspiration, her carnal secretions. Their collective pheromones permeated his bloodstream and relit his desire.

He'd been gratified that his months of enforced abstinence had not taken the edge from his ability, or his stamina. He mused on Clare's. How much more accomplished had she become in the intervening years? It was difficult to tell. It was difficult to remember; there had been so many in between.

'What are you doing now? Playing dead?'

He flipped back the sheet and smiled up at her as she stood over him, the satin robe hanging loose where the sash had slipped. She lifted the mugs before offering him one.

'And you needn't think I'm doing this every morning.'

'The coffee, or the exercise routine?'

'Careful, you'll be wearing yourself out.'

Feigning shock, he pulled back the covers so that she could slip in beside him, and he watched her protruding nipples engrave identical lines across the fabric of the gaping satin robe.

'A little washing up won't hurt you,' he said.

'It wouldn't hurt you, either. There wasn't a clean cup to be found. If I'm stopping, I'm not stopping as a housemaid.'

'Housemaiding wasn't what I had in mind.'

She smiled and sipped at the rim of her mug. 'I know what you had in mind. It's what's always on your mind.'

Leonard smirked and blew at the froth on his instant cappuccino. 'You've decided then?'

He watched her snuggle into the pillows and push at the tangle of her dark hair, feasting on the line of her body as she closed her eyes and eased back, exposing a length of neck. A soft curve stretched from the tip of her chin to the swell of her half-hidden breasts. He memorised it. A beautiful pose for a canvas.

'I could do worse,' she murmured. 'And it is only 'til Christmas, then I fly, fly away.' She turned her face towards his, so close on the pillows he could taste her coffee'd breath. 'Do you think we could put up with each other that long?'

'We could work at it.' He stretched towards her, his lips brushing hers in a tentative caress.

'It's nearly noon,' she said.

'Ah, the sheer unbridled decadence...'

Standing his mug on the bedside table he closed his mouth on hers again. She opened her lips, her tongue seeking his. They parted, and he watched her eyes circle his face, magnificent eyes, gold-flecked in amber.

'I've just made this drink.'

He took her mug and leaned across her, nestling his face in

the soft flesh of her neck. She smelled of distant flowers, of long ago springs.

'The coffee will grow cold,' she warned.

He moved his hand back across her robe, and he felt her smile into his hair as he deftly drew aside the satin to cup a breast and smother the dark nipple in milky froth.

'Then I'll have to drink it,' he said. 'Can't let it grow cold, can I?'

She was sitting on the wooden seat under the trees, the sunlight raising the individual colours in her hair. Nick eased his pace in his relief and drew up under the canopy of the Taylor Court gateway to catch his breath. He didn't want to seem too obvious, even though he was late. Hodgson had decided that a post mortem was in order and had gone on, and on, and on. It wasn't until Nick had been able to retrieve his wristwatch from his bag that he'd known the time.

But she'd waited. She'd waited nearly half an hour. A good omen.

He crossed the courtyard at a slow jog. She was reading, and didn't look up until he was almost by her side.

'I'm sorry. The game talk went on for ever.'

Alice smiled at him and the warmth he felt was stronger than the sunlight.

'I was beginning to wonder—'

'—if I'd stood you up? I wouldn't do that.'

'No, if... if you'd been hurt.'

He chuckled and rubbed at his aching shoulder. 'No more than usual.'

Concern crossed her face, and he knew he had to lighten the conversation.

'I helped score our first try. If I hadn't taken out one of their defenders our winger wouldn't have been able to complete his run. It changed the entire game. We came away 15-10.'

'You enjoy it.'

'Of course. Wouldn't play otherwise. Fires the blood.'

He could feel his blood surging as he looked at her, but that had nothing to do with playing rugby. He pointed to the magazine on her lap.

'*Marie Claire*, is it? *Fifty Ways to keep your...*' he waved his arm in front of him, desperate to stifle his original lascivious thoughts '...*your hair in place?*'

Smiling, she showed him the cover. '*History Today*. I told you. When I'm not studying I'm studying.'

Nick sat beside her on the seat, moving close, ostensibly to read the text. 'But studying what? That's what I'd like to know. You're keeping this a great secret.' He wanted to put his arm round her, at least slip it along the back of the wooden seat, but she was tensing as if expecting to be attacked.

'It's an article about ancient natural shrines, but, er... as always, everyone's idea of ancient isn't mine. Shall we get along to this museum you're so keen to show me?'

She stood before he could answer, keeping her gaze away from his, her hands busy rolling the magazine so it would fit into her shoulder bag.

'Sure,' he said. 'You can tell me all about these natural shrines that aren't so ancient as we walk into the city centre.'

'I think we'd better take the bus if this museum closes at five.' She started towards the courtyard gateway.

'Compromise,' he said. 'We'll walk between the stops until we see a bus.'

They saw a bus as soon as they set foot on Cottingham Road. It looked full, and Nick was all for letting it pass, but Alice ran to the halt and waved it down. There wasn't a spare double seat to be had, and much to Nick's chagrin they were separated across the aisle as it kangerooed through the heavy traffic.

'Perhaps Saturday wasn't such a good idea,' he mused.

'Saturday's fine. The shops will be busy, but the museum won't. No school trips. And which parents will want to bring their off-spring when they can be sitting in front of the television watching football?'

'Rugby,' he corrected. 'This city thrives on rugby.'

'Tell that to the black and ambers.'

Humour lit her eyes. She was relaxing now. He felt glad that she was, and annoyed that she couldn't with him sitting close. Something had happened in her life, something more than just losing a friend of the family in an accident. Something to do with Harkin. He shouldn't have just threatened him. He should have hit him, and hit him hard.

Leonard relaxed into the pillow with a sigh. The chill of the satin robe soothed his cheek and he pushed his face further into it to cool his brow. Last night Clare had been as he had remembered her, or wanted to remember her. It had been a reawakening of an old rapport. Their early morning joining had been deliciously impassioned, but this...

'That wasn't a groan I heard, was it?' Clare asked, jumping back on to the bed so that it rocked.

'A sigh of rapture is what you heard.'

Her face appeared in his vision amid a tousle of dark hair. An eyebrow arched as she playfully regarded him. 'You are up to this joint venture, aren't you, Len?'

He chuckled. 'You'll have to give me a few moments, I'm afraid.'

She shook her head, tutting. 'My, how the mighty are fallen.' A kiss darted towards his nose. 'What you need is a reconditioning massage.'

He felt her fingers burrowing beneath his ribs and at her insistence eased himself over. At once she was astride him, her hands manipulating his leaden shoulders.

'You've put on weight,' she chided.

'Toning of muscle.' He heard her laugh and raised his head. 'It's true. Three sessions a week in the campus gym.'

He felt her move and her hair swept across his neck. 'Doing what, though?' she whispered. 'Doing what?'

'Pining until our paths entwined once more.'

'As silver-tongued as ever you were, but more silver-headed, I see.' His pony tail was flipped over his crown to touch his forehead.

'All the rage, this shade. Treat me well and I might be persuaded to share the secret.'

She laughed again, deep and throaty, and moved her fingers down each side of his vertebrae. He expelled a breath of pure bliss.

'Relaxing now?'

'I was relaxed before. This is something else. You're very proficient, Clare.'

'Very professional. I took a course. It's amazing what I learned.' Her hands travelled up his back in small rapid movements and her body followed until she pinned him by the shoulders, her breasts brushing his ribs. 'Amazing the uses to which it can be put.'

'Like crushing me?'

'If it's your pleasure.'

The weight increased as she bore down on him, and he opened his eyelids, suddenly anxious, to find the softness of the feather pillow pressing against his eyeballs and filling his mouth.

Her weight lifted. The massage resumed, slow and sensuous, and his lungs inflated with air. He tried to chuckle, to make light of the exchange, but it came out more of a snort.

'You've definitely put on weight,' he said. 'At least a stone.' He reached behind to clutch her thighs. 'I don't remember there being this much to get hold of.'

Clare took one of his arms and began kneading the muscles. 'Ah! Your fetish is unmasked at last! You like your conquests young, innocent, and anorexic. Mere children.'

He swivelled to look at her, unsure whether the joking had turned, somehow, into an indictment. Clare gazed back with large smiling eyes. 'Wasn't I?'

'I don't seem to remember having to teach you an awful lot.'

'Well, I'm not young, innocent and anorexic now. The

gawkiness of youth has blossomed into the rounded figure of womanhood. With a woman's appetites. If I'm staying here *not-housemaiding* I expect prompt and excellent service from the in-house stud.'

The slap to his rump came without warning and made him wince.

'Do you think you are up to it, Len?' Her moist tongue slid along his spine from buttocks to hairline. 'Do you think you can hold the pace?'

Outside the Tourist Information Office, Nick stood amid a shoal of silver anchovy embedded in the paving slabs and tried to get his bearings on the map.

'This is Victoria Square,' he said pointing to the pedestrianised area with the large raised dais seating the monarch. 'So that across there...'

'... is Alfred Gelder Street.' Alice took the map from his hand and folded it. 'We need Whitefriargate.'

'White Friar Gate?'

She shook her head in disbelief. 'Marks & Spencer's and HMV?'

Nick raised a finger as if the most important information in the universe had been made clear to him. 'Of course! A history student reads maps!'

Alice rolled her eyes. 'A history student reads, period. Let me take you by the hand.'

Nick offered his hand, but she didn't enclose it in her own. Instead she began walking and he had to follow in her wake.

'Princes Dock,' she called, throwing out a right.

He'd been in the sprawling glass and chrome shopping centre often enough, and was about to tell her so when he realised that was called Princes Quay and she was probably referring to the murky waters which ran beneath the glass and steel structure.

She indicated with her left hand and swept across to lean on a wall topped by railings. 'Beverley Gate, the birthplace of the

English Civil War in 1642, where the people of Hull refused King Charles I entry to the town.'

Her formal tone made him grimace, and then he saw that she was reading directly from an information board. He looked over the railings at the tiered concrete steps and short red-brick walls four metres below them.

'Looks like a hole to me.'

She made a sound of exasperation and tapped the board. 'Look at the picture and use your imagination.'

He closed on her shoulder and she angled round against him so they could both read the small print and gaze at the layout of the mediaeval streets.

'This was the extent of the old town,' she told him. 'Everything beyond this point, all that we've covered on the bus, was rural countryside outside the walls. That,' she said, pointing across the road to a fountain surrounded in flowerbeds, 'was a dock, much later of course, and where we're standing was a bridge...'

Her words became muted to his ears. They were occupying the same space, her arm, her side, dove-tailing into his chest as if their bodies were two parts of one. And it no longer seemed to bother her, him being so close; she didn't even notice as her enthusiasm stirred her. Her voice, too, was pitched at the same frequency he had first heard in Duval's seminar when he couldn't make out her words. He revelled in it, wanting to raise his arms and bind her to him, smother her in kisses until she responded in kind. And he would lift her off her feet and carry her down the steps into the bowels of Beverley Gate, to lay her on the old brick foundations and make love to her, strong and passionate, and no one above would see them, wrapped in the history of centuries.

'Come on,' she said, side-stepping into the throng of bustling shoppers. 'Into Whitefriargate.'

Nick gripped the cold steel of the railings to steady himself, and watched as the image of naked lovers faded into the rough red bricks below.

*

'So what do you want to do today?' Clare asked.

'Sleep.'

Something cold and hard hit Leonard's shoulder, but his face was still buried in the pillows and he didn't see what it was.

'Come on. The shower's all yours. Are you taking me anywhere tonight or are we eating in? If we are, we'll have to go shopping. The cupboard is bare.'

'We can eat on campus.'

'You have got to be kidding.'

Her voice had dropped almost an octave and Leonard accepted that there would be no eating on campus.

She'd left the bedroom when he surfaced to scrabble across the bedside table for another cigarette. The packet was empty. It had been his last.

'We'll go shopping,' he called, 'if you want to make out a list.'

'Then get a move on.'

He raised himself, feeling aches in contracted muscles, and caught sight of himself in the mirror above the chest of drawers. Apart from his face, his summer tan had faded to nothing. His skin seemed translucent, almost the colour of the lank hair laying across one shoulder. Tentatively he touched his chest with his fingertips and found the parchment skin of a much older man.

The toilet flushed and Clare strode by the doorway, a bright yellow shirt flapping open over a pair of second-skin trousers and matching black vest.

'What's the hurry?' he called. He could buy a pack of Marlboro from the newsagents on the corner, he reasoned. Clare might even run the errand for him if he acted contrite. 'The local supermarket stays open until midnight.'

She appeared in the opening, her hair teased, make-up applied, bright-eyed, energised and vital.

'Sainsbury's main store doesn't, and Sainsbury's is where we're going.'

*

Nick clamped his hand over Alice's and hung on. 'I'll be losing you among all these people. You're not used to walking with someone, are you?'

'No,' she murmured.

'A loner. Nothing wrong with being a loner as long as you aren't lonely.' Yes, that was good. Sow the seeds of doubt. He purposely didn't look at her but renewed his grip, pulling her round a woman with a baby in a pushchair and a crying toddler in a harness.

'Sorry about that,' he called to the woman as they passed. He waved his fingers at the toddler, who stopped crying a moment to stare at him before taking a deep breath ready to continue the wail.

'It's my charisma,' Nick said, raising his eyebrows to Alice. 'Bowls them over every time.'

He was pleased to see her smile, even more pleased to feel her hand ease in his. Her hand wasn't cold today, not hot and sticky, but not chilled as it had been the day before. There was no electricity in her touch, either.

'I didn't know people started Christmas shopping so early,' he said, trying to keep communicating.

'The shops don't think it is.'

He noted the garishly trimmed windows. 'The shrines. You were going to tell me about the shrines that weren't so ancient. A Christmas tree's a shrine, isn't it? A left over from paganism?'

She smiled and frowned at the same time. 'Not exactly. Evergreens have always been associated with life in midwinter. The shrines I'm interested in are water based.'

He thought of the docks she'd shown him, one filled in, covered in flowerbeds, the other lapping with crumbled polystyrene and empty crisp packets.

She drew up at the edge of the pedestrianised area and gestured to their left. 'Land of Green Ginger.'

'Land of green ginger what, biscuits?'

She pointed to the street plate. 'We're entering the merchants' quarter. Look at the width of the buildings, at the pub.' She pointed again and he picked out The George, its gateway wide enough to accept vehicles.

'It has the smallest window in the city, no more than a slit, where grooms watched for coaches arriving. Horse-drawn coaches, I mean.'

He shot her a haughty expression. 'I'm not entirely thick.'

She laughed and pulled him across the narrow road.

'Silver Street,' she announced. 'If Land of Green Ginger was a street of spice houses, what do you think resided in Silver Street?'

'Banks and accountancy firms by the look of it,' he said, eyeing the bright signage.

'Money lenders, merchant adventurers, silver and goldsmiths, dealers in currency whatever the form. I've not done any research, it's a bit late a period for me, but I'm sure it would be interesting.'

Nick didn't doubt it. She pointed out the alleyway leading to Ye Olde White Harte where the Civil War plotters had discussed their deed, and then the single remaining goldsmith, the sounds of tapping coming from the shop's open door. Nick couldn't understand it. The shop fronts and recessed doorways found no latch in his memory, yet he had to have walked these streets during the year he'd been in the city. He didn't remember doing so, but must have done, and now, with Alice, the buildings were assuming new, vibrant, dimensions. The flat map at Beverley Gate was beginning to take on meaning.

'Oh, this is Lowgate. I know Lowgate,' he said. 'We went for a meal at an Indian along here, me and a few of the team.' And Louise. Nick felt the cold cinders of his life raked afresh, and purged the memory of Louise's intoxicated laughter.

Alice didn't want to try darting between the traffic, and so they crossed Lowgate at the Pelican a little further along. On the far side, narrow cobbled streets led at right angles between depressing, run-down buildings. The pavements had been laid in red brick in a herringbone design, but it didn't offset the sudden sense of claustrophobia.

'Are you sure we won't get mugged down here?' Nick asked.

'Not during the day. I wouldn't like to walk round here on my own at night, though.'

'You're not on your own,' he said.

She looked at him, and it seemed odd to have her face on the same level as his own, higher, even, he walking in the deep gutter, she on the strip of pavement. He couldn't hold her gaze.

'So,' he said, waving an arm at the cobbles. 'What happened when two carts met coming in opposite directions? Or was there a one-way system in those days?'

'Most likely there'd be no pavements. Raised stones, if that, to keep the wheels from grinding against the sides of the buildings.'

They stopped at the T-junction. 'High Street,' she said.

It looked like no High Street Nick had ever seen. It was another cobbled roadway, slightly wider than the one they'd left. To him, *High Street* spoke of shops, of commerce, of traffic. All he could see, all he could hear, was a dustcart trying to reverse in a road too narrow for its modern dimensions. When it moved, revamped warehouses rose fortress-like from the opposite pavement no more than four metres from where they stood.

'I want to show you something.'

Alice led across the uneven cobbles and through open wrought iron gates beneath an archway of scrubbed russet brick. Bond 31, the banner announced: Hull College's School of Art & Design. Nick paused to look around him. Thank God he wasn't having to study here. There wasn't an indication of life, hardly a burr of city traffic so close as to be a single street away, only the monotonous low trumpeting of a wagon trying to reverse. It made the buildings crowding the captured lane seem eerily sentient.

They passed a hanging blue sign The Neptune beside a shuttered door, and he could smell it now, decay that was not dying but alive, festering.

'You know what a staithe is?' she asked. 'It's like an embankment, a quay for vessels to load and unload. They're all along here, individually named for the lanes they open onto.'

Ahead the cobbles stopped at a square gateway nearly as wide as the lane itself. Alice led through the portal, across a narrow apron, up two concrete steps and down. Nick knew what lay on the other side. He did not need to see it. The smell was enough. Not effluence. Not man-made, despite the sprawling city. Seaweed, rank seaweed thrown up by the tidal river. And then they were standing on the planked quayside looking out over grimy barges linked by cables to the shore. Alice slipped free her hand and stepped to the edge. Strands of her auburn hair lifted gently in the river's breeze creating a corona around her head, a whisper of what he'd seen when first he'd set eyes on her.

Nick wanted to be beside her, to touch her, to explain, but not by the river's edge. He could see the river plainly enough from where he stood. He could see it moving beneath his feet through the open planks: dark, lugubrious, liquid mud.

'Beautiful, isn't it?' she said.

He didn't answer.

'All life comes from the water. The original settlement would never have existed if it hadn't been for this water. And we're not talking centuries back to the Civil War, or even the mediaeval fortifications. They're recent.'

Nick took half a step towards her, but the planks creaked ominously and he changed his mind.

'This... This is the Humber, right?'

She turned to look at him, her eyes large and bright. 'No, no. This empties into the Humber. This is the river that gives the city its name, mocking the king that bestowed his own upon it. And who remembers the king?'

She was sounding quite theatrical; it didn't seem right to Nick, didn't fit.

She squinted at him. 'You know that the city's true title is Kingston, Kingstown-upon-Hull? But it's not like Kingston-upon-Thames where the river bowed to the king's decree. Here the city's known just as Hull. It's the river's city. Just because the warehouses don't hold cargo anymore and the fishing's gone, doesn't mean that the water will relinquish its authority.'

She swung round, nodding downstream. 'See the tall structure beyond the bridge? That's the river mouth tidal barrier. Those steps we climbed, they're a tidal barrier, too, of sorts. Neither will stop the river. Eventually it will reclaim its own.' Alice turned to view, once more, the churning, viscous water.

Nick took a wide side-step on to what he hoped was more secure footing, but that plank creaked, too, and the joist supporting it looked no stronger. Both were discoloured, steeped in the river's cloying mud. Rounded banks of it glistened beneath the slatted quayside, patiently lying in wait to accept the unwary, to swallow them whole and suffocate them.

'I tried to find out about her, you know, but the records are very hazy.'

'Her? Who her?'

'The goddess. It's always a female deity who watches over the water.'

From where Nick now stood he could see Alice in profile. Her eyes had an unblinking, glazed appearance. Whatever she was seeing, it wasn't the river, at least not the twenty-first century river.

'The Humber took its name from the goddess who protected it. The Clyde, the Dee, the Severn, each takes its name from its own goddess, but the Hull... I'm not sure about the Hull.'

She turned obliquely, blinked, and focused on him.

'This is the sort of natural shrine I'm interested in. The shrine of a water goddess. I'm going to discover one, or rediscover one lost, and return it to the people, return it to the land.'

'Considering your salary, Leonard, I can't understand why you insist on buying bangers.'

'A Volvo is not a banger.'

'It is when it has a T registration.' Clare turned fully in the passenger seat to lean her elbow against his headrest and leer at him. 'There's not a Mrs Harkin somewhere swallowing huge amounts of maintenance, is there?'

'Good grief, no! I may be a romantic at heart, but actual marriage...'

Clare pulled away to look through the windscreen as they swung round the chicane of the fly-over and the road widened into a dual carriageway. On their right were the prefabricated sheds of modern light industry; on their left, half hidden behind wild-looking greenery, sat ranks of deep-sea trawlers, their rusting hulks trapped in an almost waterless dock.

'I don't know why we came this way,' Leonard said. 'It's desolate.'

'I wanted to see the river.'

'It's hardly a world-renown beauty spot. Look at it. Slate grey at best, mud-brown at worst.'

'And you call yourself a romantic.'

Leonard snorted. 'You'd need very strong rose-tinted spectacles to think the Humber romantic. The best thing about this stretch is St Andrew's Quay.'

Looking down on the geometric roofs of the retail park, Clare murmured something suitably incoherent before refocusing her attention on the river, on to a group of yachts ploughing white-tailed furrows towards the marina in the heart of the city. They passed a string of dark barges chugging upriver, to Goole, perhaps, or Selby. A high-decked yellow cargo ship glided by heading for the estuary and the North Sea. All were dwarfed by the expanse of water that stretched to the thin line of Lincolnshire, hazy on the horizon.

'If you wanted something of beauty,' Leonard told her, 'we should have come in from the other end and driven by the Humber Bridge. That feat of engineering is sheer poetry.'

Clare could see it in the distance, subjugating the centuries old artery of commerce and exploration in a single leap a mile wide.

'Concrete blocks and steel girders doth not poetry make,' she said.

'And neither,' he retorted, 'doth lines like that.'

His veined hand tapped her lightly on the thigh and rested there. She looked at it, smiled, and raised the smile to his eyes so that he wouldn't miss it.

They took the next exit, following the slip road until they were greeted by the familiar logo of Sainsbury's supermarket.

Leonard locked the Volvo's door and raised a critical eyebrow at the acres of parked cars. 'This might not have been a good idea.'

'Nonsense. Where else can we find such a tempting range of cheeses?'

'Cheeses? I hope we've come all this way for more than a portion of Stilton.'

'Of course,' Clare said, indicating that he should collect a trolley. 'You, above all others, should know that Stilton can't be enjoyed without the accompaniment of a good malt whisky.'

'Port,' he corrected, and he remembered the smell of his own malt as it had gurgled down the sink in the kitchenette.

Chapter 12

The Hull & East Riding Museum stood on the corner of Chapel Lane Staithe, but the cobbled roadway bore no resemblance to the claustrophobic alley-lane they'd used to reach the river. Museum Quarter bunting welcomed them to an area that had been opened up and grassed. Seating beckoned, modern statues stood among flowerbeds being cut back for the autumn. A steel and dark glass structure blocked all view of the river, enticing them with a sign along bright paving to the Streetlife Museum. Nick was so surprised by the change in ambience that he stood and stared.

'Not that one,' Alice said, 'not today.'

She led through clear glass doors beside them. Flooded with light, the museum shop seemed incongruous, an alien world of bright books and suspended models, of reproduction artefacts and plastic weaponry. Alice had walked through without a second glance and Nick shot forward so as not to lose sight of her beyond the jagged fitments. A uniformed museum assistant gave him a calculating look, and then he stared.

'He's with me,' Alice said. 'He's been playing rugby, as you can tell.'

The assistant let his concerned gaze linger a moment before returning to Alice and breaking into a good natured smile. 'As long as he doesn't tackle any of the exhibits.'

'Oh, I'm sure he won't.'

Watching the exchange, Nick began to tense. He stood his ground waiting for Alice to move across to him, willing her to move across to him and away from the smiling man behind the counter, a man twice his own age, as old as Harkin.

'Newtondale,' the assistant called after her. 'Did you go?

Brought back any pictures?'

Alice seemed embarrassed. 'I've not had chance yet. Work, I'm afraid. But I won't forget the photographs, I promise.'

The assistant smiled again, and nodded, then glanced across at Nick. The smile faded. Nick slipped his arm round her shoulder in an overt show of possession, bending his face close to her ear.

'So what's at Newtondale?'

Her hair smelled of lemons, her skin faintly of apples. It stirred memories he couldn't place. It stirred his desire. He watched her face turn towards his, saw her hand reach up to her shoulder to grip his fingers, not his fingers at all. Too thick, too calloused. Her lips moved as if she were speaking, and then her voice broke in with a clarity that startled him.

'...think you know your own strength.'

He released her, stepped away, looked back. There were steps leading up from the shop's floor that he couldn't remember mounting. The uniformed assistant was leaning against the counter, reading now.

'Are you angry with me?'

He returned his attention to Alice, feeling oddly out of sequence. She was frowning, her hand massaging her shoulder.

'Angry?'

'For not telling you I'd been to the museum before. You wanted the visit to be a surprise for me and, well, I've ruined it for you. Nick, are you all right?'

He took a breath to clear his head. 'Yes, I'm fine.'

'You don't look it. Have you eaten since you finished the game?'

'Eaten? Yes,' he lied. 'Just a feeling of— I don't know.'

He blinked at her, his mind finally functioning. 'You've been here before. Of course you have. You're a History Special with a bent for the Celts. How stupid of me to think you wouldn't have visited this place. You must know it inside out.'

She blushed a little. 'I should have told you, I'm sorry. But you'd gone to so much trouble, and...' Her voice trailed away.

'We can go if you're not interested.'

The locks of her radiant hair framed her face, a tumble of autumn leaves hiding her eyes from his, keeping her safe from his rejection.

'I'm more than interested.'

He watched her face lift, held his breath as her grey eyes trawled the contours of his face. He expected her to bring the shutters down, to close him out, but she didn't. Nor did she resist when he slipped his hand in hers.

'I'm all yours, professor. Where to first?'

'I'm on the wagon.'

'It's a trolley, Leonard.'

'I'm serious,' he said, but Clare was moving away, her gaze focusing on the laden shelving.

Standing amid the turmoil of shoppers, Leonard grunted in irritation. Two aisles down and they would swing into the wines and spirits. Julia had made him tip his Dalwhinnie down the drain. He'd meant to ring her. Or was she supposed to ring him? He'd forgotten. Being with Clare had swept it from his mind.

He smiled as he looked across at her, the bright yellow shirt a beacon in his grey life, an oasis in his desert. He wasn't going to need Julia now that Clare was in his bed. She'd keep the shadows from his dreams, fill his life with light. He'd paint her, he decided. He'd paint her just as she was, walking back towards him, the black top and trousers clinging to her curves, the yellow shirt flying open in the breeze her movement created.

'We'll have a special dinner tonight,' she said. 'A celebratory dinner.'

'Yes, why not.' Leonard nuzzled close, luxuriating in her perfume, as she unloaded her armful of groceries into the trolley. 'We can spend the wee hours playing strip poker.'

Clare tapped him playfully on the nose. 'Forfeits. Much more adult. Especially my version.'

Leonard grinned, his libido rising. 'Looking forward to it.'

She beckoned him after her. 'The sooner we get back, the sooner we can start.'

Leonard glanced down at the contents of the trolley as he followed to her direction. His smile faded as he caught sight of a blue and pink pack. 'Smoked salmon?'

'They're out of oysters.'

Nick smiled at the sight of the life-sized mammoth, its hairy leg being patted by a toddler held aloft by a doting grandparent.

'It's not real,' Alice murmured. 'The route starts in Prehistory and moves forward at a trot.'

Alice wasn't kidding. She looked neither left nor right at the exhibits and information boards, but strode along the winding walkways until she reached a floor to ceiling photograph of a golden man. *Face to Face with a Celt.*

'That's not real, either,' Nick said, disappointed.

'It's a picture of a celebrated sword hilt.'

There was a manikin opposite, half in, half out of a Perspex hole. Nick raised his gaze to the information board above. It was supposed to depict a chariot burial. He looked to Alice. She raised an eyebrow and turned to lead down the curving walkway. He was half a step behind when she hesitated to look around them. The few knots of visitors they'd passed had been left well behind.

'I want to go out of sync,' she said, and pushed through a door that didn't look as if it should be opened. 'Wheelchair access.'

After the subdued illumination of the other exhibits, the white light was so stark that it dazzled him. Order and authority rolled silent across the mosaics, some laid as they would have been, at floor level, others upright on the walls. Most were near complete, and Nick found them wondrous in their delicate intricacy, magnificent in the balance of their duplicated images: circles and lozenges, fish and birds and boar.

One corner had been set up as a mosaicist's workshop, complete with tools and trays of coloured tile. There were trial designs worked, graffiti-like, on the walls. In another corner was a mock-up of a sumptuous living room with beautifully carved furniture sitting amid painted plaster walls and a mosaic floor. An item of clothing lay across a stool, instilling the notion that the voyeur had missed the occupant by a mere moment. And everything was so bright: the light reflecting from every surface, the colours rich and pure.

'The mosaics are from the villas in the area,' Alice said.

'There's so many of them. I didn't think there'd be any Roman villas as far north as this.'

'Romano-British. After three hundred years of occupation the native populace was pretty well assimilated, the nobility at least. There's a map at the other side marking their position.'

He moved with her round the central mosaic, past shop fronts not dissimilar to the goldsmith's they'd passed on Silver Street, arches leading to mock courtyards so like the entrance to Ye Olde White Harte. Petuaria, the graphic said, Roman Brough.

In comparison the flat map was an uninspiring affair, the land a solid green, the sea a primary blue. The Humber was a great gash leading inland, its tributaries mere winding lines. The Hull was marked, but of its city there was no mention.

'This area—' Alice swept her hand above the Humber '— belonged to the Parisi. They had a ferry crossing the river near where, surprise, surprise, North Ferriby is today — here. The Romans eventually made it their own, the settlement, too, rebuilding it as Petuaria. It didn't look like this,' she said, indicating the wall-paintings. 'It was a major centre, even had a theatre.'

'Brigantes,' Nick breathed, seeing the word etched across the green.

'A powerful people, before and after the invasion. Their territory was vast, right across the upper Pennines and into what is now North Yorkshire. Lesser tribes aligned themselves, became part of their confederacy. The Parisi were to some extent, the Gabrovantices most certainly.'

He noticed the name high on the map, let his gaze trace the Roman roads as they swept north. Recognition quickened and he pointed. 'Derventio.'

'Roman Malton? Have you been?'

He hadn't, hadn't been north of York. Why did he recognise the name?

'It's amazing what's still left,' Alice said. 'I went there to see the spring. It's a concrete chambered monstrosity now. Man's stupidity gave half the town typhoid early last century and the spring was blamed. It had its own water goddess before Christianity supplanted her. Like most, it's now known only as Lady Well.'

Alice's tone was growing despondent, and Nick looked across at her. She shrugged her shoulders.

'The way of all things. Another few years and it will be obliterated. An unmarked shaft in the ground that local memory will fail to acknowledge. The maps will be updated and it'll be missed off, dismissed as… as a rubbish tip or something.'

She pointed to the map. 'Look at it. Roman roads, Roman villas, Roman settlements. Where are the old tracks, the Iron Age trading routes? Where are the festival sites, the pure water springs that made it all possible?'

Her eyes were bright with passion. Nick wanted to sink into them, to drown.

'At least they've got the Celtic settlements marked,' he offered.

'I'm sorry. I'm getting vociferous.'

'I don't mind.'

'My lecturers do. It's not considered a fit topic for my third year speciality. I've been told to find another. I've refused.'

'You know what you're doing in your third year?'

'Certainly. Don't you?'

She said it as if it was the most natural occurrence in the world, and Nick marvelled at her depth of conviction.

'There's a boat I want to show you.'

She led across a walkway over a mosaic, and round a corner. To one side stood a metal tank nearly as long as a swimming pool. Through the glazed sides could be seen jets of waxy water firing in never-ending sprays upon a wooden craft that was too big to be a canoe but with dimensions too narrow to be anything else.

'The Halsham cargo boat, hewn from a single oak tree. Older than the mosaics. Older than the chariot burials.'

Her voice seemed distant and he glanced at her reflection in the glass. He looked at his own. The wax dribbling down the tank seemed to give him a moustache, seemed to lighten his hair, throw it away from his face. Alice's image moved aside and his own transformed into the dark-haired man, clean shaven, with scarring on his cheek that Nick knew from the mirror in his room.

'People travel miles to see Henry VIII's crumpled *Mary Rose* being injected with wax,' Alice said, tapping at the glass. 'This cargo boat is the oldest vessel to be found in one piece in Britain. If the local BP company hadn't sponsored the preservation it would have disintegrated. And how many people are here to see it? Just us. The mosaics back there are some of the best in the country. Who comes? Who cares?'

'I care.'

'You didn't know this museum existed.' She brought a hand to her mouth. 'I'm sorry, I'm doing it again. Can you stand being bored some more?'

Leonard held the Bollinger in a chilled hand. 'If we haven't any oysters, why do we need Champagne?'

'What else would you drink with smoked salmon? It's only a small bottle.'

'It's a litre.'

'Perhaps you'd prefer an impériale,' Clare moved closer, arching an eyebrow and lowering her voice, 'then you could bathe me in it while I fed you smoked salmon from a silver cocktail pick.'

Leonard tried to remain annoyed, tried to stop the image she was painting from filling his mind. He spluttered, lost for words. Clare took the bottle from him and placed it back in the trolley. A Chablis and a good Bordeaux followed.

'I told you, I've been advised to give the vino a miss for a while.'

'So you said. Liver playing up?'

'My liver's fine.'

Clare's eyes widened. 'You've not turned into an alckie while I've been away, have you? Been given the gypsy's warning?'

'Of course not.'

'Then there's no reason for it not to be in the flat. Besides—' she lifted her shoulders and giggled '—it won't be open long enough to get flat.'

'You're intending to drink all this yourself?'

'Why not? Just because you're on the wagon it doesn't mean to say I am. Make up your mind, now. Talisker or Perrier?'

'No malts.'

'Perrier it is then. Sparkling or... *flat*?'

They were back in front of the golden man. This time Alice led down a descending walkway of diminishing illumination occasionally spot-lit to show text and illustrations on the tight walls.

A voice rose to greet them. Nick stopped. 'I know that language.'

'Latin. It's supposed to be, in their own words, how the Romans found the Celts, what they thought of them.'

Another voice broke in with an English translation. Nick didn't know any Latin, had never, except for a few mottoes, heard it spoken, or so he'd thought. He must have done, somewhere. Probably at school, he reasoned. *Julius Caesar* or something, though he couldn't remember if the play had any

Latin in it, or if his year had even covered that production.

A whiff of smoke. Nick faltered. This was the last place to be caught in a fire. He looked up, expecting to see an enclosed roof, but the panels were open to the high ceiling of the museum. The sense of claustrophobia was an illusion created with matt paint and controlled lighting.

The smoke again. This time he breathed it in. Wood-smoke. A campfire. Food cooking. People waiting. Rising anticipation made him salivate. Noises drifted towards him. A dog barking. A horse whinnying. And a voice, a small girl speaking... saying...

Disappointment tore at his chest. The tongue he didn't know. Not Latin, certainly. He felt he should have known it, but he didn't, and for a moment there was anger, and then he was inside the hut with the wood-smoke filling his nostrils and the woman bent over the kettle, stirring without movement. And his heart twisted to see her, and to hear the small girl sitting to one side of her speaking to the doll clutched in her arms. His fingers rose to his throat, searching across his collarbone.

'That's Argantorota,' Alice said, pointing to the girl. 'She's telling her doll that the tribal queen has arrived and that something will be done now. It's not the true language, though. It's Old Welsh, about the nearest. Nick?'

He was leaning over the barrier, breathing in the wood-smoke, drinking in the atmosphere of the darkened hut and its grubby furnishings of furs and baskets, its pots and drying herbs. His eyes rose to the smoke-hole, to the severed heads hanging by the hair from a line caught in the rafters. He smiled a little.

'I'm fine.' he murmured. He left the barrier and walked further along the sloping walkway.

The oak tree wasn't real, but he stopped to look, stopped to let his gaze follow its stout trunk rising from the floor, the occasional bough and spray of leaves giving a glimpse of its imagined canopy spreading beyond the reach of his eye. There were wicker farm buildings, a granary on stilts, a ring-horned goat staring. Behind, as the walkway twisted, he could see a chariot, a horse-handler, his hair stiff and white. Beside him stood a tartan-cloaked woman, her head high, her eyes fierce, if dull. Voices began, one over another: a woman, a man, another woman. Dogs barked. Chickens clucked and crowed. There was a lowing of cattle in the distance. More voices. A boy's. A whinny of a horse.

'That's Rigantimelta,' Alice told him. 'According to the information board she's called a queen, but the term is a bit misleading to our modern connotations of the word. Whatever, she's the local power. It was a matriarchal society, you understand, before the Romans crushed it and set up their own puppets. Needless to say, coming from a patriarchal society, they only dealt with men. Feminists of the world unite,' she added sourly.

Nick could smell horse sweat and ripe manure mingling with the wood-smoke, and leaf mould, and crushed bracken. He could hear sparrows and the call of a shrike, and somewhere, far away, the single desperate keening of a curlew in flight over water, water where there were no trees to send roots into the damp earth.

'Anyway,' said Alice, 'there's been a cattle raid. That's why the queen's here. The farmer and his wife – those two over there – are demanding vengeance, and the nobleman with the reins in his hands will ensure they get it. Nick?'

Her touch burned as if a blade slicing through the muscle of his shoulder, and he turned to her, to the questioning eyes so full of puzzlement, to the radiant hair that lit a face as pale as moonlight. Calloused fingers thicker than his own darted out to feed through her fiery locks. Her hand came up to stay his arm, but he had her hair in his fingers, her neck in his grasp. As her mouth opened for the cry he pulled her against him, wrapping his free arm around her back, his mouth enveloping hers. And she was his. Struggling like a lark taken on the wing, but she was his. As the breath from her body was given into his own, her struggling waned and he could taste her, could taste the fruits of the field, the game of the forest, the herbage of the stream-bank. He could feel a heart beating time against his own, strong and powerful, and he wanted nothing to part them, not clothes, not skin, not even flesh.

A sigh broke from the depths of his soul when his mouth freed hers, and he felt a rush of air tease his cheek as she drew a breath. His eyelids flickered, oddly beyond his control, and it felt as if he were waking from a satisfying dream into a contented reality. Alice was in his arms, and her arms were locked about his body tighter than rawhide bindings, stronger than an iron clasp. He slid his cheekbone along hers, to bury his face in her hair.

'I'm so pleased I met you, Alice, so very pleased.'

He stood there, with the hens clucking round his feet, and the smell of the wood-smoke in his nostrils, and the talk, one against another, filling his ears but not touching his mind. He stood there, letting the euphoria subside to a glow.

She moved against him, an altering of weight, and he opened his eyes to the gloom of the exhibits, to the stuffed horse, the plastic manikins, the polystyrene oak tree with its paper leaves. He smiled at them, and he smiled at Alice as his gaze circled her face, as his fingers unravelled from the clinging locks of her hair, still auburn in the misted light.

'You okay?' he whispered.

Her nod was as tentative as the smile she gave him, her gaze not quite reaching the level of his eyes. It seemed by common consent that they turned to continue along the narrow walkway, his arm around her shoulder. They hesitated by the potter's enclosure, the manikin kneeling by the beehive kiln reaching for broken shards of ware that would never touch his hand. They left him amid the dirt and the debris to gaze at the spot-lit displays of bead and bone artefacts, drawings and maps, the rusted spine of a sword that held no resemblance to the tempered weapon it once had been. They passed by a trench in a darkened passage, by a box of mud-encrusted objects, some as big as a hand, others as small as a thumb nail. There was a red and white pole and a theodolite on a tripod, and hanging on a nail a hard hat as bright a yellow as a warning sign.

Chapter 13

'Here? Are you mad?'

Clare inclined her head and pouted, the neon from the lamps in the car park glistening on her moist lips.

'There are too many people about. We'll be seen.'

She was kneeling on the passenger seat, her arms rigidly extended, one to each headrest, her body all straight lines and rounded curves as she concertinaed closer to the seat. Dropping her head behind a length of yellow sleeve, only her dark eyes were left visible to flash seductively.

'Security will catch us on camera.'

She wiggled with enthusiasm, making the unbuttoned shirt billow, a front edge catching on the handbrake. Despite the weak light filtering through the windows, Leonard could see the weight of her suspended breasts pulling at the Lycra of her top, her solid nipples silhouetted against the brilliance of the overlaying fabric. She wasn't wearing a bra. From the lineless curve of her buttocks, he guessed she wasn't wearing panties, either.

'You're insatiable.'

She arched her back and purred.

His body was betraying him. If he sat arguing any longer he knew he would give in to her utterly preposterous, deliciously erotic, inclinations. Sainsbury's car park! He wouldn't put it past her to step naked from the car to collect the champagne from the boot.

Dampening the image, but only a little, he drew his gaze away to turn the key in the ignition. The Volvo had barely coughed when long nails began to comb his hair, to gently rake his neck. He pulled her arm away.

'Can't you wait 'til we get back to the flat?'

'Now,' she growled. 'Now.'

She lunged close and the tip of her tongue danced along his jaw-line. Nimble fingers snapped free a button of his shirt and her hand was inside, teasing his chest hair.

'Not here,' he snapped, clamping a hand over hers.

'Where then? Has to be close. Now. Now. Now.'

Leonard looked about him. There were cars and trolleys and lights — and trees. Beyond the trees houses. No good. No good. Trees.

'I know. Off. Sit properly. We don't want to be stopped by the police.'

Clare only half sat in the passenger seat and made no attempt to fasten the belt across her body, even when they had cleared the car park and were heading back towards the A63.

'Close,' she panted. 'Has to be close.'

'Two minutes.'

'Too long. It'll ebb.'

'It won't.'

Clare began to shrink from him. 'It'll ebb,' she whined.

Leonard turned to face her, his lips a thin, fierce line. 'It *won't*.'

'You felt something in the museum, didn't you?'

'I've felt something ever since I laid eyes on you.'

'No. I mean, history called to you, didn't it?'

'Something called to me. I'd still put my money on you.'

Alice inclined her head, averting her eyes in that shy manner she'd made all her own. Her finger followed a dribble of moisture rolling down her glass, but Nick noticed that on this occasion she couldn't stop the twitch of a smile crossing her lips.

'You're embarrassing me.'

'I didn't embarrass you back in the museum.'

Her head shot up and he sprang to his own defence before

she could utter a word. 'You responded. You can't say that you didn't respond.'

'You had me pinned like a wrestler. I thought—'

'—that I'd ravish you under the oak tree?'

She didn't attempt to turn away, but glared at him, her squared shoulders rising and falling with each angry breath she took. 'I am not one of the bimbos you mentioned who so regularly flock to your side.'

It was his turn to drop his gaze. 'No,' he said. 'You're not. I'm sorry.'

An uncomfortable silence rose from the table between them, made all the more disquieting by the constant flow of scents and images that erupted in Nick's mind. The kiss had been exhilarating, her touch, her warmth, the taste of her, had lifted him beyond expectation, yet somewhere in the background had been the dull roaring of a more carnal, more bestial need.

A hint of something clammy slid across his throat, making him shudder, and he glanced at Alice, hoping for some warmth. None was forthcoming.

'I'm sorry,' he said. 'I'm sorry.'

The Humber Bridge loomed, a necklace of lights filling the windscreen.

'Not while I'm driving!'

His shirt was undone, peeled away to let the perspiration chill on his skin, and she was gnawing at his shoulders and neck. His breathing was rapid and his trousers bulging, bulging because he knew she would be delving there next.

'Clare..!'

Her nails slithered along his ribs, making him gasp.

White headlights whistled by in the opposite direction. Red tail-lights grew bright up ahead. A glance at the dashboard. Touching seventy. Where was the roundabout? He'd have to slow for the roundabout.

The Volvo shot beneath the dark gash of the bridge, its

carriageway the blade of an oversized guillotine twinkling in its own bloody light. Leonard braked hard for the roundabout, a hand automatically leaving the steering wheel to descend through the gears. His wrist brushed along a bare-nippled breast.

Watch the road. Watch the road, but his eyes kept straying as white light flashed inside the car. A gap in the traffic. The roundabout was theirs.

Up into first. As soft as silk; as hard as a coffin nail.

Down into second. A cup of dew; a twist of lemon.

Across into third. A whimper of ecstasy.

Into fourth and a foot hard on the accelerator, tearing into the tunnel of trees as the exit yawned wide. Following the dark road, bumping and twisting, pulling in his stomach as she clawed at his belt. The leather cracked. The buckle snapped. The zip grated noisily down. He dragged on the wheel, feeling the tyres spin, and bleached spectres of trees rose screaming before them. He stood on the brake as her head fell into his lap, and it was all he could manage to switch off the engine and lights.

'I don't want a relationship.'

Nick stared at her down-turned face, watched the fork in her hand turn the tagliatelle on her plate.

'Alice, you're *in* a relationship. You've been in a relationship for days.'

Her lips were slightly parted, her grey eyes wide and lustre bright.

'Alice, what's the matter?'

For a few moments he thought she was not going to respond at all, and then she composed herself.

'How... superstitious... are you?'

'Superstitious? Not at all. Why?' She looked away and he knew that he'd said the wrong thing. 'At least, I... well, I try not to let it get out of hand. I mean, they're in sort of categories, aren't they? Like, not walking under ladders, and... er...' he fought for those his grandmother had used to impart with alarm, '...putting shoes on a table, and picking up a knife you've dropped on the floor. Luck coming in threes—'

'Bad luck,' she countered. 'And you'd be my third. Everyone I touch dies.'

An image of Harkin burgeoned in Nick's mind, dragging with it the smell of paint and paper and wet clay, and a dark, pulsating desire for violence. Harkin had been touched. Harkin wasn't dead. He might have been, though, if Nick had let fly with his fists. Should have hit him. Should have beaten him to a pulp. Might do yet. Still might.

'You'll think me quite mad,' Alice said, 'everyone does, but it's true. When I first met you, all that nonsense in the refectory about reading through your essays, you were angling for a date. The next time I saw you you'd nearly lost an eye.'

Nick's anger began to fade, Harkin's face with it. His attention focused on her words, on the gravity of her tone, her gaze locked on his scabbing cheek.

'I was playing rugby, Alice. It was an accident.'

'They're all *accidents*, that's the point. I start to feel for someone and they die.' She leaned across the table, lowering her voice. 'I'm fated. I'm dangerous. And I can't control it. Stay near me and you will *die*.'

Her cheeks flushing, she was breathing hard, her hair dancing about her shoulders as she moved. Nick found it unbelievably erotic. He wanted to reach across the table, across the salad and the pasta and the garlic bread, to slip his fingers into those auburn tresses and pull her lips to his. The need in him was awesome and he could see no way of transmitting it. There she sat, her eyes wide, waiting for him to respond to prophesies of doom.

'That's a bit melodramatic, isn't it?'

Alice made fists of her hands in the air. 'Why is it no one ever listens?'

'Did the others?'

She calmed, looking at her plate almost regretfully. 'I never told them. I didn't realise. I hadn't made the connection.'

'Then who did you tell?'

She paused again. 'My parents.'

'And how did they take the news?'

'They took me to a psychiatrist.' Her gaze rose, fierce and determined. 'He said that I could not distinguish between fantasy and reality.' She leaned closer, locks of her hair falling either side of her face to flank her flushing cheeks. 'I had just watched Andrew drown — almost within arm's length of me — and that man, that man in his plush, leather-bound office, he said I could not distinguish between fantasy and reality. He said that I had a need to feel in control of my own life, a need to feel that I was controlling the lives of others.'

'Don't we all?'

'Don't mock me.'

It was Nick's turn to lift his hands in the air. 'Okay, okay. But look at it this way. You must have *touched* your parents, right? They're not dead, are they?'

'That's not the same.'

'There must have been someone you were close to when you were younger, someone you played with, a best friend?'

'He was the first.'

Nick watched her colour recede, the shutters come down behind her eyes. He wasn't sure he could tread as warily as he needed to. 'The one with the motorcycle?'

She nodded. 'I was nine.'

The age difference struck him immediately, a cold chill enveloping him. 'You used to play games with someone old enough to ride a motorbike?'

'Not exactly. He'd tease me a lot.' She raised her eyes, but they were still guarded. 'His family and mine... It was very innocent.'

Nick decided to let it lie. 'And you had no other special friends until this...'

'Andrew.' She started to say something more, but broke off.

'You have to understand that my family doesn't live in a town.

My education didn't follow the normal course of attending a local school. I didn't come into contact with people of my own age. I don't want to make it sound as if I were deprived, because I certainly wasn't, and I can't remember ever feeling lonely.' She shrugged. 'It was just the way it was.'

'But you weren't sorry to leave, were you?'

'No,' she said. 'No, I wasn't.' Her fingers closed over the cutlery. 'We'd better eat this or it'll grow cold.'

Nick laid into the garlic bread, but he was determined not to lose the thread of the conversation. He was going to get to the bottom of this, even if it did kill him.

On the driver's seat, Leonard lay with one leg over the handbrake, the other crushed against the seat belt mounting, his head wedged between the door and the steering wheel. Now that Clare had finally taken her weight from him the aches of stretched muscles, the pain of bruises, were beginning to blossom across his body. He made an effort not to groan.

In the pale glow of the courtesy light Clare squatted above him on the passenger seat, a mythical bird of prey, her breasts squashed between her knees as she wiped herself with tissues from the glove compartment.

'That was different, wasn't it?' she said.

'Most definitely.'

And it was. It was all very different from the Clare he remembered. Disentangling his leg from the seat belt, Leonard accidentally pulled it with him a few centimetres. As he saw it stretch, heard it rasp, he wondered idly if her repertoire now included bondage.

'Oh, it's beginning to rain. Come on!'

Before he'd even had chance to look through the misted windows the passenger door had opened and a blast of cold air seared his skin.

'Come on!' Clare urged. 'Nature unleashed! Let's bathe in it!'

'It's October, for God's sake! Shut that damned door.'

'It's warm. Come on. Live a little.'

In dismay he shook his head, reaching onto the rear seat to reclaim their discarded clothing. His back was to the door when Clare wrenched it open and snaked wet hands down either side of his spine.

'It's wonderful! Come on, breathe it!'

While he was still gasping she had him out into the evening air.

Raindrops splattered across his torso in a slow persuasive drumbeat, and he turned to admonish her only to set eyes on the beauty of her form as she pirouetted, bent and rose and turned, a naked ballerina dancing around him, her pale limbs glistening with rain in the faint glow from the car. It was a magnificent picture, all flashes of light against deep, deep shadow, a twisting design in abstract worthy of being laid on canvas, worthy of challenging his mastery of brush and of painting knife.

And he wanted to touch her, to prove to himself that in this form she was flesh and blood and not merely the craving of his mind. He reached out his arms and she danced towards him, slithering between his open palms, her body so hot beneath its slick transparency he fancied he could see steam rising from her skin.

As he moved with her through the softly falling rain, he didn't care about the stones beneath his feet. When she muddied her hands and drew lines down from his shoulders, he marvelled at the sensation, at the freedom of expression. The gritty debris caught between them only intensified his ardour as he lifted her on to his hips. Her teeth snapped over his pectoral muscles until the pleasure of it nudged through into pain. She wouldn't stop, was as rapacious as a vulture, and in desperation he laid her across the cold bonnet of the Volvo to thrust into her and feed from her flesh in kind.

But there was no end to it. His assault lit her appetite as if all before had been a feathered teasing. She demanded more, and more, until there was nothing left that he could give, and he staggered from her impotent, clutching at the cold steel of the Volvo to support his quivering legs. An alabaster sculpture on the bonnet, A Woman Reclining, her expression changed from puzzlement to a smile, to a grin, to a laugh. And with her laughter came the sounds of the world around them: the patter of the rain, the growl of the traffic beyond the dell, the rustle of leaves in the undergrowth so close yet ignored. The scents of the woodland swamped his nostrils: the bracken and the leaf mould, the rotting roots and the turned earth. White light from headlamps flashed behind the trees like sheet lightning, silhouetting the gnarled trunks and defoliated limbs, reaching, reaching closer each time.

Dread rushed up from deep in his gut. It was all just as in the dreams; not the dreams of yesterday, but the dreams of yester month, of the springtide when he had thrown himself on Julia's mercy and begged her to help him save his life. There were animals in the undergrowth; he knew they were there. They'd been there in the dreams, watching: hedgehog, fox, rat—

He gasped as he heard the croak. No. He'd burned her. He'd burned her in the yard behind the house. She couldn't be there. He knew she was. He'd encroached into her realm, unwittingly stepped into the domain of the woman-toad, the woman-toad with a rippled back of autumn-leaf hair and clawed human feet.

'Get in the car! Get in the car, *now!* We're leaving!'

'And... Andrew, did you call him?'

'He drowned.'

'You said. He was... your first?'

Her eyes wrinkled at the corners, deeply suspicious. 'My first what?'

Nick sat back in his chair. 'I don't know. Trying to elicit information from MI5 would be easier. You were telling me how this Andrew fitted into this scenario.'

'He is not *this Andrew* and it is not *this scenario*.'

A pair of raised hands and a contrite gesture seemed to do the trick. Alice calmed.

'He drowned. I was thirteen. We met on one of those adventure holidays: riding, climbing, boating. There was something there, between us. A rapport.'

'You were in love with him?'

'No, of course not. How could I possibly have been in love with him? I'd only known him four days when he died.'

'Perhaps I'm safe, then. You've known me six.'

'Don't joke about it.'

'I'm not, I'm stating a fact. No one else has died, have they?'

'*No one else?* How many deaths does there have to be to make it matter?'

'All I'm saying is that it is impossible for anyone — me, you, anyone — to go through life without touching people.'

A whiff of acetone claimed his sense of smell. He pushed it away.

'Maybe sometimes, maybe most of the time—'

A smell of paint.

'—there's no mutual rapport, so you don't notice.'

The stench of wet clay.

'But you still touch them...'

He reached out for Alice's hand, wanting no image to follow, wanting no grotesque darkness to pervade him. Not at this moment. Not now.

'...like you touch me. Like I touch you.'

He traced the curves of her cheeks and her brow with his sight, felt her fingers entwine his own.

'I don't know if I can do this,' she said.

'Yes, you can. We'll take it slowly.'

'If I lose you—'

'You won't.' He smiled at her. 'Third time lucky.'

'I thought you were enjoying it.'

They had not spoken on the drive back. Leonard didn't want to start now that they were entering the Avenue.

'I'm unloading the car on the double yellow lines. You can carry the shopping up the stairs while I park for the night.'

It was all coming out like an order. He didn't care. Perhaps that's what he should do, take her in hand, regain control.

Clare uttered a long sigh and arched her back. 'I enjoyed it. I thought you were enjoying it.'

'And fasten yourself up. I have enough of a reputation without having a half naked Lolita dancing about on the pavement.'

She gave a shrill chuckle. 'I'm hardly a Lolita, Len. The years cannot be resisted, no matter how one tries.'

'Just button yourself up.'

He dragged too hard on the handbrake, making it grind on the ratchets. The rain had stopped, but the tarmac road was strewn with puddles. He stepped into one and swore. The boot lid was thrown up and he heaved carriers onto the pavement. Clare stood at the wing making no attempt to help. The lid was slammed down again and he stalked round to the driver's door.

'House keys?'

He threw them across the roof.

'There's no need for this juvenile display, Len. It was bound to happen some time. You simply bit off more than you could chew.' She circled one shoulder and adjusted the comfort of a breast. Leonard glared but said nothing, leaving her standing alone on the pavement with the line of carriers.

She let herself into the house, and with two bags in each hand climbed the stairs and opened the door to his first floor rooms. Music was playing softly below, but there was no murmur of conversation. With the first of the carriers sitting in the kitchen, she filled the kettle and made her way back to the stairs. It was as she was passing the lounge that a flashing green light caught her attention. There was a message on the answering machine. Clare pressed the play button and waited for the machine to slide through its routine.

'Leonard, it's Julia. This is just a quick call to let you know that I'm back, and... and to apologise for being so short with you the other night. If you're still experiencing problems — not just the dreams, but anything at all — give me a ring. I'll be here until Sunday evening. Bye.'

Clare raised an eyebrow in interest, then wiped the message clean.

Chapter 14

The walk back to campus from the city centre had been a slow meander. Alice hadn't wanted it to end.

Inside the restaurant she and Nick had missed the rain, and they'd stepped out onto pavements glistening with the reflections of orange streetlamps and red and white car lights. Rinsed of their exhaust fumes, the trees sparkled as if clothed in May leaves. Everywhere there was a smell of cleanliness, of renewal. It didn't smell like a city at all.

The walk ended on Salmon Grove, at the gateway to Taylor Court. She dared let it go no further. Nick's need to touch her she'd found unnerving to begin with, his arm across her shoulder, his fingers feeding constantly through her hair. Then his arm would wrap around her waist, and she would be drawn into his side, as much, she'd decided, magnetically, as by the power of his arm. For his warmth was comforting. And it did feel right to be so close to him. Even his body odour was more enticing than offensive.

It was the speed of this development that worried her. She wanted to take their steps together slowly, and there seemed to be a need in him to move in haste. She wasn't certain what he would expect if she invited him into the kitchen for a late night coffee.

'You'll have a long way still to go,' she said, disentangling herself from his arms. 'I'll say goodnight here.'

She watched him look beyond her head towards Brantingham House, and felt relief at the decision she'd made.

'It's not late. I live quite close.'

'Oh? Where?'

'By that tree. Mine's the room with the balcony.'

Even as he pointed her mind was howling in turmoil. He lived a minute's walk away. Two minutes at most.

'Weird, isn't it?' he said. 'I moved into the road at the end of the last semester, but I'd never seen you around. Then, at Duval's seminar—'

She pulled her hands from his, and turned to leave. 'I'll have to go.'

'Alice—' He caught her arm. 'Don't see shadows that aren't there, Alice. Coincidences are just that; nothing more. Third time lucky, remember?'

She nodded, but could not risk meeting his gaze. Her life had been full of coincidences. None of them had been benign.

'I am tired,' she said, 'and I do need to go in.' She shrugged, making the most of an embarrassment she truly felt. 'The time of the month.'

'Oh, of course. I'll see you tomorrow though?'

It was part question, part statement. He was so certain, and she wasn't any more, wasn't certain that she could go through with this, wasn't certain that she even wanted to.

'I've a lot of work to do. I don't know when I'll be finished.'

'I'll call round.'

'Fine. Okay.' What was she saying? That wasn't what she wanted. Hands cupped her cheeks and lifted her face. Despite her roaring mind her lips reached for his. Such power. Such passion.

It was Nick who broke away, his hands snaking behind her shoulders to entrap her, his forehead coming down to rest on hers. The sigh he gave was as deep as the shudder that convulsed his body, and she was back in the museum, back in the Celtic exhibition beneath the polystyrene oak tree.

'Alice...'

'Don't do this to me, Nick, please.'

'I need you, Alice. I need to be with you. Let me hold you—'

'No, Nick. Please...'

'Let me stay. I just want to hold you, to be near you—'

'Nick...'

'—to protect you, keep you safe.'

'*Nicholas...*'

His eyes snapped open; she felt his lashes fan her brows.

'You're going too fast for me, Nick. Please, let go.'

The tension fell from him. His hands unlocked behind her back to trail around her shoulders unwilling, still, to break the contact.

'I'm sorry,' he whispered. 'Alice, I—'

'I'll see you tomorrow.' She pulled away and turned.

Her heart was racing. He'd reach for her again, pull her back towards him, she knew he would.

He didn't.

She cleared the gateway and walked between the housing blocks, her soft shoes making no sound on the brick-laid court. At the wooden seat beneath the trees she felt a need to hesitate, to look back to him, but she forced herself on towards the yellow door of Brantingham House.

First try she couldn't slide the key into the lock, her fingers were shaking so much, and then it engaged, the door giving to the pressure of her hand.

She didn't want to go inside. A breeze sang about her, ruffling her hair, and she brought up a hand to clear her face. She wanted his arms around her again, softly, gently, the touch of another human being, of Nicholas Blaketon with his scarred face and his terrible need that she no longer wanted to restrain.

A great bubble of heat sprang through her limbs and she turned to call him, but the faint glow of the gateway light showed no one beneath it. Disappointment enshrouded her, and she stood there a moment, feeling more alone than she ever had in her very lonely life.

In the deep shadow cast by the wall of Lincoln House, Nick stood among the thin shrubs watching Alice pause at the outer door. The ache within was gnawing deep, and he drew the edges of his hands along the rough bricks in an effort to divert the pain. When her hair rose around her head, and the light from the hallway suffused the dancing locks with gold, he thought his breath would leave him in a scream, but he caught it, even though his mouth was open and his head racked back against the wall.

The meal had been a sullen affair, the food, all that expensive food, tasting like pulped art-board to Leonard's palate. Clare had changed into a slinky satin number that looked more like a negligee than a dress. It hadn't turned him on. The music had been haunting, the lighting dim, until he'd snapped down the switch and flooded the lounge with brilliance.

'Leonard! You've ruined the ambience.'

'Don't pout. I don't find it endearing.'

'You didn't complain earlier.'

He watched Clare refill her glass from the dark champagne bottle, already half empty. She was smiling a lot, at her own inner thoughts, it seemed to him, but apart from that the Bollinger seemed to be having no effect at all.

He patted his shirt pocket and brought out the packet of Marlboro. It seemed very light. He flicked back the top with a practised finger and eyed the lone cigarette within. Already he'd gone through twenty.

'Is there one for me?' Clare asked, lounging back in the opposite corner of the sofa.

'No, there is not! I'm not keeping you in cigarettes as well as rivers of champagne.'

He paced the short distance to the mantel, sucking the smoke deep into his lungs. It didn't seem to help.

'I wasn't thinking of one of those, particularly. Where do you keep your draw these days?'

'I don't.'

'Not at all?'

'I've just told you, haven't I?'

'No malt. No draw. No teenage cuckoo to push out of the nest. This isn't the live-for-the-moment Leonard I know and love. I haven't travelled all this way to step into your mid-life crisis, have I?'

She shrivelled beneath the glare he shot her. With gritted teeth he stooped by the coffee table to stub out the filter in the ashtray, dislodging a couple of the earlier incumbents.

'I'm going to check downstairs, then I'm going to bed.' He made a sweeping gesture over the remnants of their meal. 'You wanted this so you clear it up. And I don't want to hear anything about your *not housemaiding*.'

What was the boy *doing*? What was he doing? Twice he'd had the opportunity to make her body his. *Three* times. What was this resistance? That such a maggot would dare to obstruct him was beyond comprehension. Was he not Speaker for the Gabrovantices, ally and confidant of Rome? The boy would learn respect and learn it fast.

His capabilities were being mastered with speed now, and the jewelled dagger was summoned easily to his clenched fist. It went into the soft belly of the boy hilt first, but the snarl of triumph which accompanied it was short. The boy bucked with such force that Ognirius felt himself unseated. Before he could renew his grip, the dagger melted from his fading fist as he began to liquefy. Desperately he tried to disentangle himself from his puny host. The exertion was enormous. He feared himself floundering, then he was free.

Scents caught him first, enveloping his nostrils and throat with their cloying, clammy moisture. He eased into them, letting his senses become attuned. Leaf litter, damp and decaying, mould spores, berry juices, the slimy trails of snails, hedgehogs' defecations, sap oozing from broken twigs, the bitter stench of human bile...

He glanced at the boy, curled in the mud at his feet, the liquid around his head steaming gently in the cold air. Ognirius sneered, and kicked out, watching his own foot and lower leg slice through the boy's unprotected kidneys. There was a groan. Ognirius stared at him.

He toed the boy gently, saw his foot enter high in the boy's shoulder. The boy murmured, but did not move. Ognirius slammed his foot down on the ribcage. He felt no resistance, but the boy cried out. His physical form was returning. He was *returning*.

The shout he gave seemed to reverberate around him, and he extended his gaze to take notice of where the boy had guided him. A roadway was close by. In a clearing iron chariots stood in ranks, glinting silently beneath golden torchlight. Buildings taller than trees shone lamplight from unshuttered windows. Beside him, next to his shoulder was the rough yellow stone of a wall, yellow light oozing from a window obscured by cloth.

And he knew where the boy had led him. He sensed her close. Sensed her waiting.

The power was within his reach, he knew it was. His physical presence was insubstantial yet, still milky pale, but the boy had felt his wrath from *outside*. He didn't need to be confined within the boy's flesh to make his mark. He wasn't going to need the boy; wasn't going to need to ride his back to fulfil the rite. He'd be able to do it *himself*.

A rasping croak caught his attention and he looked down at the boy. He needed him, yet. Didn't want him dead. Yet. But the noise wasn't the boy fighting for breath.

At first he thought it was an illusion of his mind, but it moved closer, and it croaked again.

Yslan had kept toads. Keeper of the Pool, Yslan had had toad-magic in her tongue, the tongue of the Presence, the tongue that had lain quiet and bloody in his palm.

Another movement; another toad.

Were they from the Pool? No, he'd hunted every one. None dwelt in the Pool. These were from the time of the boy. He had no ties with them yet they could sense him.

The first came closer, the second, too. A third appeared on his other side. Its tongue shot out, a straight black line. Ognirius curled his lip, unimpressed. If the boy could feel pain...

Light fell upon the group, a solid weight of silver. In surprise

Ognirius glanced skywards, too late throwing up an arm to protect his sight from Her cold and searing eye. Around him the croaking began and built in earnest so he didn't know how close they were or how swollen their number. They sounded like a plague. Retreat, he told himself, and tried to move away. He couldn't. Without the Elementals he was bound to the boy, and the rancid cur was slithering in the mud at his feet.

Clare lounged on the sofa idly listening to the return of Len's footsteps; leaden, she decided. She heard the lock engage as the flat's door snapped shut, heard Len's clump into the bathroom, the toilet flush, water run into the basin, his clump into the bedroom. The light was doused on the landing that doubled as a hall, and the bedroom door slammed shut.

She smiled at his childish fit of pique, and picked up the Bollinger to refill her glass. The bottle was still quite heavy, and she really didn't want any more. The fun had gone from drinking it now that Leonard wasn't there to watch her.

She replaced it on the coffee table, running her fingertips lightly up and down its smooth neck. It would be a pity to waste it, though; a pity to waste Len's money, spent, as it had been, with such ill grace. She smiled to herself, smiled at the wall separating them. Reaching for her bag she pulled out her phone and buttoned a number. Her call was answered on the third ring.

'It's me,' she whispered. 'Will you be free in half an hour?'

She began with a clatter of plates and a hummed tune to ensure that Leonard would hear her. She knew he'd take comfort from her *housemaiding*, that it would soothe his ire and massage his ego, but as she ran the water in the kitchen sink she quietened. With a little luck he would relax into sleep; at least into a doze.

With the crockery and glassware stored away, Clare discarded her silk shift and reclaimed from the laundry basket the trousers and top she'd worn earlier. The Bollinger she stationed by the head of the stairs. When she opened the bedroom door and turned on the overhead light, she was wearing her coat and had her bag diagonally over one shoulder.

'It's all right,' she called loudly as she made for the plate Leonard used to turn out his pockets. 'I won't be gone long.'

'Huh? What?'

Her hand closed on his key-ring: front door, back door, flat door, God-knew-what door. Enough to lock up the entire campus. She turned and jangled them towards him as his head started to rise from the pillow.

'No problem. Just come for these. Don't want to have to knock you up to get back in, do I?'

She didn't wait for a reply, but snapped off the light and shut the door on his slurred response. Scooping up the Bollinger she slammed the flat door so that it shook in its frame and she skipped down the staircase. The door to the street was shut on the call of her name and she laughed as she swung out into Cranbrook Avenue.

Through a tenfoot, left and left again, to the end and right, along the street and up the open-gated path. She didn't need to ring the bell. The door opened at her approach and shut as quickly behind her.

'Problems?'

Clare shook her head, still breathless. 'Moving faster than anticipated.' She looked the angular woman in the eye and grinned. 'It's going to work, Helen, I know it is.'

Helen let out a whoop of delight and darted forwards, arms extended to give a hug. They clasped each other a moment before Helen stepped back, wrinkling her nose.

'You smell of him.'

'Small price. Is Jenny with you?'

'I'm here. What's up?'

Both turned to watch a dishevelled figure traipse wearily down the stairs before sitting on a lower tread.

'What's happening?' she asked.

'Come on, sleepy head, find some glasses.' Clare shook the Bollinger, making it fizz in the bottle. 'Spoils of war!'

Thorned shrubs tearing at his jeans, branches and root stumps trying to trip him, Nick stumbled blindly on. There was a need to retch again, but he didn't want to give into it. His gut was burning, swollen in some grotesque hernia, pains shooting up into his chest wall and down into his groin with each jarring movement.

A kerb sent him sprawling on to tarmac. Grit scuffed and embedded into his hands. He cried out, then swore and swore again, cursing the darkness and his wavering eyesight.

He'd only wanted to be near Alice, didn't want to be parted from her. He'd no intention of looking in windows, anyone's windows, as if he were some voyeur. Yet he'd been set upon without warning, without a word of challenge. He couldn't see properly, that was what frightened him more than the pain; even though he could remember only blows to his body, not his head.

He mounted a step, saw the edge of a building, careered towards it for support but misjudged the distance and slammed his shoulder into the brickwork, pivoting himself into a wall of glass which shuddered beneath the impact. Luck was with him at last; it didn't break.

He stood on trembling legs, rolling his face across the rain-wet sheet, praying that when he opened his eyes his vision would be clear, praying that when he turned his attackers wouldn't be standing there, ready with their dull clapping, to continue what they'd started.

His sight was clear, almost, and when he wheeled around to face the shadows hardly a leaf shook in the breeze drifting over the playing field.

The playing field. He blinked across the expanse of darkness to the security lights marking out the Sports Centre. How had he got so far from Taylor Court? Why had instinct sent him here and not back to Salmon Grove?

A gasp of realisation filled his lungs with icy air and he spun back to the window to slap his palm on the glass, oblivious to the noise it made. Harkin's studio.

Is that who'd attacked him? Is that who'd been waiting outside the rear of Brantingham House? Waiting and watching outside Alice's window?

The heel of his fist crashed against the pane, making the glass wobble and his dark reflection bounce, elongating the scab on his cheek, darkening his upper lip in a show of a moustache. With cupped hands he cowled his eyes, searching each nook and cranny as if he expected the man to be lurking inside. His gaze ranged over the crowded workbench, fixed on a sphere shrouded in cloth: the clay head Harkin had been sculpting. Nick imagined it to be Harkin's own head, imagined it cleaved, imagined it exploded.

He'd sort Harkin. If it was the last thing he did, he'd sort Leonard Harkin.

Sort him, yes, sort him. His fault this. Useless piece of dung. Spineless turd. If he'd been a man Ognirius knew he would have stepped through the last time, but they were weak. All of them were so weak when they thought themselves so strong. Sort him, yes. Let him think himself strong. Let him think himself a king among men. A sky king. A green king. He enjoyed that role. The tributes, the power. Yes, sort him. He would sort him. Let him think himself a sky king, a green king, and then show him what happened with the turning of the year, what Yslan and her toads would have done beneath Her searing silver eye.

Chapter 15

It was a dream pursuing him, Len knew it was, and dreams were only contortions of the mind. But whose mind? If his, the dream would have burst upon him without warning. If hers...

He ran faster, heart and lungs aching with exertion, the sensation his only link with reality in the coal-black of the void. He could hear the dream gaining, galloping like a huntsman behind him. Or was it to his side? In front? Don't weave, he told himself. Find the light. Clare was in the light and Clare would protect him.

Except that Clare wasn't in the bed beside him. She wasn't in the flat. She'd left, left him to his fate.

The noise grew. Lights, orange and white, streaked the darkness. He drew breath to cry out, and then it was upon him, and he lay, curled and trembling, amid bracken and broken twigs.

He kept his eyes shut, tight shut, refusing to acknowledge, refusing to interact, but the woodland scents were pervasive, and, try though he did, he could not ignore the sounds.

Girlish laughter.

Occasionally the thread of a half remembered tune. The lapping of water, close by.

Girlish laughter.

Splashes. Girlish laughter.

They were in a clearing, perhaps a dozen, in a clearing amid trees, he on the further side of a pond, a pool. Light flickered across its surface, yellow and red, reflecting from fiery torches set in the ground. A shape rose in the water; arched a slender arm; withdrew. On the bank he glimpsed white limbs, pale flesh. Young girls danced, and twirled, and ran, stretching like gymnasts with the suppleness of youth.

And they were young. Very young. Some with lines so straight they could have been boys, some with breasts just budding. All of them collecting flowers, white flowers, to garland and tie in one another's hair.

Garlands were strung between trees all around them, no defence from the might of his arm or the muscle of his chest. As he stepped closer, closer, their weak stems broke against him, line upon line, until he walked into the torchlight.

Shrieks of surprise; giggles of excitement. With words of reassurance he enticed them to him, let them divest him, touch him, so he could caress them in return. And they were eager, very eager, for the pleasures he bestowed, and he accepted garlands from each and every one of them, savoured the ripening of their breasts, the maturing of their hips and thighs as childhood slipped away leaving nubile young women with appetites to match.

But they were voracious in their maturity, garlanding and garlanding, demanding ever more as they passed him hand to hand. The garlands were so heavy he couldn't lift them from his shoulders. And they wouldn't leave him, these women, these rapacious laughing women. They kept pulling him back as he tried to crawl away.

The flowers' scent was suffocating, the garlands wrapped around him, binding his head and his arms and his legs. He pleaded for relief, but they stood and sang round him, laughing at his frailty. Finally, clasping one to another, they danced on their way.

The tilled ground was stony and cold beneath Leonard's aching limbs, the remains of the leaf-crop yellow and flat, but he was glad, so glad, to be left on his own.

The sneer of contempt was harsh, and he raised his gaze to the silhouetted trees about him. Standing in the shade of the underbrush was his final painting given life. Girded in saplings from ankle to head was the sacrifice, blackthorn spines rending naked flesh, beads of red life-blood held in place by the power of will.

Leonard expelled a trembling breath. Dare he look to the face, chance meeting his reflection? The pull was too great, his only route surrender.

Dark hair, dark eyes, dark scarring — *not him* — but Leonard knew the youth by the angle of his head and the gritted teeth beneath the moustached and curling lip.

'You're bound! You're bound!'

Even as the words jumped the space between them the youth was pumping his muscles, the blackthorn spines digging deeper, the saplings shuddering beneath the strain. One snapped across his torso. Another over his thigh.

Leonard looked down at the garlands chaining him, watched as their flowerheads shrivelled to points and their stems turned brittle. The air was filled with the sound of splintering of wood, and Leonard shrank from the pain of needle-sharp spines piercing his skin.

The youth stepped from his prison as if the bindings had been flower stems, the dark lacerations now a whorling design of tattoos. Three strides and he was by Leonard's head, a heavy gold neck-ring standing proud of his collarbone, its open roundels a second set of eyes.

'I've not touched her. I've not seen her!' Leonard cried. 'She's not even here!'

The youth turned towards the women, his bloodied limbs glittering in the torchlight, his erection tall and solid. They called him in a single voice, and Leonard gasped as he saw that each was the image of the next, lustrous hair lifting in individual locks about a pale and smiling face.

'No!' Leonard cried. 'No, it's not true!'

But the youth was eyeing him, malevolence etched in every feature. Without a word he brought down his heel on Leonard's throat.

*

'Come on, Sleeping Beauty. What do you want? The wet flannel treatment?'

Nick dragged himself to consciousness, to the blinding light of an uncurtained window and Murray sitting on the end of his bed. Pain kicked in across his shoulder and chest as he lifted his hand to rub at his face. Carefully, he slid his fingers beneath the duvet to test his ribs.

Harkin. That middle-aged bastard had beaten the shit out of him, and he, half the bastard's age, had crawled away like a whimpering dog.

'Fe, fi, fo, fum. I smell the blood of an Englishman.'

Murray's idiotic expression imbued him with the persona of every friendly giant in every children's picture book. All that was missing was the knobbly chin.

Nick had a sudden image of the head on the workbench in Harkin's studio, of the mud as he'd scrabbled against the window pane.

Oh, no. Not again, surely... but he saw that the carpet was free from soil and leaf litter, and his dirty clothing lay in a neat pile by the basin.

'Are you gonna get up and give this poor dog a bone?'

He was naked in his bed, too, naked and clean. The last thing he could remember was staring through the glass at the shrouded head. Had he come back to the house and showered?

'Woof-woof!'

Nick rubbed at his eyes again, trying to ignore the pain in his back. 'What are you doing here, Murray?'

'Waiting for Little Red Riding Hood to bring along a basket of goodies. What big teeth you have, Grandmama.'

'Whatever you're on, Murray, you'd better have some left for me. I feel like Death.' He pulled back the duvet and swung his legs onto the carpet, resting a moment, his head in his hands.

'Looks as if you've had a run in with him,' Murray said, serious now. 'I've seen accident victims with less bruising than you. I came to tell you that the training sessions start on Tuesday, but looking at the state of you I think you should give it a miss for a week.'

Nick drew his hands down his face and stared at him. 'You came over here... on a Sunday morning...'

'...afternoon...'

'...to tell me something I already know?'

Murray shrugged. 'Actually I came to hear all the gory details of your night of exquisite passion, but I'll settle for a coffee until you get your head together.'

There was a prickling along Nick's spine, across his shoulders. 'What are you talking about?'

'Does the word *redhead* mean anything?'

In two steps Nick was standing at the basin running the cold tap to sluice his face and neck.

'Aw, come on... Don't start playing the coy virgin with me. You wouldn't even introduce me to her the other day, and then last night I see you entwined like love's young dream. Who is she?'

Towelling himself, Nick breathed and breathed again, hoping the pain of filling his lungs to capacity would counter the aggression building inside him.

Why was he jealous of Murray? It was true; they'd shared each others exploits like they'd shared each others joints. But Alice? He'd share Alice with no one. Not Harkin. Not Murray. No one.

He pulled the towel aside, dragging strands of hair down his forehead. 'How did you get in here?'

'Well, I know you're an Arts and everything, but if I take it slowly... You see, there's this round button on the door jamb downstairs. You know what a door looks like?'

Nick groaned in irritation and began hunting for a clean pair of briefs.

'If you press your finger to this button it sends an electric current along a wire through the wall to a bell in the hall.' Below them, faintly, the doorbell rang. Murray grinned and opened up his hands.

'Hey! Didn't know I was a magician, did you? Let's listen hard and see if that nice lady answers the door again, just as she did to me.' He cupped a hand to an ear and leaned towards the inner wall, fluttering his eyelashes as if he were a pantomime dame.

They heard the door open, heard Maureen ask a question, heard another woman answer.

Nick flung down the towel and jerked a drawer from its runners, tipping the contents on the floor in an effort to sift through the puddled clothing.

'Hell's teeth! If you moved as fast as that on the field we'd never lose a match! Oh... It's *her*, isn't it? Wow!'

Dancing on one foot as he struggled with his jogging bottoms, he couldn't stop Murray opening the door and bounding down the stairs.

Nick caught sight of his torso in the mirror, saw his muscles pumping with anger and adrenalin, blue and purple bruising patterning his skin. A sweatshirt. He needed a sweatshirt. One peeped from beneath the bed and he made a grab for it, dust and all.

They were out of the hallway and into the kitchen, Murray's voice carrying through the half-closed door.

'...friend of Nick's. We met briefly in Taylor Court the other day, but he's always the same, forgets about introductions.'

Nick burst in, slamming the door into the worktop. Murray didn't flinch. Alice jumped back in alarm.

'Ah, here's the man himself. I've put the kettle on. Are you going to organise three mugs for coffee?'

Her hair brought a golden autumn to the kitchen. Nick couldn't take his eyes from her face. He could only watch as her gaze flitted over him, absorbing the sensation as if it were a caress.

She smiled. 'Hi.'

'Hi.'

A finger prodded Nick in the back. 'Coffee?'

Drops of water meandered from his hair down his neck. One fell on to his unshod foot.

Another prod in the back, this time more forceful. 'The kettle's boiling.'

There was a click and Alice turned to watch steam billow from the kettle's spout.

Nick walked by her, breathing in a perfume not man-made. The kitchen counter seemed a million miles beyond her. Who wanted coffee? He didn't want coffee. He wanted Alice. Alone. And Murray was talking to her, drawing her away.

'He's still not going to introduce us, is he? Such a plonker. You wouldn't think it to look at him, would you?'

The mugs came from the wall cupboard in a clutch in one hand, the coffee jar in the other. Why was it such a distance to the counter?

'I'm Murray Symonds, second year Law, First team prop.'

'You play rugby, too?'

'God's only given game. And you are?'

A spoon. Nick needed a spoon for the coffee jar. It was such an effort to concentrate. The muscles in his shoulders were strung tighter than he'd ever known, his fingers numb, his actions unco-ordinated. And there, next to the teaspoons, lay the household's one and only kitchen knife, its honed blade glittering seductively.

A spoon, Nick told himself. It was a spoon he wanted.

'And your name is..?' Murray prompted again.

A hand with fingers thicker than his own reached inside the drawer. There were no spoons; only the knife, its blade filling his eyes with light.

'Alice,' she said. 'My name's Alice Linwood.'

Nick spun round to witness their handshake, her fine, pale fingers captured in Murray's thick knuckles. He slammed shut the drawer and they broke their grip. Alice hesitated.

'Come on,' Murray said, 'let's be having this coffee before we all die of thirst.' He crossed to the sink to wipe his hands on the towel hung there. 'Where are the spoons kept in this place?'

Nick stepped away from the counter back into the circle of Alice's wild-flower perfume. He could feel his shoulders easing;

the sense of touch returning to his fingertips. Behind him, he heard Murray pull open the drawer.

'Ah, here they are. Soon have a drink organised. Take sugar, do you?'

Nick watched Alice shake her head, her hair dancing about her face. 'Just a little milk.'

'Sleep okay?' Nick whispered. And he knew from her smile that she had, knew that she had dreamed of him, of him holding her. Why hadn't he dreamed of her? Perhaps he had, but couldn't recall it. No, that would be impossible.

'I didn't wake you, did I?' she asked.

'I had that pleasure,' Murray interrupted as he offered over a mug. Nick took it from his hand and passed it to her. Her fingers slid across his as she received it, and he felt his heart lurch with the sensation.

'So what course are you on?' Murray asked.

A finger prodded Nick in the ribs and his own coffee was passed to him.

'History,' Alice said. 'Second year.'

She slid her hands around the mug as if it were a bowl and raised it to her lips to blow across the surface of the liquid. Her grey eyes seemed to turn to water in the rising steam. Nick wanted to reach out and save her from drowning.

'Buried treasure and rain-sodden field trips, eh?'

'It's not all treasure. It's not all buried, either.'

'But the rain-sodden field trips are a fairly safe bet, right?'

Alice lowered her mug, her gaze only for Nick. 'It's strange, but when I find I'm looking in the right place, the weather's always good. It's going to be fine tomorrow. I'm heading for the North York Moors to do some research. If you've nothing scheduled, would you like to help?'

'Count me in,' said Nick.

'Count me out,' said Murray. 'But just in case there's need of a search party, where, exactly, are you two heading?'

'Newtondale.'

*

The twisted sheets were so damp that at first Leonard thought he'd peed himself, but it was sweat. Perspiration had been pouring from him. It still stood clammy on his skin.

He tossed back the covers, throwing off the nightmare still caught in the folds. He heard a noise, a bump next door. Someone was there. *Him?* He glanced at the alarm clock, gasping at the time. Clare. It had to be Clare. Dragging on his robe he stormed into the lounge.

'How long have you been back?'

She looked up from the magazine she was reading. 'Hours.'

'Why didn't you come to bed when you got in?'

'Well, I was going to, but you were thrashing about so much I didn't fancy ending up black and blue while you scored your goal at Wembley.'

'I wasn't scoring a goal, for God's sake. I was being murdered!'

Clare laid the magazine on her knee and raised an eyebrow. 'Were you? How interesting.'

'Why did you leave?' he demanded.

'If you remember rightly—'

'Where did you go?'

Clare emphasised her contempt. 'If I'm going to have to account for my every movement, Leonard, we may as well call it a day now.'

'You went out looking for some cock, don't tell me you didn't. What did you do? Flag down a car and drag the poor sod out into the gutter?'

Clare stood to gaze at him. 'If you must know,' she said quietly, 'I went to purchase some draw. And I think I'd better light one for you before you disintegrate completely.'

Each stood looking at the other, Clare with her calm demeanour, he a spent force.

'You're trembling, Leonard. This anger's a front, isn't it? It's not just last night, or this dream you've had. There's something seriously wrong here, isn't there?'

Shaking his head, he closed his eyes and turned away. Clare

was beside him, her hand on his shoulder.

'It'll help to talk about it.' She drew him towards her. It was such a relief to rest his head on her chest. 'Tell me,' she urged.

'I can't. Dear God, Clare, I only wish I could.'

Chapter 16

A well-polished red Citroën pulled up outside the house and Nick was down the stairs and out the door before Alice had reached the gate. Her smile of welcome said so much that he felt bereft when she turned back for the car. He caught her at the verge, pulling her towards him and wrapping her in his arms. The softness of her body, the scents floating from her skin, made up for the hours he'd spent staring out of his window at the lights of the Taylor Court apartments. It was such an effort to brush her cheek with his kiss and not make her mouth his own, but he was pleased that he didn't. She was tensing in his embrace, and he broke away to hold her by the shoulders and grin at her, full of the joy of the morning.

'I missed you.' He watched her blink at him, unsure, he thought, how to react.

She smiled, averting her gaze. 'Have you any walking boots? Waterproofs, or anything?'

'Since when has anyone needed boots to walk? Besides, you said the weather was going to be fine.'

Her face tilted towards the leaden sky. 'I've been known to be wrong.'

Throwing his jacket into the rear of the car, Nick made himself comfortable in the front passenger seat. A notice on the dashboard caught his eye.

'You've hired this. Christ, we could have borrowed Murray's Toyota for the price of a full tank of petrol.'

'But would we have been insured?'

'It probably isn't even taxed.'

He started to feed his arm round her shoulders but she forestalled him by pushing a road atlas into his hand.

'I know my way to Beverley, but beyond that it's up to you.' She turned the ignition key and the engine purred.

'You want me to map-read? Couldn't you stretch to GPS?'

'This is not the time to tell me that you can't follow a map.'

'Already you've forgotten our excursion into Hull?' He was pleased to hear her chuckle, and he settled himself into finding the correct page. 'What's the state of provisions?'

'A Mars bar, a Snickers, two ham sandwiches, two apples, a bottle of water and two cans of Coke. Do you think we can manage?'

Nick's smile was reflected back at him from the atlas on his lap. Alice had packed food for both of them, and she was beginning to relax in his company.

'Yes,' he said quietly. 'Yes, I think we can manage.'

She didn't drive through Beverley, but took the by-pass, which confused Nick, and they were heading up the B1248 before he'd pinpointed their position.

'Great help you're going to be on the moors. There's a distinct lack of signposts up there.'

At the top of the page a handful of unclassified roads zig-zagged round the edge of a dark green mass. A primary route circled it along the coast, but only one main road cut north to south across the centre. For the most part there was nothing but unadulterated green streaked with veins of blue.

'From the looks of this map there's a distinct lack of anything.'

'Don't worry. I've packed Ordnance Surveys in the boot.'

'And what do they show?'

'An awful lot of scrub and a great many contour lines.'

The plink of raindrops heralded the soft whisper of the wipers over the windscreen. Nick watched their first pass across the glass.

'Gee,' he said. He contemplated the map again, wishing that it was the Ordnance Survey and he could see the area in detail.

The rain grew heavier. Alice switched on the headlights. Nick gazed at the muddy fields beyond the hedgerow, next year's crop already showing green. He thought about the bushes that surrounded Taylor Court, of the mud at the rear of Brantingham House, and the kicking Harkin had given him.

'Do you close your curtains when the daylight starts to fade?'
'Pardon?'
'In your flat. You're on the ground floor. I was just thinking about it. Anyone passing round the back could see in.'
'There's no path at the back.'
'Perverts don't usually use them.'
'A Peeping Tom? What, again?'
Nick turned to face her. 'What do you mean... again?'
'There were sightings last year about this time. Well, maybe later. Maybe around Christmas.'
'Outside your flat?'
'Right outside my window.' She gave a shudder. 'Footprints and cigarette ends right outside my window.'

Harkin.

'Was he caught?'
'Not that I know of. Some late night revellers saw a figure skulking about and gave chase. The Police were called. That's how I know about the footprints and the cigarette ends. Cigarette ends... I ask you, how long had he been there? No other window. Only mine. I made sure I closed my curtains after that, believe me.'

Her gaze flicked across to him. 'Have you heard that he's at it again?'
'There was a rumour. Why didn't you tell me you'd been stalked?'
She shrugged her shoulders and smiled to pass it off. 'Might have been you, mightn't it?'
Nick turned back to the windscreen, seeing an aspect of Harkin's face in every bush along the road. 'It wasn't.'

Harkin. Dear God... he'd get even with Harkin.

'Wetwang,' Alice announced as a road sign flashed by.

'Malton to the left. Are you map-reading or am I doing this on my own?'

'Er, yes. Sorry.' His finger prodded at the page as if trying to gain a verbal response. 'Immediate right.'

'Got it.'

A lascivious grin spread across Nick's face. 'Wetwang... Who on earth would name a village Wetwang? Their chief hobby must be—' The words trailed away as he glimpsed Alice's frown. 'Doesn't matter. You'll need to keep to this road right through to...er...Malton? Norton?'

'Two towns separated by a river. I thought you'd been. You said you'd visited Derventio.'

There was no Derventio on the map Nick was looking at, but there had been on the wall map in the museum in Hull, in that very bright room housing the awe-inspiring mosaics.

'I didn't say I'd been. I said I knew the name.' And he did. Even now, sitting in the car, the name *Derventio* meant something to him. Exactly what, he couldn't grasp.

'Would it be far out of our way?'

'We'll pass right by its gate.' She eyed him. 'If you don't get us lost.'

Nick negotiated the car through Norton, over the railway line, over the river and up the hill. They took a right at the traffic lights and shortly after Alice pulled into the kerb to point across the road. All Nick could see was a low wall and a line of trees.

'We're here?'

'I've an umbrella in the boot, so we shouldn't get too wet.'

There was a pair of hiking boots in the rear footwell, too. Nick waited impatiently as Alice changed out of her trainers. The umbrella was retrieved and, while Nick stood holding it above their heads, Alice pulled a knee-length waterproof from the top of her rucksack and slipped her arms inside the sleeves. It was all taking so much time. She was infuriatingly thorough.

To the right of the wall was a rough track wide enough for a vehicle, and they entered into parkland easing away in an incline. Mature trees gathered in bedraggled clumps of three or four, and at the very bottom, on the other side of chain-link fencing, roofs of low industrial units stood grey in the drizzle. Beyond those the land rose gently again, revealing the stone and brick buildings of Malton crouched against the dismal weather.

'Derventio!' Alice proclaimed, sweeping her arm in an expansive gesture.

Nick blinked, unsure of what he was seeing, unsure of what he should be seeing, aware that something was very wrong. And then a trembling started in his legs, rising fast through his groin and abdomen so that he clutched at Alice for support.

'Nick? Nick!'

It was a lie. It couldn't be Derventio. Where was the stone causeway, the great gates, the white and dazzling buildings? The area was too small.

The sodden green swam before his flickering eyes. Individual grass stalks, raindrops glistening as if serrated teeth, rose in salute as his hearing was paralysed by a crescendo of sound that dulled to a throbbing and reprised, this time distinct and recognised.

A call. The solid retort of sword against shield. A lighter tinkling of metal tabs on body armour. Beneath it all, the heartbeat of the legion, the constant, rhythmic tramp of feet.

A breath brought the pungent odour of horse dung, oiled leather, bellows-charged smelting fires. Those same smelting fires had fashioned — for *him* — the gladius with the jewelled and sky-riven decoration. He made a fist, felt the hilt firm in his palm, the weight of the blade pulling at muscles long dormant.

A call. An order given. He opened his eyes to the lines of men and the dazzling buildings... but saw only dull green, the leaden sky, a clenched fist and a sword as light as air itself, fading in outline as raindrops splattered his chilled skin.

'...Nick!'

Fingertips traced an arc across his cheek and he flinched, startled, to stare into Alice's worried face.

'Nick, are you all right? You're terribly pale.'

The umbrella lay open on its side on the grass, sheltering no one. Had he been holding it? Had she?

'I'm okay.'

'Don't lie to me. You look awful. You fainted. It was a faint, wasn't it? You're not— What's the matter?'

'I don't know. I just felt...' He pulled his hand towards him; turned it palm up; flexed his fingers. '...weird.'

'Nick... Nick, what were you holding?'

The change in her tone rang alarms in his head. He flexed his fingers again, his mind racing to find excuses. 'Holding? I wasn't holding anything.' He sat up, glad that his head didn't spin. 'I get pins and needles down this arm occasionally. I must have trapped a nerve during the game. Probably need a bit of physio.' He made it to his feet. 'Jeez, I'm soaked through. You haven't packed a spare pair of denims, have you?'

'Nick, do you... do you see things?'

He turned slowly knowing that he had to hold her gaze if he was going to bluff this out. The smile he gave her was the most lustful he could manage. 'I see you in my dreams.'

'That's not what I meant and you know it.' She turned away to pick up the umbrella and furl it, despite the rain. 'Do you want to look round here, or shall we go on to Pickering?'

Her rigid stance, the anger in her tone, made Nick catch his breath. He grasped her arm and pulled her round to face him.

'But you can, can't you?'

'Don't be ridiculous.'

She tried to pull free but he twisted his fingers in the fabric of her waterproof. Its hood slipped down and she blinked against the raindrops hitting her face. 'Let go.'

'Alice... Alice, are you psychic?'

'Of course not.'

'Then what? There's something, I know there is. Tell me.'

Her fierce expression faded, her shoulders drooped. She sighed, drawing her free hand over her damp face and hair.

'Nothing so bizarre. When I was younger I... I thought I might be an empath, but it was a mistake.'

'An empath?'

She shook her head, looking as if she wished she'd never started. 'It's quite well documented, though mainstream archaeology doesn't exactly embrace the concept, as you can imagine. Empaths are people who are supposed to have a sort of gift. They are able to hold a find and images connected to the find come into their minds. Anyway, I was mistaken. I was doing what the academics always maintain. I was allowing my imagination to build on my research of the subject and fill in the gaps.' She looked at him and shrugged. 'It's very easy.'

She turned to Derventio and again swept her arm across the field. 'For a start, the trees and the modern buildings wouldn't have been here when the fortress was standing, so my mind simply erases them. We're standing to one side of what would have been the major route to the gateway — the depression over there — and that means that these grassy ridges would have been ramparts. If we go inside and walk the road-routes I can point out the principia, the granary, barrack blocks—'

'Dazzling white?'

'White?'

'Maybe... maybe reflecting the sun?'

Alice chuckled and raised her face to catch the rain. 'Not today. Do you want to walk round the rest of it?'

So they walked the site of Derventio, Alice explaining the pattern of Roman forts, Nick wondering if that's what he'd seen, what he'd heard, his own mind's eye view translated from an artist's impression in a book. The one thing it didn't explain was the sword he'd seen held in his hand, the weight he'd felt pulling on his arm.

On the grassy slope that had once been the steps of the principia, Ognirius Licinius Vranaun sat impassively watching the boy as the fine drizzle maintained him. Showing him the gladius might have been a mistake. It had certainly been a mistake to allow his rage to take such a hold, though never had he anticipated the glory of Derventio to have been brought so low as to be a cow pasture.

But the rage was a mistake. He must remember that his powers were returning, and keep such outbursts in check, especially when she was close.

So, she thought herself blessed? Ha! She'd know the truth soon now.

Rain, rain... He needed the moisture to stand outside the pool, outside the boy, but oh... was he sick of it! The Elementals had been easy to convert, his first true triumph, but they chattered incessantly and would not be still. Where was the sun that had shone that day he had stood on these steps with Gaius Senecio? They'd eaten well, he remembered, goose and suckling pig in sauces he'd never tasted the like of before. He'd known then, as he'd known from his first glimpse of Derventio, where his loyalties should lie, and the loyalties of the People. Power was due to pass to him. With Gaius' aid he had simply ensured it passed the quicker. And it had been so very, very easy.

He focused his thoughts, and the gladius appeared straddling his knees, its blade kissed by a sun of long ago. The milk-grey outline of his hand wrapped around the decorated hilt, the weight and solidity of the gift-weapon substantial in his palm. Ognirius drew back his lips as the power coursed through him, filling his weak outline with flesh and bone. Torch-lit woodland erupted around him, female screams ringing in his ears. His cry of triumph created ripples in the Pool as the bloody sword was lifted in salute.

Yes, it had been easy, laughably easy, once her tongue had laid a dead thing in his palm.

Chapter 17

Milk churns stood to attention beside a green barrow heavy with leather-bound trunks. Bright enamel signs advertised Colman's Mustard, Bristol Cigarettes and Yorkshire Relish.

'When you said we should come to Pickering and *let the train take the strain* I was thinking in terms of an Intercity, not something out of a 1930s film set.'

'Nick, you're an ungrateful individual. If it hadn't have been for this weather I would have driven on to the Hole of Horcum and yomped you across the moor.'

'Yomped me, eh? You never know, I might have liked it.'

There was a shrill whistle, and young and old surged forward, vying with one another for the best position to watch the arrival of the steam engine. Hidden from view by the bend in the line, Nick could hear it grunting, only its smoke, light against the darker sky, betraying its progress. The concrete platform started to vibrate beneath his feet, startling him momentarily into believing he was back at Derventio. The engine strove into view: blood-red buffers below a charcoal-black face, grey smoke heaving in lumps from its stubby chimney, white steam hissing from between its wheels. Shutters clicked on cameras all around, and the air was filled with the smell of soot and oil and burning coal. As it slowed, steam escaped in a sigh to cloud the carriages trundling behind. Finally, with a shudder, it was still.

Nick felt a tap on his arm and he turned to find Alice laughing at him.

'Your expression! I'll have to buy you a notebook so you can write down its number. Come on, let's see about tickets.'

Faces bright with elation, passengers streamed by as Nick paused close enough to touch the engine's matt black hulk.

Steam hissed over his trainers: a monster, gently snoozing. Uniformed men wearing leather caps guarded the secrets of its footplate, imparting knowledge to those who crowded near: to men old enough to be their own fathers, to babies too young to speak brought close by doting parents. Crouching low, Nick peered between the bodies to glimpse the open firebox and the burning coals within. Such power harnessed. There was no resemblance to an Intercity.

The little crowd stepped back, half of them walking with the fireman to watch as he descended between the tender and the first carriage to uncouple the two. With an ear-splitting shriek and a cloud of steam, the engine shuddered forward as far as the buffer stops. The points were changed. With a grunt and a snort and a sliding of wheels, the engine reversed down the parallel line to the other end of the carriages.

'I would never have thought it of you,' Alice whispered fanning two tickets in front of Nick's eyes. 'You're like a devotee paying homage at an altar. Can we climb aboard now?'

The buffet car was open. Over a cup of coffee Alice showed him a leaflet explaining the route and the timetable.

'It'll take half an hour to reach Newtondale Halt. We should be able to find the spring and be back at the platform for the return train at just gone three. With a bit of luck we'll have time to drive on to Stape before it gets too dark. There's a spring there, a little way into the planted forestry. The Roman Road ran right by it, but the modern road is a hundred metres west. There's bushes there hanging with offerings just as there'd have been in Celtic times.'

'Says nothing about a Roman Road here,' Nick said, tapping at the leaflet. '*Waymarked walks to explore coniferous forests of spruce, pine and larch.* No mention of teashops, either.'

Alice snorted. 'Make the most of the drink before you. I'm not even sure that the spring is on one of the designated walks. I did remind you to pack a machete, didn't I?'

'I hope you're joking.' He watched her eyebrows arch. 'Oh, great,' he said. 'Tell me the worst.'

Alice spread an Ordnance Survey map across the table and tapped it three times with a finger nail. 'Railway line. Newtondale Halt. The spring.'

Nick could see words printed across a green background covered in tree symbols and criss-crossed in Forestry Commission tracks, but with the constant vibration and swaying of the carriage he found it difficult to focus on the fine detail.

'You're telling me that X doesn't exactly mark the spot?'

'No, but bearing in mind the constricted contour lines and the fact that this ridge here is called Killing Nab Scar, I suspect that the spring is the source of that stream.'

'As long as you know where we're going.'

He sat back in his seat to watch the trees rush close by the window. Most were spindly silver birch, the bright bark of trunk and branch displaying to perfection the yellows and russets of their leaves. His hand lifted to follow the locks of Alice's hair as she folded the map.

'You know,' she said, 'I think the sky's brightening. We might even see some sunshine. It could be an omen.'

Leaning towards her, Nick drank in the soft perfume of her skin and hair. He brushed her cheek with his own, tracing his lips along her jaw-line. She turned to him, more startled than consenting, but when he laid his mouth on hers she did no more than back into the seat. She tasted wondrously sweet.

He drew away to watch her blink at him, her face a mask of doubts.

'You can respond,' he whispered. 'It is allowed.'

She glanced behind him to seats he knew were empty.

'Do you feel anything for me, Alice?'

'We're on a train.'

'So? You're safe with me.'

She turned towards the window, trying to ignore him. He nibbled at her ear. She pulled away.

'And I,' he murmured, 'know that I am safe with you.'

She swung back on him, her grey eyes tense. 'You know

nothing of the kind.'

'Third time lucky,' he reminded her, and he knew that she believed it. Or wanted to.

Shadows filled their carriage as crowding pines tapped dark fingers against the window. The land itself rose in craggy outcrops to peer through the glass.

'We'll be arriving soon. We'd better get ready. The train won't stop for long.' She slid the rucksack across to him, and he stood to shoulder it.

The train didn't stop long. No sooner had Nick noticed the guard standing further down the slatted wooden platform, than the man was lifting the flag in his hand and climbing back aboard. There was a whistle and the carriages edged forwards, the vibration from the engine travelling through the platform until it trembled up Nick's legs. A small girl waved at him from the window of a carriage. Automatically Nick raised a hand in return, but she disappeared in a burst of orange and yellow as the sun reflected off the glass. He let his hand fall as his gaze took in the length of the platform. He and Alice had been the only passengers to alight.

'The clouds are definitely thinning,' Alice told him. 'I've got a good feeling about this.'

Nick squinted towards the sun, and then around him, all around him, at the blanket of variegated green and yellow. Opposite, across the railway line, mixed woodland dipped and soared in a jagged cliff-face, a natural barrier stretching left and right. Behind him, but not quite as close, another ridge swept up to touch the sky in the darker green of pines. Between the two, a cover of alder, rowan, and shrubs he couldn't identify, hid the ground as perfectly as if it did not exist. He couldn't even see turf through the slats of the wooden platform for the growth of fern and gorse. Newtondale Halt seemed to be suspended in mid-air by the fingers of Nature. There was a haunting, half-hearted whistle from the steam train and Nick looked up to see the receding dot of the guard's van take the distant curve, and the green vegetation close in behind it.

'You've got that timetable safe?' he asked.

'Yes, and my wristwatch is working. I'll get you back here before the last train.'

'The one at just gone three?'

'There's one at half past five, too.'

He stepped to the fence at the edge of the platform and peered at the thick undergrowth below. It would be dark by five, so dark they wouldn't be able to see a hand before them. He hoped that Alice had had the foresight to pack a torch.

It was Alice who led the way to wooden steps, Nick following to descend through the leafy canopy to a shaded mossy track.

'It doesn't look as if it's rained here. Not for weeks.' She pointed to a Fire Hazard sign and a stook of long-handled beaters. 'This way. We should come to a Forestry road fairly soon.'

Nick didn't begin to relax until he saw the white of the loose stone roadway through the trees, feeling more confident when its man-made solidity was biting into the soles of his trainers. He breathed in the woodland fragrances and listened to the birds singing, pleased that he'd shed his jacket back on the train and tied it to the rucksack. The steep-sided valley seemed to be concentrating the sun's warmth as if it were a summer's day. He only wished he'd thought to bring sunglasses to cut down the glare from the white road.

Alice, too, seemed to be feeling the sudden heat. He watched as she pulled her sweater over her head, his gaze following closely the line of breast and neck beneath the figure-hugging top she wore. As she knotted the sweater round her waist, he increased his step to slip his arm around her back and press his lips into her hair.

'How are we doing. Lost yet?'

'Oh, ye of little faith.' She consulted the map. 'Beulah Wood is to our left; Pifelhead Wood to our right. If we'd walked the other way when meeting the road we'd have come across Yaul Sike Hole, which I think might be a sinkpit. We'll have a look on the way back. Could be interesting.'

'A sinkpit is interesting?'

She turned to peer at him and he grinned as if he'd meant it as a joke.

'The ridge above us is Killing Nab Scar, though I've seen it written as Killing Noble Scar. It makes me wonder if it might have been, especially considering there's this spring beneath it.'

Nick chuckled. 'Might have been what? A place for killing nobles? Our ancestors didn't go in for that sort of thing, did they?'

'It's as likely to be where the Neolithic residents stampeded large game over the precipice. It'd be far easier than running them down with flint weapons.'

'Neolithic? You mean, woolly mammoths and sabre-toothed tigers and stuff?' An image of the mammoth in the museum came to him, the toddler reaching to pat its hairy leg. Somehow it no longer seemed so cuddly

Alice shot him a withering look. 'History begins with the invention of the combustion engine, does it?'

'Round here it seems to have begun with the railway.'

'You should look at a map occasionally. This area is littered with howes and cairns and standing stones. Not far from here there's an east-west trading route that was ancient when the Romans sliced a road through it.'

'Okay, okay. You're so easy to wind up, Alice. Where's your sense of humour?'

She regarded him testily before increasing her step. Nick sighed and lagged behind. What had he said that had been so wrong?

Ahead the roadway divided, the left fork rising up the steep hill before looping back on itself among the conifers. The trees on part of the hillside had been felled. Stumps and dead branches littered the site in dusty brown humps, almost the same colour as the ruptured soil. To Nick it looked more desecration than management.

Alice drew to a halt, her face tilted towards the skyline.

'It's up there somewhere,' she said, but her voice was so quiet that Nick wasn't sure if she was talking to herself.

She moved ahead, keeping to the right fork where pines crowded the road as if in protection of themselves. The curve of the railway lay nearby, Nick knew, probably only metres away, but there was nothing to be seen through the interlocking branches. To fight for a path through he would probably need that machete Alice had teased about. He wasn't even carrying a penknife.

Without warning she darted left to crouch at the shallow ditch part-clogged with trimmings from the hewn trees.

'Water,' she said.

Nick drew alongside to watch her dabble her fingers in the clear liquid, prodding at its yellow sediment.

'We're here.'

'We're here? You mean... this is *it*?'

Alice didn't answer, but turned away, quickening her step as her gaze scanned the hillside above them. Nick slung the pack from one shoulder to the other to ease the pressure on his bruises and started after her, but she was moving fast now and he realised that he would have to jog to catch up.

'Hey, Alice!'

'It's here!' she called, and without even a wave she vanished into the trees.

Nick bolted forwards, desperately keeping his gaze fixed on the point where she'd disappeared. His panic was short-lived. A dusty track lifted steeply from the roadway. Beside it a dark green sign pointed in white lettering: *Newtondale Spring*.

Nick climbed. The track divided at a junction. Another sign. *Newtondale Spring* leaped out at him and he didn't wait to read the rest, just followed the arrow left. And up.

The track hugged the contours of the hillside, giving no more forward view than ten or fifteen metres. He'd hoped to glimpse Alice ahead of him, but it was as if she had never passed that way. Pine sap was strong in his nostrils, now, cloying in his throat. His thighs were aching with the continuous upward thrust, his ribs from the beating he'd received. The shoulder he'd hurt playing rugby demanded relief, and he paused to transfer the pack again.

'Alice!'

He waited, breathing hard, for his call to be returned, but all he heard was a rushing, like water, a hissing, like steam. There was an ominous crack, and he looked up to the canopy to find the interlocking branches sawing at one another overhead. There was not a breath of wind where he stood. There hadn't been a breeze on the roadway below.

'Alice!'

Fixing his sight on the disappearing trail as if it were a try-line, he filled his lungs and ran, up and over and down and round. At the shoulder of the hill he slid to a halt on the rough matting of pine needles. Alice was bounding towards him down a stairway cut into the edge of the hillside. She stopped when she saw him, her hair writhing about her smiling face, her eyes large with excitement.

'It's here! Nick, it's wonderful! Can you hear it? Come on!'

Turning on the narrow path, she leapt from step to step, climbing up the face. Nick followed more slowly. The trees to his left were thinning, falling away with the landscape, those on a level with his head offering their spiked tips to his view. He checked his ascent to glance down. Almost vertically below he could see the white roadway they had walked along, a thick chalk line snaking through the trees. His foot squelched as he placed it on the next riser. Wooden rungs were pegged to hold the soil, but they also held water seeping from the bank above.

'Alice, be careful!'

He climbed after her, the weight of the rucksack dragging him towards the drop.

As the conifers thinned, straggly alder and rowan took their root space. Nick paused to look upwards, seeking sight of Alice. Dwarf oaks crowded the ridge, their gnarled trunks masking the contorted faces and twisted limbs of men falling from the sky, their flowing hair raked back in thin leafless branches.

'Nick, come on, I want the pack. You can admire the

landscape from up here.'

He gazed at Alice standing below the ridge. Where had she appeared from? Why hadn't he seen her before she spoke? As he watched she stepped back, her autumn-shaded hair and pale top fading into the surrounding foliage. And he heard it. Not this time the rush of wind through the leaf canopy, but water tumbling over rocky ledges.

Grasping at uncovered roots as a safety line, Nick climbed the final, near vertical, metres to the ledge. A seat awaited him, incongruous in its normality, a bench transported from any city park or manicured garden lawn.

'It's better than I'd dared to hope. Better than anything I've ever seen. It's absolutely fantastic!'

Nick eased to his left, following the sound of Alice's voice and the thrashing of the water. The hillside fell away. Wooden decking came into view, a guard rail; in miniature the halt on the railway line now so far below. As his feet trod the spaced boards, he felt the vibration of the water's power rising up through his thighs, and the world turned so bright a burnished gold that he had to shield his sight from the glare of the liquid bursting from the rock.

'Isn't it marvellous?'

'I— Christ!'

'Christ wasn't even born when people stood around this in awe.'

Nick let the pack slip down his arm and drop on to the boards. His eyes were growing used to the brilliance of the colouring, which was not the water itself, as he'd first supposed, but the rock and vegetation it flowed across. The noise was deafening, the entire spectacle a constant battering on his senses. It took him a moment to bring it all into focus.

'I don't understand,' he said. 'If this is natural, why are the rocks so angular?'

'Read the information board. Cisterns and a well-house were built in the 1600s. These are thought to be the last remains.'

'Cisterns?'

'For bathing. For taking the waters. There's even a cup — look — which is beyond words in itself.'

It was certainly beyond words for Nick. Alice was freeing from the guard rail the most battered orange plastic beaker he'd ever seen. Looped in its handle was an overlong bootlace which had once, itself, been orange.

'You're never going to drink the stuff?'

'Of course. It's a mineral spring rich in iron. That's why the rocks are this colour.'

'Oh, sure... And dioxins, and pesticides, and Christ knows what else.'

Alice stepped on to the wide shelf cut into the rock-face and crouched to fill the beaker.

'I keep telling you, Nick, Christ has nothing to do with it. There will always have been a cup here. Most likely the original was the top of a human skull.'

She took a draught and gasped. Nick was beside her in a stride.

'It's cold enough to freeze your throat.' She passed the cup to him, but he shrank from it. 'It's all right, honestly. The water won't harm you. This is a healing spring.'

'Oh, yeah?'

She smiled and dipped her fingers in the beaker. 'Most often it was used medicinally for joint problems, eye ailments, that sort of thing.'

Her hand reached for his face. Water dribbled down his torn cheek, first paralysing the scar tissue and then searing it with heat. Icy fingertips painted lines across his forehead and over one eye, following his latest facial injury. Nick leaned into her delicate touch, his breathing growing shallow, his gaze intent on her face, tracing caresses of his own. Her auburn hair was lost to the rock's leaching colour, her pale eyes to the silver cascade.

'Will... Will it heal bruises?'

'I'm hoping so.'

With trembling hands he reached for the buttons of his shirt. Alice's calm expression changed to one of dismay as his chest and ribs were freed of the garment. The beaker slipped in her hand, spilling the last of the water.

'Nick... Nick, what happened to you?'

He didn't want to explain. He wanted only for her to touch him with her ice-bound fingertips, anoint him with the fire-filled water.

'Why didn't you say? If I'd known I would never have brought you up here. Nick, you must be in awful pain.'

The only pain he felt was an ache within his soul that only she could soothe. He dropped to his knees, reaching out a hand to lift water from the shallows. The cold clamped about his wrist, striking up his forearm in an attempt to drag him further in. The temptation to submit was strong, but he resisted, lifting his numbed hand to Alice's face to smooth away the frown.

'I'm not hurt,' she murmured.

'You are inside, I know you are.'

Heat lit in his fingers as he touched her skin. It built to a fire along his knuckles and in his palm as he traced her cheekbone and her chin, easing to a tingling as the paralysis faded and his fingers caressed down her throat and over her collarbone.

She dipped between his reaching hands to rise again, and his body shuddered beneath the onslaught of liquid ice as it cut over his shoulders and down his back, over his shoulders and down his chest, the anaesthetizing cold penetrating each aching muscle, each bruised rib. In its wake the fire came, scorching impressions of her fingers into his flesh, and into his desire.

As his mouth sought hers, her name eased from his throat, a sibilant invocation, and he fed his fingers through her auburn hair and inside the neckline of her top to ease it from her shoulders.

Her drawn breath mirrored his own as his hands cupped her breasts, but he tasted no salt on her skin as he made them his, his tongue caressing and teasing until she anchored her nails into his shoulders and arched her back in her need.

At the unfastening of her jeans her hand stayed his.

'Nick— I'm not on the pill.'

'I know.'

'But I don't—'

His finger stilled her lips as, in turn, he gently kissed her nose, and each eyelid.

'Taken care of.' He raised his head to glance about them, at the vivid green of the over-hanging foliage, at the sun-kissed brilliance of the iron-rich waters at their side. 'What better place for us than here.'

Ognirius watched the lovers below, his ire seething but impotent.

Why here? Why *here*?

In any other place he would have ridden the boy and given vent to his frustrations. She would have known, then, the meaning of power, the meaning of control, the meaning of submission, as Yslan and her acolytes had learned it at the Pool.

But this... this *concern*.

The vibration of the water was pulsing through the earth beneath him, resonating through the neck ring, its vapour rising on the breeze to sustain him as it sustained the foliage beside him. But was it, was she, the source of his concern, or was he sustaining it himself? He twisted the rings at his fingers, adjusted the torc at his neck.

He'd planned for so long, tried so often to pass through; failed because of the miserable creatures that had come within his grasp. This time was different. This time nothing had been left to the gods' sly intervention. With these two, hand-chosen and nurtured, he would pass through. So why was he here, hiding his presence among the dripping oaks, instead of riding the boy and making her body his own?

He drew his gaze away. Beside him the bark of the gnarled oak offered a contorted face, a clawing hand. He tried not to look, not to remember, but the dwarf oaks crept closer, grew taller. The day turned to night in the vision of his youth, torchlight glimmering on the sacrificial victims suspended in the grove as they twisted under their own weight, gaping mouths and hollowed eye sockets turning to greet his approach.

And then there was the torc lying heavy on his collarbone. He fingered it again, fingered the thick hollow roundels sealing each end of the twisted strands of gold. It was growing in its solidity, in its colour, as he was growing. He remembered the rite that had placed it round his neck, marking him with the authority of the People. Yslan had hailed him that day. But he'd chosen Rome. And when her tongue was lying in his hand he'd had the torc removed.

Ognirius pulled his thoughts away to look into the open blue of the sky above, a sky he'd surfaced so often to gaze at, to swear to, to decry.

Blue sky.

A bag. A sheath.

The sky was blue.

The boy's seed had not reached its mark.

The sky was blue.

Where were the Elementals he commanded by his will? Where was the rain? Why was there this... this *concern*?

Chapter 18

Nick awoke with a start. Instinctively he clasped Alice to him as she lay in the crook of his arm. Tendrils of her auburn hair retreated across his chest as she stirred.

'We've missed that one,' she murmured.

The shriek of a whistle rose from the valley floor, forcing a chorus of small birds to wing.

'The train!'

'There's another.'

As she moved against him, he became aware of her body, the softness of her skin. Momentarily his libido surged. He kissed her shoulder, easing his open palm down the contours of her spine.

'You all right?'

Raising herself on to her elbows, she looked at him. He smiled, but could not hold her gaze, and let his attention slide down her throat to the heavy fall of her breasts. He wanted to hold them. Instead, his fingertips caressed in a butterfly's touch.

'You keep asking that.'

Her lips reached for his, and he was thankful to be able to close his eyes for their gently teasing kiss.

'Were none of your other bimbos virgins?'

'You're not a bimbo.'

'I'm not a virgin, either — now.'

Nick grinned because Alice was grinning, but he could not sustain the forced humour and gathered her in his arms to pull her down on top of him. Locks of her hair swept across his face as she giggled. With her weight pressing against him the rough timber decking bit into his back, pieces of grit, sandwiched between, skewering into his flesh. The cacophonous roaring of the spring forced itself into his senses once again and he winced, more against the noise than the discomfort.

'I've made a mess of your shoulders,' Alice murmured. 'As if you aren't bruised enough—'

She gasped as he hugged her closer still, wrapping his legs around hers, capturing her completely. He rained kisses upon her cheek and her neck and her shoulder, trying to rid himself of the memory of that moment, that stark moment, when she'd turned rigid in his arms trying to muffle her cry of pain — and he'd realised. She'd been telling him, though, hadn't she? Why hadn't he listened? There'd been no enjoyment after that; he'd wanted only for it to end. And the blood... He raised a hand behind her back to glance at it, half expecting to see the dark liquor clinging to his skin as it had when they'd washed it away into the waters.

Alice kissed his cheek. 'Nick...' She flicked away her hair, it falling either side of her pale face, the same tumultuous rush, the same iridescent colour as the waters from the spring.

'Nick... you didn't hurt me. I mean...' She stroked his cheek, guiding her hand lightly down the vertical scarring.

He kissed her fingertips and smiled. 'It'll be better next time.'

'I'm a willing student,' she whispered. 'You'll be able to teach me.'

He shook his head. 'That's sex, not love. Love is...' He reached forward to capture her lips with his own. Love is... *a willingness to give your life*, but he knew she wouldn't appreciate hearing that.

The door mechanism snapped on the last of the students and Leonard pulled the pack of Marlboro from his shirt pocket. Leaning heavily against the shelving unit carrying thinners, he blew smoke rings at their warning signs, not moving until the air was thick around his head and he was drawing on the cork filter. The tab he ground into the illicit ashtray of a foil mixing dish. Another cigarette was lit.

With conscious ceremony he switched off the computers, printers and plotters, blowing smoke at each piece of humming machinery prior to its whining demise, until only the fizz of the fluorescent strips was left to assault his hearing. If there had been another light source available he would have cut those, too. He stared up at them, wishing for years long past and a bank of north-facing skylights. Finally he focused on the line of gently twirling gulls suspended from a wire slung across the studio.

Cardboard bloody gulls. The propounded textbook theories, the dynamics of flight and its applications in the engineering industry, were as fleeting as world peace when the only image which steadfastly filled his mind was an afternoon craft hour in some grubby primary school. If he had known at the start that his dreams of a fine art career would come to this...

His heavy eyelids closed and he dragged on the cigarette until it, too, was ready to be ground into the tinfoil dish.

Nick had still been tying his trainers when Alice emptied the rucksack on the decking. Beneath their scant provisions had been a camera, a notebook, a trowel, a five-centimetre paintbrush, and now she was screwing together lengths of telescopic red and white tubing.

'And what, exactly, is that?'

'A collapsible ranging rod.'

'Which surveyors use?'

'Which archaeologists also use. I need some photographs before the light fades.'

Straightening his collar, Nick ran his fingers through his hair and posed. 'Will this do?'

Alice laughed, and picked up the camera to look through the viewfinder. 'Oh, it's deceiving. To the eyes it still seems light here, but the metering is quite low. I wish I'd brought the tripod now. Using a flash against this water will wreak havoc.' The shutter snapped. 'There. Explorer extraordinaire, though you would have looked better with a waxed moustache and a pith helmet.'

'Let me take one of you.'

'I don't need one of me. I need pictures of the spring.'

'You didn't need one of me, but you took one. Now I don't need one of you, but I want one.'

He closed the gap between them and took the camera from her hand, planting a kiss on her brow in exchange. 'Now go strut your stuff beside the falls, dear lady.'

Picking up the ranging rod Alice stepped across the decking and onto the rocky shelf. 'It's set on auto,' she called behind her. 'You shouldn't have any difficulty. Can you get the top of the crevice in line with my head? And the stone cisterns in on the left?'

'Oh, listen to her! She thinks she's directing a $60m epic while taking the starring role! Trust me.'

Nick raised the digital camera and concentrated on the LCD screen, but the picture was hard to make out, indicator lights flashing green then orange down its side.

'Does this have a faster setting?' he asked.

'That is the fastest. Be careful not to shake the camera. Just get on with it, Nick. I need to make a full account of the spring before the light fades any more.'

The internal zoom moved in and out as if confused about its true target. He held the shutter halfway down in an attempt to make it focus. It didn't help. One moment Alice was visible, the next all he could see was the red and white ranging rod. Her head had melded with the rushing water, the light colour of her top with the surrounding foliage.

'What are you doing to the camera?'

'Nothing. It's doing it—' There was a click. '—automatically.'

She walked across and took it from his hand. 'David Bailey, eh?'

'He's older. You'd not mistake us.'

'I'm sure I wouldn't. Here.' She passed over the ranging rod and waved him back towards the spring.

'Alice, what's happened? You're freezing.' He grasped her hand, then reached up to her neck and cheek. 'Alice... it's as if you've been dipped in the water and come out dry.'

She shrugged him away. 'Don't fuss. It's nothing. Bad circulation, that's all. I've had it for years.'

'Don't tell me not to fuss.' He pulled her sweater from the safety rail and drew it over her head. Her face sprang from the neckline and he bent to kiss her chilled lips. 'If I don't look after you, who will?'

The sheeted clay head stood on the workbench Leonard called his own and to which he would allow no student access. He had set himself a deadline, and in truth the head was nearly completed, but he couldn't face working on it yet. It had been a strenuous day. The enthusiasm of the first year students had not permeated the remnants of the weekend's frenzy. The initial euphoria of Clare coming back into his life seemed to have dissipated as quickly as the bubbles in her expensive champagne, though it was barely three days. The nightmare of the forest nymphs was still uncomfortably close, and felt, if anything, more real. He had hoped to be able to work the dread from his system, but it lingered.

Another cigarette was lit on the stub of the last, and he walked round the untidy studio seeking physical labours to occupy his hands and his mind. Bins were emptied into waiting black sacks; discarded artcard returned to the paper chest. He rewashed brushes, sharpened pencils. The tall glass window overlooking the sports field dimmed through deepening shades of blue, camouflaging the last of the rain-washed mud on the outer surface. He was pleased to see it fade. The work of drunken yobs, without a doubt, but the smears had pulled at his attention throughout the day. It was as if someone, something, had been trying to get into the studio.

The cigarette finished, he again pulled the pack from his shirt. Only one remained. He held it in his fingers, stuffed it back in the pack, the pack back in his shirt.

This was ridiculous. What was he playing at? The head was nearly ready: the face-mask, the jaw-line, the classical nose. The curls had refused to hold, but the clay should be drier now. Why hadn't he done as he'd first intended and completed it over the weekend? Clare would have understood. Clare would have brought her wine and her damned smoked salmon and made a picnic of the enterprise.

He brought forward the life-size head, patting its winding cloth with his palm. Too dry. He should have wrapped the entirety in clingfilm. Sweeping up the spray bottle, he pumped a light mist over the cloth. The last thing he wanted was for any of the clay to be transferred to it as the head was unwrapped.

Tentatively he caught a fingernail beneath the leading edge. The cloth lifted at his touch and he grasped it between thumb and forefinger, gently teasing it from the layer beneath. The cloth was long enough to enshroud the head three times, keeping the clay moist despite the centrally heated studio. He sprayed again, the fine mist chilling the back of his hand. The cloth unwound steadily, its once white threads blotched a fungal red-ochre as if covering a bloody wound.

Leonard caught his lower lip between his teeth as he concentrated on the final layer. Another misted spraying. A tentative separating of cloth from clay, sticking plaster from skin.

It was free. He breathed again, depositing the soiled cloth on the workbench beside the plinth. The head was facing away at an oblique angle, giving him an almost full sight of the rear. There was something very wrong with the hair, but he'd known that when he'd enclosed it in the cloth at the end of the previous session. The classical finger curls had been straightening as he'd worked on them. Dried out they looked as stiff as a hedgehog's spines.

Even as he released the catch he knew the sculpture was rotating under its own weight. Instinctively his hand reached out to steady the plinth. He faltered. The hairs on the back of his neck were starting to rise, mirroring those of the sculpture.

It wasn't just the hair. There was something wrong with the cheek. A long gash had been etched from eye to chin. As more of the face came into view he recognised the swelling of a bruise over one eye. A scream built in his chest, a pressured pain, but his throat constricted and would not let it pass. Birds pecked at his face and head, and his flailing arms careened into shelves which fought him in their turn, loosing canisters and palette knives to bounce up from the tiled floor and attack his shins. Bags of powdered paint followed, splitting on impact to scatter autumn colour underfoot.

Through its own weight, or will, the head kept on rotating. There was nowhere in the littered studio for Leonard to flee its searching eyes. On hands and knees he scrambled into an alcove, pushing aside its contents, until his nails were tearing at the plaster wall. He collapsed on one thigh, whimpering from a cramped chest and aching arms. There was no escape.

The eyes, the carefully crafted eyes of sightless smooth perfection, had been torn away. In their sockets were carved the bulbous spheres of a seeing youth hell-bent on his destruction. He knew who it was, knew beyond a doubt, but could not draw his gaze away.

When a moustache began worming from the clay to cover the upper lip, Leonard could not believe what he was seeing. When the lips drew back from gritted teeth, Leonard screamed.

Not only did Alice want photographs, she wanted measurements, each checked and double-checked. Then came the sketches, pages and pages of them as every angle was covered, in close up and from distance; the fall of the land, the conifers and the ground cover, the gnarled oak trees on the ridge.

'Alice...'

'I'll be ready when I'm finished.'

'Alice, it's getting dark.'

'We'll not miss the train.'

It wasn't missing the train that was making Nick uneasy. Again he looked up to the soft glow of the sky and the encroaching darker cloud. There was going to be a change in the weather. He could feel it in the air. He couldn't say why he knew, he just did, and it worried him.

A short, high-pitched bark raised through the trees. Nick glanced warily about him. In the growing gloom the conifers were staggering closer. Bushes seemed to be creeping where, in the sunlight, gaps had stood in the foliage. Colours had drained to a deep grey-blue. Every item had taken on a fuzzy edge, individual shapes becoming a vibrating amalgam.

'Let's go,' he said.

'In a minute.'

'Now.'

He began to push their belongings back into the rucksack. The woodland echoed with another eerie cry.

'A fox,' Alice said. 'Did you hear it?'

Nick looked at her as she passed him the sketch pad. It hadn't sounded like any animal he would want to stroke.

'Come on, my night vision isn't all that good and we've got to get down this hill.' He thought of the steepness of the drop and the tips of the pines waiting to skewer him as he fell.

'This woodland holds nothing that will hurt you, Nick.'

A movement flickered in his peripheral vision, and he swung round to peer into the gloom. Shapes danced before his eyes making it impossible to be certain whether or not the undergrowth had moved.

'You are more at risk walking the streets of Hull.'

There was a crash, a splintering of wood. He shouldered the pack and glared at her. 'So what was that? A rabbit playing at being a lumberjack?'

She kissed him softly on his cheek, capturing his gaze in her own. 'It'll be a deer. It's dusk, Nick. Animals will be coming to drink.'

Her grey eyes seemed to glimmer in the twilight, her auburn

hair as radiant as a setting sun. He wanted it to move, to lift in individual locks about her head as he'd seen it lift before, but he knew it wouldn't. It had been a figment of his obsession, and his obsession was now a part of him. He thought of telling her, but she would think that he was mad. Perhaps he was, standing in a woodland on the edge of an abyss with the darkness gathering. If something happened who was there to call on for aid? He dare not check his phone in case there was no signal.

'I love you, Alice.'

She blinked. 'It's a little early, isn't it, for that?'

He raised his hands to her face, drawing his thumbs along the contours of her cheekbones. 'Sometimes,' he said, 'sometimes a person just knows.'

'But I know him!'

Clare pressed the malt into Leonard's hand and watched him drain the glass in one gulp. He was still shaking, his sweating face lobster-red. She hadn't asked, but she'd guessed that he'd run all the way across the campus from the studio. He'd taken a few minutes to be able to speak, despite his claims that he worked out in the gym.

'You're saying that over the weekend someone has managed to get into the studio and vandalise the bust you're working on.'

'No. Yes. I *don't know*.' He hung his head, wiping at tears with his forearms.

Clare refilled the glass, offering it to him again. His grasping fingers reached, then hesitated, his anxious expression turning to one of renewed panic. In a vicious lunge he slapped it from her hand to send it spinning across the lounge.

'Where's that come from? I've told you, I shouldn't be drinking that. He can get to me through that. It's Julia I need.' He looked at the phone. 'Why hasn't she rung? She said she'd ring. I have to ring Julia. I need her.'

He rose from the chair, but lurched sideways. Clare caught him and sat him down again.

'Later. I'm sorry to say this, Len, but at the present moment all you are doing is raving. Calm down and let's get this story straight before we start ringing anyone.

'Now... is this defacing of the bust anything to do with the dream you had on Saturday night?'

The change in Leonard was dramatic. He quietened, eventually nodding his head. Clare walked round to the other side of the chair and sat on its arm.

'This has been going on some time, hasn't it?'

'I've got to speak to Julia. She'll understand.'

Clare draped her hand across his shoulder and drew his head into her breast. She stroked his hair.

'Julia... Where is she?'

'Oxford.'

'Well,' said Clare, 'she's not going to be an awful lot of help down there, is she? Let's try to sort this out ourselves.'

'We *can't*. You don't understand.'

'That's because you're not explaining yourself.'

'It's *him*.'

'Who him?'

'I don't know his name, but he's reaching for me... because of *her*.'

'Who her?'

Clare watched him close his eyes, refusing to say.

'Are they both on campus?'

He nodded.

'Both students?'

He curled into the chair.

'Ah...' It was a picture with which she was familiar, and it explained why there had been no cuckoo in the nest on her return.

'You've had a hard day, Leonard.' She laughed a little. 'You had a hard weekend. You should rest, you know. Go to bed. Go to sleep.'

'I can't *sleep*. He'll come. *She'll* come.'

'Not while I'm here.'

She jumped as he grasped her round the waist, burying his head further into her breasts. 'You mustn't leave me. You mustn't leave me for a *minute*.'

'I won't, I've told you, but you do need to sleep, Leonard. It's only going to get worse with lack of sleep.' She trawled her fingers through his long hair. 'How about I come to bed with you?'

'You can think of sex at a time like this!'

'I was thinking more of giving you a massage.' She began on his neck with the fingertips of one hand. 'You're so *tense*, Len. There's no wonder you're in such a state. I'll give you a massage and watch over you all night if you wish. Do you want anything to eat first? When did you last eat?'

He dismissed the suggestion with a wave of his hand.

'Something to drink, then, to take away the taste of the whisky? A herbal tea. Go into the bedroom and get undressed.' But he sat in the chair with his head in his hands until she returned with a steaming cup. One swallow and he tried to give it back to her.

'Drink it all, Len. You've got to be able to relax. You're doing yourself no favours like this. I've cooled it down. It's quite drinkable.'

From behind his chair she worked gently at his shoulders, watching him sip at the liquid before finally gulping it down.

'There,' she soothed. 'You'll feel a lot better soon.'

In the bedroom she helped him out of his clothes, stripping herself to her underwear, but it was as if he did not even notice. Despite his earlier protest, though, he welcomed the soft touch of her fingers, and she had barely begun when he started to relax.

His breathing eased, became shallow. Clare turned off the bedside lamp, leaving only the light from the landing to filter into the room. Sitting on the edge of the mattress, she waited for signs of restlessness. When none appeared she covered him with the sheet and redressed.

'Obviously you skipped lunch as well as breakfast,' she

murmured. A faint snoring was his only answer.

In the lounge she pulled her phone from her bag and punched a number, her hand slipping into her pocket as she waited, her fingers crushing the sharp fragment of pharmaceutical foil into a tight, unrecognisable, ball. She'd need some more. The strip was almost finished.

Chapter 19

For a moment he thought he lay in his own bed in his own room, but the light was too dim, and there was a clicking noise he couldn't place. Then the scents of forest flowers assailed him from the pillow and he spread his limbs, luxuriating in the warmth that was Alice's single bed. The only imperfection was that Alice was not sharing it with him.

Raising himself on one elbow, Nick pushed back the edge of the duvet. Wrapped in a white kimono, Alice was sitting at her workstation, the light from the computer screen sheening her a ghostly silver-grey. Apart from the occasional click of the mouse in her right hand, there was no other sound.

His gaze caressed the rippling fall of her hair, the gentle curve of her shoulders, a pale leg extending into the shadow beneath the table. He wanted to capture her in that pose as a photograph, to look at her hour after hour and not sense the passing of time. Yet he wanted her with him, now, clasped in his arms, the heat of his passion burning a path through her soul.

He whispered her name, murmuring it again and again, gifting it to the air as a never-ending chant... *Alice 'n' Alice 'n' Alice 'n' Alice...*

Her hand faltered. Her head inclined, and she swivelled her chair to smile at him as he reached out a hand towards her.

'Alisss...'

'And good morning to you.'

Her brisk salutation broke the charged atmosphere. He blinked, rubbing at his face to feel a growth of sharp stubble.

'Is it?' The curtains were drawn at the window, only the faintest glimmer of orange from a distant streetlamp intruding.

'Morning, or good?'

'Alice, what are you doing over there?' He threw himself back into the pillows, extending his arms above his head to touch the two walls crowding in on the narrow sleeping space. 'What are you doing over there when I am aching for your touch? I am bereft. I am distraught.'

'If I remember rightly, I was kicked out of bed.'

He sat up and looked at her. 'You're kidding me?'

'No.'

'An aberration.' He watched amusement dance in her eyes.

'Some sort of dream, I think.'

'Scoring tries at Twickenham again.'

She shook her head. 'More a nightmare. It was deep, whatever it was. I tried to wake you, but you wouldn't rouse. I didn't like to try too hard. Anyway, you settled, and so I left you and...' She gestured to the computer.

Nick couldn't remember any dream, or any nightmare, though others came to mind easily enough. 'Did I... say anything?'

She turned back to the screen, her hand automatically reaching to guide the mouse. 'You didn't utter the names of any ladies, if that's what you mean.'

That wasn't what he'd meant, but he felt wounded just the same. Tossing back the duvet, he captured her by the shoulders and buried his face in her hair.

'You're the only lady in my life.' He kissed her. 'You are my life.'

'Do you say that to all your—'

He pressed a finger to her lips. 'I'm serious, Alice. I've never been more serious.'

'I'm sorry, I simply never thought of you as being a romantic.'

'*What?* You mean you can't see romance emblazoned on my forehead, shining from my eyes? All these kisses we've shared and you've never noticed the rose gripped between my teeth?'

He watched her smile grow to fill her face with ease and humour. Before she could react he caught hold of the chair, threading his arms behind her shoulders and beneath her knees to hoist her aloft and swing her round the narrow room. Laughing with delight, she clasped him to her until set down on the soft pillows.

'I didn't save the program.'

'Save me instead.'

Licking his dry lips, Leonard regarded the smoking tab between his yellowed fingers. He'd get one more drag from it, maybe two. A full packet had been smoked, an entire twenty, since he'd woken bathed in perspiration. He'd wanted to ring Julia, but Clare had been adamant that the studio had to be confronted first.

'You can't crawl away and hide, Leonard. I'll be with you, right at your side. We'll go together.'

Barely able to master a cohesive thought, he'd appreciated her decisive strength. What he hadn't expected was for her to hold him as close as an arresting officer. It had irked him to begin with, but as they'd passed the gateway to Taylor Court he'd been grateful for her body shielding his.

The studio door opened and anxiously he peered up the short flight of steps to see Clare framed by the light from the fluorescents.

'I think you'd better come in.'

The dread returned. His chest began to tighten, his mouth growing uncomfortably dry as he stepped across the threshold. He wanted to be anywhere, anywhere at all, but in that studio.

Hatred for the tall shelving units burst upon him. They made a labyrinth of the place. He wanted to put his shoulder to the nearest and force it from its mountings, to send it crashing into the next, and the next, toppling them as if gigantic dominoes until every one lay flat and he could survey the entire room, wall to wall, in a single sweep of his gaze. He needed to know that nothing lurked there.

The anger ebbed as quickly as it had swept in, leaving him trembling, the crushed filter-tip burning his thumb and forefinger. Clare went ahead, disappearing round the edge of the first rise of shelving. Leonard hurried after her, not wanting to be left alone.

His wooden bench stood in its allotted place, artcard in an untidy pile at one end. There was his metre rule, his name in bold black marker ink along its length. A scatter of pencils lay alongside raised spots of hardened glue and ringed coffee stains, but there was no plinth, no red-ochre stained cloth, no clay head. Leonard ran his tongue over cracking lips. The tiled floor was clear of debris. Sculpting knives and packets of paint were sitting neatly in their places on the shelves to either side. Above, cardboard gulls twirled slowly from a wire.

Clare rattled phlegm in her throat to catch his attention. Beyond her shoulder the window gave a view of the sports field, uninterrupted by any smearing of mud on the glass. He couldn't take his eyes from it, dare not focus on Clare.

'I... I didn't imagine it,' he said.

She gave no answer, just looked at him, her face expressionless.

'Don't tell me I kicked you out of bed again?'

Alice turned from the computer to smile at him. Nick liked that smile. How easily it came now, making her face much fuller, easing the tension from across her eyes.

'No, nothing like that. I just woke first and... well... I'm not used to sharing a bed, and it's so narrow—'

'—and I'm so big?'

He watched her lips twitch ruefully, but she wouldn't be drawn, and returned her attention to the screen.

Pulling up a pillow, Nick propped himself against the wall. Daylight flooded between the partly opened curtains. Beyond the window birds were singing. The soft beat of music from a radio was carrying through the thin wall. Someone was moving on the floor above. A toilet flushed close by. Over every noise lay the dull clacking of computer keys interspersed with the occasional clicking of a mouse. It was warmer now that the heating was on, but he'd gladly suffer the natural chill of the night for the benefits of its silence to be alone with Alice.

'I can be a terribly jealous lover.'

'I'll give you no cause.'

'Then how is it that every time I wake you're giving your body to a machine and not to me?'

'That's a positively indecent accusation, Nicholas Blaketon. And it's not true.'

'Oh yes, it is.' He propelled himself from the bed to crouch behind Alice's chair, his fingers tapping in quick succession at her shoulders and neck. As she squirmed beneath the onslaught, he brought his mouth close to her ear. 'Don't tell me that this isn't erotic.'

'It's ticklish!'

'It's all in the interpretation.'

His teeth nibbled at her earlobe, his tongue following down the side of her throat as his fingers drew wide the neck of the silk kimono to lay bear her shoulders. She drew a breath and held it until her lungs could take no more, quivering beneath his feathered touch.

How quickly he could arouse her now; he never would have believed it. His erection surged at the thought of her need of him, and as his tongue caressed her collarbone, his hands took possession of taut, ripe breasts. Her hand rose to his face, fingertips lingering over eyebrow and cheek. It rose again, the nails to rake his stubbled jaw, stoking the passion churning in his belly. When the hand rose for the third time the fingers slid behind his head to find leverage in a fistful of hair. She pulled, arching and lifting her breasts towards his gaping mouth, dragging him bodily down to devour her.

'Oh, come on, Mr Harkin. Give us a break here. I'd like to get through this course without contracting lung cancer.'

Leonard squinted at the pimply youth before thumbing his

lighter and bringing the cigarette to his lips.

'And it's against the law,' added the short brunette.

Others had stopped working to look his way.

'What is this?' he demanded. 'Insurrection? You spend each lunchtime stuffing yourselves with cheese burgers and greasy onions and you complain about a little smoke damaging your health?'

'It stinks.'

'Onions always do,' he retorted.

'It's dangerous,' voiced another. 'Just about everything in this place is inflammable. There isn't even a proper fire exit.'

There was a rumble of unity.

'Oh, for God's sake... Get back to work. I'm closing down in twenty minutes.'

The pimply fresher swung round to face him. 'Twenty minutes! This is supposed to be a full hour's tutorial, though scant tuition there's been that I've noticed.'

Leonard felt a growing pressure in his chest. Perspiration began to prickle and ooze beneath his armpits. 'Oh, you've noticed that, have you? Have you also noticed that the only requirement today is to draw a few curves and a couple of straight lines? Anyone who needs individual tuition to do that must have bribed their way through their GCSEs, never mind their 'A' levels. You've now fifteen minutes to get the job completed.'

There was a chorus of groaning and all but the pimply youth turned back to the work in hand. Leonard stared him down. 'And if I want to smoke ganja in my fucking studio, I fucking well shall.'

'Your bruises have disappeared.'

Nick tensed the muscles in his chest wall as Alice's fingertips fanned over his ribs. 'It doesn't feel like it.'

She kissed his nose. 'Oh, dear. Was I a little rough?'

'You were intensely passionate.' He hoped she would think

the same of him. Her breasts bore the marks of his teeth, her belly his fingernails. He'd meant to be passionate, but it was as if some primal strength had broken free and had been riding him as he had been riding her. He did not want to dwell on what he might have done if she hadn't cried out.

Her fingers stroked his eyebrow. 'There's not a bruise anywhere. I told you Newtondale was a healing spring. The goddess has smiled on you.'

His own hand rose to touch the length of scarring on his cheek. 'She hasn't quite healed everything.'

'You want the moon. Come on. My stomach thinks my throat's cut. We'll have to raid the kitchen.'

Nick picked up the knotted condom, inspecting its contents in the dimming light. There would be one or two other things they'd need if they were going to keep up this pace.

'Stand there and don't move.'

The brunette's suspicious frown was not missed, but Leonard didn't care what she thought or if she reported him direct to the Vice Chancellor. He didn't want to be in the studio alone. The day had been enough of an ordeal. The very last thing he needed was to be caught there as the daylight faded into dusk. And that was exactly what was happening beyond the window, the louring rain clouds spitting their venom and dragging in an early night.

He moved fast round the studio, snapping off the power to the computer hardware, keeping one eye on the brunette as she edged towards the door.

'Not yet,' he snarled.

Why couldn't Clare have met him now instead of at lunchtime? He should never have allowed her to take him into the McCarthy. He needed something to calm his nerves, she'd said, to stop the shakes, but it had been more like liquid courage to face the afternoon. And he shouldn't have had it, even though it wasn't malt, even though it was only one, he shouldn't have had it. He was laying himself wide open.

The door gave on its spring. She'd left him! He spun round, clutching at the shelving in panic, but the brunette hadn't moved. A moment later she was joined by another girl — a girl with raven's wing hair and coffee-silk skin.

'Hi! Have you finished for the day? Is it all right to bring these in?'

He glanced at the grocery box in her hands, at the file of papers laid on top, at the slow altering of her expression as she exchanged a look with the brunette.

'You suggested I use a corner of the studio,' she said with lessening enthusiasm, 'as a work area, to build—'

'—the crucifixion.'

'Yes.' She tried for a half-hearted smile. 'For a moment I thought you'd forgotten.'

He had. How could he? Sensuous, erotic, Choutelan. A child-woman ready to be—

He dragged in a rasping breath and moved towards her, fanning the air with his arms. 'Not now. Tomorrow. I'm closing the studio. I have to be somewhere. I have to lock up.'

Unseen, the door snapped shut, and he paused to focus on the empty space where the brunette had stood.

'It won't take a minute,' Choutelan was saying. She'd deposited the box on his bench — *his* bench — and was riffling through her file of papers.

'Not even a minute. Not now. Tomorrow. Come tomorrow.'

The box. The box was standing on his bench where the head had stood on its plinth.

'I've considered your suggestions... about the Christ figure not being original—'

The box was large enough to carry the head.

'—I thought I'd take the concept of the spiritual sacrifice a stage further backwards—'

He could sense it, see it, turning inside the box. It's glaring eyes, its snarling lips, the worming moustache.

'—paganism being sacrificed on the altar of formalised

religion. What do you think?'

She was tapping a paper, bringing his attention to a sketch in her hand. He looked down at it. Focused.

The studio filled with the cries of gulls hanging from a wire, but he knew it was issuing from his throat. His fist tore the paper from her hand, sent it fluttering towards his feet. He stamped on it, stamped on it, again and again. It was *his* painting, *his* nightmare, wrapped in coiling blackthorn. He pounced on his workbench, punching the grocery box to the floor. He *hadn't* imagined the head grinning at him; it *hadn't* been a monster from his mind. It had turned on its plinth, looked at him, *spoken...*

The box crumpled beneath his weight as he jumped on it.

...he'd flatten the clay head, flatten the brown face, distort it, leave it looking like a body dragged from a peat-bog.

The cardboard wall split, spilling out its contents. Leonard reeled back. There was no clay head. Uncoiling about his feet, snagging on his trousers, was a spool of thick wire, its barbs bloodied with rust.

On the bed, Nick sat with one hand twisting locks of Alice's hair, the other forking a shared tinfoil container of nasi goreng into his mouth. Across the duvet, in the light of the small bedside lamp, lay spread soy pork, shrimp crackers and rice noodles.

'I can't believe I'm doing this.' Alice dipped a finger in the sauce. 'A picnic that's surreal. And I can't believe you went to the door like that.'

'What's wrong with me? I'm dressed, aren't I? He'll have seen a lot worse than a fella wearing only a pair of jeans.'

'An unzipped pair of jeans.'

'They're zipped. They're just not belted. I didn't want to make it too hard for you to tear them off again.'

'Your rice will grow cold.'

'Just as long as you don't.'

They paused, ignoring the food to taste each other's lips.
'How many condoms are left?'
'One.'
'We'd better save it then.'
'You're cruel to me.' He kissed her cheek.
'I know.'
'Leading me on.' His teeth tantalised her neck.
'Shameless.'
'And me such an innocent.' His tongue found her cleavage.
'Nick?'
'Mmm?'
'Eat your food.'
'I'm trying.'

She laughed, and tapped him lightly with her fork. He lay his head in her lap, begging to be fed. She obliged with shrimp crackers and soy pork.

He'd never felt so content. The silk kimono covering her thighs seemed peculiarly cool, the material almost damp. He closed his eyes and felt himself floating, buoyed by it. Alice's fork scraping at the tinfoil dishes conjured ghostly birds calling from afar, the squeaking of the bed springs as she moved, water lapping against a shore. And the smell, the scent of flowers, cloying in his throat...

'Hey, sleepy head!'

He juddered into wakefulness, to find a weight across his chest and a bright moon-face staring down at him.

'It's all right, Nick. Good grief, you look so shocked. What is this? A guilty conscience?'

He rubbed at his face, refocusing on Alice, her complexion paler than ever caught in the white light from the bedside lamp.

'...drifting off.'

'Drifting? I've never known a person sleep so much. You must be wearing yourself out.'

*

Leonard punched the buttons on the phone pad and pressed himself further into the acoustic hood to escape the noise of milling students. How could he have left his mobile at the house? He always carried it, always. The engaged tone seeped dully down the landline. He slammed the heel of his palm into the wall above the pay-phone.

'No! No! What can she be talking about?'

He hung on to the cradle, breaking the connection. The handset he tapped against his cheek, beating a rhythm against the bone.

'Come on, Julia, come one. Come on, Julia, come on. Come on, Julia, come on, get off the fucking phone.'

The cradle was released and the buttons stabbed by a rigid finger. He held his breath, waiting, waiting. The engaged signal filled his ear.

'No! No!'

He fisted the cradle, cutting the line, and pressed the back of his hand against his teeth, feeling the indentations on his flesh. It was growing dark outside, he knew it was, but he dare not turn to the window to see. He had to go through the campus, through the trees and the shrubs, to get back to his house on Cranbrook. But would he be safe there, with the vines scrambling over the back wall, creeping over the grassed area from the pond in Taylor Court? He'd got rid of the debris, hadn't he, from the dustbin fire? Yes, he had. Yes. Not even her ashes remained in the yard. But where was the head? Where was *he*?

Punching at the buttons again, he missed a number in his haste and had to redial.

'Come on, Julia, *please*. Even your voicemail. Julia, even your voicemail. It's all I ask, all I ask.'

The dull tone repeated.

'No! No!'

He cried out, hitting his temple on the hood as he recoiled from the weight of the hand on his shoulder.

'It's okay. I didn't mean to scare you. Calm down. Are you all right?'

A youth. Dark-haired. Same build. No scar. No scar. It wasn't him. The darkness beyond his shoulder! The darkness at the window!

When the youth turned to follow his gaze, Leonard darted by him, leaving the phone dangling by its wire.

Letting the kitchen door swing shut behind him, Nick started back to Alice's room, smiling to himself at the blonde's expression when she'd caught him depositing the empty takeaway trays in the bin.

In the corridor he paused by the full length mirror, admiring his reflection in the glass. The unbuckled jeans and naked torso matched well the growth of stubble and scarred cheek. It gave him, he thought, a touch of repressed savagery. The blonde had certainly seen it. Not only had he chosen timid Alice, but he'd wooed her and won her and was now shagging her rigid. Superstud!

Alice was back in front of the computer terminal. Nick closed the door and leaned against its wood, not quite believing that he could be forgotten so soon.

'I had this vision of returning to find you flaunted across the bed pining for me, not shackled to that bloody machine again.'

'Don't take it so personally. I had a thought, that's all. Just wanted to run a program through the database. It'll be over in a moment.'

He drew up behind her, slowly massaging her shoulders.

'Nick, let me do this.'

'I'm not stopping you. Am I stopping you?' The screen changed through a number of maps showing different coloured icons, the series flashing through so rapidly that he couldn't assimilate the information. He withdrew to lay on the bed behind her. 'It's a wonder your eyes don't melt.'

'Every spring, every cairn, every tumuli, each Celtic trackway and Roman road is on this. I know there's a correlation. I know there is.'

'Alice... for God's sake.'

He stared above him at the shelves overhanging with books. If it fell he'd be crushed to death. Books were everywhere. Knowledge was everywhere. What flat walls were left hung with maps. It wasn't so much a bedroom as a tomb crowded with grave goods.

'I don't understand why you hide yourself away here, Alice. I always thought the rooms in this complex were supposed to be fairly luxurious. It's as claustrophobic as living on a shelf in a library.'

'There weren't quite as many books in this library when I moved in last year, and there certainly weren't as many papers.'

'So why take it for a second year? Why not move to somewhere with more space?'

She swung round, her expression startled. 'I can't. It's—' She shrugged and faced the screen again. Nick propped himself up on a pillow.

'It's what?'

'Difficult to explain.'

'You think I'll laugh.'

'You'll think I'm mad.'

Nick chuckled. 'It takes one to know one.'

'I knew I wanted one of these rooms as soon as I received the information pack from the university. Why? Because of the house names. Ferriby, Brough, Lincoln... They're all Celtic or Romano-British sites. Brantingham had a villa. We saw part of its mosaic flooring in the museum. It's why I chose to come to Hull rather than Durham or York.'

'You passed on the historic city of York... for Hull?'

She turned in her chair, her expression full of impish fire. 'You want to hear something truly bizarre? I passed on Cambridge.'

Nick felt his smile fading but couldn't halt the change. 'You were offered a place at Cambridge and you came— How many 'A' levels did you gain, Alice?'

'Oh, you're not going to start sounding like my parents, are you? I told you, I've had no other hobbies. When I'm not studying, I'm studying. It's always been the same.'

'But... *Cambridge*...?'

'A waste of time. How could I possibly have driven up on to the moors and back again all in one day? Can't be done, can it?'

'Am I catching this straight? Your shortlist was Durham, York and Hull... because they ring the North York Moors?'

'I said you'd think me mad.'

'Just so you can find some forgotten spring?'

'Do you listen to anything I tell you? It's not just any old spring. I am looking for the site of a shrine—'

'—to a Celtic water goddess. I listen. I just don't believe it.'

'You listen, but you don't hear. You're reading English. Are you telling me that you aren't touching the mediaeval romances?'

He shrugged. 'I missed a few lectures last year.'

'But you must know the Arthurian legends.'

'Sure. I'm not exactly on first name terms with the cast list, but I know of them.'

'King Arthur lies dying. He gives instructions for the sword Excalibur to be taken and cast into the lake. Not any old lake, you understand, *the* lake. The sword is tossed into the air and a hand — a female hand — rises from the waters to catch it and take it beneath the surface.'

'A Celtic water goddess.'

'Absolutely.'

'I don't believe it. You look sane.'

'I am sane.'

'You can't be, Alice. You're looking for Excalibur.'

'I am not looking for Excalibur. If I'm very lucky, very lucky, the site may excavate sacrificial finds: pot shards, knife-shanks, spear-heads, horse harness, even; anything that was of great value to its owner. A sword... a sword was the ultimate possession, even for the nobility. A good swordsmith was regarded as a magician, a sorcerer. There's more chance of finding a gold neck torc than a sword.'

The computer beeped and she turned back to the screen. Her shoulders sagged. 'At this rate there's more chance of winning the national lottery than finding either.'

Nick stared into the rippling fall of her auburn hair, his mind a dull howl of impossible connections. The muscles in his right arm contracted beneath a pulling weight and he looked to his clenched hand. There was nothing held there. But there had been, at Derventio. At Derventio he'd clasped a jewelled sword and watched it fade into the daylight.

Chapter 20

Noise of a hair-dryer woke Nick. He was in bed alone again, and a sudden, leaden despair threatened to overwhelm him. The curtains hung partly open, and as he listened to the high-pitched whirring, he draped an arm over his eyes to ward off the daylight. At least she wasn't shackled to the computer. He tried to feel grateful for small mercies.

Peering round the edge of the wall beside the bed, his nose came close to a full mug of coffee. An empty mug stood beside it. He waved to catch Alice's attention, and miraculously the hair-dryer fell silent.

'Good morning,' she said. 'No need to ask if you slept well.'

'This coffee mine?'

'If it's still drinkable.'

She untied the belt of the white kimono and slipped the silk from her shoulders. Nick watched expectantly, and was surprised to see that she was wearing underclothes. They weren't lacy, but he still found them alluring, and he rubbed at his face to drive away the last traces of sleep. By the time he'd gained his feet, Alice had pulled on a long-sleeved T-shirt and was zipping up a pair of jeans.

'You going somewhere?'

'Lecture at 9.15. Shall we meet for lunch?'

'Lunch?'

'Mm. How about Zucchini? One o'clock?'

'Alice... You're leaving me!'

She looked bemused. 'Only for the morning. I've a lecture.'

'What about my lectures?'

'Nick, I wouldn't ask you to miss your studies to keep me company. It would be—'

'—*company?*'

'It would be wrong. Selfish.'

He covered the narrow space between them, taking her by the shoulders.

'Nick...'

Her eyes were brighter than he'd ever seen them, her hair a living mass of colour, each lock fashioned from separate writhing tendrils. As he rolled a thumb over the bloom in her cheek his irritation dissipated. 'I love you.'

'I know,' she said, 'but we can't spend the rest of our lives locked in each other's arms waiting for food to be delivered into us.'

'Why not?'

'It's madness.'

'I've been touched by a madness ever since laying eyes on you.'

She lifted a hand to stroke his cheek and he caught his breath. 'Alice, you're freezing. Are you ill?'

'Of course not.' She broke their embrace to shrug. 'Not if you discount the low blood pressure, the poor circulation, and the fact that I need to take tablets to supplement a salt deficiency. And you were thinking you'd picked yourself a bargain.' Playfully she tapped out a tattoo on his stomach with her cold fingers, sending him scurrying for the sanctuary of the bed.

'I'll see you at one,' she called, and the door closed behind her.

Leonard awoke with a shudder, automatically gripping the arms of the chair to steady himself.

'It's all right. It's only me,' Clare whispered. 'I've brought you a coffee. Be careful, it's hot.'

He wrapped his hands round the mug, pushing his face into the steam and burning his tongue on the liquid.

'I warned you it was hot,' Clare said. 'How do you feel?'

He didn't want to talk; didn't want her fussing.

'You did sleep, you see. Nothing came, did it? Nothing came to get you. You may as well have slept in the bed with me. At least you would have been comfortable. At least you would have had some decent rest instead of being cramped in this chair.'

They'd all come, separately or in groups; a mouse first, an incongruous little grey mouse. He hadn't even realised that she'd sent it; equated it with the mice that ran occasionally in the walls, that he trapped with baits of chocolate. But she had sent it; it had led the others: the hare, the rat, the snake, the boar. He'd nearly pissed himself when the boar had walked from behind the sofa, its flat snout edged in glinting tusks. And the stench of its coat... He'd known that they were apparitions, persuaded himself that they were apparitions. And then he had walked through the wall, naked and filthy, the clay head on top of his muscled shoulders, the moustache worming from above his lip. And behind him, behind him, as pale as moonlight—

'Leonard, mind the cup; you'll spill it.'

At his feet, Clare was bending to pick up a tartan throw.

'I tried to keep you warm, but every time I laid it across your lap you fought it off. It's only a rug, Len, nothing more sinister than a rug. How about some breakfast? I've scrambled some eggs.' She looked at him. 'Toast then. How about some toast? Leonard, speak to me, or so help me...'

He managed to nod and she brought the toast, but it was long cold and so brittle it disintegrated at the first bite.

'There's something wrong with the phone. I tried to call the doctor last night—'

'I don't need a doctor. It's Julia I need.'

'Oh, you're talking now, are you? You frighten me half to death with all this weirdness; you pound about the flat half the night wailing to yourself so that I have to calm your tenants, and now, when I'm trying my level best to understand, to help you even, you dig up this long lost love, who at least had the brains to trash you, and you tell me that it isn't a doctor you need it's this fucking Julia! So who is she? She'd better be some sort of nubile shrink, that's all I can say, because that's the sort of doctor I think you need.'

Tears formed in his eyes, blinding him. 'I'm sorry. Please don't shout at me, not you, please. It's all getting so out of hand I don't know what to do.'

Clare crouched beside the chair, her fingers delicately covering his wrist.

'I'm the one who should be sorry, Len. I didn't mean to shout. I know you're going through something horrible. I want to help, I really do. But how?'

Wiping at his cheeks, he fought to control his breathing. 'I'm not sure you can.'

'There must be something I can do. I can ring you in sick, call the faculty head. It'll give you some breathing space.'

'Yes. Yes, I— I can't teach today.'

'Right, I'll do that. I'll go to the shops, too.'

'Cigarettes. I need cigarettes.'

Clare nodded towards the overflowing ashtray. 'Yes, I can see you do. You look as though you've smoked half a carton during the night. I could hardly breathe when I walked in here. I opened a window.'

Leonard shot to his feet. 'You mustn't open windows. You mustn't.' He stumbled across to the bay to heave on the sash and slam it back into place.

'Calm down, Len. It's only a window. For God's sake, you've got to get a grip.'

'You mustn't open any windows, not any, do you understand?'

'Yes, yes, if it makes you happy. Now come and sit down before you fall down. You're shaking like a leaf.'

He lifted a hand in front of him, watching it tremble with mounting alarm.

'Come and sit down,' Clare repeated, patting the chair. 'Your coffee's still here. You just need to come round slowly, that's all.'

Nodding, he moved towards her. When he was settled, she replaced the mug in his hands.

'I'll go to the shops, call the faculty, and arrange for an engineer for the phone. I won't be long.'

'Phone?'

'It's not working. I told you, or tried to. You bit my head off.'

'I'm sorry.' He put out a hand. 'My mobile—'

'It's dead, Len. You left it charging on the draining board. It must have fallen into the sink. I found it in a pan of water.'

Gently she tapped his hand with her own. 'Keep calm. I'll be as quick as I can, Len. Just relax.'

He didn't watch her leave, but stared at the answering machine. There were no lights showing on it. Raising himself, he moved across to the telephone on the wall. There was no tone when he lifted the receiver. There'd been a tone the evening before. He'd called Julia as soon as he'd got in. Her voicemail had responded at the second ring; a sure sign that she'd not been home. Just running across the campus from the Union to his house, he'd missed her. But she'd ring him back. After the message he'd left, she'd ring him back and tell him what to do. Except that she couldn't, could she? The phone wasn't working. It was working last night. Why wasn't it working now?

Dragging the small table away from the wall he followed the wire down from the handset to the socket. It had been chewed. Close to the skirting, it had been chewed. Coloured wires were showing through the casing.

Apparitions. One had been real. Into his flat. How? The window. The open window. Chewed the wire. *She'd* known, known he'd called Julia.

Leonard grasped at his chest as a bubble of air caught and expanded, spreading pain across his ribs.

Calm down. Calm down. Get a grip. Yes, get a grip. It's not night, no. Daytime. Only threats in the daytime. Only fear in the daytime. Julia. Julia would be calling. She'd know his phone wasn't working. She— *She wouldn't be able to get through.* Calm down. Calm down. Ring her. Julia would wait for him to ring her. But his mobile was dead. In the kitchen. He never charged his mobile in the kitchen.

*

Nick felt more himself after the shower, a bit groggy, a bit hung over, as if he'd had a heavy night. Though he'd had a heavy night, hadn't he, and he smiled to himself at the memory. Thankfully he didn't have a lecture at 9.15. Pity about the one he'd passed on the day before. No matter. Bernie would have missed him and taken notes. Bernie had better have taken notes or he'd end up in the same deep shit he'd been in last year. Except that this time it'd be for keeps.

The steamy mirror above Alice's basin shone back a patchy reflection. The harsh fluorescent created dark shadows round his eyes, deepening the scarring on his cheek. He scratched at his stubble wondering if the itching that had erupted with the shower would stop if he left the flush of growth a couple more days. He'd never tried for a beard. He'd tried for a moustache once; his sisters had made his life unbearable. He fingered his upper lip, made faces in the glass. A moustache might suit him. He'd see what Alice thought.

Moving away, he pulled on the light cord. As the tube lost its power the cubicle seemed to lose its heat. He shivered in the sudden change in temperature, catching a sideways glimpse of his reflection backed by woodland and flaring yellow light. He swung back to the mirror, hesitantly reaching out to wipe away the condensation hanging on the glass. His face. Alice's bathroom. His eyes were playing tricks. His eyes had played tricks at Derventio. He hung his head. He didn't want to think about it. Closing the door behind him, he dried his chilled hand on his trouser thigh and refused to think about it.

'What do you think I have here — a database of all his previous whoring pieces?'

Clare shut her eyes and tried to keep her voice level as she spoke into her mobile. 'He's determined to contact her.'

'Well I'm going to need a sight more information than *Oxford*.'

'Have you checked with the colleges?'

'Of course I have, but do you know what I sound like? *Do you have a lecturer with a first name of Julia?* She could be anyone. She could be a cleaner for all we know.'

'She's not a cleaner.'

'It was a joke, Clare. We should have invested in a pin mike. We could have kept tabs on his dreams with a pin mike.'

'And how would we have explained that away? Oh, I keep forgetting. You wouldn't have had to, would you? It's not you fighting in the trenches.'

There was a pause before Helen's voice returned to her ear. 'There's no point the three of us falling out over this. It's only a minor hitch.'

'Well let's hope it stays minor, because if he gets her up here we're fucked.'

The line filled with Julia's modulated tones and Leonard leaned against the acoustic hood of the phone booth, his knees weak. Why was her voicemail message so long? Why was there never anything on it for him?

The final elongated beep sounded shrilly in his ears and he withdrew the half-smoked cigarette from his lips to garble a message into the handset. He cut the connection, drew on the cigarette, and punched the number to Julia's office. There'd be no bullshit from her tight-arsed assistant, no putting him on hold, or stonewalling him with tales of never-ending appointments which couldn't be interrupted.

'Mr Harkin, I've been waiting for your call.'

Leonard couldn't believe the response. 'You have? Then put me *through*.'

'Mr Harkin, Ms Marshall isn't here. She's out at a private consultation. I've been—'

Leonard removed the handset from his ear and struck it against the Perspex hood. 'No. No. *No!!*'

'—conference she may not have it switched on. Mr Harkin, are you listening to me? Please calm yourself and listen. This is very irregular. Ms Marshall never divulges the number of her mobile. She said that I was to give the number to you. Have you a pen?'

Leonard patted his jacket and trousers. Nothing. Turning to scan the reception area he grabbed the arm of the first student who passed within reach.

'Pen! Pencil! Anything!'

The wide-eyed girl handed over a biro and hurriedly made her escape.

He nestled the handset between chin and ear so that he could write the number across the back of his hand. 'Give it to me!'

The assistant was still speaking when he cut the line to punch the mobile's number. It was answered on the first ring.

'*Julia!!*'

'It's all right, Leonard, I'm here. How bad is it?'

'I'm being hunted, Julia. *Cornered.* It's *imminent. I need* you.'

'I'm coming up, Leonard. I'm coming up to Hull tomorrow.'

'*Too late.*'

'It won't be, Leonard. It won't be if you listen and do what I say, *exactly* what I say...'

Nick stepped out of University House straight into the path of Murray Symonds.

'Your excuse had better be damned good.'

'And good morning to you.' Nick transferred the polythene carrier to his other hand and pushed his change into his jeans' pocket. 'So what's crawled up your arse?'

He caught a thick finger in the chest, the stabbing power of a prop forward behind it.

'If you want to stay on the team you come to the practices. And don't think of giving me any lines with *forgot* in them.'

'Oh.' Nick crossed the tiled floor and pushed through the outer doors onto the concrete terrace. He had forgotten about the rugby training; inconceivably it had slipped his mind— right up to the moment that morning when Alice was pulling on her clothes to leave.

'Are you going to pass on Thursday's meeting, too? I'd like to know now if you are.'

'Maybe. I don't know.'

'Oh, great. I get lumbered with that selfish prick on right wing and my number one fly is incapable of making a commitment.'

'Commitment? It's only a game, Murray. The team's only a poxy—'

'I was made captain last night.'

Nick faltered on his way down the steps. 'Congratulations.'

'Thanks. I know it's not Twickers, but it's liable to be the best I'll ever see. And we were so close last year, Nick, so close.' Murray's fist grasped space in front of him, the stem of an elusive silver cup. 'It's the first match on Saturday. Hornsea at home. I want you to wear the shirt.'

'Okay. I'll be there. Thursday, too.'

'Good man!' Murray's slap on the back changed into a shoulder hug. 'I've been wondering whether to make a few changes, perhaps introduce the haka instead of Hodgson's pre-whistle huddle. You know, fire the warrior spirit a bit?' Splaying his legs, he took a couple of the steps, orchestrating it with the slapping arm movements and Maori chant.

'Well,' Nick said, 'being built like a brick shit-house you and Bernie Colwyn would probably look good. I'd look a right plonker. What do the others say?'

'I haven't broached it yet. I thought I'd see how we did on Saturday. Oh, I've a tidbit that might interest you. Louise turned up for the practice—'

'I don't want to talk about her.'

'—but she wasn't looking for Toby Medavoy.'

Nick shrugged clear the enveloping arm. 'I told you—'

'Yeah, yeah. So who do you want to talk about? Whatsername... the wraith?'

'Her name's Alice.'

'Yeah, suits her. Alice through the fucking mirror.'

'*Through the Looking Glass*.' Nick smiled, glowing with the memories that were pouring through his mind. 'Actually it's been more like *Wonderland*.'

'Moorland, don't you mean? A cosy little drive for two, never to be seen again. I thought she'd had her evil way and buried you in some bog up there.'

With a turn of speed that surprised them both, Nick let loose a right jab to his shoulder.

'Hey! You're getting a bit too handy with those fists of yours.'

A commotion made them focus on the terrace they'd left moments before. It was Harkin — just. The dishevelled silver hair stood out from his head as if electrified, his bright eyes so wide as to distort his ashen face.

'I know you're coming!' he yelled over the parapet. 'I know, but I'm ready. I can take you on. I can take you *all* on now! And don't think you'll escape her either, because you *won't*!' His hand lifted from the wall to jab in Nick's direction, his bloodless lips curving into a sinister grin.

'The new king inevitably turns into the old king. You'll not survive her touch! No one survives her touch! But I will! I will!' Pulling away from the edge, Harkin began to run along the terrace towards the elevated walkway.

Nick could only watch, his mind numb. In his peripheral vision he could see Murray turning to look at him with wide eyes of his own.

'Tell me you don't know that madman. Tell me he's not talking about the wraith.'

Chapter 21

Nick sat close to the plate glass window of the small café in the Wilberforce building. He was early, but he'd meant to be. He needed time to think, and his room no longer seemed the haven of peace he'd envisaged when he'd moved in during the early summer.

The last half hour he'd spent with a razor in his hand, trying to coax the dark stubble above his lip into a more meaningful moustache. The beginnings of the beard had gone immediately. Despite the difference in colour, and the cutting scar down his cheek, he'd seen the likeness of Harkin's grizzled jowls staring from the mirror, and Murray's forceful questioning had returned with the persistence of a vulture separating flesh from bone. It was time, Nick knew, to face a few facts.

Harkin had not seduced Alice. That truth had been made clear at Newtondale spring, but he'd pushed it from his mind because it meant that he'd been in the wrong, and the violent feelings he had carried for Harkin — still carried — needed him to be in the right.

Yet was he entirely off line? Alice had been stalked the previous year — Cigarette ends had been found beneath her window. Did Harkin smoke? — and who had laid into him as he'd stood there himself? He'd not *seen* Harkin, certainly; he'd not *seen* anyone, only felt the blows and heard the clapping. Had he been mistaken about that, too? Could the sounds have been slow manic laughter?

It was easy to recall the image of Harkin leaning over the parapet, finger pointing. He had certainly looked manic. Mad even. Or high on some sort of amphetamine cocktail. But Harkin had known who he'd been accusing, and even Murray had realised he'd been talking about Alice. This lack of insight was eating at him. He needed to know their connection.

Alice greeted him with a full-mouthed kiss, stroking her fingers down the line of his closely shaven jaw. She didn't seem to want to break the contact, and despite his keenest resolutions Nick found himself raising his own hand to her dancing hair, his entire body reawakening with the need to possess hers.

'I missed you,' she said. 'I couldn't concentrate on the lecture for thinking of you.'

Their lips met again in a tentative touching before she drew away to sit in the chair opposite.

'Have you ordered yet?'

He shook his head. She wasn't the same person he'd first approached in the refectory. She held herself erect now, full of self-assured poise, and she was glowing with vitality. He'd lit something within her, something that was flourishing under its own momentum. It was wondrous to watch. And he was a part of it. It was all down to him.

'Shall we eat?' Her gaze flitted over his face, her smile changing by degrees, becoming salacious. 'Are you hungry, Nick?' Her pale eyes grew as bright as sun-kissed water. 'I am,' she said. 'Did you go shopping?'

Vibrant conversations from tables close by faded from Nick's hearing as his mind replayed memories of her touch and his body begged for more.

'The only priority.'

'Well, Nicholas Blaketon, let's go eat.'

Cloud-cover had drawn in again, raindrops splattering the pathways in churlish indecision. Hand in hand they ran behind the buildings and into the shelter of the birchwood walk.

Ognirius held the woman's hand as the boy held it, smiled at her with the boy's lovelorn devotion, but it was a sickly pretence he could not stomach long. Closing his eyes, he detached himself, transferring his essence to the droplets of water as they fell through the air. He imagined he was a birch, and a birch he became, snagging the woman's hair in his brittle finger-twigs, slapping the boy in the eye as the couple swept by him. In their euphoria the lovers merely giggled. He answered through the throat of a jay, a harsh, deriding laugh incongruous against the city's foliage.

Halfway up the stairs Clare hesitated to gaze at the ceiling. It sounded as if the bailiffs had moved in and were tearing the place apart. Twice she'd been back, twice finding the flat empty. Where had Leonard been? She'd have sworn to anyone that he'd not venture out.

The latch had been dropped on the door to the landing. She used the copy key with quiet care, uncertain of what she'd find. The door opened, at once hitting an obstacle. She squeezed through the gap, coming face to face with the slack-jawed mouth of a rolled up carpet.

The narrow landing was crammed with furniture, all of it, Clare realised, from the lounge. Two dining chairs sat one inverted on the other. Encroaching into the kitchen space, the battered gate-legged table was piled high with books, cushions, and the empty vivarium, itself now an overflowing receptacle for the bric-a-brac Leonard hoarded but refused to dust. On top of all laid the aging carpet, its backing of foam perished, crumbling at the merest touch.

A screech of wood being dragged over wood made Clare turn to the closed lounge door. Leonard was inside; she could hear him singing softly, or was he talking to himself in a sing-song tone? Shadows flitted beneath the bottom of the door. More noises escaped from within. He was moving the heavier furniture. From the echoes it sounded as though the room had been stripped bare.

'Leonard? It's Clare.'

The singing stopped, the movement, too.

'It's Clare, Leonard. Can I come in?' She glanced at the carrier in her hand. 'I've brought the cigarettes you wanted.'

'Clare?'

She heard her name clearly enough, but it sounded more a wavering question than a relieved greeting.

'I'll just open the door, Len.'

The floor was bare to the boards. Leaning into the opposite corner was a tower of his possessions. In the centre of the room stood the sofa. Behind the sofa stood Leonard, his wide eyes fixed, not on her, but on the landing beyond her shoulder. Encircling the greater mass of cleared floor space, Leonard and the sofa, passing directly in front of Clare's feet, was what looked like, what was, a red plastic washing line.

'Did you lock the door to the street?'

She raised her gaze to him, but his attention was still fixed on the landing.

'I dropped the latch, yes.'

'The flat door?'

'It's locked.'

'Good, good. Can't be too careful now. Everything will be all right if we're careful.' He raised a hand to beckon. 'Come in, come in. Shut the door. Don't touch the circle. Step over the circle, step over it. You'll be safe in here. You'll be safe in here with me.'

Replete, Ognirius lay back against the window, using the dappling raindrops and the shadows of the beech to camouflage his presence, to camouflage his arm draped along her pale thigh.

Such orgasms were wasted on the boy, wasted; a gelded hedgehog had more capacity. He raised his hand to deal the boy a blow that would restore the colour of the bruising, but his temper held. The child would cry out and leap from the bedding, forcing her to move as well, and he didn't want that.

He wanted to lie a while, his eyes feasting on the full breasts and flat stomach, his fingers nestling in the liquid warmth of her engorged inner flesh. A waste on the boy, an utter waste, but she was coming to fruition, and Ognirius knew there could be no delaying until he'd acquired strength enough to stand alone. It irked him to accept it, but he still needed the boy.

'Are you okay?' she asked.

The boy grunted. Ognirius sneered at him, watching with ill-grace as the woman's hands stroked wide circles over the boy's back.

Her eyes widened, and she tapped the boy lightly, starting to disentangle herself from his limbs. Smiling, Ognirius withdrew his hand to taste her secretions. There was, after all, something in favour of the sheath the boy wore. Her flavour, her scents, remained true.

He watched her pull materials from a bag and start to write.

Yes, yes. Nearly there. Nearly there.

The boy raised his head; dragged his shoulders after.

'Oh, God, Alice... What is this with you?'

'I've an idea I want to pursue. If I don't put it down I'll lose it.'

'Again? Now? *Here?* I thought being separated from that damned computer you'd give me your entire attention. Come back to bed.'

He rolled over on to his back, displaying his flaccid genitalia. Ognirius threw back his head, fighting to restrain a mocking laugh.

'That was something, though, wasn't it?'

The boy pulled himself on to the pillows, holding aloft the discarded, heavy, sheath.

'I thought you were going to suck me dry, Alice. I don't know where it all came from, I really don't.'

Ognirius slid his sticky hand along the length of his own rigid penis. He was ready. The woman would take it. He looked to the boy and curled his lip.

*

Clare sat on the sofa, smoking one of Leonard's cigarettes. Two butts lay at her feet, crushed into the floorboards. Neither had been dropped by Leonard.

She'd waved the cartons under his nose, even opened one and split the cellophane on a pack. All he'd said was, 'Later, later.' By her calculations he should have been tearing out his hair with craving, but he'd hardly noticed when she'd blown smoke in his direction.

Again her gaze wandered round the bare room. Not only had the pictures been removed, but so had the telephone. All that remained were the retaining screws set in the wall by the door. It was better than she, any of them, could ever have hoped. But how to use it, that was the question.

'Are you going to explain all this to me, Len?'

She stood to peer over the back of the sofa. He was on his knees, talking quietly to himself while drawing shapes with a thick black marker on the boards beneath the bay window. When he didn't answer she moved around the furniture, the soles of her shoes grating on the fine layer of white granules spread on the floor. Already she'd wet a finger and discovered it was salt. There was a thin line of it running along the window sill by his head.

'Leonard…' She stepped on the logo so that he couldn't continue. 'Leonard…'

He looked up at her, his eyes dark-ringed and bloodshot. 'Got to do this,' he said. 'Got to be finished before the daylight fades.'

'There's hours yet 'til the daylight fades. And we've got electricity, Leonard. It isn't as though there'll be no light at all.'

He gestured for her to move and she noticed marks on the back of his hand. He was even drawing on his skin. She shook her head in disbelief and tapped at the red line encircling the room.

With terrifying speed Leonard lashed out with his fist, numbing her leg. 'Don't touch it!'

She hopped away from him, her own fists raised ready to retaliate, but he was scrabbling on the floor inspecting the line.

'Mustn't be touched,' he kept telling her. 'Mustn't be disturbed. It'll keep them out.'

Clare gazed at the red plastic washing line. '*That* will keep them out? Leonard, who are *them*?'

Painfully straightening his contracted muscles, he stood to look at her in amazement. 'You went to the meetings. You were there for the rituals.'

'When? Leonard, are you talking about when I was here as an undergraduate? For God's sake, it was years— Oh. The Mother Ear—'

'Speak no names!' he commanded. 'To name is to imbue with life. It is to summon!'

Clare looked back to the floorboards at her feet, to the layer of salt, to the ring of plastic-coated rope. Degrees of protection. Surely not? All those inane pronouncements about nymphs and faeries and the cycle of natural life. Did he actually believe it? He did! Of course. Why hadn't she realised? October. Halloween. Samhain. She glanced to the calendar to check the phase of the moon, but it no longer hung from its nail.

'Aes Sidhe,' she said. 'You're being hunted by Aes Sidhe.'

'Oh, Clare, it's worse than that. Much worse.'

Nick lolled against the pillows, looking out of the window. The beech seemed eerily stark with the neon street light behind its reaching boughs, as if, should he close his eyes for more than a moment, it would shatter the glass and stake him to the bed. And he was tired. Always he seemed in need of sleep.

Tentatively he reached for the edge of the curtain, drawing first one and then the other, forming barriers across the window. He switched on the bedhead light, but it didn't dispel the creeping chill. At a corner of his untidy desk Alice sat writing in a quick, jerky hand, her shadowy hair cloaking her pale shoulders.

'Alice...'

'Mmm...'

'Alice, do you know a lecturer named Harkin? Leonard Harkin?' He watched her raise her head as if in thought. 'Grey-silver hair, ponytail, fifties probably? Maybe sixties?'

'I don't think so. What's his specialty?'

'I'm not sure. He works out of Loten. Some sort of artist.'

She turned to look at him. 'Artist? The nearest my group gets to art is Art History. It's not a module that's ever interested me. Besides, Loten houses Estates Management, doesn't it?"

In his mind's eye he could see the studio through its window, see the cloth-wrapped head on the bench, white wing shapes slowly twirling from a wire.

'Did you ever belong to the Mother Earth Society?'

'The *what?*' She laughed, her hair flicking about her face. 'Pseudo-Celtic rubbish. One part New Age, one part Golden Age, ten parts fertile imagination and, I shouldn't wonder, a great excuse for an orgy.'

'Orgy?'

'Think of all those handmaidens dressed in little else but flowers.'

A lascivious grin crept across his lips. 'I'm thinking, I'm thinking.'

He ducked beneath the duvet as one of his English books sailed through the air towards him. When he surfaced Alice had returned to her writing, though how she could see what she was doing in the gloom he had no idea. He watched her a while, willing her to look at him, willing her to come to him. She remained intent on her work.

'Are you cold?'

'No.'

He padded over to slide his hands down her arms. She jumped with the shock.

'You're warm,' she said.

'Alice, I am not warm. It's you who is freezing.'

He switched on the main light and unhooked a padded jacket from the peg on the back of the door. Even as he was cosseting her with its soft fabric he wanted to let it drop and wrap his own arms around her, give her his warmth, his body.

'You know, for a student you have an amazing aversion to seeing people study.'

He smiled into her hair, breathing in its tantalising scents. 'Only you. Only you.'

She turned in his arms, offering her lips to his, her breasts to his lowering hands. The jacket began to slip from her shoulders.

'This will not keep them at bay,' Clare told him. 'For a start, the circle's the wrong colour. You should have bought a white line.'

Leonard shook his head. He was by the door now, still on his knees, still marking sigils on the floorboards. 'White is her colour. This is a battle, Clare. Red for war.'

She wanted to ask who was *her*, but she'd broached that once already and received a silencing glare in return. To name was to imbue with life, to summon.

'Besides,' added Leonard, 'it's only one night's battle. Tomorrow the war will be won.'

He sounded so confident that he could only be counting himself the victor. Against the supernatural? The folk of the hollow hills? Clare knew that she was missing something vital.

'What happens tomorrow?'

'Julia arrives.'

A long stream of cigarette smoke left Clare's nostrils. She looked to the wall where the phone had hung, then back to Leonard rising unsteadily to his feet.

'Julia from Oxford?'

'Yes. And I shall be so glad, Clare. I shall be so glad.'

He stepped back into the circle, visibly relaxing.

'Come and sit down, Len. You look all in.'

'Soon. One last job.'

From behind the sofa he brought a long thin packet. 'My idea. It should be a wand, of course, but I don't have one now, and these seemed a good replacement.'

Thumbing his cigarette lighter, he applied the flame. A thin trail of smoke began to curl towards the ceiling, filling the room with a cloying scent.

Clare stubbed out the half-smoked cigarette and pulled free another incense stick.

'Let me help,' she said. 'Two people must be more powerful than one. Pity we're not three.'

'We will be three when Julia arrives. The power of three to be invincible.'

Clare gave him a rueful smile. 'The power of three,' she echoed.

He offered the lighter's flame, but Clare's gaze was only for the back of his hand. It hadn't been a sigil she'd seen there. It was a telephone number.

Chapter 22

Now that they sat in the restaurant of The Goodfellowship, Nick's irritation was beginning to dissipate. He hadn't wanted to leave the comfort of his room in the Salmon Grove house, the comfort of his bed, especially the comforts of Alice's flesh, but she'd been adamant as soon as the front door had opened and the hall had filled with voices, never mind the drizzle, never mind the long walk down Cottingham Road.

'So what are we celebrating?'

Alice shrugged, but her eyes were dancing with amusement. 'Our good fortune? Our being together? Our great sex life?'

'If it's so great, why have you dragged me out here?'

'Because, Nicholas, to use the colloquial, you look shagged.' She smiled at him across the table. 'How about a bottle of wine?'

'Do we run to bottle-of-wine money?'

'Don't worry about it.'

'Oh, I'm not. You obviously don't. Meals out, hired cars, a personal library to rival the Brynmor Jones...' He sat back in his chair. 'So who in your family is the merchant banker?'

'My father's an accountant. Don't look like that. His work is very staid and low key. The way it's been continually told to me, and believe me *continually* is the word, almost as I was taking my first breath covenants were drawn up to mature in conjunction with my leaving home for university.' She waved her hands in a vague dismissal. 'It's what accountants do best.'

'My father's a line manager at a bottling plant.'

'Does he bottle anything interesting?'

'Chutney. And I never want to see another jar in my entire life.'

Her eyes widened as she tried to stifle her amusement. Nick

basked in the warmth of her good humour, smiling with her.

'I didn't mean— Oh, Nick I'm sorry.'

'Don't be. Chutney does that to people. My Mum works in a DIY superstore. She had to take on extra hours just so that I could get here, so you'll understand that life is a bit frugal on this side of the table.'

Composed now, Alice nodded. 'Of course. I do understand.'

He watched her ease away to survey their surroundings and change the subject. 'I like it in here,' she said. 'All the wood, and the space. And it's not as noisy as in The Mare.'

Nick followed her gaze, taking note of the restaurant's furnishings. It reminded him of the pine-clad McCarthy bar, even the pale woods adorning the Taylor Court apartments. Very much the pale woods of the Taylor Court apartments. The unexpected similarity caused a tightness in his chest. They'd passed under trees to gain entry to the restaurant. Through the windows he could see their heavy limbs shielding the lights from the car park. There'd been shrubs crowding the door, too. One had scratched him. He twisted his wrist to look at the red weals on his hand. Hairs started to rise on the back of his neck, the prickling that had been absent for so long. Perhaps it was coincidence, all of it. Perhaps she just preferred trees and pale wood decor.

'I also wanted us to come out for a meal to sort of assuage my guilt.'

He looked at her and watched her pale cheeks tint pink.

'In the beginning I didn't think it would matter, then I delayed telling you. I'm on a field trip with the history group tomorrow. It's a postponement from last year.'

'You're leaving me *again?*'

'For the entire day, I'm afraid. I knew you wouldn't be happy.'

It was irrational, he knew it was, but a surge of jealous howling was building within him as if a physical entity. Harkin's face filled his mind, wild-eyed and pointing; the clay head wrapped in its winding sheet; the smell of paints and thinners, musty earth and rotting—

'Nick...' Alice reached across the table to take his hand. 'I should be back about six, seven at the latest.'

He slipped his fingers through hers, anchoring himself to her. 'I've been picked for the match on Saturday. I'm training tomorrow evening.'

'We can meet afterwards.'

Rain lashed his back, gripping him with cold and melding his shirt to his skin. In the darkness caught in Alice's eyes, a girl holding a red and blue panelled umbrella stood on the sideline. Nick didn't want to see her; didn't want to acknowledge that she was there, waiting.

'Come to the field, Alice. Come see me train. You'll be lucky for me. You will; I can feel it.'

Switching off the buzzing fluorescent and working in the light from the desk lamps hadn't helped. A band of pressure was spreading from the base of Julia's skull, aiming to cross above her ears and meet behind her eyes. Driving would be beyond her if she let it reach that point, and she hated taking painkillers for a simple headache, it was such an admission of defeat, but her own neat writing was shifting on the page as if viewed through a rippling tide. She had to get through this. Maeve had been good enough to stay on. She couldn't just throw in the towel and leave the job half finished.

Closing her eyes, Julia took a series of three deep breaths, letting the exhalations stream from her lungs, purging the tension.

'That bad, eh?'

Julia smiled at her administrator. 'Busy week.'

'Tell me about it. The phone never stops.'

'People are reaching.'

'Half of them don't know what they are reaching for.'

Julia refused to be drawn. 'This one can be put back a fortnight; this one I'll have to ring myself. How's the schedule looking for a week Monday?'

Maeve handed over the diary. 'You're not intending staying in Hull that long, surely?'

'Difficult to say.' Julia's manicured fingernail skimmed down the page. 'Perhaps we could ring Mrs Sillitoe and ask her to—'

'How many clients do you wish to lose?'

'None.'

'So don't shunt them about as if they were freight wagons.'

'Yes, Maeve. No, Maeve.' She passed across another file. 'Any Thursday for that one.'

'The longer you stay in his company the less you'll be able to function, you know that. Look at you now, and you've only spoken to him on the phone. Remember what happened when he was here in the spring.'

'Maeve, I can do without this.'

'He's not worth it, Julia.'

'Everyone's worth it. Read the Mission Statement.'

'Not if their character is knowingly flawed or their mind is seriously cracked. And he's both.'

'People can shed destructive tendencies as easily as they can give up eating chocolate. And everyone knows how simple that is, don't they?'

Maeve shut the drawer to her desk. 'That was below the belt.'

A warning note shrilled from Julia's bag: her mobile phone. Maeve made a soft clucking sound and shook her head.

'Talk of the devil and the devil appears. I knew you shouldn't have given him that number.'

It wasn't Leonard. It was a young woman so tearful that Julia could hardly understand what she was saying.

'Leonard Harkin? Yes, I know him. Please calm down—'

'—kept saying your name, saying *Tell Julia*—'

'What's happened?'

It started insidiously at the edge of her shoulders, but Julia was so intent on catching every word of the girl's disjointed phrasing that she ignored the warning signs. Muscles began to contract sending the tendons in her neck into rigid spasm. Maeve was right. The very mention of Leonard was setting up a tension loop.

'— not sleeping — tearing the flat apart — frightened — called the doctor — Leonard kept shouting — took him away — wanted you to know—'

Julia raised her gaze to Maeve watching beyond the desk. 'Who took him away? Where's he been taken?'

'— doctors — I don't know — *awful* — got to go—'

'No, don't hang up. Tell me your name. Give me a contact number.' She reached across the desk for a pencil.

'— can't — uni phone—'

'Oh, yes. Of course. But you will ring me as soon as you hear where he's been taken?'

There were only sobs from the girl now. She sounded very young, absolutely distraught. Julia started to feel angry, for the girl, for Leonard, *at* Leonard. Why wouldn't he *learn*?

She caught herself. Anger would help no one. And it was her fault. She should have driven up to Hull when he'd first phoned.

'Please listen. It is important that I know where he's been taken. Use this number. Any time. I'll—'

The line was cut. Julia looked at the handset hoping that there was something she could do.

'And..?' Maeve prompted.

Her defences down now, pain was sweeping through Julia's head making her wince and hunch her shoulders. 'I think he's been Sectioned.'

'Sounds about right,' said Maeve, and she picked up another file.

'Come to bed.'

'I have to make a few things ready for the morning, I told you.'

'Switching on your laptop is making a few things ready?'

'I'm just checking my e-mail. You're very hostile, Nick. If you're tired, go to sleep.'

'I don't want sleep; I want you. I want you now. I want you all tomorrow. I don't want to share you with anyone.'

'You sound drunk. I think that wine's gone to your head.'

He didn't answer. The computer beeped to gain her attention and the screen displayed its report. There were no e-mail messages.

Raising her hand to switch off the machine, Alice turned, instead, to squint through the shadows to the bed. Nick's open mouth betrayed the haze of sleep enveloping his senses. Any sudden noise might rouse him. Although she found his touch exciting, his overwhelming need to possess her every breath was curtailing her work. The prescribed syllabus she wasn't particularly bothered about, but she needed to pursue her search for the shrine. If she could make a breakthrough, if she could pinpoint its location to within a manageable area, she knew that he would help with the field work. He'd like that, she'd like it, making love by a lakeside with nothing but the earth beneath them and the moon lighting their passion.

Quietly, she thumbed through the stack of folders beneath the window, choosing the one containing maps. As each was withdrawn, its cover was angled to the steely light from the laptop's screen. Alice had examined the Ordnance Surveys a hundred times before, pored over their detail for hour upon hour. The moors were huge, the national park itself over five hundred square miles. In trying to home in on a likely area she had placed her faith in technology, in the ease of its storing and sifting of minutiae, but the place she was seeking didn't have its basis in logic. It was a shrine. Its basis was in belief. It had been a sharing of that belief that had focused her investigation on the North York Moors, that had brought her to the city with its name devoted to water, to Taylor Court with its house names echoing sites of the Romano-British and the Celts before them. Who had named the city? Who had named the apartment houses? Had it been a leap of faith, with no basis in logic? Had it just seemed *right*?

The workstation was too cluttered to lay out the folded maps and so she knelt on the carpet to deal them, thick playing cards, in a tight semi-circle below the window. Resting back on her heels, she closed her eyes and took control of her breathing: long, deep inhalations to slow her heartbeat and disconnect her mind. But her mind refused to disconnect. The hum of the computer pervaded her concentration. Whether or not it woke Nick, it would have to be switched off.

The single click might have heralded the end of the technological world, it was so loud, so final. Quiet rushed in to fill the noiseless space. No floorboard creaked above. There was no murmur of traffic from outside; not a footfall of a human or the call of an animal. Two lights shone through the thin fabric above her head: one pale neon, the other bright silver. Alice reached up to draw back the curtain. The waning moon shone directly onto her face, onto the fan of maps on the floor. She smiled up at it, serene and ancient, the eye of the Goddess to which all water deities acquiesced, the eye of Mother Nature. Easing her breathing, Alice allowed her senses to float on its light.

Clare cast an eye over the congealed contents of the take-away trays abandoned on the floor. 'Do you want me to get rid of these?'

Leonard shook his head. 'We mustn't keep leaving the circle. There's no knowing what we might bring back into it.'

'I wasn't suggesting going beyond the flat door, only to the kitchen.'

'Don't you listen? I said we mustn't leave the circle.'

'Yes, Leonard. The circle.'

It had taken all her skills of persuasion for him to accept that they would need supplies for the body as well as the mind to successfully mount the night's vigil. It had also given her the opportunity to ring Helen. It was up to her and Jenny, now, to keep Julia in Oxford out of their hair.

Pushing at the nearest tray with her toe, Clare listened to it grate on the salt-encrusted boards. Already the clutter was beginning to mount. Beside a large bottle of mineral water stood two mugs, three gaudy plastic carriers and an overflowing ashtray. She'd been pleased to note that he'd chain-smoked during the time she'd been away. What with those and the incense sticks he'd renewed, the room was thick with a blue-grey fug.

Stretching out her legs, she tried to make herself comfortable in the corner of the sofa. Leonard was perched on the edge of the seat, biting his nails and staring at the door.

'You know, if I'm to help you through this night, Len, I really need some information. This *her* you keep referring to... Is this the same *her* with the argumentative boyfriend you mentioned? Oh— the *him*.'

Leonard nodded quickly.

'You met her through the, er... *club*?'

'No, no. Nothing to do with it.'

The catch in his voice told her otherwise, so did the sheen of perspiration on his forehead.

'Like I was nothing to do with it... until you introduced me to its... secrets?'

He covered his face with his hands. 'Oh, Clare... if I could only roll back the years. I'm being punished, I know I am. *Aes Sidhe. Faerie Folk.* How quaint it sounds! How ludicrous! We didn't know what we were playing with!'

'Naïve young women, Leonard, that's what you were playing with, anorexic virgins hardly out of childhood.'

'It wasn't like that.'

'Of course it was. All that talk of solstice magic and the goddess within, you were re-enacting your youth: free love and peace, flower power and hallucinogens. You're nothing but a dirty old man in a multicoloured raincoat.' She rose to prowl about the room.

'Clare, I thought you were here to help me.'

'Like you helped me by paying for the abortion?'

Leonard shook his head, bewildered. 'Abortion?'

'You don't even remember, do you? There's been that many

of us.'

'Yes, yes, of course I remember. You... you wanted the abortion. It was your decision.'

'It was no decision at all. I wanted my life back.'

She looked at the dusty cobwebs slung across the cornice, at the scratched and faded wallpaper. 'How many of us have there been, Leonard? How many lost careers? How many ruined lives?'

'What are you talking about?'

'How much are you having to shell out in paternity?'

Leonard sprang to his feet, his fists clenched. 'Are you blind?' He extended his arm towards the sigils on the floorboards. 'Does this mean nothing to you? I wasn't giving life to children, I was giving life to *her*. I opened a portal. Don't you understand that? She's coming through!'

'Who is, Leonard? The goddess within?' Clare had moved to the other side of the sofa, and she leaned across to taunt him. 'If to name is to summon, let's call her forth. Which is she, Leonard? Brigantia?'

'*No—*'

'Andrasta? Prytania, herself?'

He lurched across the back of the sofa, his arms outstretched to catch at Clare, but she was expecting it and ducked.

'What did you think you were? Some sort of Father Sky figure returning each academic year to sow the seed?'

He tried again, but Clare was too agile for him.

'The King of the Green dies each autumn, Leonard. I'm surprised at you overlooking an important fact like the corn dolly being buried in the field after the harvest.' She watched his breathing become rapid, his eyes to stare. 'She won't have forgotten, though. She will have marked every blasphemy, waiting for you to make her powerful enough to exact retribution. Even now you're helping her, Leonard. You're walking *widdershins*, Leonard, directly into her embrace.'

A cry left his lips and his face drained of what little colour it contained. For a moment he looked about him as if not knowing where he was, and then he started to walk clockwise round the sofa: once, twice, three times.

Clare stepped out of the circle to stand by the door.

'Where are you going?'

'Leaving you to your fate,' she said, and she snapped up the light switch, plunging the lounge into darkness.

Her name was screamed as she left the room, and then light flooded beneath the door into the narrow hall. He'd been desperate enough to reach across from the circle to turn the power back on. Clare merely smiled, and ran her fingers over the dusty cover of the fuse box.

Rise up, boy, rise up and take the crown of green. Nurtured for this moment, rise up to do the duty you were summoned for. Let us walk together, you and I, along the path between the trees as I once walked alone. Let me show you a true man of worth.

The familiar prickling was in neck and in shoulder, spine and in ribs, feathering to a tingling in thighs and arms, toes and fingers.

Nick wasn't certain how long he'd lain awake gazing at Alice. The room was suffused with a silver-hued light, making the robe she wore shimmer, ghost-like, as she knelt on the floor. Her back to him, her head bent forward as if in supplication to the uncurtained window, she was offering an hour-glass of sensuous curves that fired a need so deep Nick believed the yearning would never be extinguished.

As he closed his eyes tree shadows filled his inner vision, the scent of woodland, the scents of Alice, calling him, drawing him down to join her.

Slipping from the bed, light through water, he crawled behind her to match her pose and fill his lungs with her flower fragrance.

Naked, he crawled, amid bracken and leaf mould, a shadow in the darkness, the woodland odours thick in his nose. They were in the clearing amid trees, he on the further side of the Pool. Light flickered across its surface, reflecting from torches set in the ground.

The white silk of her robe felt damp to his touch, as slippery as ice. His fingers twisted in its edges, ensuring his grip, peeling it slowly, slowly, from her throat and her shoulders, lifting her body back to meet his, trapping her arms in the folds of the gown.

Others would be ready. He must wait for the signal, wait, but his heart was thudding in anticipation. He wanted the Keeper now, she who held toad-magic in her tongue. He wanted Yslan for himself.

Her chilled flesh drew fire from his fingertips each time he touched her. Each time he touched her drew a murmur of contentment from her lips. She offered no resistance as he pulled her back further, their bodies horizontal shadows in the moonlight, the silk robe liquefying around and between them as his mouth closed on Alice, fraying at her neck with his tongue and his teeth.

A call. A woman's voice. The smell of smoke, the crackle of fire. A shout, more urgent. A crump, a whoosh, hardly audible, and yellow light filled the clearing, reflecting from his arm, from the honed blade of the gladius tight in his fist.

She tasted sweet, of honey and soft fruits; smelled of crushed yarrow and mint. As his muscles took the strain of their weight he immersed himself in her flavours.

A cry on his lips, a pounding in his chest, he was running, running through the garlanded trees as the acolytes fled from one into another, their white robes turning red beneath the rapine and the slaughter.

Every skeletal ridge and dip he devoured, first with his fingers as she lay taut over him, then with his flexed palms. Along each rib, over the flesh of her hips and the flat expanse of her belly to her groin, as far as he could reach and back again, gliding, gliding, round her breasts, teasing the soft flesh until the nipples stood proud.

Yslan. Before him stood Yslan, her eyes blazing defiance, a toad croaking alarm at her feet. Her lips parted to denounce him, but not a word did she utter as he fell upon her to prise open her jaw.

Tightly he gripped her, pumping his muscles to increase the pressure of his hold, rolling her beneath him as the liquid gown lapped around them, wrapping his legs about the powerful muscles of her thighs.

His cry of triumph rang through the clearing as he held aloft his trophy and she squirmed, choking, beneath his foot. So warm in his hand, it felt, so small, so silent. He painted himself in its blood before dropping to his knees beside the Keeper, her body both altar and sacrifice.

Bursting from his own skin to enter her, he licked at the sheen glistening on her back, feeling the ridges and whorls through his tongue as she spasmed in ecstasy beneath him.

Once he killed her, his hands around her throat. Twice he killed her, the gladius an extension of himself raping through her organs. Thrice he killed her, holding her beneath her own sacred waters, drowning the Keeper in her own bloodied Pool.

His senses ignited in a fiery conflagration as he flooded her with his light and his warmth, his youth and vitality, enriching her chilled inner flesh to bring fertility and rebirth.

His. Everything would be his. Leadership of the People, the power of Derventio. All would be his unchallenged now that their ties to the Presence had been severed and he could lead them to the deities of Rome.

His searching hands found her breasts engorged, flowing with nectar to feed his thirst, her belly so rounded he couldn't match her girth with his arms. Sensations waxed, to shine iridescent and wane, only to wax and shine again. Stronger. Ever stronger. He clung there, flesh sealed within flesh, no longer knowing, or caring, who he was, or had become, as the water lapped around them and the flower scents filled heart and mind.

*

Mustn't think. Mustn't think.

Keep the mind free. Don't focus.

Breathe deeply. Keep serene. Serene. Serene.

Don't sleep! Don't sleep!

Panic rose in a wave of giggling hysteria. Leonard fought it all the way, clamping his teeth on the noise so that it escaped only as a nervous whinny. Even so his hand shook, the pale flame from the lighter guttering dangerously.

He glanced at the window, at the strong orange neon filtering through the curtains from the streetlamp outside. Why were there no noises? Where was the traffic which prowled mercilessly along the route each night? What had happened to all the rowdy students leaving the campus bars, returning to their digs from the clubs in the city? Where were his tenants? Why was there this silence?

He took a shuddering breath and looked about the room. Shadows danced on the walls around him, playing tag with the weak light. No matter where he looked they were more marked, more angular, at the edge of his vision, daring him to see, to recognise, to fear.

And he did fear.

What would happen when the gas gave out and the lighter died? How would he keep them at bay? Would the circle suffice on its own in the dark?

He lit another incense stick and blew on its smouldering tip. It gave no light, but its red glow offered comfort, and he was grateful for every mercy. Julia would arrive in the morning. He needed only to see out the night.

Muscles were tight, joints stiff, but he rose with care to step to the edge of the circle and align himself with the first of the cardinal points. Lifting the make-shift wand, he began drawing sigils of protection with the fragrant smoke.

*

The scent of the flowers was very strong. Or was it the scent of Alice? Nick could not isolate one from the other. They had been searching for a spring without water and had stopped to eat in the meadow. She had feasted on him, and he on her. Satiated, he had lain on the cool turf as she had blanketed him in flowers: in buttercups and daisies, in speedwell and clover, and a host of other sweet-smelling blooms for which he had neither name nor recognition. He knew only that they were soft, and light, and compelling, and that Alice was with him, touching and smiling, and there was not a worry in the world that could break their peace or disrupt their harmony.

The moon, full and white, looked down on him from the dark, dark sky, and he blinked as he awoke, uncertain where he was or who was rousing him. The moon's smiling face resolved into the smiling face of Alice, and he smiled back, taking the hand that was offered and rising to his feet. Together they walked through dew-damp grass, he naked and shadow-patterned, she adorned in a white silk gown that flowed about her limbs and glistened, ghost-like, in the moonlight.

His chest felt tender. He looked at the weals cut into his skin, at the bloody scratches patterning his limbs. Trees bent their heads, their angular boughs creating a lattice of black shadow and silver light.

There was a movement ahead on the well-worn track. A hare stood in their path, stared, and ran on. A hedgehog grubbed in the leaf litter, stopped at their approach, then turned away. The toad stood as still as a rock, its colours a covering of lichen. Nick gazed at it as they passed, but it did not blink, and it did not move. It was the toad from Alice's courtyard, he knew it was. He wanted to draw her attention to it, standing there sentinel, but his toes dipped into cool water, and the Pool was in front of them, its surface partly wreathed in skeins of mist, bubbles from its feeder spring rising to its centre.

Alice stepped into the water, still holding his hand, still smiling, the moonlight suffusing her russet hair. Nick stepped as she stepped, his hand caught in hers, the cold reaching up his thighs as the ground shelved away, reaching up to his waist, to his chest, to his shoulders. His hand stayed secure in hers, his gaze safe in the benevolence of her smile. He knew what he was doing, felt no fear of what would come. He was with Alice. The water lifted her auburn hair, draping it around her head in individual locks, just as he remembered it the first time he had seen her.

And the water stung his eyes, glazing his vision, filling his ears and dulling his hearing. Down, down. Nick looked at her, moonlight seen through water. He knew peace. Contentment. Liberation. Opening his lips, he let the sweet liquid pour into him, let it bubble down his throat and into his lungs, water hissing over red hot stone.

Leonard crouched back into the corner of the sofa, hugging his knees into his chest and holding out the wavering flame of the cigarette lighter. His gaze was fixed just beyond the sofa, at the point in the mist-shrouded pool where the lovers were disappearing, their descent as rhythmic a movement as if on a staircase, their eyes locked upon each other even as the water filled their nostrils. Auburn hair was floating out around her head, rising and rippling on the currents they were creating, a halo of fire on ice-cold liquid. As Leonard watched, her moon-round face turned from her lover's, the pale eyes seeking his own, the gaze never wavering as her head disappeared and the mist swirled in her wake.

Leonard drew a breath so thin and deep that he began to hyperventilate. The lighter shook in his hand as he watched a single set of bubbles rise from the water, thickly at first, and then not at all. The silvery moonlight faded, the trees drew back into the walls, the water seeped away. Only the smoke from the incense sticks remained, swirling gently over the floorboards. Leonard's breathing eased. He'd survived. He'd *survived*!

A floorboard creaked as he moved on the sofa. A second creaked when he hadn't moved at all. He lowered the lighter to inspect the boards. They seemed solid enough. He crouched, touching one with his fingers.

The noise came again, distinct now. It hadn't been a creak he'd heard, but a croak. He raised his gaze in time to see it lift its legs and step to one side — a mottled toad half as big as a football — except that it didn't move. It remained where it was. A second toad, the image of the first, had stepped aside. There were two of them.

Not toads. Not toads as he'd kept toads in the vivarium, the ones he'd gassed and dismembered and burned. There was something in the eyes, in the shape of the head. His gaze followed the line of the ridged body, down the muscled green legs to—

His scream reverberated off the walls to fill his head with noise, the pressure making his eyes bulge. The toads remained unaffected. They stood a moment on their human feet, blinked at him with lustrous pale eyes, and croaked in unison. And each lifted its legs to step aside and reveal a duplicate. The four Alice-toads stood a moment, blinked at him, and croaked in unison. The four became eight; the eight sixteen. The single croak grew loud. Leonard retreated into the corner of the sofa, his jaw sagging open, the pulse in his ears a continuous note. The sixteen became thirty-two, became sixty-four. Leonard shut his eyes as they croaked in unison.

'Julia! Help *me!*'

His free hand was in his mouth, stifling his sobs, but his fingers didn't taste of salt. He looked about the floor for the coarse white granules. There was no salt on the floorboards. The pool had leached away his last protection. The Alice-toads croaked again and raised themselves on to their toes, bloating their bodies to twice their normal size.

In the yellow flicker of the lighter flame, Leonard saw their backs begin to glisten. Then the lighter failed.

Chapter 23

Music was drifting softly from one of the other rooms, from the floor above maybe, maybe from the second storey. It wasn't a tune Nick recognised. It floated in and out of his subconscious as he lay on the bed, the sheet of paper in his hand.

He'd woken to find himself naked, his cheek nestling against her silk kimono, her flower fragrance filling his senses. He'd waited for her to come out of the bathroom, or back from the kitchen. She hadn't. Finally, he'd raised himself from the pillow and found the note.

> Gone to Map Library, then bus.
> See you tonight - Love you, Alice.

He'd lain back on the duvet, holding the paper to his chest, watching the sunlight dapple shadows on the wall beside the uncurtained window. Tree shadows. Lattice lights. The remembered warmth of the dream consoled him, offered comfort in her absence. He recalled every sequence, smiled again as she smiled at him, shed a tear, a single tear, when she took him by the hand and drowned him in the pool.

He was through. He was *through* — at least part of the way.

Nothing of the transfer had been as he'd planned. Yslan had been in his mind as she'd been in his hand, but the boy had been blind in his weakness. No grieving. The outcome was all. Riding the woman's blood, he would fill her heart and mind as he was filling her womb.

Ognirius steadied himself within her. He wanted to surface,

to draw his form outside her flesh and watch her, coax her, bruise her, just a little, as he'd bruised the boy aplenty. But he wasn't strong, not as strong as he'd been within the boy. Perhaps it was the exertion of the transfer, perhaps the difference in host. Perhaps he'd left something of himself within the boy. He'd take advantage of that, enjoy himself now the boy could be discarded.

Slackening his grip, he let the woman's pulse be his pulse, let his body mirror hers. If he could not yet rise and be himself, he would become as his host, hear with her ears, see with her eyes, taste with her tongue.

The sensations confused him. It was as if he were back in the Pool, the water glazing his eyesight and dulling his hearing. It had happened with the boy, certainly, though not to such extent. But the more he thought on it, the more he saw the sense. What was a human but an illusion of solidity, fragile skin wreathed about a body of liquid gore? With the gladius in his hand, he'd taken apart enough to know.

He concentrated, focusing his vision to hers. Where was she? What was she about? Ah! Better than he had dared to hope. He would pass through. So very soon now, he would pass through completely and be free of them both.

They were stepping stones arranged in a horseshoe beneath the window, five Ordnance Survey maps neatly folded within their covers. Five maps and a gap where a sixth should be laid. Nick sensed that the gap was significant. Alice had gone to the map room, hadn't she? She'd taken it with her. No, it was more than that.

He knelt on the carpet, crawling close enough to touch them. A tingling was building in his shoulders, but faintly, almost an echo of the sensation he understood so well. The gap was significant, he knew it was. He deepened his breathing, let his eyelids droop. The scents of Alice rushed in to overwhelm him. He could smell her, taste her, hear her cries of ecstasy, feel the flesh of her hips in his groin, her breasts in his hands. They'd made love there, over the maps. He opened his eyes to gaze at the stain on the carpet. They'd made love there, with no protection.

It was another full attendance at the afternoon relaxation circle and Julia was pleased that she'd not cancelled the meeting. She was concerned about Leonard. His location was proving elusive, though away from the campus he would undoubtedly be safer, both from himself and whatever he believed was pressing in on him. Besides, as Maeve had pointed out, others were relying on her. She had fought hard to convince sceptical GPs, and the contract from the Health Centre was still in its probationary period. She couldn't afford to throw away her reputation over a man who exaggerated his every breath. She wished, though, she wished so very fervently, that she hadn't gone along with his psychosis.

Clapping her hands, she began to separate members from their initial cuppa and conversation. Within a few minutes everyone was seated and she was able to switch on the music. At the first tinkling notes most present closed their eyes and cradled their hands across their laps, well used to the routine. Maxine's head began to nod. Julia felt she hardly needed to lead them now. Most were perfectly capable of leading themselves.

'Breathe in. And out. In. And out. Slow. And deep. Slow. And deep. Concentrate on the *sound* of my voice. On the *rhythm* of my speaking, and *allow* yourself to sink *deeper*, and *deeper*, into relaxation...'

Her own eyelids became heavier as she took the group by the hand, leading them along the well-used lane, through the break in the hedge, and into a meadow of sweet-smelling flowers. It wasn't the meadow she was expecting; the colours were of a slightly different hue, the hillocks more pronounced, but the sun was shining, and she felt very warm, very light. The narrow track was there. It led down, down, beneath shady oaks and ash to the edge of a mist-shrouded pool. Someone was swimming. She could see an arm rise and fall through the swirling mist. A woman's arm, beckoning. A pale arm, almost translucent, beckoning, beckoning...

'No!' Her eyes sprang open. Julia could see the circle, the group, the inclined heads. Between them and herself, as if a pastel-shaded painting on glass, was the pool, and the mist, and the beckoning arm.

'No!' Aware of the alarm in her voice, she steadied herself, her gaze darting round her group seeking signs of distress. They were all with her. All safe.

'We mustn't go in. The water's too cold; we mustn't go in. Not today. Back up to the meadow, now. Hold hands, hold hands tightly and go back up to the meadow.'

One of the group raised her head. Another opened her eyes. Julia could see them quite clearly through the pastel-shaded glass, but the pool was still there, between them, shrouded in mist. The arm was still beckoning, not beckoning but waving, not a woman's arm but a man's, not waving but—

Three rasping coughs were followed by a great whooping breath that seemed to fill the room with sound and commotion. Maxine was clutching at her throat, her eyes wide and terror-stricken. Julia stood, her concentration centred solely on her distressed participant. The painting loomed large as she stepped towards it, shimmered and dispersed as she cut through it to the woman's side.

'Someone get a glass of water,' she called. 'You're all right, Maxine. You swallowed the wrong way, that's all.'

She was holding her by the shoulders, patting her back. Others were standing, looking. Some were talking in low, serious tones. A glass was brought and Julia stood aside. She had to smile for them, had to show that nothing was amiss.

'Everyone else okay? Yes? Well... That was a bit of a shock to us all, wasn't it? Brought us round a little faster than anticipated.' She turned her smile into a grin. 'It certainly sent my heartbeat soaring.'

The ladies smiled at each other. One nudged her companion and chuckled, relieving the tension for everyone. The coughing stopped.

'How are you feeling, Maxine?'

'I thought I was drowning.'

Julia looked down at the woman with the ashen face and felt her own smile grow taut enough to shatter.

With trembling fingers Julia fitted the key into the steering lock, but she didn't turn the ignition. She was in no condition to drive. For long minutes she sat fighting the urge to cry.

She couldn't believe it, *still* couldn't believe the power of the vision. Immersed in her hectic schedule, she'd banished the far past, thought of it only in terms of Leonard's current state of mind. He hadn't been exaggerating. Something was out there pressing in with such force that it could reach nearly 200 miles and still be capable of sweeping along non-sensitives. What might have happened if she had not broken the link? Maxine had believed she was drowning. Someone had been drowning in the pool. She would never forgive herself if it was Leonard.

Rummaging in her bag for her mobile, she thumbed his landline number, but the ringing tone droned on and on. The girl wasn't there. She tried his mobile; not even his voicemail kicked in.

She closed her eyes. Leonard was such a manipulator, such a drain. He would lie, and smile, and smile while he was lying. But he'd been there for her. The years had altered him, but they could not alter that truth. If he had been so easily dissuaded where would she be now? What would she have become? Her parents had thought her mad; she had thought herself mad. The doctors called in to help her had *believed* her mad.

A shudder ran through her as images of Seventies' psychiatric treatment danced about her head. She would have been left a zombie. Leonard had saved her life as well as her mind. No matter how health care had improved, wherever he'd been taken there would be no one who believed a word that Leonard spoke.

She tapped her office number.

'Maeve, I want you to drop everything and ring Hull. Call every hospital, every evaluation centre— I know you've done it once. Do it again. Call Personnel at the university. Call the Police if you have to, but find out where Leonard has been taken. And cancel all appointments, Maeve. Regardless of what you find, I'm starting the drive north *now*.'

Wherever Clare placed her feet the stairs creaked. She only hoped that Leonard was so exhausted that his sleep would be too deep to register the noise.

When Julia's secretary had rung the *HullFire* office seeking information about Leonard's whereabouts, Jenny had been as evasive as she could, but it was clear that the tear-filled phone call made the previous day had only served to stall the inevitable for a few hours. Julia Marshall was driving up from Oxford. Their concerted attack on Leonard Harkin was over; it was time to pull the plug and disappear back into the ether. The decision hadn't been unanimous, but Helen had been talked round.

The copy key fed into the lock and turned with oiled ease. Clare pressed the door into the rolled carpet and squeezed through the gap. A cloying scent gripped the back of her throat, and her eyes began to water as she fought the urge to cough. Leonard must have burned every incense stick he'd bought.

The cluttered upstairs hall was dim, despite it only being mid afternoon, and Clare felt irritated that she'd not thought to bring a torch. The door to the bedroom was open, just as she'd left it, but she peered through the crack between the door and the jamb to be certain that the bed stood empty. Leonard must still be in the lounge.

Her holdall lay slouched on the floor beneath the window, fresh clothing and the books she'd carried as camouflage already stacked in its gaping maw. She didn't try to be tidy, simply placed a foot on top of the bulk and dragged the limp sides of the holdall around her possessions. A strategy for a quick escape had been pre-planned, though none of them had expected the need for it to arise so soon.

Her toiletries she rescued from the bathroom shelf, her soiled clothing from the laundry bin. She checked the kitchen as best she could. Nothing of herself had to remain in the flat. The only dubious facet was the fuse box in the hall, its cover hanging loose, its main switch turned off. To return the switch would be to flood the lounge with wattage enough to wake him, and wake him was the last thing Clare wanted. If only the individual circuits had been marked she could have isolated the room. She left the switch as it was, refastening the cover.

As the pungent scent began to claw at her throat again, she picked up her bag and shut the door to the stairs after her. In the small car park behind Salmon Grove, Helen would be waiting with the car. In Paragon Station a train would be pulling in to take her south, then to the Tunnel, and back to Paris. Let Julia Marshall pick up the pieces. There was always another day, another year. Leonard Harkin was on the slippery slope and there was only one way for him to slide.

Alice flew down the steps of the Cohen building into the damp evening air, running along the pathway until it opened on to Salmon Grove, only slowing when the sheaf of photocopying tucked beneath her arm threatened to float away on the breeze she was creating.

She'd found it. She'd missed the field trip, but who cared? She'd found it, she knew she had. She hardly dared admit it to herself in case it was her imagination filling in the gaps, but it couldn't be, not now. And she and Nick had been so close when they'd visited Newtondale, so close as to almost touch it. The whole thing was unbelievable. Derventio, the Cawthorne Camps, the road over Wheeldale. She'd kept ignoring the

Roman connections as irrelevant — the shrine would be centuries older — but they were as tied to the shrine as the later Christian houses which ringed the moors with their ruins.

Ever since beginning her search for the water shrine she had visualised it as covering a small area, hardly bigger than any of the springs she'd visited over the years. But why should it? The known goddesses of the Clyde and the Dee had protected great tracts of water and surrounding land. Because there was no lake, no navigable river, she had concentrated on looking for something small when it was obvious, now, that it was the area itself that had been sacred, not in the same league as the isle of Mona, perhaps, but enough for the Roman army to subdue it and the Christian Church to suffocate it. And she wouldn't have made the connection at all if she hadn't been shown that badly-drawn map. That single, simple, cross, almost marking the spot as if it had been treasure. She couldn't believe it. No other map showed the remains of a religious building on that site. She could still hear the misgiving in the assistant's voice.

'There's a note attached to that one. The map's been proven a fake and can't be relied upon for its accuracy. I'm not sure why it's been archived; probably its age.'

'Few maps of the time can be relied upon for their accuracy,' Alice had replied. 'Few of the maps of the time have survived. If I can just transfer it on to a modern Ordnance Survey I'll have a ballpark grid reference, and with a grid reference I'll be able to call up the relevant databases for more information, find out which of the religious houses it belonged to.'

The woman hadn't looked convinced, but Alice knew that it was possible, as long as the information had been placed on a database. At least her own terminal wasn't constrained to the opening hours of the map library. If she needed to work all night, she would.

It was a good turn out for the training session, probably due to the fact that it wasn't raining. Nick hesitated in the doorway, knowing that he didn't want to be there. He'd left Taylor Court sometime after midday, trailing from the Salmon Grove house to the Sanctuary and back to the house again in an effort to kill time and stop himself worrying. It hadn't worked.

He and Alice had had unprotected sex. He could no longer think of it as *making love*. *Making love* was the idyll, the culmination of gratifying sensuality with none of the drawbacks: no AIDS, no STIs, and certainly no off-spring, no baby. He wanted Alice, he wanted to be with her for the rest of his life, and children were sure to put in an appearance sometime, that was the norm, but could they handle it so soon? She might not have caught, of course, he'd kept telling himself that, and even if she had there was that three-day fix available from the Med Centre, wasn't there? But why had she gone that morning, leaving only the note? That's what he couldn't understand. Why hadn't she said something? Surely, surely she knew?

He'd stopped at Brantingham House on the walk across to the Sports Centre, but it had been as silent as the grave with not a light shining from a window. No one had answered a bell, or his fist on the glass. If she'd been there he wouldn't have come to the training session.

Murray gave a wave of acknowledgement and Nick started to walk over to him, but he turned away to resume his discussion with Hodgson. Further down the changing room Bernie Colwyn was reliving part of some game seen on satellite for the benefit of a captive audience. Sitting on a bench by the showers Toby Medavoy was already in his kit, fastening the laces on his boots. He glanced up as Nick approached, but the forced rapport of previous days was missing. A natural enough response, Nick decided, if Louise had given him the elbow, especially if she had cited himself as the reason. He wondered, momentarily, what Louise was playing at, before deciding that he didn't care. He just didn't want to see her on the touchline at the end of the session. He wanted to see Alice.

*

The computer beeped. Another blank. Alice tried not to feel despondent, but her options were running out. If the only map showing the religious site had been deemed a fake by some eminent academic, no matter how thin the reasoning, it was likely that no database would hold any information on it. She checked her e-mails and the bulletin boards she'd contacted, but no one had picked up her queries. If only she'd had a name, something to link it to one of the leading monastic houses, she could have focused her attention there. More and more it was looking as if her only course was going to be to hire a car and walk the site, if she could find it. Even then, with the man-made deforestation and the erosion of centuries, there might be little, or nothing, to see.

She set another search in motion and checked the time. She needed to speak to Nick and it would be hours, yet, before his return. She might go to the Sports Centre. She might yet go to the Sports Centre.

Out on the rugby field they completed their dual circuit beneath the floodlights and began stretching exercises to warm muscles. Nick's ached. No matter which way he leaned he felt a twinge, in his back, his shoulders, his thighs, and after the run he was tired enough to keel over and sleep on the grass.

The inevitable cones were set out and the ball was passed at a run. Murray took over after that, stamping his authority as captain and splitting them into groups. Nick found himself with the two wingers and a full-back to practise punting. Toby Medavoy was quick to partner himself with one of the others, and in pairs they separated down the length of the field to improve their aim. Nick tried not to think of Alice, not to keep looking to the sideline or the bright entrance to the Sports Centre, but she was filling his mind. He'd removed his watch and had no idea of the time. She had to have returned from her field trip by now, had to. It had been dark for hours.

Eventually they got to playing a shortened game. Nick hadn't the heart for it. He couldn't get his wind and was feeling queasy. He hoped to keep out of the play, but the ball kept coming within his reach.

Bernie took him out the first time, catching him a glancing blow which pivoted him on his heel before he was up-ended. He watched his boots rise into the air as his head went down and then everything turned black as Bernie followed through with his weight.

The second tackle he never saw at all. He felt the contact in his upper thigh and he was down, his nose ploughing the turf. Someone grabbed a handful of his shirt and dragged him up, tightening the neckline across his throat, but he was released before he found his feet. The game moved forward, leaving him behind.

Gratefully, he stole a moment's respite. When he opened his eyes he saw that the floodlights had failed. The game was continuing regardless, with spectators on the pitch holding flares to light the way. There were white-winged gulls swooping and twisting through the tracking smoke. The noise was excruciating, with shouting and cheering and high-pitched screaming. It was like an international at Twickenham, but strangely slow, oddly surreal. Nick stood, unable to make sense of it.

An insistent light caught his peripheral vision. Alice was on the sideline. His spirits rose to dip immediately. There was not one person, but three. Alice on the right, her hair flat and controlled in the light which arced behind the triad, Louise on the left, standing there watchful, and in the centre, with his arms possessively round both their shoulders, stood himself.

Nick staggered back. No, not him, like him. More body weight, a full moustache. Flashes of recognition from a darkened mirror, a waxed glass. He watched fingers thicker than his own feeding down to cup a breast. The scarred cheek curved in a grin and there was a mania in the expression, a mania he'd seen in Harkin's face. Nick forced his unresponsive limbs to move, but was stayed by a call. The ball had been punted down-field towards him. It was coming out of the night sky, spinning on its axis, wreathed in a net. Not a net. He caught it with a grunt and clasped it to his shirt. Too heavy, covered in slime, in gore, the same russet as the hair. He held the head at arm's length, a scream erupting from his throat, but they were upon him out of the torchlight, tattooed and naked and bloody, with shouts stronger than his own.

Alice cried out as she saw the pack run over him, hid her face in her hands for the time, the interminable time, it took the players to rise to their feet and free him. He didn't move.

She ran on to the pitch as the team crowded round, shielding him from her sight. She pushed her way through to fall on her knees by his side. Laid on his back, one arm was caught beneath his ribs, one leg tucked up at an awkward angle. Lifeless.

'Nick!'

She reached out to hold him, only to be dragged back with admonishments.

'Someone do something!' But she knew there was nothing to be done.

Third time lucky, he'd told her. Third time lucky, and she'd believed his every word. None of it was true. It was Andrew all over again, dragged from the water. It was the great emptiness of Mark and the constant revving of his motorcycle. She'd killed them. She'd killed them all. And someone was laughing. Unbelievably one of the players was laughing.

Chapter 24

Laying the mobile in her lap, Julia gazed through the rain-streaked windscreen at the lights of the motorway service station. From her enquiries Maeve had discovered that Leonard was officially absent from his teaching post due to ill health.

'Beyond that nothing. It's as if he's disappeared into thin air. What do you think?'

Julia hadn't wanted to think. The headache had intensified as she'd cut the call. She was feeding it herself, she knew that, using it as a blocking device to keep at bay whatever was out there, pressing in with evermore strength the further north she drove. The chill.

It wasn't some figment of her imagination, some banal southern cliché about the northern weather. She'd been born into it. It had blighted her early life, her teenage years. Such was its normality that she hadn't even recognised its hold until she'd escaped.

Again she consulted the map. The M18 was close now. Her finger traced along the route as it fed into the M62, past the Humber Bridge and onto the final stretch into Hull. So close to York. So close to the moors and the National Park. Why couldn't Leonard have stayed in the south, away from its grasp?

The light was very bright. Someone was talking to him, a soft murmur of sound, as soft as the fingers tracing along his cheek. The light resolved into a face, a smiling face of dark hair and brown eyes, of moist, painted lips.

'Welcome back, Nick.'

The face came closer.

'Can you see me okay?'

The moist lips came closer still.

'Nick?'

'Get away. Get away from me.'

He turned his head and pain shot along his shoulders and down his back. He could smell her perfume, sharp and insistent. Man-made. Not a flower scent.

Murray's head filled his vision, his expression questioning. 'Nick?'

'Get her away from me.'

Murray's gaze lifted. 'Call the nurse.'

Nick heard a rustle, a clack of heels. Perfume trailed on her shadow.

'Nick, you're in hospital. There's a few bruised ribs, nothing horrendous, but you've been drifting in and out for hours and making no sense at all. Nick, can you understand me?'

'Alice...'

Footsteps returning. The same clack of heels. The same insistent perfume. A woman in white, not Alice, blinding him with light.

'Mr Blaketon? Nicholas? Follow the light. Let your eyes follow the light. Ah, good. Pleased to have you with us at last. You've been giving your friends quite a turn.'

She moved away.

'I suggest a few minutes only, and then let him sleep.'

Footsteps leaving. Scent, coppery, blood on his tongue.

'Murray?'

His face came into view again. He wasn't in isolation this time. Behind him were yellow curtains, a rail, a window.

'Keep her away, Murray. I don't want her here. I don't want her.'

He saw Murray glance away, then his face came closer, his voice an aggressive hiss.

'I think you're being bloody ungrateful. Louise came with you in the ambulance. She walked you through A&E, and X-Ray. She's filled in more damned forms than for UCAS.'

'Alice. Where's Alice?'

'Good question. That useless piece of work took one look at you and ran.'

The university had been surprisingly easy to find, despite the initial signs sending her to the halls of residence instead of the campus proper. Her intention had been to park the car and walk, but Cranbrook Avenue presented itself while she was searching for the entrance, and Julia brought the car to a halt on the double yellow lines outside Leonard's address.

With trembling fingers she cut the engine. The house was in darkness; at least, there were no lights showing at the front. She wanted to let go the tension she'd used to fuel the mental barriers, to relax and let the chill envelop her so that she could know it for what it was, but she'd manned those barriers too long and too hard for them to fall away so easily.

There were two bells inside the porch. She pressed both simultaneously, maintaining the pressure until a light shone in the hall behind the opaque glass. The door was opened by a bare-footed youth wearing only boxer shorts and a grey T-shirt. He smelled of stale sweat and garlic.

'My name's Julia Marshall. Leonard's ill. I need to see him, and I need to see him now.'

There was no attempt at objection. The youth opened the door wide and pointed to the stairs. 'I don't think he's in. I've not heard anything since we got back.'

'How long ago is that?'

The youth shrugged. 'A couple of hours.'

'Come with me,' she said.

'Are you kidding?'

'No, I'm deadly serious.'

She reached for the banister. The contact gave her an odd, clammy sensation, and she wished she'd been wearing gloves, but she faltered only a moment to look up into the darkness at the top of the flight. She had to do this, for Leonard's sake, but she was pleased when the youth followed her up.

He stood shivering on a lower tread as Julia beat the door with her fist.

'Have you a key?'

'Of course not. He's our landlord; we're not his.'

Julia watched as he hugged himself, moving from foot to foot. It wasn't just her being sensitive now. Even the youth could feel the chill. Dear God... Leonard.

'What's that odour?' he asked. 'Incense?'

She'd been smelling it ever since mounting the stairs. Incense, certainly, and some scent she couldn't grasp. Why couldn't she glimpse something? She needed to relax, to step outside of herself and feel.

'How many are downstairs?'

'There are three of us.'

'Rouse them. We need to break down the door.'

Tree shapes in the darkness. Lattice lights of flaring yellow. Streaks of white that he knew were not gulls shrieking an alarm. Wood-smoke in his nostrils was threatening to fill his lungs and asphyxiate him. He didn't want to be there, knew it wasn't him who was there, but The Other, knew there was nothing he could do to break away.

A screaming woman ran close by, veering through the tree shadows, the remains of her pale clothing flapping as if a broken wing. He tried to lift his arm to hide his eyes, but muscles fought against a weight. In his right hand he held a sword, the decorated hilt shining through the colours of the rainbow as he turned it in the light from the flames. The blade was dripping gore, but it was his hand that fixed his attention. Fingers thicker than they should have been were gripping the hilt and turning it in the light. His fingers, his hand, his entire arm as far as the biceps, was covered in blood that was not his own.

What had he done? Not him. Mustn't think that it was him.

The Other.

Walking. They were walking, stepping over a bloody headless thing that could not have once been human, no. Water. He could hear water lapping, see reflected flames burning in its surface. Someone was standing in its shallows, a woman in white, standing as serene as a marble statue in its shallows.

Mud squelched cold between their toes. Water rose above their ankles, sucking at their legs. As they raised the sword, the woman turned towards them.

No!

At the end of his bed, shimmering in the half-light of the darkened ward, stood a nurse in a white uniform.

'You're all right, Mr Blaketon. It was only a dream.'

Julia expected to be engulfed in a crushing dread, but once the wood began to splinter she found herself coursing with a cold serenity that drove the tension from her muscles and numbed her aching head. It was the young men who were anxious, looking to her for decisions and leadership. When the door finally gave onto the pungent darkness, it was Julia who pressed through the gap.

The electric light didn't work and she sent one of the youths to her car for a torch. The kitchen, the bathroom, the bedroom: each was given a cursory glance before she laid her hand flat on the closed door of the front lounge. There were no vibrations at all. Turning the handle, she let herself in.

The fug was strong enough to make her eyes water and the youth behind her cough. The stick of torchlight was too narrow to gain a full view of the room, and she moved it slowly across the bare boards, hesitating over sigils, a red plastic rope, a half-empty take-away tray, the skin of its discarded contents crazed as if ice had formed. The yellow light jumped when it met a shoed foot. From behind her there was a gasp.

'Stay here,' she said. 'Touch nothing.'

Moving closer, she swept the beam over a leg, two legs, ran it along the torso to the head. The torchlight jumped again, and this time the cry came from her own lips. His eyes were tiny in a bloated face, his open mouth filled with a swollen, purple tongue. The corpse on the floor didn't look like Leonard at all.

'It's a hell of a drastic way to ensure you're not picked for the game tomorrow.'

Murray held open the door as Nick lowered himself carefully into the rusting Toyota.

'It was a joke,' Murray told him. 'You're supposed to laugh.' He closed the door and moved round to settle himself in the driver's seat.

'Are you sure you're okay? Only you look grey. They're releasing you too soon, if you ask me. We can go back inside if you want.'

Nick shook his head. 'Bad night.'

'Tell me about it.' The engine coughed, shuddered and finally caught. Murray drove out of the hospital grounds into the city traffic. 'You positioned yourself under that punt as if you and it had been made for each other, and then you just held the ball away from you like you were trying to hand it to the first bugger who swept up. I couldn't believe what I was seeing.'

Nick stared out of the side window, refusing to be drawn. Visions, that's what they'd been. Not dreams, not even nightmares, least of all the last. He'd seen that sword before, resting in his hand in broad daylight at Derventio.

'Have you spoken to Alice?'

'Why would I possibly want to speak to the wraith?'

'Stop calling her that. Have you seen her?'

Murray turned his eyes from the road to glare at him. 'Start getting arsy and you'll be walking back to the uni.'

'What about Louise, then? They were standing together on the sideline.'

With The Other fondling their breasts.

Nick grimaced back a surge of bile. The Other was real, he

knew it was. Worse, he feared it was a part of himself. Or had been.

'She never cropped up in conversation. All Louise talked about was how you and she had fallen apart, and how bad you were looking, and how she was worried about you—'

'Oh, save the emotional diarrhoea. She's so distraught that the first thing she does is jump into bed with Medavoy.'

'I suggest you save the righteous indignation. I seem to remember you laying her out in full view of the entire team.'

'She's probably fucked the entire team.'

Murray was watching the traffic and didn't respond, but there was something in the bunching of his shoulders and his grip on the steering wheel.

'Did you take her home last night?'

'Of course I did. I'm the one running the fucking taxi service, or hadn't you noticed?'

Nick looked through the windscreen and didn't say anything.

'Don't start giving me the silent treatment. I had a thing going with Louise before you.'

'*Jesus.*'

'Okay, so she sleeps around. So do I. I enjoy it. Why shouldn't she? We're students for Christ's sake. We've our entire lives to get hitched to a relationship. But with you she has a point. Ever since the pair of you split you've been going downhill all the way. Ever since you got hitched to the fucking wraith.'

'You call her that one more time—'

'Me and you, we've shared a few spliffs, sank a few Es, but whatever you and she are downing together it's killing you, Nick. Can't you see that? Don't you look in a mirror? You've taken on her pallor, that look across the eyes. She had her claws into Harkin, didn't she? All that ranting from the terrace of the Union building. You're starting to look like him. Obsessed. And he's dead, Nick. He's history.'

The anger Nick was stoking evaporated. 'Harkin's dead?'

'The corner of your road was blocked last night, well, early hours of this morning. I was leaving Louise's and caught the blue lights. We decided to walk down to see what was breaking. I mean, I didn't know who lived there, but she did.'

'My road?'

'Cranbrook. Opposite side to you, on the corner. I'll drive past it.'

Just behind Taylor Court. Nick couldn't believe how close Harkin lived to Alice, to him.

'And the uni's jumping with rumours,' Murray persisted. He took his eyes from the road to look at Nick. 'Like, would you believe...*Satanic Rites*.'

Murray indicated onto Cranbrook. Ahead cars and vans were parked on the double yellow lines. 'Christ, they're back. They'd gone this— Oh, shit.'

It wasn't the authorities. It was the media.

A uniformed policeman was standing beneath the porch, and a barrier carrying blue and white tape had been set in the gutter running round the house onto Salmon Grove. Murray had to take it slowly into the junction so many people were milling about. One woman, carrying a fluffy microphone, knocked on Nick's window.

'Are you a student at the university? Will you talk to us?'

Nick refused to meet her gaze, even as she trotted beside the car, tapping on the glass.

'Keep driving,' he told Murray.

'I will. I will.'

Vans carrying satellite dishes were parked up the kerb on the patch of grass close to Taylor Court. Oblivious to their safety, people stood out in the road as their car approached. Lights flashed on hand-held cameras; one shone bright above a shoulder-mounted video.

Murray gasped. 'I'm not stopping here. We'll get eaten alive. You're coming back to my flat.'

'I need to see Alice.'

'You want to lead this lot to her door? You can ring her.'

*

'No, I'm not from Hull. This is the first time I've visited the city. I told this to the uniformed officer, the one I gave the statement to at the house last night. This morning,' Julia corrected.

She gazed at the detective sitting opposite her. She mustn't stare at him, she mustn't. He'd jump to the wrong conclusions. Closing her eyes she shook her head.

'I'm sorry if I'm a bit short but I'm terribly tired, you must understand that. I put in a full day's work yesterday and then drove up from Oxford. I stayed with the Police as long as they wanted me. They were very good about finding me that hotel room, but I didn't exactly get much sleep.'

'Yes, we're, er, sorry that we had to move you. Hopefully you won't get pestered now.'

'The nerve of that man. Was he from one of the tabloids? How did they get to know so quickly? How did he know how to find me?'

'The usual way. Someone rang them. In fact, the way it seems to be panning out, someone rang every media outlet in the country and started feeding them juicy information. It's a wonder the city isn't gridlocked.' He altered his weight in his seat. 'It's a pity, too, that that someone didn't think to feed it direct to us.'

She noted the change in his tone, saw, again, the occasional flickering, very faint, above the curls of his sandy hair.

'What sort of juicy information?'

'The sort tabloids relish. Most of it, of course, will be pure fiction, and that's what I hope you'll be able to help us with: separating the fact from the fiction.'

He lifted the top sheet of stapled papers and scanned the handwriting. 'There are plenty of people who can give us details about his day to day life: colleagues, neighbours, students...' he smiled at her '...but no one who's known him so long, who can give us his background in such detail. I hope you don't mind.'

When the first police officers had arrived at Leonard's house and seen the state of his lounge they'd turned unnaturally quiet. Julia hadn't attempted to hide anything; it would have only made things worse. She'd given her statement to the young constable knowing that would be only the start, and spent the rest of the night deciding which facts she could disclose and which she'd better keep secret. The possibility of a media frenzy hadn't entered her mind.

The detective began to skim over her statement and she took the opportunity to study him unobserved. The flickering was still faint, but it was enclosing his head like a hood, tendrils licking at his shoulders. It could no longer be dismissed as a reflection from the fluorescent lighting.

'You're not a native of Hull and have never visited the city before, even though Leonard Harkin has lived here for several years. Is that right? Oh, yes. Here it is. You're from York originally, and that was where you first met him. In the 70s.' He raised his gaze and smiled. 'Flowers and bells and free love.'

'I think you're mixing the decades.'

'Mmm,' he said, and she knew that it had been meant.

'We lived together for some years, moved south, but the relationship didn't last. I wanted stability, to stay in the south. He wanted to return north. He used to be a keen walker, a naturalist. He illustrated a number of books. He sent me copies over the years.'

'An amicable parting, then?'

'I was barely seventeen when I met him, he not much older. We'd both matured. Grew apart as we grew up, I suppose you could say.'

'You never got back together, even for a short time?'

'No.'

'And neither of you married.'

Julia wasn't sure where this was leading. From all that had happened, and her lack of sleep, she felt somewhat unco-ordinated. A sense of self-preservation had made her enter into a first stage relaxation so that she would be more able to interpret his signals, but she'd never expected to see his aura. She'd never expected to see anyone's aura ever again.

'You kept in touch,' the detective prompted.

'For a while, yes, but our correspondence declined to the usual Christmas card, and even that fizzled out. I had no idea that he'd taken a post at the university here, not until he contacted me at the beginning of the year.'

'Why did he contact you?'

'He said that he'd been thinking about me a lot and decided to get in touch. It wasn't until he visited me in March that I realised there was more to it, that he was heading for a breakdown.'

'You have a medical background to be able to make such an assessment?'

'My business card is in your hand, detective.'

'Ah, yes. Hypno-therapist.'

'Stress management. Leader in relaxation techniques. As well as my private, and corporate, clients, I'm attached to two medical centres in the Oxford area. I help people who are overcoming heart attacks, strokes; people who are being weaned off tranquillisers, those on stringent medical diets. I could, if you wanted, help you to give up smoking.' She looked pointedly at his nicotine-stained fingers.

'I'm sure you could,' he said. 'Did you try to help Leonard Harkin give up his addiction?'

'Leonard didn't want to give up cigarettes.'

'I was thinking more along the lines of controlled substances. Class A to be precise.'

Julia stared at him. The detective stared back. His aura was intensifying to a discernable glow.

'Did you know that he had a predilection for young women?' he asked.

'Predilection?'

'Some people, if they were of a mind, might call it preying, and where better to prey on young women than to stand as an authority figure on a university campus, especially if he were offering drugs in exchange for somewhat, shall we say, dubious sexual favours?'

'I don't believe that.'

He flicked over the statement and looked at her again.

'It says here that you drove up to Hull because you feared for his mental stability. Why didn't you ring the Humberside Police and get us to check on him? If his mental stability was as bad as you thought, we could have gained him medical help. Why waste vital hours driving all the way up from Oxford? Or were you more worried that the drugs he was using could be traced back to you?'

She heard his voice on the line and the tears came again, streaming down her cheeks as her heart swelled with relief.

'Speak to me, Alice. Are you there?'

'Nick... Nick, are you all right?'

'Yes, I'm fine. It was just concussion. They kept me in overnight for observation. How are you? Your mobile's switched off. Are you okay? It's taken me an age to get through on this phone. Cindy told me that you'd been besieged there. I tried to come to see you, but we couldn't get out the car. I'm at Murray's place.'

His breathing grew heavy down the line, as if he were cupping the mouthpiece close. 'Alice, we've got to talk. And you've got to be frank with me. Something very weird is going down. Alice, do you remember telling me that you once thought you might be an empath? That you thought that you could see things?'

A cold prickling started to run along her shoulders.

'Alice, are you there? Are you listening?'

'Yes.'

'I know this sounds crazy, but I've been seeing things, weird things, horrendous things. Alice, I think you might be in danger.'

Her voice was a mere breath. 'It's not me. It was never me.'

'What? Speak up, I can't hear you.'

'It's not me who's in danger.'

'You know!'

She gripped the phone tight, closed her eyes tighter still. 'I've always known. I told you, and you made me believe it wasn't true. It is. Nick, you mustn't come near me.' He started to say something, but she moved the handset away from her ear and shouted. 'Stay away from me! Don't you understand? Stay away!'

Slamming down the phone, she turned back for her room, tears filling her eyes. Cindy was blocking her path.

'Are you having trouble with him again?'

'It's on! It's on!'

The shout from the open kitchen door caught their attention. Someone was turning up the volume on the television.

'*...of Hull. Police were called to a house close to the campus where lecturer, Leonard Harkin, was found dead in suspicious...*'

Alice stared at the photograph filling the screen.

What went through her mind when she saw Leonard Harkin's room? Did she think the marks on the floor held ritual significance? Had he ever spoken to her about the Mother Earth Society? Covens? Witchcraft? His hoard of pornographic pictures? No, of course she wasn't being formally interviewed. She was adding to her original statement, helping the police with their enquiries.

It went on for ever and Julia felt she couldn't call a halt without it seeming that she had something to hide. Throughout, his aura had kept strengthening, either that or her ability to interpret it. But the detective had given her a vital piece of information. Someone had been with Leonard when he'd died; someone who left lipstick smears on stubbed out cigarettes. The detective hadn't used the exact words, but Julia was in no doubt that she wasn't to leave Hull. She didn't want to leave Hull. She wanted to find Alice Linwood before the police did. She wanted to take her south before it was too late.

Chapter 25

Despite the onset of evening, and the double yellow lines, media cars were parked along Cranbrook Avenue, though there seemed to be only one journalist out on foot, talking to the policeman at Leonard's gate. More vehicles stood on the side street. As Julia drove round the corner a man wearing a disposable white jumpsuit walked out of the walled rear yard, and she realised that the media would be sitting there for days. Everyone was working on the premise that Leonard had been murdered. Perhaps they weren't wrong. She would have to be careful.

Parking her car by the administration block, Julia made her way through the campus towards the Taylor Court residences where she knew Alice Linwood had a room. The unfamiliar walkways were thronged with students and, it seemed to Julia, a great many uniformed security staff. At a distance their individual auras were undetectable, but up close... up close she kept her eyes trained on the ground.

She realised she had taken a wrong turning as soon as she noticed the vans with their satellite dishes parked beyond the tiny birchwood plantation. She was heading for the road back to Leonard's house, and it was there, at the edge of the leafless trees, that she first felt it. Not the chill, but an amalgam of emotions which grew more intense as she trod the winding path: rancour, malice, vicious supremacy. It howled from a house across the road, from an upstairs room. She saw shapes beyond the shadowed glass, bursts of light, yellow and red, angular flashes of white. Leonard had told her that the girl had sent a guardian to warn him away. So close to Leonard. Alice Linwood had bound him within an eternal triangle. No wonder he'd been unable to defend himself.

The trail of the guardian was so well-worn as to be almost luminescent on the pavement. Ignoring the vehicles and their inhabitants, Julia followed it directly in to Taylor Court. At the covered gateway the signature began to change, overwhelmed by the chill reaching out from Brantingham House. It was so integral to the courtyard that Julia sensed the brick-laid paving was no longer anchored to its solid foundations, but was floating, as if a raft, on a liquid base. Ahead, caught in the yellow light from the porch lamp, two men and a blonde woman were arguing on the semi-circular steps.

Julia faltered. She was no longer following the guardian's trail. He was there, in front of the doorway, his violence a fiery aura around him.

'What do you mean, she's not in? I spoke to her on the phone not twenty minutes ago.'

'And left her in tears. Again.'

The young woman crossed her arms in a deliberate show of defending the doorway. Julia felt a sudden dread for her safety and hurried closer.

'Don't you understand?' she heard the guardian say. 'She's in danger.'

'Too true,' the blonde retorted. 'From you, y'bastard.' Her face lifted and a finger shot out towards Julia. 'If you're here sniffing for a story, you can get the hell out of it as well!'

The young men swung round, the guardian stepping out of the shadow of his bulkier companion. Malevolence reached out with his gaze, but it was the sight of him that confounded Julia. He was stooped, holding himself awkwardly as if in pain, his scarred face the colour of parchment. It hadn't just been Leonard. Through Alice Linwood the chill had been feeding from them both.

'No, I—' Julia came as close as she dared. 'I'm a friend of Leonard Harkin. I came to see Alice.'

As she knew he would, the guardian reacted. It was a relief to see his companion catch at his arm.

'Alice didn't know Harkin.'

'She did.'

They all turned to the young woman blocking the doorway. She seemed taken aback by the attention, and awkwardly gestured behind her.

'Alice recognised his picture on the television.' She glared at the guardian, her self-assurance returning. 'Just after she cut the call to you. She sort of freaked, kept saying that he wasn't a lecturer, that he was a gardener, a gardener of all things, that he'd dug a pond.'

'He did,' Julia confirmed. 'Where the seat is. I made him fill it in. It was part of the obsession, part of her link to him.' She was keeping a wary eye on the guardian. His aura was changing colour, his violence subsiding, being overtaken by a spurt of confused anguish. She'd never seen anything like it. He was radiating his emotions.

'What link?' the young woman demanded.

'He knows,' Julia said gently. 'She's doing the same to you. What's your name?'

'His name's Nicholas Blaketon,' his bulky companion answered. 'And you're right about this obsession with the wraith. I don't care what anyone else believes, I think she's weird. She's certainly got some kind of hold over him.'

Julia held her breath as the guardian caught him a backhanded blow to the chest.

'She's in danger, I tell you. Why does no one listen to me?'

The thick-set young man curled his lip. 'Try that again, you prat, and I'll fill you in where you stand. You're getting far too frisky with those fists.'

'Please, we must remain calm. It's feeding from your anger.'

The bulky companion swung his attention to Julia. 'What is?'

Julia ignored the question and looked purposely at the woman on the step. 'Do you know where Alice Linwood has gone?'

'No idea. Staying one step ahead of him, if you ask me. She lit out with a bag and a rucksack as if her life—'

'A *rucksack?*'

Pushing the girl aside, Nicholas Blaketon strode into the house. His companion looked at Julia, shook his head and followed. Julia brought up the rear, trying to calm the girl, trying to stop her from confronting the guardian. As soon as they entered the inner corridor Julia let her go.

The smell of wood sap was forcefully intrusive. Twigs were breaking beneath her feet, a flower fragrance filling her nostrils. It was difficult to keep to the reality of the corridor. The chill was seeping, wet, from the wood-lined walls. They were in single file, hacking through the thicket to the source, kicking at the portal. Very close, they were. It was drawing them. The source was drawing them all, just as it had during the relaxation session when Maxine—

Julia cried out, but her warning was lost beneath the sound of tearing wood as the door splintered along the line of the lock and burst open. She took a breath, expecting them to be engulfed in water, but not so much as a trickle met Nicholas Blaketon as he crossed the threshold. Elbowing the others aside, Julia stood in the opening, afraid to venture further. Her breath was misting in front of her face, the cold tearing at her lungs.

'It wasn't Leonard,' she gasped. 'It was you I saw drowning in the pool!'

The guardian turned to face her, his eyes wide.

'You've got to get out of this room,' she told him, 'away from here, from Hull. You've got to leave now, come south with me. We can outrun it if you come south with me now.'

He shook his head. 'Alice—'

'It's too late for Alice. She'll *kill* you. She's killed Leonard. God knows how many others are dead because of her.'

'No! It's not true!'

Julia saw the violence rise in him and took a step back as he advanced on her, his right fist out before him as if he were holding a weapon. He was. She saw it in milky outline. A rod of some kind. A short-bladed sword that faded with his violence.

'*It's him.* If you can see me drowning, why can't you see *him*?

She's the one in danger. He's going to kill her at the pool. He's done it before. I was there. I was covered in blood.'

'What the fuck—?'

'Murray, she was going to the map library. She knows where the shrine is. That's where she's running to. We've got to find her, stop her from reaching it. He's waiting for her there. He— He could even be taking her there.'

Julia raised a hand. 'Why would she run, Nicholas? Why wouldn't she wait for you?' She watched him falter, shaking his head. 'She believes it, doesn't she? She's trying to protect you. She believes you'll die if you're close to her.'

'She's got it wrong.'

He turned in the narrow space between the bed and the computer table, spied something on the floor beneath the window and fell on it: a pile of Ordnance Survey maps. On his knees, he spread them on the carpet in an arc, his back to her. The angle of his head, his shoulder, the way his feet were tucked beneath him, it brought images of Leonard at the same age, poring over his own maps, following contours, measuring ley lines, searching, always searching for that nameless elusive.

And the wet beaded on the walls, dripped from the shelving, puddled around the maps encircling him, keeping them afloat while it covered his feet and rose up his thighs.

'Nicholas, get out of there!' Julia turned to his friend. 'Get him out! Get him out!' She beat her fist on Murray's chest, saw his shocked expression, knew he'd believe her mad, but he moved, strode through the door, walked through the water as if it wasn't there.

'Nick, come on...'

His arm was shrugged away. 'There's only five. There should be six. One's missing. I don't know which one it is. Murray, help me!'

'Okay, okay. Let's be logical. One's missing. She went to the map library.' He checked his wristwatch. 'It'll still be open. Take the maps. They'll know which one's missing if it's a sequence. They'll know what she asked for, what she was looking for.'

Julia watched in shuddering relief as the guardian swept the maps into his hands and splashed through the water to the dry of the corridor. Murray followed, hesitating at her shoulder as his friend headed for the outer door.

'That do you?'

'You mustn't let him go,' she said. 'You mustn't let him follow her.'

'How the hell am I supposed to stop him?'

Julia trailed after them, a ghost in her own life. Nicholas Blaketon had looked so much like Leonard, the maps spread in a crescent around him. The room was a rectangle, the water in her mind filling it from wall to wall, yet still the sense was circular, as circular as the vision of the pool where she'd seen him drowning. She'd told Leonard that he would be protected inside a circle, but the circle had been a trap. She'd reached out from Oxford and killed him as if with her own hand. She had done to Leonard what Alice would do to Nicholas, unless she could stop him from following her, and she wasn't sure that she could.

Her feet were cold, her hands, too. The chill was unrelenting, stronger than she'd ever known it. Or she weaker. Older and weaker.

An argument was developing at the counter. How easily Nicholas slipped from anxiety to frustration to violence. He was spreading maps on a table, one rolled, one folded. Something about an historic counterfeit, that the girl had been told it was unreliable, but Julia knew that it wasn't a fake, couldn't be a fake. She could see threads of mist nudging from beneath the edge of the rolled parchment. It was building into skeins, writhing down the legs of the table. Dragging aside her gaze, she stared at the carpet, her hand to her mouth, desperate to stem her fear. The source was reaching out for them. Only she could see it, and no one would listen.

The guardian blocked her view, his weight leaning to the left. He lowered on to his haunches, their faces almost level. The anxiety, the frustration, the anger, had been replaced by the cutting chill of the source.

'You can see without the need for touch.'

It wasn't a question. His gaze was fixed, his eyes unblinking. Terrified, Julia shook her head.

'Don't lie to me,' he whispered. 'Don't ever lie to me.'

Tendrils of mist were coiling about his feet and lower limbs, rising in fingers behind his shoulders to caress his neck.

'I need the location. I need Alice.'

His breathing was altering. He was sending himself into a ragged trance, reaching deep inside himself. For what? Dear God, for what?

'Don't do this, Nicholas.'

His dark eyes glittering, his scarred cheek rising in a grin, the guardian began pumping his muscles, exuding the controlled menace of the psychotic.

'Think what delights I could bring by my touch.' His hand reached towards her face, thick fingers extending in a fan.

Julia scrambled across the chairs to get away from him. 'I'll find her! I'll find her!'

She hid behind Murray, using his bulk as a shield. 'Keep him away from me,' she whispered. 'Tell him to give me a minute. I can't function.'

She was trembling, with cold and with fear, as bad, worse, than when she'd been young, when the visions had come every night, every day, and they'd said that it was her imagination, that she was an hysteric, that she was insane.

The library table had changed from a rectangle to a circle, its wooden apron deep, its legs short. Mist was pouring from the wooden cauldron's rim. Ice had crazed over the wet surface of the rolled map, distorting its lines and its icons. Julia brushed her hand across, melting it to water, but its inked details ran one into another making it unreadable. The more she touched, the more the water rose, seeping up from the parchment, filling the cauldron, pouring from its rim as the mist had before it, falling to the floor to wet her feet, to rise up her ankles with a terrible, seeping, cold. The guardian was behind her, mirroring her stance, his breath an icy threat on her neck.

She couldn't function like this, couldn't. Why didn't Murray keep him away? It was a table, a table. There were maps. They were dry. She had to make herself believe the reality and ignore the vision.

But the water rose relentlessly, bubbling, as if from a spring, running onto the modern Ordnance Survey, running in a line, a line of clear liquid, to puddle and spread from a single centre.

Julia jabbed her finger in it. 'There!'

A pencil came across her arm to mark the place on a map that was dry: the guardian, quiet now. The librarian pulled the parchment from a table that was square and the mist disappeared, the water, too. Julia was left reeling; it had all happened so fast.

'I trust you will all now leave,' the librarian snapped, 'before I call Security.'

Nicholas was folding the Ordnance Survey. 'I need the Toyota.'

Murray looked at Julia.

'Give him the keys,' she said.

'You told me—'

'Have you seen nothing here? Give him the keys!'

The keys were passed. Julia pulled out her wallet and tossed over her paper money. Without a word Nicholas scooped up the notes and strode towards the door. Murray started after him, but Julia clasped his arm and refused to let him follow.

Chapter 26

She'd known Leonard Harkin. He'd been there, every day, landscaping the pond area. But a lecturer?

She'd spoken to him. He'd made her smile. Had they talked about the Romano-British links to Taylor Court? Of her research? Alice couldn't remember. She must have done. And now he was dead. Not Nick as she'd feared, but this Leonard Harkin who had been there, every day, grubbing a pond from the earth in front of the house, talking to her, smiling at her, walking with her as she crossed the campus. So innocent. So calculated it made her shudder.

Nick was in danger from her and he would not accept the truth of it. Andrew and Mark she had been unable to warn; this Leonard Harkin she didn't want to think about, but Nick... She had to put distance between them, had to keep him out of her life. One of them had to escape.

Ognirius revelled in the woman's panic, in her disjointed thoughts, in her surges of adrenalin. Echoes welled up from long ago: the screams of the acolytes, the gurgling croaks of Yslan at the Pool. He could smell the smoke from their burning dwellings, see the yellow flames painting bright their open doorways. He had felt energised that night, so energised he could have touched the stars. And it had been only the beginning, the first stage of the plan he and Gaius Senecio had devised together. When the Foreigners had marched into the stockade to decree his be the voice of the People, giving him the power, it had fulfilled his every dream. No one could speak against him, not while he was backed by the might of Derventio, the might of Rome.

*

The rain hit as Nick crossed the bridge. It jumped out of the sky and pounded the windscreen as if the earth had turned over and the river was emptying itself on the car. He fought the unfamiliar instrument panel, trying to find the Toyota's wiper control. As the blades scored an arc through the deluge, the glass filled with the stone frontage of a building and he thought his heart would burst. Dragging on the steering wheel, the car began to turn, only for it to aquaplane away from his control. There was a blinding flash of headlights and the Doppler effect of an elongated car horn. The offside tyres hit the kerb and the car tilted sideways to fall back on to its four wheels and shudder.

Nick let out his breath. The engine was still running. The steering wheel still turned. He was sitting in the path of oncoming traffic, but somehow nobody had hit him. What speed had he been doing across the bridge? Where the hell was this? Malton? What speed had he been doing to reach Malton so soon?

Steadying himself, he waited for a gap in the traffic before making an ascent of the hill. Not until he was passing the cold fields of Derventio did he notice the oil warning lamp blinking at him from the dash, and the needle of the petrol gauge nosing into the red.

Pickering and its rolling vale had been left behind, the road narrowing the higher it climbed, its rough metalled surface awash. Each time she left the shelter of the conifers the wind attempted to throw the hired car into the ditch.

Alice checked the speedometer. Fifteen miles an hour. With neither cat's eyes nor white markings, even on full beam she could hardly make out the road ahead for the siling rain. If a deer jumped out in front of her neither of them would have a chance.

She'd filled the rucksack in a hurry, giving no thought to where she would sleep, that night or any other. She'd not be able to return to the campus for days; Nick would be sitting outside her door. She tried not to think of him. To think of him was to pull him to her, to endanger him. She had to find somewhere to sleep. If she'd brought the down bag she could have pulled the car off the road on to a forestry track, but she'd just brought her weatherproofs and they'd only keep her dry, not warm.

White light flashed in the rear view mirror and was gone. It flashed a second time. Alice peered into the silvered glass, but there was nothing there. The steady gradient was deceptive, though. There were dips in the narrow road. Again light was reflected in the mirror. She hadn't been mistaken. Another vehicle was coming up fast, despite the weather.

Trees crowded in at the muddy verge. Her headlights picked out the lighter wood of logs, trimmed and stacked for collection. By them, a gap. Alice swung on to it, hoping the following car would see her in the poor visibility. It tore past, high on its axles, kicking up spray in its wake.

Driving was much easier keeping its rear lights in view, and Alice rose through the gears using the off-roader as a guide. She wondered where she was exactly, how close to Wheeldale Moor. There was no shelter up there, not even trees.

Ahead, brake lights shone and disappeared. The Land Rover had turned off the metalled road. Alice slowed as she drew level with a rutted drive, at its end a security lamp. She saw figures run from a vehicle to a farmhouse porch. Slamming on the brakes, she leaned on the horn and reversed.

The warning light kept blinking red on the shadowy dash. Nick had topped up the oil when he'd stopped at the petrol station, though God knew he'd made it by seconds before it closed. The attendant was noting figures on the pumps and hadn't taken kindly to his plea for the power to be switched on again.

The fold of twenties in his pocket had come as a shock. For long moments he had stared at them before adding more fuel to the tank. Inside the cabin the warmth made him realise how ill prepared he was. His jacket wasn't even rainproof. He peeled away another note to buy a plastic raincoat, a wool ski hat, some chocolate and a torch. It wasn't until he was back in the Toyota that he noticed the lack of road atlas. He'd driven north on memory alone.

And the warning light kept blinking red on the shadowy dash. If he could get to Pickering on the road signs he could follow the Ordnance Survey map. Alice wouldn't cross the moors in the dark, not in such weather.

'Why didn't you find a bed & breakfast in Pickering?' The thin-faced woman had introduced herself as Rosemary, her husband as Phil. 'It was lucky we'd been out to the cinema or we'd be well in bed by this hour.'

'Should be in any case,' her husband muttered. 'Some of us are up at five.'

'Half past, don't exaggerate. Put the kettle on for some cocoa.' She turned back to Alice. 'You look as if you could do with a cup. A bit of supper, too?'

Phil shuffled towards the open kitchen door. 'Aye, well...'

Rosemary kept her smile in place, but the tension was unmistakable. Alice's heart sank. It reminded her of her parents' home.

'Ignore him,' Rosemary whispered. 'He didn't enjoy the film.'

Nick kicked at the tyre in his frustration and shouted into the driving rain.

'Bastard!'

The rhythmic thunk, thunk, thunk, coming from the rear of the car could not be ignored, and he had slowed looking for somewhere safe to park. There had been few vehicles after

Pickering, and he'd certainly not passed any since leaving the main road, but that didn't mean that some milk tanker wouldn't come tearing along and ram the Toyota from behind as soon as he turned off its lights.

Dragging the woolly hat over his head, he fought the wind for the plastic raincoat he'd bought. Even though he'd picked up an Extra Large it hadn't been made to take a jacket beneath. The two middle buttons he forced through their holes, but he gave up on the rest.

Murray was a pilfering slob. The Toyota's boot was a stinking tip of empty beer cans, mildewed clothing and discarded takeaway cartons. Beneath it all was a traffic cone. Everything had to be removed to enable him to reach the spare wheel in the well under the flooring. He tried to heave it out, only to find that it was secured in place by a rusted wing nut. The tool roll gave up an adjustable spanner, but his fingers were numb and wet, and he had to use both hands to gain a purchase. All the while the wind sawed at the boot lid, threatening to close its jaws on his ribs.

By the time he had the spare leaning next to the flat, his body ached and his jeans were glued to his legs. He played rugby in the rain and had never thought much about it, but here he wasn't moving. He was wet and cold, and the cold was sapping. When he made a fist a pain shot along his right arm and shoulder, and he couldn't breathe deeply without feeling his ribs. At the hospital he'd been assured that he'd sustained nothing worse than bruising. He wasn't so certain any more.

In the boot he flashed the torch around the well for the jack. There wasn't one. An oily rag, some sweet papers, that was all that had been hidden beneath the spare. It had to be inside the car, under one of the seats or the shelf beneath the steering column.

Nothing.

He opened the bonnet, nearly losing it to the gusting wind. The beam was flashed over the engine, into every crevice. There was nothing wrapped in plastic, nothing fastened to the chassis supports. He slammed down the bonnet.

'Murray, you bastard!'

Supper was bread, cheese and pickle, all of it, Alice noted, home-made, and despite never having tasted cocoa, the drink was warm and satisfying.

'A history student, are you?' Rosemary repeated. 'Our son's at Cardiff studying engineering. He's in his last year.'

Her husband grunted. 'And he'll not be back here when he's done, neither. Not for him getting up at five every morning. You after the ghost road, are you?'

Alice blinked at him.

'Across the moor,' he said. 'The legion.'

'Take no notice, dear. He's trying to unnerve you.'

'It's not some long-dead Romans she needs to have a mind for, but the weather and the iron workings. Label it a National Park and idiots from the city think they can tramp these hills as if it's full of flowerbeds.'

'Phil!'

'Well... Break a leg up there, young lady, and you won't be found for weeks. Shouldn't be on your own.'

'I'll be sure to leave a note of the route I'm taking,' Alice told him.

'Aye, well, that's as maybe.' He stood. 'I'm going to bed.'

Alice watched him leave before turning to his wife. 'Is there a history of supernatural sightings in this area?'

'Unexplained, perhaps. I wouldn't say supernatural. Mind you,' she inclined her head towards the curtained window where the rain was hitting the glass with the force of tossed gravel, 'sitting in electric light listening to that lot can be quite eerie on occasion. Sitting listening to it in nothing more than candlelight would be enough to send most folks batty.'

*

The plastic raincoat was leaking along a shoulder seam. Either that or the water was trickling from his head to his jacket collar and through the material to his skin. His hands were so cold his fingers wouldn't bend fully, and the continual slapping of the raincoat against his sodden jeans felt as if it was leaving great weals on his legs. He'd calculated five miles on the Ordnance Survey map he'd slotted beneath his jacket, and five miles was nothing. He'd run more than that during a training session. Every step he took, though, was marked by the squelching of his trainers. The inner soles were beginning to disintegrate, pieces of the foam-backed material rubbing between his toes.

Pausing a moment, he flexed his aching leg. He couldn't go back. Where were the vehicles to pick him up? Besides, Alice was ahead. Five miles, that's all. Just five miles. There was nowhere to hide a car. He'd come across it and she'd be there. She was scared. She wasn't stupid. She wouldn't cross the moor in this.

With the aid of the torch he trudged the narrow road, trying to keep to the nearside tyre track worn into the metalled surface. The puddles were fuller there, but the over-sized stone chippings less numerous. His feet needed all the help they could get.

Pictures of The Other kept rising in his mind, filling him with disquiet; pictures of The Other leaning over Alice's shoulder, cupping a breast, his grin a lascivious sneer. The Other had been with them, a part of him, when he'd been making love to Alice. Whose hands? Whose tongue and teeth? Nick didn't want the answers, couldn't stop the questions. And the vision of the bloody sword grasped in his hand — *his* hand. The screaming, the stench, the sight of Alice standing in the water... Had that been the past? The future? Was the past about to repeat itself?

A tear trickled down his rain-wet cheek. He felt stupid for releasing it, weak and useless in the face of so much he didn't understand. Alice was in danger. He clung to that belief.

*

Elementals clashed against the dwelling in noisy disarray, finding chinks in the wood and stone to mewl and whine for his attention. Ognirius snubbed them with contempt. What need had he of wind and rain, so long his sole companions? He was a man restored now, or would be soon.

Drawing himself from the woman, he inspected his form. Colours were growing brighter, no longer milky pale. There was substance to his flesh, spongy yet, but all was returning. He peered at his forearm, at the short hairs as russet as a hind's on his skin. He stroked them, marvelling at their texture, at the detail, all the detail: the standing veins on the back of his hand, the calluses on his fingers, the glint of gold tight against his knuckles, sensed the weight of the torc about his neck. Such workmanship, for him alone. He sighed, a breath across a reed-filled pond. So many jewels left behind, so much tribute through his hands he would never see again: captives for his blood-lust, maidens for his bed-lust, children for the slave ships in return for wine and silken cloth. And who had dared to speak against him with Yslan gone and the Foreigners at the gate?

His lip curled as he thought of Gaius Senecio. Such tales he had told, of the luxuries of Rome a hundred-fold more than Derventio could offer, of the tribute funding a villa bigger than all enclosed by the People's stockade, of the welcome awaiting him, of the ride along the Processional Way. Just one more wagon-load; just one more season. And then, like hail on a summer pasture, he had gone, taking the tribute, the ship, taking his men.

Derventio deserted. He'd thrust a blade through the liar who had brought the news. A mistake, true. The first voice was raised before the man was cold, and then all were yapping, like the dogs they brought to hunt him. And She... *She —*

Bunching his fist, Ognirius turned and slammed it through the bedding into the woman who slept beneath. She shrieked, and opened her eyes as wide as Yslan had opened hers. He wanted her to see him, to know him for what he was, what he could do and would do, but as she whimpered he drew into the shadows. There was a better way to torment her than with the bruises he had dealt the boy. She coveted the gladius. They all coveted the gladius.

Turning to the elementals, the rain and the wind, he coaxed them towards him with praise and honeyed words. Together they would build a vision where even the trees would return.

There had been no crossroads shown on the map, Nick was certain, but that's where he was standing, at the centre of a crossroads with no signposts to mark the way. Nothing showed in the beam from the torch, nothing but the worn metalled roadway and the torrential rain, each drop a silver crystal in the light. Had he mistaken the road on the map? Had he been on the wrong route, even driving the car?

He pulled the Ordnance Survey from inside his jacket. The strain snapped the buttonholes on the raincoat and it flapped open, its edges whipping him across the cheek. He tried to tent it around himself to protect the map, but the wind was too strong, his hands too cold. Holes appeared along the paper's creases, ripping as the gusts sucked and eddied around him. For fear of losing it, he gathered it into a bundle and stuffed it inside his jacket.

What use was a map that he couldn't read? Alice wouldn't cross the moors in this. She'd be somewhere warm and dry. He was the fool. She feared she would cause his death, and it would happen if he carried on. He'd be found in some ditch, dead from hypothermia. He needed shelter. He needed warmth. There had to be farms up here. It was moorland, not an arctic waste.

Which junction? He'd take the left, he decided; give it ten minutes, and if there were neither buildings nor light he'd turn back and take another route.

The stone wall beyond the verge dissolved into moss-covered blocks littering the ground, beyond that was nothing he could discern. To his right regimented rows of conifer blacked out any sign of a horizon. Ahead, tufts of grass and weeds were growing through the worn surface of the road. Potholes deep enough to twist an ankle lurked beneath the puddles. Stones bigger than his hand thrust up through the crumbling asphalt, the foundations of the road. This route was leading nowhere.

He missed his footing, twisted, caught himself before he fell, and stood upright. Disorientated now, he didn't know which line was ahead and which back the way he'd come.

His blisters were killing him, his back, his leg, his shoulder. He was so cold. He couldn't go on. It was useless. What the hell did he think he was doing?

Shutting his eyes, he sank to his knees among the puddled stones, grateful for the relief in his feet. The rain pounded on the plastic raincoat, a sound that grew steadily more rhythmic. There was a vibration beneath his hands, a prickling between his shoulders. He opened his eyes knowing that the sound was not simply the rain. Something was coming along the roadway, something big. A lift, at last.

He stood to flash the torch, and realised that although the downpour remained the same, the road underfoot did not. Gone were the potholes, the eroded foundations. It wasn't asphalt, or chippings pressed into tarmac. The camber was noticeably higher, and at the edge, close to where he stood, a wide gutter ran with a stream of churning water. Beyond— beyond the trees were gone. No, they were there, at the extreme of his vision. He could see... branches waving. Not conifers, deciduous trees.

A call, an answer, another call. Nick killed the light and kept very still. The solid retort of metal against leather. Not a vehicle. The regular tramp of feet. His chest seemed to crumple. When he blinked he was bent so far over as to touch the roadway with one hand. Filling his lungs with air, with fire, he dragged himself up, half-limping, half-running up the roadway looking for a place to leave it, a place, a delve, anything, anywhere to hide. The sound was growing louder. He knew what it was. He'd heard it at Derventio. Just a flash, that's all there'd been, when he'd seen a jewelled sword in his hand melt into the daylight and thought that his mind was playing tricks. But this wasn't a flash. He could hear singing now, a low-pitched single voice, an answering chorus of many; singing to keep the rhythm of the march. They'd see him. Dear God, they'd see him. Ahead— ahead was something, something close to the roadway waving white, a marker beneath it.

A single tree stood by the roadway, hardly taller than himself, a mere shrub devoid of leaves but waving strips of cloth, leather straps, a woven cord with a trinket attached, spinning in the wind. Nick drew breath as Alice's explanation returned clear to his mind: *The spring's near Stape, a little way into the planted forestry. The Roman Road ran right by it but the modern road is a hundred metres west. There's a bush there hanging with offerings just as there'd be in Celtic times.* And there, at its roots, a stone trough with a hood intricately carved. Nick stared at it, blinking through the rain. He reached out to touch it, to gather into his palm its bubbling, dribbling water welling up from within, welling up from the earth.

A call.

The singing died.

Nick glanced along his shoulder, saw a flaring torch, and jumped the churning gutter to be swallowed by the darkness. He didn't look back, but kept running, through scrubby trees and matted undergrowth, briars ripping at his trousers, shredding the plastic raincoat, branches flailing at his chest and head until he lost his balance among tussocks and fell. He didn't get up, but squirmed into the liquid mud beneath twisting roots. They'd not see him here in the darkness, not follow him in the darkness, even if they'd glimpsed him on the road. But what if they had dogs? Did they have dogs? Could he hear dogs?

*

Alice could hear dogs, far off; big dogs, hunting dogs. There was a crashing of undergrowth, of groans and stumblings, of air being dragged into raw lungs, her lungs, causing a fire in her chest, and on her arms and her legs, something whipping them, and she was running through a wood, a forest, through trees which grasped at her, running for her life because the hunting dogs were hunting her.

Not her. A man. A ghost at his side, she was running with him, seeing with his eyes, sensing his fear, his determination.

There was a Sanctuary. He knew the path, had trod it years before, but it was overgrown now, so overgrown. The Keeper was gone, gone to his hand, but the Presence would be there, locked among the thorns. The Presence was all powerful. She would embrace him, surround him, protect him. He still had the gladius, the jewelled and flashing blade. She would take it in payment. She could not refuse him. She would protect him, disarm his enemies, turn them to stone, to pillars of fire, to hares to be hunted by their own dogs, to be torn screaming limb from limb, to have their entrails laced across the branches while they still breathed.

Alice tried to shut it out, the rage, the horror of the man's thoughts. She tried to pull herself free from his mind, from the nightmare she knew was a making of her own subconscious. She saw the bedroom, faintly, reached for it... But there was a fire in her lungs, pain from her arms and from her legs as the thorns dragged at her flesh, at his flesh, and she was behind his eyes again, trapped in his body, running along a track she could scarcely see.

The howling of the dogs was closer. They were coming to tear him apart. Each sinking of teeth, each crushing of bone and tearing of flesh would be her bone, her flesh. Fear of him became fear for him. He had to escape. She willed him on, breathing with him and for him, taking his pain as her own. Her desperation fuelled him; she could feel the difference in his stride.

He faltered. She gasped for air as he gasped for it. Her legs were near to collapse. They were looking for something, another path, and then the sword came up into her vision, its hilt glinting in the night's weak light, its blade a blur of shadow against the silhouetted trees as it swept through tangled briars.

They were running again, down an incline. The trees were thinning, the land softer underfoot, water and mud squelching as they ran, forcing between their toes, splashing up their legs, burning into their broken skin.

Ankle deep now, they were standing at the rim of a pond, a pool, not a ripple stirring its surface. Trees crowded the edges as if they had backed away in deference to the spreading liquid, leaving a ring of sky so brightly starlit that Alice drew breath in wonder at the spectacle. His heart, too, was soaring.

They splashed across to a fallen tree, its roots lost in the darkness of the woodland, its leafless boughs reaching across the centre of the pool. Their left hand grabbed at a jutting branch and they heaved themselves up, he and she together. The trunk was covered with moss, and the water cascading from their legs turned the surface to slime. It was difficult to keep a purchase, but his balance was better than hers and they did not fall.

She heard it as he did, a single slapping of the water, but his wits were quicker, and she could only follow on his movements as the sword was brought up two-handed against the leaping dog. Its dark shape grew to fill their vision, the starlight catching the bared fangs, coating the glistening tongue with frost. It did not yelp as the blade parted its ribcage. Blood spurted hot along their arms as they turned along the axis of the animal's leap to heave the body from the blade. It flew by their shoulder as if still under its own momentum, landing on the jutting branches to be impaled there, dripping gore into the dark liquid below.

Their hunters were crashing through the woodland, men as well as dogs, yellow fire-torches flashing between the trees. The pool filled their senses, his and hers together: the scent of rotting wood, of peaty earth, of lichen and moss and a host of other natural matter he could discern as individually as night and day but which came to her a composite in the starlight.

Most of all there was the Presence. And Alice knew where she was; what the sword was for. This was the shrine.

Anticipation made the hairs rise on their skin. It powered his blood and fired his sexual desire. Alice caught her breath as the sensations rippled through her. Then he was calling, as if a name, with a voice so deep and challenging that it reverberated down her larynx. Again he called, definitely a name, followed by words fast and rhythmic. Not speech; verse perhaps, an invocation. The sword was taken in both hands, its blade pressed flat across their thigh. Strength such as Alice had never known was applied to break the blade, but it did not even bend.

The dogs were close; Alice heard them splashing at the edge of the pool. What was happening? This was not how it was supposed to be.

The weapon was lifted to shoulder height. A second invocation — Alice could hear the panting of the dogs, the cries of men — a third invocation, and the sword was tossed skywards to meet the twinkling stars. It turned as it rose, twisting along its length, the jewels set into its pommel blinking and winking against the darkness of the woods. Its thrust exhausted, it began to descend, out of the sky and the stars, down through the column of silhouetted trees, and into the yielding water with less sound than a pebble's drop.

On tip-toe they stood on the narrow trunk, head given back, arms outstretched, every muscle tensed for the moment, the coming of the Presence.

There was splashing, much splashing. A dog barked so loudly that Alice winced. She thought she felt its breath hot on their legs. A spear flew by them.

A great whoop of indrawn breath. A gasp. Eyes widening to the brightness of the stars, to the silence of the pool below their feet. He called afresh — a great shout filled with horror. The name again, fear gripping the tone. He screamed the name, bellowed it, fists clenching in anger. He railed at the Presence, stabbing at the air in front of them as if it were a person, seething abuse at an unseen form which gave no answer.

They did not see the dog. They felt its weight, its claws at the flesh of their backs. Alice tried to break away, to escape the fate that awaited him, but she was bound to him the tighter. When the great fangs burst through her shoulder the night turned red to her eyes and she screamed until her lungs had no more air to make the noise. They were falling, the weight of the dog bearing them down, twisting in the air as the sword had twisted, man and ghost and dog. The cold waters of the pool enveloped them, breathing fire into their wounds. And still he railed at the Presence, cursing and swearing vengeance, until the bubbles frothing from their lips sparkled no more in the starlight, and the chilling liquid poured into their lungs, water hissing over red hot stones.

Water gushed around him, making his body a sodden island beneath tree roots that were his shelter. They'd gone, whoever they were. He'd not lifted his head to see, had hardly dared to breathe. They'd gone, that's all he knew, their singing, the sound of their stride, fading into the distance, sucked away on the rain-laden wind with the barking of the dogs which seemed, now, only to be an echo in his mind.

And still Nick lay there, the water rising around him, deadening his limbs with its cold, deadening his mind, until it swirled mud into his mouth and threatened to drown him. He spat out the mess, coughing to clear his airway as he crawled out of the delve beneath the tree roots to collapse on a bed of heather.

He thought of Alice, of her auburn hair rising in locks about her head, of the texture of her skin, of her mouth hot on his, of The Other, an arm around her shoulder, a hand cupping her breast, taking possession. He opened his eyes to the rain. Taking her where? To the pool to be gutted?

He dragged himself up on unsteady legs, on to feet which had lost all feeling. Which way? What did it matter? The torch was gone. He could see no more than a stride ahead. Alice was all that mattered.

With the first step he spoke her name in his mind. With the second he spoke it aloud. With the third he shouted it to the wind, a challenge to The Other. He kept chanting it, over and over, as he forced his body to respond, to walk, to keep on walking. Find a road. Find a farm. Find Alice and keep her safe.

Alice 'n' Alice 'n' Alice 'n' Alice.

The scream was overtaken by a fit of coughing, and she dragged whooping breaths through tubes filled with mucus. Malevolent shapes stared from the gloom as she clung to the sheets, desperate not to slip back into the water. Far away a name was being called. She thought it was him, invoking the Presence above the surface of the Pool, but it was her name uttered long and sibilant; Nick in her mind, or Andrew.

Dear God, let it not be Andrew drowned so many years ago, water running from his closed eyes, weed clinging to his face. The vision appeared as she thought of him, and she buried her face in the pillow to escape. But there was no escape from the throaty roar of Mark's motor cycle as he rode it round and round her bed, his severed head streaming yellow light all over her.

Behind the images and the noise, behind the sickly smells of meadow flowers and exhaust fumes, rain beat against the window, mimicking grotesque laughter.

The tumbled stones of a wall caught him across the shin before Nick realised it was there. Beyond the wall was a road, and across the road, across the darkness, was a light. He stood a moment, not daring to blink against the rain in case it was snuffed out by his mind, but it remained constant. At last! A farmhouse, at last.

He walked on, faster now, a limping jog, gritting his teeth against the pain, one foot on the verge, one on the puddled roadway, his eyes always on the light. Slowly, very slowly, it was moving from his side to in front of him. The road was curving, leading him towards it.

The light came from a security lamp. Nick almost laughed when he recognised the silhouetted petrol pump, the old Shell emblem sitting high above its rusted shoulders. The garage was closed, but at least it wasn't derelict. He walked down the side, past a lean-to housing a tap and an air hose. There would be a bungalow at the back where the light was mounted. The owner would be there, in bed, but home.

There was no bungalow. Not even a caravan. Nick stared in disbelief at the expanse of weed-strewn asphalt. The brilliance of the security lamp mocked him from a position high on a steel post. What was it doing there? There was nothing to protect.

Around the front once more he peered through the window of the tiny office. A till stood open on a counter filled with chocolate and packets of sweets. Behind, cans of oil shared a shelving system with tins of soft drinks and a box of crisps. There was a swivel chair with a jacket draped over the back, and away in a corner, supporting two half pint mugs, the chrome facia of a mobile gas heater glittered at him.

Nick licked his lips as he stared at it. He knew the door would be locked; he did not even try it. Turning aside his face, he angled his arm to drive his elbow through its glass.

Chapter 27

Nick counted three twenties on to the cluttered counter.

'Don't need all that,' the man murmured, his anger, now, replaced by embarrassment.

'It's not just the window,' Nick confessed. 'I used all the gas, and I've had some chocolate and a can of Coke, and... and I'm hoping you'll be good enough to get me back to my car with a jack.'

'You look as if you need running to the hospital in Whitby.'

'I'm not that bad, honest.'

The man laid the wrench on the counter, and for the first time since he'd woken to see the weapon menacing his face, Nick let the tension ease from his muscles.

'I really wouldn't have broken into your—'

'It's all right,' the man said. 'Got a lad your age myself. Sort of daft thing he'd do, walk across a moor in weather like that. Better get you back to the house. Clean you up and feed you.'

A shaft of sunshine broke through the clouds to light the interior of the office, making Nick squint against its glare. *The weather's always good when I'm looking in the right place.*

'No time,' he said. 'I've got to find someone. It's very important. She's on the moor.'

'Which moor?'

'I don't know.' He passed grazed knuckles over contorted pieces of Ordnance Survey map he'd managed to dry. 'I had it marked, but I can't find it now. I know this sounds crazy, but I've got to find her. She's in danger.'

'If she were out on the moor last—' The man looked at him askance. 'Your age? Reddish hair?'

'Alice.'

*

She wore her padded jacket against the breeze, and knee-length gaiters kept most of the moisture from her trousers. Even so, in the sunshine and the wind the heather was drying quickly. Not so the peat beneath, which squelched liquid up the sides of her boots.

Alice had been grateful to get out on to the moor. Despite the dawn and the change it brought in the weather, traces of the nightmare still clung to the farmhouse walls, ambushing her from unexpected corners. Rosemary had fussed over breakfast, asking if she had slept well or if the storm had kept her awake. Alice had lied. Of course she'd lied. How could she tell anyone about the nightmares which pressed so far into her reality that the two could not be separated? When she'd been younger she'd told her parents, expecting love and understanding in return. Her parents had nearly had her Sectioned. She hadn't told Nick, not the whole truth, hoping that it would be different with him. And it had been, for a while.

She pushed thoughts of him away. It wouldn't do to draw him to her. Too many had died already and he had to remain safe.

Squinting up into the sunshine in an attempt to cleanse her mind, she shook off the rucksack to bring out a compass and the Ordnance Survey map she'd marked. The old map in the university's library had been declared a fake, but she didn't believe that coincidence had brought it to her attention. The nightmare in all its horrendous detail stood testament to that.

She took a bearing and shouldered the rucksack for the trek across the great sweep of moor. Blossoming violet and purple beneath an almost cloudless sky, it was difficult to visualise the undulating landscape cloaked in trees, but each step she took caused wet peat to squelch up the sides of her boots, reminding her too easily of the nightmare. Humming to herself covered the sound.

*

Parked in front of the stone farmhouse was a green Vauxhall he didn't recognise, but the hire company's name emblazoned across the rear window was familiar. Nick's elation was short lived. Sitting in the kitchen was a woman with a face as grey as the stone flooring beneath her feet.

'She left two hours since.'

'Where? Did she say where she was going?' Nick felt a hand clasp his shoulder.

'Be calm, now. We've got the Land Rover. Rosemary, did she leave a route like she said she would?'

'Oh, yes, but you'll not be needing a map. She's making for the pond.'

Nick swung round. 'Yes, a pool. You know where this is?' He saw the exchange glance. 'What? What is it?'

Phil wouldn't hold his gaze. 'Fenced it this summer. Always losing sheep to it. Stupid animals.'

Nick took a breath and held it. 'It's not just sheep, is it?' he said. 'People drown there, too, don't they?'

Alice studied the Ordnance Survey, then the photocopy of the parchment map she'd been warned was a fake. The pool in front of her was roughly rectangular in shape, about three metres by four. At such a size she had expected it to be shown on the modern map, but it wasn't. Perhaps it was seasonal, dependent on rainfall. If that were the case it had to be fed only intermittently by a spring, if at all. So why, in all the acreage of the open moorland, had someone taken the trouble to fence it?

She set down the rucksack, careful of the sheep droppings lying thick where the heather gave way to grass. The lie of the land was deceptive, the heather hiding much. If the mediaeval map was to be believed, the place had been occupied by members of a religious order, but where were the stone foundations of a building? The area would still have been wooded, if less thickly than the nightmare suggested. Had it been a wattle and daub construction, a habitation so transient as to be mentioned on only a single map?

She walked alongside the stick and wire fencing, all the way round, seeing the water from every angle. She knew what she was looking at: a monastic fishpond, hewn from the stony ground with picks and wooden spades, weeks of back-breaking labour. Hardly a feature of a temporary encampment.

A memory of Leonard Harkin flashed through her mind, of him kneeling in the flowerbed in front of Brantingham House, digging out a pond. Why? Where had the water come from? Where had the water come from for the fishpond? Why had this place been chosen at all?

All of them! Every one of them! They followed the sheep like sheep themselves. Even she he had nurtured from birth so that her eyes would be clear. He should blind her as she stared into the false water. Eviscerate her where she stood and strangle her with her own entrails.

Wrenching free from her, Ognirius stepped into the glaring light of day. The sun's rays burned his form transparent, the cool wind chilling his anger and the remnants of his soul.

There were no trees.

It seemed to have been his closest thought for longer than a man could name his forebears. There were no trees. Without trees there were no birds, and no bird's song to break the desperate keening of the wind across a land so long shaded from his sight. A desolate land, he had reasoned, but now that he could see it plainly, he knew it to be a land full of imperial colour. And against it, tendrils flashing as a beacon in the darkness, her gold and russet hair was writhing in the wind.

Calloused fingers reached and separated, feeding through the flowing locks, through her scalp and her skull. She had run with him as he had run; now the trees would rise again in her mind and she would walk with him through that memory to the place they both desired.

*

Phil allowed the Land Rover to roll to a halt and turned off the ignition. 'On foot from here. You going to be okay?'

Nick didn't answer. He felt bruised and sick, both from the motion and from fear. People died on these moors; stories handed down the years, Phil had told him. Accidents. Peat-cutters, shepherds, lead miners. Accidents, all. Coincidence. Except that Alice didn't believe in coincidence. Nick had once, but not any more.

Pain burned through his feet and up his legs as soon as he began walking on the uneven surface. Blisters had burst during his night crossing of the moor. He'd dressed them as best he could, but his ankles would be a bloody pulp before he'd covered half a mile. Better his feet than Alice. Gritting his teeth, he nodded at Phil to lead the way.

The shallow depression held no heather, only close-cropped grass and clumps of tall, thick-stemmed reeds. In the cleft where Alice was kneeling was a single bed of sphagnum moss, its tiny leaves so pale a green as to be almost translucent. Trowel in hand, she scraped away the surface covering to reveal moist peat thick with fibrous roots. That, too, was cut and scraped aside. A hand's depth down she hit stone.

He couldn't see Alice. He could see the fencing, though, silhouetted against the sky. It wasn't as substantial as he'd expected, and looked oddly sinister in a land of rounded curves where no vegetation grew taller than his knee. It reminded Nick of iron railings around a grave.

Phil hadn't said a word to him during their walk, though he'd looked back several times, and offered his arm once, when the pain in Nick's sodden feet and calves had got too much and he had overbalanced, falling to his knees. His fingers had sunk into the soft wet peat beneath the heather. The smell of decomposing vegetation had risen to fill his nostrils, not flower scents, and as he'd drawn free his hands there'd been a glucking noise that had turned his stomach. He'd found his skin stained brown, the debris of decay clinging to them, like the blood and gore of the nightmare re-enactment. He threw the slaughter from his mind. He'd reach Alice in time. He made himself believe it.

Phil didn't look back now, but increased his stride, opening the gap between them. Nick shouted for him to wait, but his voice was whipped away on the buffeting wind, or Phil was refusing to hear him. Despite the burning, tearing pain, Nick broke into a jog. He wanted to be first to the pond, to see the water, to see whatever it held captive.

He heard Phil's anguished cry and felt his chest being crushed, watched the farmer as he mounted the fence and disappeared into the fold of the land. Losing his footing, Nick scrambled the last few metres on hands and knees to pull himself upright against a fencing post. Phil was standing by a clump of rushes, knee-deep in black water.

'It's all right!' he called, waving his arm. 'It's not her. It's my bloody sheep. Two of them.' He looked down and shook his head. 'Forcing their way through the fence now. I don't believe it. What's the matter with the stupid things?'

Nick turned away. Alice wasn't there. Her rucksack wasn't there. Where was she? This was the place she'd marked on the map. Or was it? They hadn't brought a map, they'd been so certain.

He stumbled to the far end of the fencing, clung to it as the wind flung his hair into his eyes and tore at his jacket. What would she be wearing? What colour should he look for? There wasn't another soul on the moor, nothing to see but the bright glow of purple heather sinking and rising and waving in the wind as the land undulated in every direction. Alice could be in any dip, in any gully. He could walk right by her and never know. Letting go of the fence he began to shout her name.

*

At first Alice thought she'd hit bedrock, but the colour was wrong, the texture. This wasn't stone natural to the area; it was granite.

The slab was nearly half a metre wide and, once cleaned of its peat covering, the marks of man-made dressing were clearly visible. She made the hole bigger, digging beneath the granite's edge to reveal a purchase for her hands. There were definitely other, irregular shaped stones beneath.

She heaved, once, twice; it didn't budge. There was nothing close that could be used as a lever. Was she going to be thwarted because of her own frailty?

Heat surged through her as nerve-endings tingled in a fan across her torso. Alice gasped at the sensation, swaying on legs that seemed uncertain of supporting her body's mass. Fingers gripped one edge of the slab. With the noise of a sucking drain, it lifted to roll aside.

Alice fell back, resting on the edge of the hole to wait for the trembling in her limbs to fade. She opened her eyes to a layer of peat-dyed stones, each twice, three times, the size of her fist. Rising between them, water was mixing sediment into a thick paste around the soles of her boots.

She hadn't been wrong. It was a spring, the source. Its throat had been blocked to dam it, to change its route.

Pulling up the stones, she threw them aside to create a spoil heap above the cleft. The more stones she removed the faster the water welled up, not peat-stained now, not thick with sediment, but running clear. Pausing, she cupped a hand to take a sip. Sweet. It was sweet.

The wind carried her name and she stood to look around her. It couldn't be Nick. She was hearing a memory replaying in her mind.

The water was rising fast now, over her boot tops, lapping at her socks. Her feet were so chilled she couldn't feel them, the cold reaching up her calves, her gaiters no use at all. She should have brought waders, was going to need waders for this; she wasn't equipped.

Sunlight played on the bubbling surface, creating lattice patterns, creating rainbow colours. She heaved aside more stone, each piece gripping the one beneath as if through suction. The lattice patterns lengthened, the rainbow colours grouped. Someone was shouting her name. Nick? She stood again, easing her aching back, to look about her.

Shaking the circulation into her hands, she hunched over the water to reach for another stone, and saw it. Unmistakable. The decorated hilt of an implement, a weapon. She kept telling herself that it couldn't be, that her eyes were deceiving her, that any item sacrificed to the waters would have disintegrated centuries before. But it looked... She thought of the moment in the nightmare when the sword had been tossed into the air and had twisted, catching the starlight as it made its descent. It couldn't be that sword, couldn't be. She reached out to move a stone, revealing more of the blade. She touched it, felt metal, cold and hard beneath her fingertips.

Her name again, on the wind. Definitely Nick. He shouldn't be there. Shouldn't have followed her. It was dangerous. His life was in danger.

Her hand broke the surface of the water, reached down to the hilt, grasped it, felt it substantial in her hand, the weight, the awesome weight of a weapon made to kill and sacrificed for life. A tingling began at the back of her neck and ran across her shoulders, round to her collarbone, building to a solid pressure. And she was pleased, so very pleased that Nick had followed her. She and him together. For ever.

Touch it, yes. Imbue the illusion with substance, with life, as you imbue me. A little further, yes...

Ognirius closed his hand on hers, wanting to urge her, wanting to feel the heat leap from her flesh into his. The torc about his neck was vibrating, sending a tingling along his shoulders and his arms, surging along his ribs and down his spine, filling his body with an elation that was bordering ecstasy. He could hear the boy, could hear him calling her, that hollow vessel that thought himself a man.

Come this way, boy. Come this way and see a true man of worth.

The gladius. The woman had the gladius in her hand and was lifting it out of the water into the sunlight. Around her ankles, around his, the water began swirling into a vortex to sink away between the stones. The gift, given so long ago, was finally being accepted. At last he was passing through.

The boy was close, half a javelin's throw. Ognirius took a moment to grin at him, to relish the wide eyes and horrified expression, as he twisted his hand and arm in a gesture of violation designed to fill the boy's throat with bile.

Yes, boy. Fall on your knees and sob, boy. Sob for the air in your lungs as you watch me cleave hers from her chest and make you eat them.

The ground began to tremble and the boy fell to his knees. Ognirius turned from him, his attention solely for the woman, his left arm across her throat, drawing her into his chest, his right hand lifting, ready to take the gladius from her fingers. A whistling cut the air, more shrill than a score of ritual pipes. The moment was upon him, *his* moment. Silver water rose in a geyser to surround him and her together, and she shuddered in his grasp. It was as if her entire life-force peeled from her, reuniting him with his soul, with his flesh, with the warmth of blood that made him live and breathe as he had lived and breathed before. He had passed through. Yes! He, Ognirius Licinius Vranaun had *passed through*.

His fingers curled around the hilt of the gladius that was his by right and honour, but it did not leave the woman's hand. Despite his grip across her throat she began to turn towards him, a groove digging sharply into his forearm by some object around her neck. A torc. She wore a torc as he wore one, the style, the decoration an exact copy, except... except that hers was the silver of moonlight, and his... His he'd had removed.

His hand rose to his own throat, naked now as it had been

naked then. The torc around her neck glinted yellow in the sunlight, filling his senses with belief, and with dread, as his gaze rose to her face. Her mouth and cheekbones were moulded smooth by the force of the water, her hair the only colour to his sight, each lock as dry and curled as autumn bracken and lifting about her head. Her eyes opened to reveal the glazing of a sun-kissed lake. He saw Yslan in her features, and the acolytes, one by one, those he could no longer give a name to, as he could no longer give a name to Her. She had been with him through the centuries, feeding from the dark tribute of his rage as he'd fed from it himself.

Pulling back, he tried to step from the geyser, tried to let loose the hilt of the gladius. Both held him. He watched the sword tarnish in his hand, watched it being eaten by rust, dissolve to grains and fall away, its sky-riven decoration liquefying into rainbow hues to light Her eyes and tint Her lips. Those lips smiled upon him now, and he knew with graven certainty that it was not he who had passed through.

The whistling turned into a scream, a very human scream, a man's scream, which carried on and on with an intensity that filled Nick's skull despite his hands clasped tight to his ears. His image, The Other, was being shredded from the legs up. In front of Nick's eyes he was being shredded, but slowly, so very slowly, each drop of water a twisting diamond blade of crystal, the combined spray arcing over the heather as tainted hail, as sleet, as snow, to land blood-red and dissolve into liquid gore, to craze with ice and freeze around him, on him.

Nick's instinct was to run, but it was himself he saw, himself, as the torso disintegrated, as The Other's throat was torn apart, silencing the scream. The jaw followed, the mouth, the scarred cheek, the staring, terror-filled eyes, until only the hair, not even the hair, remained.

The whistling built again, a constant siren, and the silver geyser burst skywards stronger than before, fountaining into rainbow-lit planes catching the sunlight, moulding and sculpting the shape of a woman, a voluptuous, pregnant woman with hair that lifted in a shimmering curtain of wind-borne vapour.

Alice.

Her name left Nick's lips in a gasp of awe, but his chest filled with panic as he saw the head turn, a thick ring of pale gold glinting at its neck as an arm branched away to reach for him. He tried to scramble backwards but could find no purchase on the icy peat. Crying now, sobbing her name as the outspread hand closed on him, water cold beyond belief rained down to freeze on him, snatching his breath as it soaked his clothing. Beneath him the ground began to liquefy. The weight of the water started to ebb, dragging him, as if a returning tide, towards the growing pool. He snatched at scrubby heather to anchor himself, pulling its roots from the sodden earth, his last and only lifeline.

The whistling faded. The hand, the arm, withdrew. The power of the geyser subsided, the female image falling away in individual silver drops until there was no more than a harsh bubbling in the centre of the pool. And Alice. Alice was floating face down in the water, her auburn hair writhing about her head in a fiery mass.

Nick splashed into the freezing liquid to grab at her wrist and drag her on to ground soaked but solid. He swept the clinging locks from her face ready to clear her airway, to give her mouth-to-mouth, but her right temple was a bloody pulp, her sightless eyes wide open.

Chapter 28

His hired car had been left at the farmhouse. Phil had offered to loan him the Land Rover, but Nick wanted to walk across the moor, wanted there to be no one but himself and its solitude, its vast horizon and constant wind tugging at his hair. He wanted to do this alone, needed to do it to bring some sanity back into his life. His parents had understood; closure they had called it, as if Alice had been a girlfriend, as if her death had been an accident, all a set of coincidences folding into a pattern.

Every decision had been taken from his hands. He was not Alice's next of kin; her parents had been brought north to formally identify her body. The post mortem had gone ahead without his knowledge; the inquest opened and adjourned without his presence. A blow to her head, water had taken her life, flames had then taken her body, the triple death of the anointed. Nothing was mere coincidence. People he didn't know, people who didn't know him, had cremated her, leaving him without a grave to mourn beside. And he needed to mourn, to make sense of what had happened, of what he'd seen.

The undulating land had lost its purple hues, the heather drawing into itself ready for the midwinter solstice, but he found the place as he knew he would. It drew him, as it had drawn Alice.

The pool was not as Nick remembered. It was wide, now, circular, a small lake, its water as clear as window glass rippling from a column of bubbles rising at its centre. He'd brought flowers, wild flowers with a scent that lingered in his mind, but there were offerings there already, tied to saplings newly planted around its rim: red ribbon, white cloth, a garland of daisies, desiccating in the wind and the weak winter sunshine.

Nick wanted to say something to the water but could not find the words. Instead he fanned the flowers he'd brought and laid them on the surface, pushing them towards the centre of the pool. The water numbed his fingers, sending fire along his wrist, and he plunged in both hands to cup the liquid and cascade it down his face and neck. Bone-chilling, it was, just as it had been at Newtondale when Alice had poured water over him to heal his bruised flesh, and he had taken her in his arms and they had made love that first time.

Tears mixed with the water spilling down his cheeks, and he fell on to his knees in the liquefying earth to cry her name. She'd reached out for him, had wanted to take him with her, but he'd been paralysed by the demise of The Other, unable to place his hand in hers as he had in the dream when she'd walked him into the pool.

How many times since had he wished that he had joined her; how many times had he feared that he might? Murray had visited him at his parents' home with tales of rugby triumphs, but Nick knew he'd neither play nor watch the game again. Julia Marshall had visited him, but there was so much they dare not say, even to each other. She'd urged him to stay at his parents' home in the south, knowing that he never could.

The single croak was followed by a splash, and Nick wiped at his eyes with the back of his hand to clear his vision. The long legs were scissoring through the water, its green and russet colouring a blur as it dived beneath the drifting flowers. A frog, perhaps; perhaps a toad. Definitely a toad, but its feet... He couldn't be certain about its feet, hadn't seen them properly. Instead he concentrated on the flowers slipping, now, beneath the surface, the clear liquid easing over petals and leaves to shape a face, smiling up at him, tendrils of auburn rippling on the current.

Author's Note

This is a work of fiction. The people depicted in this novel never lived except in the mind of the author. The places are real. They have been neither relocated nor renamed, and are described as true as this fiction allows. Tread carefully. We walk on yesterday, and yesterday is only a heartbeat behind us.

When next visiting a chrome and glass shopping mall and pausing to toss a coin into a fountain, consider: you are not wishing for 'good luck', but are enacting a ritual at least three thousand years old, invoking the continued bounty of a female water deity.

If you enjoyed this novel, please consider leaving a short review with your retailer. Read on for an excerpt and the Prologue to Book Two – *The Bull At The Gate*.

Excerpt from
Book Two

The Bull at the Gate

Trying to get his life back together, Nick takes a short-term contract in York, a walled mediaeval city of crooked half-timbered houses and tight cobbled streets where re-enactment groups thrill the tourists. When a colleague is reported missing the police suspect foul play, and when the investigation uncovers the macabre deaths in Hull, Nick becomes a suspect.

But York was once the Roman colonia Eboracum, with a fortress that garrisoned both the infamous Ninth Legion and the Sixth Victrix, and where the stains of older, sacrificial, deaths lie buried deep in modern cellars, desperate for escape.

~~~

Nick spasmed as he woke, fighting off the clinging duvet, fighting off her outstretched arm. His back rammed into the headboard that rammed the wall with a dull thuck, leaving him nowhere to go. Alice was at the bottom of his bed – *his bed* – not some meadow, not some sunlit warmth of flower scents. The yellow lamplight from the ceiling was shining down on her, the white fluorescent from the bathroom cutting across her. She was *here* – and he was hyperventilating, his heart straining in his chest.

He sucked in air in a whistling stream but it was so cold, searing at his lungs as if liquid ice. Alice was in his room, in his space, in his time, her hand outstretched across the duvet, water cascading from her fingers. The bed was sodden, he realised, the carpet awash. It was coming off her everywhere, her hair and her face and her jacket and her arm—

Nick blinked. It was the jacket she'd been wearing when the geyser had engulfed her, when he'd dragged her from the pool.

'Alice...'

She was trying to reach for him, her lips moving, her head turning to one side and back to face him; reaching for him across the bed, her lips moving, her head turning, then back to face him; reaching for him with her right hand, water cascading from her bunched fist, soaking the duvet, it splattering from the bed onto the floor. Each time she reached she cut a little further through the bed, through the mattress, through the duvet, reaching for him, her lips moving, her head turning to one side and back to face him... edging closer and closer...

His fingers clawed at the bedside cabinet for his mobile – grasped it and hit the programmed button. He could hear its ring even before he'd got it to his ear, ringing and ringing and ringing and—

'Sh-yeahsh-sceenn.' It didn't sound like Julia, didn't sound like anyone. There was a cough, but the signal was echoing, drifting. 'Nick? Is... ou? Of cour... matter, Nick?'

He couldn't feel his feet, he realised, couldn't feel the bottom of his legs. He pulled them up to his body. His jeans were sodden, stiff. There was an odd crusting on his shoes. He reached out to brush it off.

'Speak to me, Ni.... What's the maaa...'

It was ice.

'Nicholas, it's nearly four... morning. I have worrrrk... Talk to me if you'rrrrr...'

He stared at Alice, at her reaching arm, at her turning head, at the bed cutting through her just above her knees.

'Nicholas? Nick? Arrrr... hyperven... *Breathe*, Nick, *breathe*. You're okay. I'm... talk to me. I'm with... You are not alone.'

She was reaching for him, her arm outstretched, water cascading from her, ice crazing across the duvet, rising in splinters as he pushed the covering away from him with his feet. His back was to the wall and she was reaching for him, coming ever closer.

'Alice!'

'What? Breathe, Ni... can do this. Get closer tooooo... far

away.'

He glanced at the handset fixed to his cheek, heard the long interrupted echo of Julia's words. Breathed. He was *breathing*. He could breathe if he didn't look at Alice. With his free hand he pulled at a pillow wedged behind his hip, pushed it onto his legs in an attempt to stem the water.

'Alice,' he said into the mobile and this time he knew he'd said it true.

There was another echo, a whine. Let Julia hear him! 'Alice is—'

'You've been dreaminnnn...'

'She's *here!*'

Again an echo, a whine.

'Nick... Alice is dead.'

'I *know*.'

Prologue

The light behind was fading, the darkness pressing in, pushing the silence so close that he feared he might suffocate in it. He began to lick his lips and immediately raised his chin, stretching his spine as if on parade. A son of the Victrix harboured no anxiety. It was time, and time did not wait.

Reaching for the boulder barring his route, he felt the facets of its surface disconnect as his knuckles sought its limit, felt its chill and its weight as he took it on his forearm, heard the clink of stone as it shuttered as smoothly as segmented body armour. Bending his knee in the first supplication he swung himself forward and under, relaxing his arm so the stone hanging returned to position, chinking as it solidified behind him.

His fingers checked the ties of the bags at his belt, the solid contents of the larger bumping at his hip as he turned in the narrow, rock-hewn passage. He eased his stance with care, his shoulders and bent head brushing the rock above. Its protrusions were sharp, and he'd bloodied his scalp once before.

Taking a breath to steady himself, he reached out a sandaled foot, feeling for the edge of the hewn steps. He knew their alignment, their unsteady gait, the way the third tipped the unwary towards the wall, almost smoothed in that place by flattening, bloodied, hands desperate for balance. Down one, down two, guiding his fingertips along the slope of the rock at his head, careful with the third step, safely to the fourth.

The air had chilled. Or was he sweating? He wiped his hands down his tunic to maintain a dry grip.

There was a turn, to the left. He knew it by heart, felt for the edge of the wall, the edge of the step, comparing his descent with the map in his mind. He stopped. Was his imagination offering visions to overlay the darkness? No, it was a flicker of reflected light; he was close.

Down, down, the rocks above closing on the steps below, making him bend further, but he would not crawl; it was unseemly to crawl, even though his thighs pressed into his ribs, his face between his knees. The river of light!

Fighting a rising smile, he breathed more easily. The water glimmered a coiling yellow across his path, but soundless, as if only a picture in his mind. He knew it wasn't, knew to step into it would mean being swallowed, dragged beneath the rock walls by the current and into the bowels of Orcus' domain.

He concentrated on re-balancing his weight, stretching out his left leg in semblance of some wary spider feeling its way, reaching for the unseen step below, hearing the nails on the soles of his sandals etching lines into the rock, their strapping biting at his ankle and calf. He wouldn't slip, he told himself. And he didn't.

Light flooded his eyes as he took the last steps, blinking away his blindness, aware that the tight rock walls had opened in a chamber.

'Who crosses the Blood of Luna?'

The deep, demanding voice caught him by surprise and he winced as the sudden sound amplified off the rock walls, echoed from the vaulting, seeming to come from everywhere. He snapped upright, parade straight.

'I, Tadius, initiate.'

He stared into the darkness, at the two flames issuing from small lamps, marking the first set of pillars.

'Who knows this man?'

Two more lights flared, marking the next set of pillars. From the blackness beyond emerged the head of a giant Raven, its glossy feathers shimmering in the lamplight as it floated towards him. No body showed, only its head, its piercing eyes regarding him as its bulbous polished beak opened and closed with a faint but determined clack.

'Advance!'

On the command Tadius took two paces forward, his fingers fighting to undo the bag tied at his belt, to free the deep cup inside. He knew by its weight some of the grain had spilled into the bag, but there was no refilling it now. Holding it with both hands he straightened his arms, offering it and its contents to Raven. He watched Raven's head jerk towards him, cocking left to peer at him with one eye, cocking right to peer at the vessel with its other, but it did not dip its beak. Instead it came closer, walking up to him, by him, round him, its feathers brushing his arms, his cheek, his neck, the shining, clacking beak so close that Tadius could smell its breath. It seemed to him that all the entrails of all the carrion it had consumed were close enough to regurgitate, and he parted his lips attempting to strain the rancid air through his teeth so that his own bile would not rise and unman him.

In front of him again, it turned in shallow jagged movements — eye, beak, eye — and stabbed. The polished beak moved so fast in the weak lamplight that Tadius did not see it strike but felt its sharp beak rip across his knuckles. He wasn't sure if he cried out, he prayed not, and was quick to raise his arms from the jarring blow, to re-present the cup, hoping he'd let none of the grain fall. Raven's head was jerking away, round, back, ready to dip again. Tadius gritted his teeth in readiness for its beak slicing his other hand, but it dipped with accuracy, jabbing through the grain to the bottom of the cup, once, twice, then lifting its beak to the darkness above the lamplight, clacking and shaking it as it moved to the left to become still beside its column, beneath its lamp.

'Welcome, fellow Raven!' boomed the voice.

Tadius let his arms relax, tucking the cup in the crook of his elbow to allow himself the opportunity to check the blood running down his hand. He'd understood the duck to be enough for the sacrifice prior to his descent. Obviously he'd been wrong. What else had he misconstrued? He'd only proven his true standing. He wasn't halfway through the ceremony.

Twin sets of lights began to flicker in the darkness, each

bringing a section of column to his view. Beneath, alternating between the columns, appeared the symbols of the hierarchy Tadius had come to expect. The oversized helmet of Warrior called a muffled welcome, the eye-slits of its full-faced guard blanked. Then Lion stepped from behind its column, its partly human face diminutive, swallowed by its mane and ears. To the left came Persian, a cluster of stars about its enlarged eyes, a scythe across its over-sized shoulder. Behind appeared Sun-Runner, a radiated crown upon the yellow mask of its head. In its hand was a cone-torch which burst into flaring life as it was raised, momentarily suppressing the flames of the oil-lamps with its brilliance and illuminating, far behind, the silvered blade of the weapon that brought death to the sacrifice and freed life across the world. Tadius watched it glimmer and fade into the darkness as the flame from the torch diminished. He noticed, too, the dark space before him and felt a frisson of anticipation for what lay ahead. When completed, he would be the one to return to the dark space to light the lamps there and show the hidden columns.

'Advance!'

His feet obeyed. Raven stepped forward to take the cup as he passed. To his left and right he could hear the muted slap of naked palms on stone couches lost to the darkness. The noise would build to a crescendo as the rite reached its climax, and the thought energised him as he passed Warrior, and Lion, and Persian. The smouldering torch of Sun-Runner barred his way, the smoke catching at the back of his throat, testing the clarity of his eyes, but he was close enough, now, to see the indistinct shapes of the relief trying to emerge from the gloom to meet him.

'What has been brought?'

Tadius' attention snapped back to Sun-Runner.

'Silver coins have been brought.'

'For what have the silver coins been brought?'

'To honour the goddess whose name cannot pass my lips.' He shaded his eyes with his bloodied hand even though, in truth, he could not see her countenance.

'Which goddess?'

'The goddess who guards the night. The goddess who commands the waters.'

'Show the silver coins.'

Tadius drew loose the smaller bag from his belt and tipped the coins on to his palm. Sun-Runner brought the spluttering torch close so that their glint might not be missed.

Something was said that Tadius did not catch, and Sun-Runner spun away. There was a low thud and lamp-light blossomed both to his left and above. In front of him Luna looked down, not at him as he'd expected, but away from the relief, towards the light to his left. He followed her dulled gaze to see part of an arrow protruding from the rock wall, its feathered fletching writhing yellow and white in the guttering lamplight. From the wounded rock, water was dribbling into a basin carved from the wall.

'Now.'

The word seemed to be hissed, he wasn't sure. Should he say something or speak only in his mind? *Luna accept me, protect me, shroud me in your light.* He threw the coins. Most went into the basin, some tinkled against the rock wall.

'Present.'

He opened his arms wide, felt hands come around his waist from behind, felt his belt removed. His sandals were untied, removed. He took a breath as the hem of his tunic was raised and he angled his head so the cloth didn't catch on his chin. The air was very chill, he a sheen of perspiration. The stone couch before the altar had been draped with his gown. On top had been placed the lamp, his sign of office, as yet unlit.

The shock of cold as icy water was poured over his head made him gasp, silently he hoped, though after the third libation across his shoulders he couldn't stop shaking.

'Where's your stamina, *Raven*?' Something was trailed across his chest. It took him a moment to realise it was Sun-Runner's whip. 'Or do you wish us to call you *Consort*?'

There was a sneer to the voice now. The whip trailed across his shoulder blades.

'Or is that not enough? Should we pay homage to *Sun-Runner*? Perhaps to the Great One, to *Invictus Sol*?'

Tadius felt the short hairs on his neck begin to rise. He must not speak, must not raise his gaze. This was the rite, he told himself, part of the ordeal.

'You, who brings a *female water fowl—*'

He didn't hear the rest, his mind a howl of distress.

The thick grip of the whip hit him across the chest and Sun-Runner's golden mask closed on his face. 'You are Deceiver! May your arms be dressed in black. Where is Consort?'

Hands grasped his wrists and lurched him forwards a step. The couch was bare stone now, he the sacrifice, it the altar. He wouldn't fight them, he told himself. Let it be over; just let it be over.

The sound of grating alerted him, stone moving across stone. The couch was hollow. He felt his eyes widen as the lamplight tried to pierce the gloom within, the dank gloom of the sarcophagus.

'No!!'

He fought them then, but they had him - Lion and Persian and Warrior – and the skin peeled from his shoulders and heels as his flesh was pressed tight into the chiselled stone, and the slab pushed over his body until it reached his eyes. The last thing he saw was Sun-Runner's facemask shining down.

'Bring forth Consort! In Luna's name, bring forth the Consort!'

But Tadius never heard the demand. When the cover slid fully to rest the sound of his screaming weakened to an indistinct resonance, though the echo of it boomed around the cave until it weakened too.

Raven came to listen at the small hole drilled in the slab's surface, cocking its head to peer with an eye, until Sun-Runner returned with the libation dish and began dribbling water into the hole. Raven clacked his beak and pecked for fallen grain. At the foot of the sarcophagus it cocked its head to peer again, this time at a hole close to the base, where no water ran free.

About The Author

Linda Acaster is an award-winning writer of five novels, over seventy short stories in a variety of genres, a wealth of magazine articles on writing fiction, and a guide to writing short fiction. She lives in northern England, a stone's throw from an ancient spring.

Other works include:

The Bull At The Gate – the second in a trilogy of paranormal thrillers set in northern England

Nick has moved temporarily to York, a walled mediaeval city of crooked half-timbered houses and tight cobbled streets where historical re-enactment groups of Civil War Parliamentarians and Viking longshipmen thrill the tourists. But deep in the crypt of York Minster sit the foundations of an earlier occupation, the Roman fortress of Eboracum that garrisoned both the infamous Ninth Legion and the Sixth Victrix.

As one of Nick's colleagues is reported missing and the police begin to ask awkward questions about Alice, an artefact from the Temple of Mithras appears on his desk. A clever reproduction, or a 1700 year old relic looking as new as if it had been made yesterday?

Availability: coming soon – paperback & all-formats ebook.

Beneath The Shining Mountains – a Native American historical romance set on the northern plains c.1830s. Moon Hawk wants Winter Man not notice her, but why would a man with so many lovers want to take a wife? Challenging his virility is to play a dangerous game. In a village of skin tipis where every word is overheard their escalating game of tease and spar soon spirals beyond control, threatening Moon Hawk and her family with ridicule and shame. From buffalo hunting to horse raiding, this is a story of honour among rival warrior societies and one woman's determination to wed the man of her dreams. Heat level: sensual. Availability: all formats ebook & paperback.

Reviews: *...vibrant, funny, poignant ...I loved learning about their customs and rich culture...beautiful love story, realistic and sensual...should be listed with the classics ...*

Hostage of the Heart – a mediaeval romantic suspense set on the English-Welsh border in 1066. Rhodri ap Hywel, prince of the Welsh, sweeps down the valley to reclaim by force stolen lands, taking the Saxon Lady Dena as a battle hostage. But who is the more barbaric: a man who protects his people by the strength of his sword-arm or Dena's kinfolk who swear fealty to a canon of falsehoods and refuse to pay her ransom? Betrayed as worthless, can she place her trust, and her life, in the hands of a warrior-knight shielding dark secrets of his own?
Heat level: sweet. Availability: all-formats ebook & mp3 download.

Reviews: *...a page-turner by anyone's standards... an exciting, nail-biting tale, full of high stakes and adventure... a heart-warming romance with a good dose of intrigue...*

Contribution to Mankind and other stories of the Dark – a short collection of previously published dark fantasy and science fiction stories.
Availability: all-formats ebook.

Reviews: *...from the slightly whimsical "Our Tyke" with its tale of a supernatural friendship no one expected, to the title story about organ-donation and a deadly feud, these are stories which will leave you looking over your shoulder...*

Reading A Writer's Mind: Exploring Short Fiction – First Thought to Finished Story – an aid for beginner and intermediate writers seeking to improve their fiction-writing skills. It includes the deconstruction of ten stories in a variety of genres from Romance to Horror to Twist in the Tail.
Availability: paperback & all-formats ebook

Reviews: *...the author's concise but comprehensive work on approaching short fiction now has a permanent place in my library... I've learned so much about characterization from this book that it has already coloured the way I craft my stories...*

Linda Acaster also writes in the Western action genre under the pen name of Tyler Brentmore.

For current information and sample chapters
or to sign up for a newsletter:

http://www.lindaacaster.co.uk
http://lindaacaster.blogspot.com